LANY MARIE

THE REBEL HEALERS

CHRONICLES OF A FRACTURED SOUL

EMPOWER
P   R   E   S   S

An Imprint for GracePoint Publishing (www.GracePointPublishing.com)
GracePoint Matrix, LLC
322 N Tejon St. #207
Colorado Springs CO 80903
www.GracePointMatrix.com
Email: Admin@GracePointMatrix.com
SAN # 991-6032
Library of Congress Control Number: # 2021905456
ISBN-13: (Paperback) # 978-1-951694-44-9
eISBN: (eBook) # 978-1-951694-43-2

Books may be purchased for educational, business, or sales promotional use.
For bulk order requests and price schedule contact:
Orders@GracePointPublishing.com

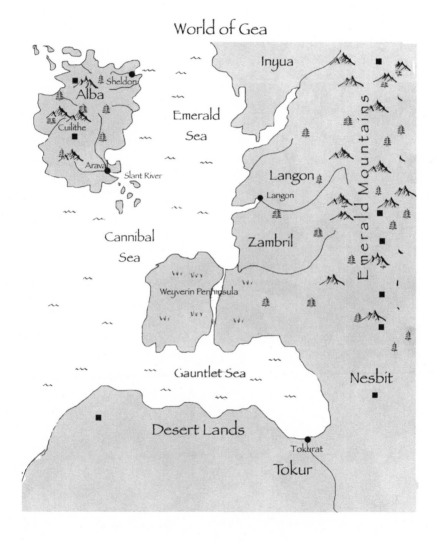

Dedicated to those who know they have a role in making the world a better place, but don't think they can and are afraid to step into their destiny.

PROLOGUE

THE THREE SISTERS: A TALE OF CREATION

From Cleric Paul's translations

I n the beginning, the Great Mother Goddess birthed three daughters, Gea, Shara, and Earth, in that order. As a gift to her offspring, She swept her hand through the Universe and pressed the dust she had gathered into a sphere. She handed it to the young goddesses.

"Divide this planet between yourselves and embrace your part as if it is you, which it is." As she spoke, three beautiful worlds took shape. As She blessed each daughter and imprinted the essence of each goddess into a world, the Great Mother said, "You are responsible for the life and well-being of all who live here as if it is your life, which it is. Care for these creations as if *they were your own children. You are the life of this creation and it bears a resemblance to you. Be worthy of it."*

At first the young goddesses marveled at the wondrous gift from their mother and spent eons admiring how each world reflected the essence of the Mother Goddess. Each sister watched the creatures of the air, land, sea, and the spirits from other realms move about in her world and compared what she noticed with her siblings. The worlds were beautiful and abundant, just as the sisters were beautiful and abundant. The Great Mother was pleased and praised each daughter for how well they tended their charges.

The young goddesses grew in stature and wisdom. Their mother had imbued each of her children with subtle differences, likened to personality traits, so that each engaged with and perceived life from a slightly different perspective.

Willowy, sensitive Shara loved the water. She shaped her world into vast oceans and waterways that cut paths through her landmasses like a gigantic set of canals. She loved the creatures that thrived in Her waters. She spent days traveling through her world in an oyster shell chariot pulled by six dolphins. Her watery steeds cavorted through the waves and inland passageways. Inspired to give her dolphins sport, Shara created so many small, winding, and watery passages between land masses that soon her world became filled with islands of all sizes and shapes.

Voluptuous, sensuous Earth, not to be outdone by Shara, created large continents and distributed them around Her globe. Earth loved her dry lands and continually shaped the terrain like a potter shaping clay. She squeezed together some earth and formed majestic mountains. She grew lush forests and expansive grasslands. She put snow on the highest peaks and drew rivers with her fingernail. She loved the creatures that roamed her lands. Dressed in her finest silks and sampling fruity delights dipped in chocolate from her plant kingdom, Earth lounged on a mountain top where she could look out over her world. She brushed her fingertips across the treetops of her rain forests and ruffled the needles on her evergreen trees just to smell the pungent aromas. She blew across the open grasslands and marveled at how the grasses changed colors. She traveled her world on a cloud pulled by four eagles.

Elegant, wise Gea opted to retain a balance between the elements in her world. She was the balancer and the peacemaker. Above all, she wanted her creatures to live in harmony and enjoy their lives. To her sisters, Gea's world seemed boring, and they frequently chided her about it. Gea would just smile. She watched her sisters' friendly competition to gain the favor of their mother. Occasionally, she would suggest something one of them could try, or intervene in an argument. Mostly, she just watched, content with the world she had been given. Gea loved every creature, no matter what it was. To her, they were all valuable and played an important role in making the world complete. Unlike her sisters, who thought she was silly, she instilled Divine magic into her world. It took root and permeated every life form, giving every beast, rock, and tree a spirit. Truth was, every creation on Shara's and Earth's world also had a spirit, but because Gea anchored that wisdom into the fabric of her world, the knowing could never be lost.

As time passed, the continual reshaping by the sisters created distinctive worlds. Shara and Earth each became consumed with making her world more magnificent than the other's and a friendly competition turned into a rivalry. As the goddesses focused more of their attention on certain aspects of their creation, the frequencies also changed so that no longer were all three worlds connected, at least to the ordinary observer.

One day, Earth rested on a mountaintop and gazed out over her creation. She smiled. The patchwork of green, brown, tan, and blue pleased her. More sensual and companionable than either of her siblings, Earth wished she had someone to share it with. She thought of Gea and Shara but shook her head. She didn't like water as Shara did. It was too deep and emotional. And Gea... well, Gea just wasn't exciting enough.

Lonely, Earth became saddened and started to weep. Her tears flooded her precious lands, eroding her mountains and gouging deep gorges. She cried even more.

Gea came to her. "Sister, you must restore your heart. You are destroying your beautiful world."

Earth flung herself into her older sister's arms and cried. "I have no one with whom to share my beautiful world. I have some of Shara's sea creatures, but I want something special. Unique." She pleaded with her sister. "Share with me some of your human creations."

Gea looked long at Earth. "I would be happy to share with you the humans from my world. I will also share them with Shara. We must maintain a balance to keep stable our planet, upon which each of us live and thrive. You will need to oversee your humans, for as you care for them, they will care for you."

Earth nodded enthusiastically. "I'll watch over them. I'll do everything you tell me. When can I have them?"

Gea called Shara and Earth to her homeland. They sat at the top of the world and looked over Gea's lands and seas.

"Let me give you two pairs from each region. You must learn how to take care of them before I give you more."

The sisters took their prizes back to their domains and placed them in the most hospitable environments. They watched over them like first-time mother hens over their broods of chicks. Earth and Shara were ecstatic.

Gea and the Great Mother were pleased and soon seeded more humans. For a period, they thrived.

But Earth wanted more. She watched her creatures mate and have offspring. She wanted to know what that felt like. She decided she wanted a mate. Someone who was her equal. Someone with whom she could create little Earths. One day, a stranger named Kurat arrived.

"I can make your home the loveliest paradise in the whole universe," he said with a winning smile. "Together, we will fashion more worlds like this one. Together, we can rule the galaxy." His handsome features glowed with a golden light.

Earth admired his muscular form and imagined becoming a Great Mother of her own clutch of planets and stars. Yet, a tiny tickle inside warned Earth to be careful. She held back, and decided to test this charming god.

Kurat was particularly interested in her creatures, especially the two-legged ones. "These creatures can become the most powerful in your realm. Why do you keep them small?"

The question took Earth aback. "What do you mean? All my creatures are equal. I love all of them equally. None are better than another. Each plays a different role in my world. I don't want to disturb the balance. It has been working perfectly for eons."

The man took Earth in his arms and kissed her. "And you have not been happy. I felt your plight from across the galaxy."

Earth had never felt the touch of a god, such as this man. She forgot about her creations and surrendered to the seductive charms of the stranger from far away. She fell into a deep sleep. When she awoke, the stranger was gone. She searched everywhere, but there was no sign of Kurat. Then she noticed her creations. Instead of her animals and humans mingling and foraging alongside each other, the humans had clustered into groups and hunted their animal friends. And each other!

Earth was shocked. She transformed into a woman and walked her lands. She mingled with the animals in the forests and on the plains and listened to the trees and mountains. They all said the same thing. "Kurat has stolen the heart of our home and transformed it into his likeness. There is a hier-

archy now, among species, and the males of the two-legged ones have claimed superiority. We are no longer safe. Please help us."

Earth shape-shifted to become an eagle and spied upon the human camps. It was true. The males appeared to subjugate the females, mating brutally with their women as the urge drove them, fighting and killing each other and killing their animal friends. Their attitude towards the land that had provided so generously had turned possessive. She noticed that rather than find a peaceful resolution, they quickly resorted to violence. She abhorred violence and the despoiling of her creations!

Earth fled to Gea. She cried and cried. "What have I done? I have ruined my world. What can I do?"

Shara and Gea tried to console Earth.

"I'll destroy my world and start over," she declared.

"If you destroy your creation, Sister, you will also destroy us and our worlds. We will help you restore the balance. But the damage is done. We have to build on what remains."

Gea, the wise, elder sister, continued, "We cannot go in and cast out what has been seeded into the hearts of the inhabitants of your domain. Instead, we have to set up a way for your world to evolve and shift its frequency out of what Kurat has entrained. It will take time. We must let this cycle play out. Then you will have recovered your beautiful realm again." Gea patted Earth on the shoulder. "It won't be easy. You must be strong and dedicated. And patient. We will aid you in this task."

They spent days absorbing the ancient wisdom of Gea's Heartland, formulating a plan. "It's risky," Gea said. "If it doesn't work, all of us will be destroyed."

Shara added, "You must keep the Goddess alive in your world. People must live by listening to their hearts and remember that they are not only united as a species, but one with all life forms in your world, ours, and the cosmos. When people forget they are all children of the Great Mother and lose their connection to Her, and magic is replaced by the intellect and the need for empirical proof, we will have failed."

"Support the females of your populations. Imprint into them the Great Mother's wisdom and the memory of the Goddess. Don't let them forget it." Gea handed Earth and Shara a bowl of crystals. "Plant these around your realms. They provide a link between our worlds and will help to amplify the Mother Goddess's Divine Love in yours. Protect these crystals. They are your lifeline to the Mother and critical to your survival."

Heartened, Earth returned home. She was determined to undo the betrayal by her lover. She transformed into a wise woman and went from clan to clan. She chose a woman from each village, imprinted her with the wisdom of the Goddess, and declared her leader of the clan. She blessed her priestess to protect her from the males who would depose her. To ensure the message survived through the generations, Earth gave specific instructions to each of her priestesses on how to erect sacred schools that taught those with the talent the mysteries of the Goddess. She made changes in women's bodies so that they would always have a connection to the Goddess, no matter what they had to endure. This wisdom would pass down through the maternal line and, over many generations, tame the changes that Kurat had implanted into the males of the human species.

Based upon Gea's guidance, Earth dictated one Divine Truth to her priestesses. "Everyone — every human, animal, plant, rock, or tree — everything seen and unseen — all of us are children of the Great Mother and are alive with the spirit of the Great Mother. They are Divine expressions of Her. As such, everything is animated by the same force — the Great Mother. All creations serve and are equal in the eyes of the Mother, and all are sovereign, free to choose their life path. Remember this above all else, and let it be your guide."

Earth watched over her humans. She wept at how she saw, over and over, her women being treated as Kurat had treated her. Taking what wasn't his to take, degrading women, treating them like slaves and property to be bartered for what could be gained. Using charm or force — it had the same result.

Earth withdrew to her mountaintop. She didn't want to know. It saddened her. Sometimes she would weep and the world flooded. Other times she became angry and massive storms swept across the lands and seas, destroying anything in their wake. She could feel the life being sucked from her. She begged her sisters for help.

Gea came to where she lay, cradled in an enormous volcano. Steam rose around her and the mountain rumbled ominously.

"I'm trying to be patient, Sister," Earth said. "I get angry at what Kurat did to me and my world, and at my human creatures who rape and pillage me without any consideration of the consequences or the harm they are doing to me. They bicker and fight over resources, believing they don't have enough. They have abused my abundance, thinking wealth equals possessions, power, and control over others. They don't realize the waste they create all on their own. They have brought the world to the brink of annihilation several times with their energy weapons and senseless disregard for the dangerous substances with which they meddle, poisoning me and my creations. Males still subjugate my women, degrade them, and think of them as the lesser of their species. They would rather fight wars than find peaceful solutions."

Earth sighed. She stretched out her arm and jabbed the earth. It shook. Quietly, she said, "Magic has been lost. A flower becomes a combination of petals, stamen, and chemicals. Forgotten is the essence of the flower and acknowledgment of the transformative effects of a flower's beauty on one's psyche, the calming or stimulating effects of her scent, and color frequencies that merge mind and heart."

"All but a few outcasts have forgotten the Goddess, the Great Mother. My priestesses have almost all been destroyed, replaced by male dominated organizations who claim to be the spokesman for the Divine. In reality, these organizations serve as just another way to control people through fear. There are

only a handful of my lineage that remember. Sadly, my beautiful and abundant realm has become a wasteland and the playground for the Dark Lords." Earth sighed again. "Sometimes, I feel like igniting all the volcanos and bringing an end to the two-legged ones."

Gea sat beside her sister and put an arm around her shoulders. "I know, Earth. This scourge of unconsciousness, aided by the Dark Lords, has invaded Shara's world and mine, as well." Gea hesitated.

"What is it, Gea?"

"Kurat has visited Shara's world, too."

Earth sat up abruptly. The land beneath her rumbled. "What has he done to Shara?"

"He came to her disguised as an albatross while she rested on an island watching her dolphins play. He tried to woo her, but she saw through his illusion. He came back again, disguised as a salmon. Not knowing his true nature, one of her servants brought him to her on a platter. She was about to eat him, but one of her dolphins leapt onto the table and consumed him. The dolphin died immediately. Aggrieved, Shara cast him out, forbidding him to return.

"When cold-hearted Kurat enchanted you, you didn't know that he had allied with the Dark Lords. In retaliation of Shara's rejection, he ordered his servants, the Lizard clans, to invade her world. The clans act like locusts, swarming from planet to planet, breeding, and consuming all life and resources to raise

11

their offspring. Kurat, with his Lizard clan allies, plans to become the master of the Galaxy." Gea patted Earth's arm. "Don't feel bad, Sister. He has raped many a realm, leaving his mark upon the few that have survived. What he couldn't claim with charm like he did you, he takes by force." Gea shuddered. "Evil creature. Even if he is a child of the Great Mother."

"What can we do?"

"We must work together to survive. I have an idea." Gea started humming a melody. "Do you remember Mother singing this to us when we were young?"

Earth nodded. "It is her creation song. Let's get Shara and sing it together, and recreate our worlds."

Earth made space for Gea to settle beside her and the two goddesses started singing. Soon Shara joined them. They sang for days, for centuries.

Earth relaxed. Before her, she noticed subtle shifts in the terrain. She felt subtle awakenings in her body. She smiled. "My priestesses, the Spirit Women of Shara, and the Gra'Bandia Healers awaken. We shall prevail, Sisters. Thank you."

ONE

ELLARA AND CLERIC WILSON

Sheldon, Alba

"I command you to leave." Cleric Wilson blocked the doorway to the sleeping room. "Begone, witch!" Shoving me with one plump hand, he raised the other to make the sign of the cross to ward off evil.

I stood my ground and peered around him to the woman moaning on the sleeping mat. Basilee, once healthy and vibrant, now barely moved. A quick glance at the midwife sponging Basilee's forehead and shooting angry glances at the cleric alerted me to my patient's dire condition. Basilee's mate, Patrick, paced back and forth, crossing his hands over his heart in the customary position to petition the Goddess.

I knew how important this baby was to Basilee and Patrick. After years of trying, this was their first child brought to full term. Swallowing several times to suppress my apprehension, I ducked under the clergyman's arm and squeezed past his ample waistline, pleased at the way he cringed away from me. I hastened to Basilee. Her pulses were thready, as were her feeble contractions. The midwife and I exchanged frowns. We had worked together for many years on difficult birthings. Placing my hands on my patient's belly, I sensed the distress of the baby. As I invited life force to flow through me and into the mother and child, I asked softly, "How long?" I pulled a dropper bottle of tincture from my medicine kit.

"Since early this morning. The baby is breech and I cannot tend to her." The midwife cast a scathing look at the black-robed man. Then under her breath, "When he went out to relieve himself, we were able to convince his assistant to send word for you."

"You should have fetched me sooner."

Basilee moaned weakly as another contraction gripped her body. The Natuan cleric, who professed to be the best physician in the land, glared at us. "Stop. You can do nothing. It's too late for her, and for the unborn babe. She's in God's hands now."

I parted Basilee's lips and dropped the herbal formula into her mouth.

The doula's hands moved expertly around Basilee's belly. "We need the Goddess's help," she whispered. "Basilee and the child are at death's door."

I looked at the stony visage of Cleric Wilson. This was the first time I had come face to face with this new vicar who called himself God's physician. If he witnessed a successful birthing after he had proclaimed it hopeless, both the midwife and I would be accused of being witches and arrested, and I would likely be murdered like many of my sister Gra'Bandia Healers. I sighed. I had pledged to serve the Goddess and accept the consequences.

The man must have read my thoughts. "Since the new laws have *finally* outlawed your archaic Goddess tradition, you are forbidden to practice your craft, Healer. You break the law by being here and helping her. I will finally have the evidence I need to have you killed."

Cleric Wilson had arrived in Sheldon three months ago with the arrogant Captain Sengy, who quickly killed our Peeress and her pair'ti and proclaimed himself the omnipotent ruler of our province. Lord Sengy had forced the physician upon my patients, and many women had died. To help those who had not, I followed behind him and repaired the damage his methods had caused. It appeared that the palliative practices of the Natuan clergymen consisted mostly of having faith that the One God would heal the malady. It relied very little upon actual herbal, physical, or wound-tending care. Even if this man had been trained in the latest scientific education about the human body, as he professed, he didn't have a clue about organizing and harmonizing the energies in body systems to bring about life and health.

I placed a hand on Basilee's and let the Goddess energy flow into her. "Bassie, stay with us."

Basilee opened her eyes and feebly squeezed my hand. "Thank the Goddess you are here, Ellara."

The cleric approached, glaring at me, and growled, "Her soul is prepared to enter the grace of the One God. I will not allow her salvation to be contaminated by the demonic work you do."

I raised my hand and, palm outward, pushed it towards him as if I could expel him from the room through sheer will. "Leave us. We have work to do!" As I moved toward him, he backed away, crossing himself. I nodded to Patrick to follow the physician and keep him out of the room. Satisfied that the cleric's fear of Gra'Bandia Healers could be used against him, I closed the door and wedged a chair against it to guard against the clergyman witnessing what was required.

Once we were alone, I softly sang the calming song my mentor, Nana Magog, had taught me as I lightly stroked Basilee's belly, relaxing her muscles so the midwife could turn the infant. As I sang, I opened to the Goddess and called upon Her Gra'yia to give this mother and child the vitality they needed to endure the birthing. The life-giving force of the Goddess's love flowed through me, and the doula manipulated the baby into position.

The contractions strengthened. I propped Basilee so she could lean against me and push. In my mind's eye, I watched a channel of light open through the birth canal and the infant pass quickly into the outer world. The girl-child cried lustily.

Fists beat upon the door. "Open up!" the cleric demanded.

"Bassie, are you alright?" Patrick called.

"Patrick, you have a healthy, beautiful girl," the midwife responded.

Patrick's shouts of joy punctuated the clergyman's pounding on the door and demands to enter.

"We'll let you in when we are finished," I said.

We ignored the cacophony outside and supported the mother while she delivered the placenta. We cleaned and purified Basilee and the baby in the traditional way. The midwife put the infant into Basilee's arms. The Goddess's Loving Radiance continued to flow through me until mother and newborn felt strong.

Basilee smiled adoringly at her baby, stroking her as the babe suckled noisily. "Just look at her! She's perfect," she crooned. She hummed softly. By the time we collected the bloodied cloths and cleaned the birthing area, the infant had fallen asleep, content in her mother's embrace.

Before the midwife opened the door to the enraged physician, Basilee caught my arm. "Thank you, Ellara. None can do what you can. You truly are a gifted Healer. You took a great risk by calling in the Gra'yia of the Goddess. I was prepared to die, but I know it would have been hard for Patrick." She chuckled. "I'm the one that keeps the business and home going." She squeezed my hand. "I will keep this secret, even if we have to endure their exorcism ritual."

She referred to an order by Lord Sengy demanding that the Natuan physician must tend to the care of the body and spirit. Families who were discovered to be using Gra'Bandia Healers were taken to the manor house for a torturous exorcism. This made the inhabitants of the region reluctant to call, at least openly, for a Healer's services.

Cleric Wilson burst into the room and inspected the recovering mother, who was returning to her feisty self. He turned accusatory eyes to me. "What demonic craft is this? She was at death's door. I anointed her so she and the babe could go to the Natuan afterlife." He leaned closer. "What bargain did you make with the devil so she could live?"

I stared at the man, appalled. "No bargain. You would have let an innocent mother and her unborn child die because of your ignorance and hubris. You are not following the precepts of your religion, Cleric." We glared at each other. *Is he really trying to rid our country of the Goddess tradition by letting women die, as the rumors claim?*

"She was beyond saving."

I pressed my lips together to hold back the incendiary words that threatened to escape. Instead, I said, "It appears that perhaps the Natuan physicians do not understand women and childbirth as well as they proclaim."

The self-important man jabbed a pudgy finger at me. "You Healers lead your people in barbaric ways. We will rid this island of heathens just like we did in the Emerald Mountains. Alba will be converted to the Natuan faith, as the rest of the world has been!"

Moving with a speed one would not expect from such a rotund man, the physician grabbed my arm. An electric shock coursed through my body. I felt his fear and something else with which I was unfamiliar. I wished I had my daughter's ability to see auras.

"Ellara Ruark, I'm arresting you for the practice of witchcraft. Your trial will be short, and you will be cast from the cliffs!"

"I did nothing illegal. You have no grounds to charge me."

He sneered. "Not even that scholarly Cleric Paul, a traitor to his holy vows, can free you this time! Paul's time is coming, and he will not be welcomed into the Natuan heaven because of his associations with you!" He dragged me from the small cottage and into the custody of Lord Sengy's Natuan mercenaries.

TWO

ROKAN AND THE GRAND MASTER

Suzerain's Palace, Tokurat, Desert Lands

S mall dust devils stirred by the desert breezes were the only signs of life along the darkened streets. Cloth walls, securing the closed food and merchandise stalls, flapped lazily. Laughter came from a nearby shuttered building, and the melancholy notes of a shawm, a common reeded flute of the Desert Lands, accompanied by low chanting, drifted from somewhere in Old Tokurat. Even at this late hour, not all citizens slept. This was my time, an hour for clandestine meetings, assassinations, and spying.

"Master Rokan." The soft call came from the shadows opposite my lair. Creeping from the shadows, the servant continued, "The Suzerain wants to see you immediately."

"Come on," I grunted. I strode toward the palace of Tokur's head of state, the servant trailing behind. Detecting a change in his footfalls, I spun around as the man leaped at me, dagger in hand.

I dodged the thrust and with my longer reach, grabbed the man by the scruff of his neck, and tightened my fingers in a pincer-hold that was both painful and incapacitating. In seconds, the servant's appearance dissolved into a low-ranking Droc'ri sorcerer. "I have no patience for you, Brother." I snarled. "You cannot defeat me."

The man thrashed. "You're an old man, Rokan. You are too weak to remain the Grand Master's Henchman. Step aside and let one more capable do it."

"You think you can kill me to get my position?" I snorted and leaned in, inches from his face. "I am your Master, Brother." I squeezed my fingers against the arteries of his neck. Releasing him, I let him slump to the ground in a faint.

I continued towards the palace, muttering to myself, "Old indeed! I've only lived two hundred years. I'm in my prime! Irksome underlings, perpetually making me prove my superiority."

I skirted wide around the broad lamp-lined entry through which dignitaries passed for an audience with the Suzerain. Instead, I chose a narrow, paved path that led to a quiet side door opening into a network of passages within and beneath the palace. A servant paced the corridor near the entry. When he saw me, he stopped moving and lowered his head, his fingers twitching nervously. "Master Rokan, the Suzerain wants to see you immediately."

I don't want to see him now, I thought. I just braved the high seas to accomplish his distasteful tasks while he eats grapes and sips rose water in his favorite garden. I dismissed the frightened servant. *I'll see Garrick when I am ready.*

Instead of heading to my private sanctuary beneath the palace, I chose another corridor that led to the servants' quarters. I tapped on a door. It opened immediately. A lithe, black-haired young woman smiled enthusiastically and pulled me into her small room.

A recent addition to the palace servants, Sophia, was a pleasing combination of loveliness and intelligence. Of all the servants I had used, she served me the best. I rewarded her dedication generously, with custards and other delicacies from the Suzerain's table, as well as jewelry and trinkets I came across in my travels.

Wordlessly, she led me to her bed and slid off my shirt. She knelt behind me and pressed strong thumbs into the muscles along my spine, kneading upwards and out along the tops of my shoulders.

"Rokan," she murmured in a soft voice, "You smell of the sea. Are you still working on the conquest of Alba?"

I nodded. Sophia had relatives in Alba and was particularly interested in the events taking place there. "The Natuan clerics are forcing out the Goddess tradition. My magic broke through the Goddess's shield which protects the Alban merchant fleet from Bruce the Terrible and his pirates."

"And now Bruce the Terrible can attack them? Is that what has made you so tense?"

I sighed. "I spent two miserable days at sea with the man." I snorted. "Bruce is an overbearing moron! He has no class and is nothing more than a two-bit pirate. His magic is pitiful. He can barely calm the sea or call the wind. He couldn't break through the magical shields around the Alban ships. I had to do it for him. I should have never awakened his feeble magical abilities."

Sophia shuddered. "I'll never forget how that beastly man captured me. I hated serving him on our way to Tokurat, but I saw what happened to the women who refused." She exhaled raggedly and took a minute to recompose herself. "I am glad you are not like him or the other sorcerers."

She reached towards a small bed stand laden with bottles of scented lotions and herbal infusions, a comb, hairpins, and a few pieces of jewelry. She picked up and uncorked a small container, releasing the sweetly pungent aroma of evergreen trees mixed with frankincense, lavender, and several herbs. She had made the infusions from samples I brought back from her homeland in the north where evergreens grew. "Here, let me soothe your aches with this oil. I made it especially for you."

As she rubbed the ointment into my skin, the angst from the days with Bruce the Terrible faded away. "You always succeed where others fail," she remarked as she worked along my arms. "You deserve respect and reward for all the sacrifices you make for your master."

The atmosphere surrounding us shifted as her heart opened and a pale mist emanated from her and filled the air. I inhaled the ephemeral nectar of her emotions, smiling to myself. My charm was one of my best tools. It was so much easier to feed on a willing partner.

I pulled her onto my lap and kissed her. Meeting her gray-eyed gaze, I touched her forehead, drawing the symbol for sleep, and added the dream that would feel so real to her that she would brag to her friends about her incredibly sensual time with me. Sleep also promoted recovery of the energy reserves that I drained.

I had not engaged in physical mating for over one hundred years. I had discovered that, while pleasurable, it often took more time and energy than I could spare. Husbanding my strength for magical purposes had become my priority. Harvesting another's vitality, the unseen essence that animated a person and allowed them to work, eat, and live, was far more effective and efficient. Along with an ecstatic lift, I could sustain my magic and negate the need for sleep. Replenishing my spirit with another's life force was much faster than eating and sleeping, as others did. I preferred the northern women, especially those raised in the Goddess tradition. Their essence had an unrestrained quality about it. Unlike women of the Desert Lands, in the north they were free to live and love as they liked.

As Sophia drifted into her erotic fantasy, I kissed her again, my magic drawing forth her life force in a gossamer thread. I inhaled and savored the substance recharging my body. Suspecting I would be interrupted before I could be satiated, with a swift movement of my fingers, I drew all of her vitality and amassed it into a pulsing orb before me. Her body went limp, and she stopped breathing. All I had to do was ingest her entire spirit, and I would have the energetic sustenance I needed for the next several days. But a good servant was hard to come by, and Sophia knew how to please me without expecting anything in return or becoming jealous of my other lovers.

I pursed my lips and blew most of her spirit back into her body. Immediately, her breath and muscle tone returned to normal. *What fragile creatures we are.* It is so easy to steal the life of another without the other even suspecting. Unlike other sorcerers who fed on human life, Garrick being the most wasteful, I never took so much of my lover's life force as to kill her. Instead, I sipped from my victims, and they fed me for months — after which they ultimately died. Garrick went through a dozen servants a week!

I had barely begun to fill myself, depleted as I was by the intense effort of breaking through the protective barrier on the Alban frigate, when someone pounded on the door and thrust it open.

The Droc'ri sorcerer took in the scene and appeared to delight in interrupting my pleasure. "The Grand Master commands you to his presence. Now."

I lay back on the bed and willed myself not to kill the man.

"The Grand Master is furious with you, Rokan," the sorcerer said. "He may finally eliminate you, and then I can take your position."

I snorted as I slowly shrugged into my shirt. This Droc'ri had already tried to assassinate me a dozen times. *I should just exterminate him and be done with it!* But the curse the Healer, Ellara, had placed on me so many years ago drained my magic so thoroughly that if I were to kill someone, I would need to consume the life essence of a dozen servants to replace what was lost. The cost to do what used to be so easy now made me appear weak.

I left the young woman's room. The Droc'ri messenger followed behind. "I can find my way, Sid. Go on." I turned to wave him away.

At that moment, a half-dozen brown-robed sorcerers emerged from side passages and swarmed around me, curved assassin daggers glinting in the torchlight. I cursed silently, wondering why I hadn't sensed them.

I backed to the wall and warily faced my attackers.

"You again!" I growled. This was not the first time Sid and his cohorts had tried to eliminate me. "You think that killing me will make you that much closer to becoming Grand Master?" I lifted my head, wearing a smug smile, trusting that my relaxed posture would confuse my opponents. I stared each man in the eye, projecting an attitude of invincibility, while my fingers moved swiftly at my side, weaving a protection spell around myself.

"Yes," Sid replied. "You've had that privilege far too long."

"Come on, Rokan. We know you hate working for the Grand Master. How about an eternity working for the Dark Lords in the Tiarna Drocha instead?" another man taunted. Someone hurled a spear of fire.

I lifted my hand, palm outward, effortlessly blocking the feeble attack. It dissipated harmlessly around me.

"Is that the best you can do?" I took my time while I read each one's energy, counting on my reputation as an efficient death-dealer to weaken their resolve. This wasn't their first attempt, and I knew what to expect. So did they.

The man who spoke was afraid of me. I could sense it. So were the others. Finally, I grabbed my blade and leaped at the weakest member of the group. Buffeted by his companion's blows, I swung the man around, using him as a shield.

Men pressed me from all sides. Daggers slashed at me and some nicked my arms or thighs. The man who had been my shield soon hung like a ragdoll in my grasp. His dead weight slowed me down. I hurled him at several attackers, knocking them down, and attacked those remaining with a single-minded focus.

Fighting assassin-trained sorcerers was not like a typical tavern brawl. Not only were they highly skilled in the art of killing, but they used magical powers as well. However, these foolish men didn't frighten me. They annoyed me.

Using a prized spell I had formulated long ago to gather the magic cast against me, I used my attackers to strengthen me and increase my agility. I smelled their fear and sent it back to them, amplified.

I dodged a black lightning bolt and hurled my own at the feet of my assailants, anchoring the men's feet to the floor. Unable to move, they sent unseen hands to squeeze my throat. Tendrils of invisible energy wrapped around my chest. Other strands wound around my legs in an attempt to hobble me. Instead of entrapping me, the cords dissolved where they touched my body, and drained the magic from my opponents.

When they tired, I slipped a hand into my pocket. My fingers touched my traveling talisman. I imprinted the stone with a location and silently said the words that summoned the gateway to the frigid lands in the far north. With a wave of my hand, I cast the sorcerers into that darkness.

Leaning against the wall, I caught my breath. I inspected the blood-soaked rips in my tunic and automatically summoned the magic to heal my wounds and restore my clothing. It would have been better if I had killed them. It may take a while, but those Droc'ri would be back. Again, I cursed my invisible link to Ellara, brought on by what I had once taken from her.

A palace servant trembling at the end of the hallway beckoned. "The Suzerain awaits you," he squeaked.

I sauntered along the darkened corridors that led deeper under the citadel to Garrick's secret chamber. I knew the longer I delayed, the more annoyed he would become. It was risky to anger the Droc'ri Grand Master, but his fury would cloud his mind, making him easier to deceive. That suited me just fine. He thinks he can order me about like he did when we were growing up. And he has the gall to send his minions to assassinate me, not once, but twice in one night! He deliberately waits until I am enjoying the intimate companionship of one of my favorite ladies before he summons me. I usually talk with him in the garden, and this could probably wait until tomorrow.

Outside the room, I paused, produced a magical mirror to inspect my visage, and clamped shut a silver brooch to hold my hair behind my neck. I tugged on the hem of my tunic, ensuring that every wrinkle was removed, and took a deep breath, shifting my expression into one of indifference. I dismissed the servant, knowing the grim fate Garrick would have for him if he entered. Cowering, the man backed away with surprising speed. I sighed. *I'm tired of this life as a Droc'ri sorcerer. I wish...* No, I dared not even think of the wish that broke every Droc'ri code.

I strode hurriedly into the room. A solitary oil lamp on the table in the center cast a man's shadow onto walls of solid white marble. "Forgive me, Master," I said breathlessly.

A thin, bald man sat on a gold, velvet chair before a table. Garrick Solan, publicly known as the Suzerain of Tokur, and secretly, the Grand Master of the Droc'ri Order, yanked elaborately embroidered, deep-blue silk robes closer around him, annoyed. The fingers of his other hand reflexively stroked the jeweled hilt of a curved dagger that hung on his gold braided belt, alongside a small silk purse. Expensive leather slippers adorned his feet, and many rare, large gemstones glittered from slender fingers. A gold band encircled his head. Though he used an illusion to present himself as youthful, his somber features couldn't disguise that this man was much older than he appeared. He exuded an air of power and authority.

"You're late!" Garrick, in his Grand Master role, snapped. "What's your excuse this time, Rokan?"

I cast a glance at the maps on the table. Alba's was uppermost, and he had drawn the dagger symbol for the Droc'ri, the one each brother bore as a tattoo, boldly on the sheet. I had been to Alba many times and knew the expansive isle to be a paradise, rich in resources and with a temperate climate for farming. The vast, enchanted forests in the Heartland were rumored to contain the wisdom of the Cosmos, and Alba possessed unparalleled wealth in its diamond mines.

I stood at a respectful distance from the table and my master. I averted my eyes from the body of a servant lying on the floor, eyes bulging and mouth wide in a voiceless scream. Flies buzzed around the corpse. What a waste, I thought. I had never liked to squander resources, and servants were another form of wealth.

Garrick noticed my expression and commented sourly, "It's much quicker than what you do."

I pushed aside my loathing for my master and stood a little taller. I wore an ordinary brown tunic that emphasized my muscular physique. Tight dark trousers defined the anatomy in my crotch and hinted at what pleasure could be had if Garrick followed his inner urges. I tucked my thumb into the woven gold and silver belt, a symbol of my status in the Droc'ri Order, but kept my fingers away from the equally splendid cousin to the Grand Master's dagger fastened there. I deliberately dressed simply to demonstrate my lower rank and provide a subtle statement about my master's excesses. Garrick's gaze raked over my body and lingered in the nether region. I straightened just a little, satisfied by the tiny smile Garrick wore.

"Your messenger said it was urgent. What has happened, Master?"

Garrick waved a hand dismissively. "I see you survived my test. I have to give my underlings practice in assassination. And I knew if you survived, you would not kill them." He shook his head. "You've lost your edge, Rokan. You'll never succeed me as Grand Master."

"I don't want to succeed you, Master. *You* are a good Grand Master: cunning, ruthless, and an excellent example for the rest of us. I could never emulate you."

Garrick smiled. His tone turned silky. I tensed. "You've been gone over two days. Is Alba finally mine?"

I hesitated. He would not like my answer.

He leaned forward, his gaze boring into me. "You have failed me, Rokan. I gave you a simple task to destroy the Goddess's hold over Alba, conquer the country, and add it to my empire. Alba and her Healers are all that stand in the way of my becoming Grand Master of our world, Gea."

I pressed my lips together, fearing what I might say. When I had control over myself, I said tightly, "I was seeing to the prophecy, as well as to your interests in Alba."

"Ah, yes. The prophecy. I can't have some fractured Healer who is not a Healer interfering with my plans. Have you located her?"

"Not yet, Master." I lowered my head submissively. "The prophecy says the Healer will be mated to a captain from the sea. I have assassinated all the men but one who fits this description. The last captain has unusually strong protection. But he will join his friends in the Otherworld very soon. You can be assured of that. This will disable her ability to destroy the Droc'ri Order." *Then Ellara can't fulfill the prophecy, and I can use her to satisfy my own goals. I can't let Garrick know about Ellara.*

"Find her," Garrick growled. "I must make certain she is eliminated." He thumped his fist on the table. "You were to bring me *all* the Healers, Rokan, and yet you have brought me only a few. How are we to find the true Healer from the prophecy if you do not round them up?"

"There is a ship on its way to Tokurat now with women escaping from Alba. Some of them are Healers, though they will deny it. We will soon ferret them out."

Garrick fingered the map of Alba, pulling it closer. He tapped his forefinger on a forested area in the center of the map. "What are you doing about the secret Gra'Bandia Council meeting in Alba's Heartland? I want those Healers most of all. They can still pose a threat to me."

"Yes, Master." I grimaced inwardly. He asked the impossible. *He expects me to find every last Healer so he can kill her.* Aloud I replied, "The Heartland is protected by powerful magic, and the Droc'ri cannot enter. The Healers come from all over the world and most travel instantly through space as I do."

"Excuses, excuses. Perhaps I need another sorcerer who is more willing to serve me."

"Master, I know you are wise and all-seeing, but leaders and citizens do not always follow your timeline. The actions you have initiated in Alba are bearing fruit already. The country is falling as we speak. You have Alba and the rest of the world in the palm of your hand. You will achieve your conquest of Alba and global domination within a matter of weeks."

Garrick rubbed his hands together gleefully. "Splendid! I will finally be free to leave this barren desert and take my rightful place in Alba as Grand Master of all the peoples, lands, and seas of this earth. Our magic will finally work everywhere. The Droc'ri will become strong again, and people will fear

33

us." He waved a bejeweled hand at me. "And I'll allow you to become Suzerain of Tokur as your reward."

I lowered my gaze. As a loyal Droc'ri, this should be welcome news. But Garrick as Grand Master of the world? I couldn't allow that. And I had no intention of becoming Suzerain to Tokur. There were much more hospitable places to live than the hot, dusty, poor Desert Lands.

He tapped his chin. "Send an imp with a message to Lord Garth's sorcerer in Alba. Have Lord Garth put a generous bounty on the Healer witches for their capture. Tell him they must be kept alive and brought directly to me! One last thing." Garrick twisted his hand and made a beckoning movement. I felt my vitality drain, and my legs weaken. Garrick inhaled the tendril of my life force and smiled. "Don't be late next time! And don't try to deceive me, Rokan. I know you better than you know yourself!" He finally dropped his hand. I slumped, clutching at the wall, and suppressed the anger that threatened to blast through my self-control.

I leaned against the cold stone, struggling to get my legs under me and cast another glance at the maps on the table. Alba is all that stands in the way of his global control. I scowled. *There is no way in the Tiarna Drocha's eternal hell that I'll let that vile gombeen escape this desolate land and become Grand Master of the world!* I have a better plan.

THREE

ELLARA AND CLERIC PAUL

Sheldon Vicarage

I had been arrested a handful of times in the previous months after Cleric Wilson had gotten wind I was a Healer. The previous times, though, I had been freed almost immediately with the aid of Cleric Paul, Sheldon's scholarly representative of the Natuan faith. He had been able to argue there was no evidence of lawbreaking. This time, as the days passed in the cold prison, I wondered if the new physician had been right, and not even Cleric Paul could liberate me.

Six days passed in my dingy cell before the lock rattled and the door groaned open. I stood, thinking I was to be released. Instead, a guard spun me around, roughly pulled my hands behind my back, and shackled my wrists and ankles. A stout rope was threaded through the metal bands, and one of the guards grabbed the loose end.

In the dim light, I discerned the red uniforms of Lord Sengy's soldiers. Where were the Alban guards who had been my custodians?

"What's this?" I protested. "Unhand me!"

"Silence, Witch."

They tossed a thin cloak about me, the hood covering my head and half my face so I could only see the floor. They dragged me out of the building and thrust me into a waiting cart. Two men sat on each side of me, holding my arms. Two more guards sat on the driver's bench. The wagon bumped and jolted on the cobblestones. At least the warmth from my captors eased the chilly night. Salty air indicated we were nearing the Sheldon port.

Dockworkers called to each other, and their curses mingled with the clunks of windlass gears and creak of wood. Dread ate at me. I wished my pair'ti, Sam, were here, but he was still at sea, racing towards Sheldon. I contemplated trying to escape. I was wedged between two strong men, who had tethered me with a sturdy rope as if I were a dangerous, wild beast. I smiled wryly as I imagined myself as a fierce grimalkin threatening my captors with a few swipes of my claws.

"Stop! Release her!" came Cleric Paul's reedy voice. I craned my neck but could only see the backs of the driver and his companion.

The cart came to a halt. "Out of my way, old man."

Cleric Paul approached the guards, waving a piece of parchment. "Release her!" he panted. "She is not guilty of the charges against her!"

"Who are you?" the irritated guard snapped. "You have no authority over us." He slapped the horse's rump with the reins, but the cart didn't move.

"Cleric Paul, and your vicar."

The guard snorted. "We only answer to Cleric Wilson."

"It doesn't matter. Lord Sengy signed this writ for Ellara's release. You are required to follow your commander's orders."

"His orders were to take her to the waiting ship going to Araval and deliver her to Arkheim Aleas." The guard snatched the order for my release, held it up to the torch wedged on the side of the cart, and sneered at the elder. He started to tear it up. "You won't cheat us out of our share of the reward for her capture. You're just a graybeard. You can't stop us."

Cleric Paul drew himself erect. He lifted a hand skyward, and his reedy voice became full. "May the One God smite me down this instant if this writ is not true and legal." With his other hand, he pointed at the soldier. "May He cast you into Hell if you dare to defy His commands!"

The guard paused in ripping the document.

Silence reigned as everyone watched to see if the One God would actually strike down the clergyman. He remained standing proudly.

"Lord Garth and Captain Sengy, and all of you soldiers, have sworn an oath to the Natuan Ethnarch, our earthly representative of the One God and leader of our faith, to uphold the Truths of the One God. These Truths have been ignored and falsely interpreted by some for their personal greed and aggrandizement. Those who do so, or help their superiors do so, will be punished for eternity!" He lowered his upraised hand but still pointed with his other at the guards.

They shifted uneasily.

I clinked the metal shackles together.

Cleric Paul indicated to me. "Remove her restraints."

My captors gave me a hostile look as they jerked my arms, releasing the catches in the irons binding my wrists and ankles. I slid out of the cart and rubbed my wrists. Tossing the rope and the manacles into the wagon, the men climbed aboard. The driver savagely whipped the horse into action.

Cleric Paul put a bony arm around my shoulder. "You're freezing, Ellara. Come, let's get you home."

Attended by a handful of Alban regimentals, Cleric Paul guided me to his humble residence, overrun with books, leather-bound manuscripts, ancient scrolls, and statues. He invited me to sit in the only available chair and have some tea and a little sustenance.

"It was not so easy to get you released this time, Ellara. Cleric Wilson made a good case against you. The Peers acquitted you, but Lord Sengy refused to honor their decision. You are lucky you have such loyal patrons willing to defend you, despite the costs to themselves."

I sat up. "Is Basilee alright? Has she or her baby been harmed?"

The old man shook his head. "They are fine. Lord Sengy is a bully, and he is not as smart as he thinks. It seems that even he must adhere to the laws he claims to uphold, and Cleric Wilson could not absolutely prove you used the Goddess's magic, since he was not in the room to witness it. Even though practicing your art is supposedly forbidden, depending upon how one interprets the Natuan Code, Healers are not forbidden from wound tending, herbal treatments, or anything that does not require the use of the Goddess's power. Even the latest edict disbanding the Gra'Bandia Council and its leadership role in Alba only restricts a Healer, or anyone else for that matter, from engaging with or associating with the Council. It does not prohibit a Healer from practicing. Only the Natuan Code does. It was argued that the mother's survival was a result of the herbs you gave her and the midwife's skill."

He smiled to himself. He poured a steeped tisane into a cup and handed it to me along with a plate of sliced cheese and bread. A sly grin crossed his thin features. "Cleric Wilson would have known that if he had done his research." He shook his head again. "We can be grateful that whoever wrote the latest edicts was *not* an Advocate."

I perked up. "Are you saying that the recent proclamation does not authorize the soldiers to hunt Healers and abuse women?" The bite I was about to take crumbled between my fingers and bits of bread and cheese fell on my lap. I salvaged what I could while listening intently.

The scholar nodded and chuckled. "It took time to dig through all the volumes." He motioned toward a stack of journals and charters beside his chair.

I suspected that the academic had thoroughly enjoyed outmaneuvering Cleric Wilson with some obscure yet essential facts. The elderly vicar had once been arrogant himself, but over the years of our friendship, he had learned humility. He still loved a passionate debate, and his mind was as sharp as a Heartland-forged blade.

"Ironic, isn't it," I said. "*You* accused me of practicing witchcraft the first time we crossed paths. Remember?"

I had encountered Cleric Paul twenty-five years earlier, when I was newly pregnant with my daughter, Margot. We were both attending a complicated birthing where he had pronounced the mother and child beyond saving. I reminded him of the story.

He laughed. "You accused me of meddling in something I didn't know anything about. I was stunned that you dared to accuse my God of not knowing anything about childbirth. You suggested I should leave that work to those who did. If I could have captured you, I would have had you burned for those blasphemous words! You're lucky Sam hid you on his ship.

And the Peeress of Sheldon forbade me from pursuing you. You Goddess worshippers are a stubborn lot!" He harrumphed.

I finished the cheese and dabbed up the remaining crumbs on the dish with my finger. "The way of the Goddess has worked since the beginning of time. We will not give up the practices that help us to thrive. Besides, you had no legal authority to punish me even if you did capture me." I sighed. "Who would have guessed we'd become friends — considering the difference in our philosophies. I have enjoyed our discussions. I've learned more about the Goddess tradition from you than from the scanty lessons given by my mentor, Nana Magog." I sloshed the tea leaves around the bottom of my cup. "What can we do about these new ordinances, the empty threats and invisible shadow these decrees bring?" I indicated the wall of manuscripts. "There must be a solution in one of those venerable tomes."

"Remember this, Ellara. The Goddess cannot be destroyed. There are those who see the new ordinances as an excuse to persecute you, despite what the documents actually say. They will make your life and the lives of all the Goddess-born miserable until you are no longer."

I protested, "I don't want the traditions and sacred sanctuaries of the Goddess desecrated in Alba as they were in the provinces of the Emerald Mountains during the Religious Wars. I don't want the citizens of Alba to become slaves to an unseen master who exploits their talents for his own gain. Nor do I want Alba to become overrun with patriarchal beliefs that restrict women from exercising their natural talents freely and powerfully in partnership with their pair'ti." I leaned back in my chair. A stack of loose paper on the desk covered in Paul's precise lettering attracted my attention.

Cleric Paul took a sip of his tea and cleared his throat. He noticed my interest in the documents on his desk. "You must leave Sheldon tonight. Lord Sengy informed his commander, Lord Garth, that he finally had a good case against you. He won't get his reward until you are safely in Araval and in the custody of the Natuan Arkheim. That's why he delayed your release. There was a ship waiting to transport you to Araval. You are not safe here. Or anywhere." He indicated a wash-basin in the kitchen. "Cleanse the grime of the dungeons from yourself." He pointed to a cloth sack on the counter. "I have collected a change of clothing and your traveling cloak. You dare not go to your house. They will look for you there, first."

As if on cue, we heard the distant clatter of horses' hooves. I darted under the desk to hide behind a stack of books while Cleric Paul peeked out his shuttered window. "The patrol is heading towards your house, Ellara. When they get tired of waiting, they will come here." He motioned me to hurry. "Finish eating, and you need to leave."

While I washed and changed into a clean tunic and split woolen skirt, the cleric rummaged among the papers on his desk. He collected the stack of sheets and waved them at me. "This is my translation of everything I could find about the Goddess's teachings, and some of the Droc'ri's. This is my life's work." He caressed the document. With his free hand, he rummaged through a jumble of cloth and leather bags, wooden boxes, and paper wrappings shoved into an open closet to one side of the desk. "There is a Droc'ri prophecy. Only a few know about it."

"What is this prophecy?"

Cleric Paul extracted a leather tube from the clutter. He continued, "The first I heard of it was when I was assigned to the Emerald Mountains during the Religious Wars and overheard a Droc'ri talking with his companion. They were anxious about whether their Order would survive and speculated as to the prophecy's meaning. I have spent years trying to find out what the prophecy actually says. I have finally found what I think had spooked the Grand Master enough to urge the Natuan Ethnarch to cast out the Goddess tradition and convert all the citizens of the provinces to the Natuan faith. This started the Religious Wars. The Grand Master continues to take aggressive action against the Healers."

"What does the prophecy say?"

"The prophecy refers to a fractured Healer who is not a Healer. It promises that this Healer and her mate from the sea will bring down the old traditions, which one could assume means either the Goddess's or the Droc'ri or both. It is foretold that she will restore the Great Seal, which will close off the Dark Lords' hold on this world, and unite the people of the world into the Radiant Lady's family."

"Do you know who this Healer could be? Does Nana Magog know about it?"

43

"Nana has been searching for the full prophecy as well. It is not among the Goddess's teachings. From what I gathered, a Droc'ri scholar discovered the prophecy in their profane Book of Tornaad, which defines the Order's code. There's something else. The Droc'ri brotherhood is dying, ironically, by their own evil practices. They are partly right when they blame the Goddess."

"Dying? Is that part of the prophecy?"

The old man lifted his watery eyes to meet mine. "Yes and no. There is more." He collected the pages and carefully rolled them into a thick scroll. He tied the parchment with a thin strip of cloth and reverently lifted it. "It's all in here. This contains everything I have learned about both the Goddess and the Droc'ri traditions. This is the literal translation from the ancient dialect. It is not easy to read, even harder to understand, and the meaning is obscure. But I know you can glean wisdom from it. The Grand Master believes that their Order will be destroyed if he does not find this Healer first. He will hunt you and your Goddess-born sisters to destroy you all. He is particularly interested in finding the Healer of the prophecy. So is the Gra'Bandia High Council. You must tell Nana Magog what I have told you and have her present this information to the Council."

I imagined telling this unsubstantiated theory to a bunch of crusty, senior Healers like Nana Magog and smiled. "They'll think I'm crazy if I don't have proof. They would listen to you more than me. Have you talked with Nana Magog?"

He nodded. "Nana listened, then said she didn't agree with my interpretation that the Droc'ri Order is dying." He gently shoved the document into the receptacle and pressed a watertight cap over the opening. "But she's a wily old Healer, and I think she took my words to heart."

He handed the tube to me. "When you go to the Gra'Bandia Council, you must get the old Healers to realize that they failed miserably in the Religious Wars. They need to create an alternative to the Gra'Bandia Triunes. The past Triunes were not structured the way the Goddess intended." He tapped the tube. "If the Council sticks to their matriarchal tradition, and doesn't share the Goddess's Gra'yia with their masculine counterpart, the Healers will be destroyed, and our world will be overrun with ungodliness. Not only will the peaceful and sustainable ways of the Goddess be obliterated, but the Natuan religion will suffer, as well." He took a sip of cold tea and frowned as he ran a finger around the rim of his cup.

In the silence that followed, the manuscripts that filled his house seemed to whisper to me. *"Origins. Origins."*

Cleric Paul handed me a satchel filled with bread, cheese, fruit, and a flask of water. "You and I each answer to a different higher authority, yet we have learned to work together and share our wisdom. You must leave Sheldon. You should have gone with your children when they escaped a few days ago. Or left for the unlawful Gra'bandia Council meeting in the Heartland before being captured. I can't keep coming to your rescue. It will be your death if you are not more careful." He stopped, as if in thought. The clock ticked steadily where it sat on the mantle.

He tucked packets of rare herbs into a small medicine kit, wrapped a half dozen scones in a cloth, and put everything into the satchel I held. The thin man opened his arms, inviting me into a hug. "This is farewell, Ellara. I don't have much longer to live." He chuckled. "I was once like Wilson and thought my God was superior to the Goddess. You taught me otherwise. I have valued the many stimulating exchanges about our respective spiritual codes, and have lived a longer and happier life because of your Goddess-enhanced healing ministrations."

A wave of sadness passed over me. This was to be our last encounter. I had grown to care for the wise man. I hugged him, saying, "Thank you for everything, Paul. I will remember you with fondness."

"Now go, before that worthless physician stirs Lord Sengy into action. You'll find your horse behind the vicarage." Cleric Paul patted my back. "Stay alive. Don't get caught." He peered into my face for a moment, then chuckled. "I bet you are the Healer of the prophecy!"

I shook my head. "You must be joking. I'm just a country Healer and nothing more. I'm definitely not part of a prophecy."

Cleric Paul smiled. "I would not wish that fate upon anyone. Take care of yourself and when you encounter the Healer of prophecy, help her."

I hugged him one last time, then listened carefully before opening the door. I stepped into the still night. I had pressed my luck with the arrogant, self-appointed lord of our district. But I didn't want to leave without saying goodbye to my beloved pair'ti, Sam. I reached with my Far Sight and saw his ship would be docking soon.

FOUR

ROKAN AND ANYA

Inyua

My office beneath the spacious halls and gardens of the Suzerain's palace offered a welcome relief from Garrick. I leaned back in my chair and shut my eyes. Garrick had given me an impossible task: infiltrate and spy upon the secret meeting of the Gra'Bandia Council and capture those Healers in attendance. No sorcerer had ever figured out how to overcome the robust protection of the Alban Heartland to enter the sacred forest. In fact, using the Droc'ri magic in Alba was virtually impossible because the potent essence of the Goddess permeated the whole island.

I took a deep breath and stared at the marble walls of my dimly lit office. I had erected a shield that gave me seclusion, although I suspected that Garrick somehow penetrated it and spied upon me. Rarely did I have any visitors, nor did I speak aloud in the room.

The space was large enough to hold a desk and wooden chair, three freestanding bookshelves, another more comfortable chair, and two oil lamps on side tables. The musty smell of old manuscripts blended with those of herbal formulas and lamp oil. An array of talismans and crystals lined the top shelf of the bookcases. I kept my desk free of clutter, and everything had a place. An untidy environment distracted my focus and could lead to fatal mistakes. The white walls served as scrying tablets, and I often played out scenes on them for analysis. I relished my solitude and thought of this chamber as my silent refuge from Garrick and his miserable games. It was the one place where I could perform my Droc'ri tasks alone and uninterrupted.

I spied upon people and gathered information to be used against them. This was one of my primary duties for the Grand Master. I analyzed and extracted the motivations of those I spied upon and strategized the next steps. I excelled at what I did, and most of the time, I was right, though Garrick never gave me credit. My other duties consisted of assassinating those the Grand Master deemed must be eliminated and executing plans to expand his domain.

I muttered a few words and swept my hand in front of the marble wall, conjuring a bird's-eye view of Alba. Unlike previous times when everything was enshrouded in a fog, I could discern distinct green areas, a few mountains, and rivers. I smiled. The enchantment I had placed in their mines a few months ago was doing its job and eroding the Goddess's hold on the island. That I had been able to break through the protective shield around one of the Alban ships just a few days ago was also a sign of Her weakening influence. The force was still too strong for me to enter the sacred forest though.

What was I going to do about the Healers at the secret meeting in the Heartland? Capturing them at Cuilithe was not practical. I needed an agent at the Council who could identify the Healers so I could catch them one at a time. Additionally, I wanted to subtly manipulate the Council to a plan that benefited me.

I mentally reviewed a list of the Healers that would attend and finally hit upon one living in Inyua, Bruce the Terrible's frigid homeland. Long ago, I had saved the woman from drowning in the icy fjord waters. She had been one of my mentors at the Scholars' Guild in my younger years before I endured the Rith Bac'Croi. The ritual not only blocked my connection to the Goddess and all She represented, but also pledged me, body and soul, to serve the Dark Lords — forever. Part of the ritual included giving a fragment of my soul to the Dark Lords for 'safekeeping'; a nice word for insuring my commitment to them. In this way, I could draw power from them. I slid up my sleeve to stare at the Droc'ri dagger tattooed on my inner forearm, a reminder of that cursed day. In the cross of the dagger's hilt were symbols indicating each rise in status. Four of the five positions of power were filled. The fifth and last point of power, the Grand Mastership, would be a circle at the base of the hilt. Mindlessly, I pursed my lips as I gazed at the empty place, then shoved my sleeve down and returned to my task.

Anya was one of a few scholars with whom I discussed intriguing findings in my research over the years. She contained a wealth of information not commonly known about the Goddess. I smiled. I knew just the bait to get her to cooperate.

I left my sanctuary and walked to my adobe hut in the dilapidated section of town. I rummaged through the clothing in a trunk in the corner and found baggy trousers, a tea-stained shirt, and vest. I dressed, then shrugged into a threadbare woolen long coat that bore the Scholars' Guild sigil and wrapped a colorful scarf around my neck. In the mirror, I looked like a typical professor.

Holding my travel crystal, I imprinted the desired destination. After incanting a few words, the air split before me. I stepped into a wintry landscape and shivered. I pulled my thin covering tightly around me and wished I had opted for a heavy cloak. Why anyone would want to live in a climate where winter gripped the land far into spring was beyond my comprehension.

Heavy clouds smothered the feeble daylight and the horizon blended with the snow-covered ground. I turned around, scanning for the craggy peak with rocky cliffs so sheer that snow could not cover them. When I spotted the black and white mountain, I put my back to it and walked towards a woodland, where a village lay next to the sea. I headed towards the small cottage at the edge of the forest that housed the retired, scholarly Healer, Anya.

Thin wisps of blue-gray smoke blended with the ashen woods behind her small dwelling. The house was silent. I knocked.

In a few minutes, the door opened. The elderly woman instantly recognized me. "What do you want this time, Rokan?"

I laughed. "Anya, I came for another of our bracing debates over the Goddess's teachings."

"Hmph!" The spry old lady invited me in and indicated I sit by the fire. "You look cold. Not used to our weather, are you, Rokan?"

I shook my head and rubbed my hands together in front of the fire. "I just stopped by to see how you were faring."

Anya turned her back and reached for a cup. I moved aside as she lifted the kettle from the hearth. While she poured the water and dipped the small herb basket into the cup to let it steep, I meandered around her home, picking up a book from the table and stopping near the hooks by the door that held her travel cloak. I turned to ask Anya, "Are you going to the Gra'Bandia Council meeting in Alba?"

The Healer looked sharply at me. "There hasn't been a meeting of the Gra'Bandia Council since the Alban king disbanded them!"

I took the proffered tea. "I heard there was a gathering of the Healers, and I'd have thought surely you were going."

"I wouldn't tell you if I were!"

I sipped tea and drew two thin vellum sheets containing line after line of hand-printed text from my pocket. "I brought this for you, Anya."

She reached for the pages. Scanning the document, her eyes lit up. "Where did you find this?"

"Under some books in the Guild's archives. I thought of you when I found them."

"These are some of the lost teachings!" She looked longingly at the sheets as she handed them back to me. "I can't keep these. You must return them to the archives where you found them. I will not be responsible for their loss."

"Anya, I know how much satisfaction you get from studying the Goddess's history. These pages talk about the Goddess's warriors, the Gra'Bandia Triunes. The Gra'Bandia Council needs to form new Triunes to battle the current rise of the Droc'ri."

Anya picked up the pages again, moved to the window, and squinted at the words. She inhaled sharply. "This is indeed different from how we were trained!" She closed her eyes and slowly nodded her head.

I warmed to the topic. "This document describes the original purpose of the Triunes and how they were *intended* to be formed. From your experience, do you think this kind of Triune will be more effective against the Droc'ri than the ones you made during the Religious Wars?"

She snorted. "How are you invested in the kind of Triunes we create? The Goddess selected trios of Healers — specially trained women — to unite into one powerful force to channel Her radiant energies and protect the provinces in the Emerald Mountains. They worked for decades until you and your Droc'ri Brothers discovered how to destroy them. I always suspected you were instrumental in that, Rokan. Why do you want to resurrect them? Does your Grand Master think the Gra'Bandia Healers are foolish enough to repeat something that doesn't work — so you can finish destroying us?"

When I didn't say anything, she nodded to herself. "The High Council Doyen, Camila, is set in her ways and will want to repeat our mistakes. She won't consider any alternatives. That woman will bring down the Goddess tradition single-handedly through her narrow-mindedness." She glowered at me as if it was all my fault. She was partly right.

I tapped the pages. "The Droc'ri killed the Healers' mates, making the three women vulnerable to capture and death. These teachings tell of a different configuration for forging the Triunes that will make the united trio invincible."

Anya harrumphed. "Men cannot host the Goddess. If they had the power of the Goddess at their fingertips, the world would be destroyed." She pointed an accusing finger at me. "Look at the chaos the Droc'ri bring upon the world. Men like you have to prove you're better than everyone else. Only women can understand the nature of the Goddess."

"Not all men are that way," I retorted. "I'm not power-hungry or greedy."

Anya laughed. "You deceive yourself, Rokan. What would you be if you were stripped of your magic or authority?"

I ignored her comment. "You have to admit that when the Religious Wars started sixty years ago, the Healers were strong enough to defend their regions from the soldiers. But that didn't last."

"No. The Droc'ri leaders' egos couldn't stand that the Goddess was mighty enough to resist their efforts." Anya set her teacup down carefully, then continued, "We had to scramble to find something strong enough to combat the dark magic you wielded. You had a straightforward goal. Kill the Goddess and her servants." She waggled a finger at me. "Try as you might, we are still here and a burr in your side. We will always remain. You can *never* destroy the Goddess or her servants!"

"That's quite a claim. What makes you think you can survive? The Dark Lords are stronger than the Goddess. They always have been."

"You forget, Rokan, that we held the Droc'ri sorcerers at bay for fifty years. The Triunes worked."

"Yes, but it took three women to one sorcerer. It seems to me that the Goddess is weak."

"Hah! You don't understand the Goddess, Rokan. Unlike the Droc'ri, who in their obsession, are dead set to rid the world of the Goddess's influence. She didn't want to destroy you." Anya shook her head. "The Doyen of the Gra'Bandia Council does stupid things, and the Droc'ri have no vision except for their personal aggrandizement. The Droc'ri are immersed in the very fear that they spread around the world." Her stern gaze returned to me. "The Grand Master can't see that by eliminating every Healer and person incarnated into the Goddess-born lineage, he destroys his Order as well." She pointed an arthritic finger at me. "Remember, Rokan, every sorcerer of the Droc'ri *is* Goddess-born, just like the Healers, and the untrained ones who carry the lineage. Don't think you can cast out the Goddess so easily. The Goddess teaches tolerance. That's why the intention of the Triunes was to protect, not to attack and destroy the Droc'ri."

"I never did know the real reason why you disbanded."

Anya looked away. "You killed our pair'ti. Our beloveds, who embodied the Sacred Masculine element to balance the Goddess's Divine Feminine. This was a fatal flaw in the Triunes." She fixed me with her gaze. "But that won't happen again! We will rise anew!"

"How are you going to do that? There are not many of you left. I know just about all of the retired Healers scattered around the continent and in Alba. How can you restore the balance this time?"

Anya pressed her lips together.

"Perhaps you could take these pages and let the Council see for themselves that the Triunes will work," I suggested.

Anya drew herself upright and glared at me. "Rokan, do you think me a fool? Even though it is forbidden for a Droc'ri to associate with a Healer, and vice versa, I tolerate you because you were my best pupil and are not as arrogant and dim-witted as your Brother sorcerers. However, I will not let you manipulate me. I question your motivations and what you really want to accomplish by giving me this information."

"I don't want the Goddess tradition to die." At her skeptical look, I added, "If all the Healers were gone, and the world was dominated by ignorant sorcerers like our Grand Master, Garrick, there would be nothing of interest for me, no reason to live. I thrive on challenges, and Healers have many to offer."

"Like hunting us down?" Anya interrupted sourly.

I nodded. "You notice that I find you, but don't capture you."

She harrumphed. "You keep us like mice in a cage, Rokan." She looked as if she had more to say. She took a sip of tea instead.

I continued, "Some of the Goddess's teachings make more sense than the Droc'ri code, such as Her teachings of balance, as opposed to the Droc'ri mission of Her lineage's complete annihilation. You have helped me find the defects in our Order, and I have pointed out your flaws. We need to keep the cycle going." I leaned forward. "Admit it, Anya. You enjoy a good debate. There can be no contest of wills without an opponent." I leaned back and smiled smugly. "I'm right, and you know it."

She tossed the papers on the table. "I'm getting too old for these games, Rokan. Find someone else to test your wits upon."

I pointed to the vellum. "Consider this a loan. I will be back to collect it in a few weeks, after you have had a chance to study it." I rose to leave. "Thank you for the tea, Anya."

She will unwittingly play her role for me at the Council gathering. Now, I'll enlist Felicity to gather the names of the Healers attending. I stepped out into the cold.

Back in warm Tokurat, I returned to my sanctuary beneath the palace, grateful for the warmth radiating from the stone edifice. What made Anya so sure that the Healers would overcome the Droc'ri this time? Had she discovered something I hadn't? I was sure she would take the papers to the Council and show Doyen Camila and the others. I suspected Camila's strict adherence to tradition would stop any modifications to the Triunes, which would please Garrick and doom the Healers. Too bad. The lost teaching contained a provocative solution. One that I could exploit to become more powerful than Garrick.

My dreams evaporated the moment I saw Garrick's servant waiting in the corridor that led to my office. I groaned. *Now, what does he want?*

As I entered Garrick's favorite garden, I tensed. I knew I'd be blamed for whatever had angered him this time.

The Grand Master sat on a ruby velvet settee. A decanter of cucumber water and a dish of dried apricots rested on a carved wooden stand alongside the sofa. The sickly-sweet scent of rose from bushes lining the tiled pool lingered in the air. Garrick smiled at me as if everything were fine. He must be very displeased, indeed. "That ship of Alban women and Healers that was supposed to come here went to Langon, and her passengers have scattered throughout the mainland provinces. How could you miss that, Rokan?"

I swallowed. "I was tending to the Gra'Bandia meeting, Master. My sources assured me the ship was en route to the Desert Lands. I had every reason to believe that was true. I will find out why they docked in Langon. Have no fear. We will round them up soon. It is easy for us to move on the mainland."

Garrick shook his head and crooked his finger. I watched as a tendril of my life force drifted towards him. He inhaled deeply. Garrick had made a practice of finding some reason to punish me in this manner for the last several years. It didn't really hurt, but it humiliated me. I dared not complain. Protesting would embolden him to discipline me harshly.

He leaned towards me. "I will hold you to that promise. So, do you have a plan to capture the Gra'Bandia Healers at the Council assembly yet?"

"Yes, Master. One attendee will disrupt the gathering and force Doyen Camila to resurrect the Triunes that we so easily destroyed. I have another who is making a list of the Healers and their mates so that I can capture them when they least expect it. It will take time. We must be patient."

"It's always later! I want to see results today, now!" He stabbed the air in my direction with the finger of one hand. The fingers of his other caressed the hilt of his dagger. "It's your job to keep me informed *and* to seize the Healers as you are instructed. *My* agents told me about the Healers escaping in Langon. You've been letting me down, Rokan." He shook his head. "If I didn't know you so well, I might think that you are trying to thwart my rise to global power." Passionately, he closed his fingers around an imaginary ball. "This planet and everything on it, is mine! I'd hate to have to turn you into an imp for not performing your duties adequately, Rokan."

"I will find those who were on that ship and bring them to you, Master." I clamped my jaw. *Maybe you should do it yourself for a change. But no, you won't soil your hands with work, nor will you budge from this palace, afraid for your life.* Ha! I waited for him to dismiss me. Finally, he did.

Immediately, I walked to my hut in the old part of Tokurat. I preferred to travel the astral planes from the privacy of my abode, away from the palace and Garrick. I lay on my sleeping mat, and after calming my mind, entered a meditative state that allowed my spirit to scan the people and places around Gea efficiently.

I turned my attention to survey the sea. Among the merchant ships, I saw the vessel of Ellara's pair'ti sailing toward Alba. I surveyed Sheldon in an attempt to see Ellara before continuing on my search and then traveled effortlessly about six hundred miles southeast to the Langon province. With my spirit, I could see people and places, but it was almost impossible to identify a specific person without knowing what they looked like or possessing an object imprinted with their energetic signature. I speculated about whether Ellara's daughter, Margot, might be among those escaping Alba. After all, it was her father's ship that had carried the refugees to Langon. If I could find her, she could lead me to the others.

I had been trying to capture Ellara for many years. She had power and I wanted it. When Margot was a toddler, I tried to steal the child. If I had been successful, the mother would have come willingly to rescue her, and I could have entrapped her. But Ellara had saved her child and shoved me over a cliff. Only my feeble magic had saved me from falling to my death. Apprehending Margot now could still lure Ellara to me. I counted on Ellara doing anything to protect her children.

From a pocket inside my tunic, I extracted a smudged, thin sheet of folded paper with the hair I had stolen from Ellara and Margot. This fragment would allow me to track the mother and daughter anywhere around the globe. Focusing on it, I sent my spirit to find Margot. Some distance from the Langon port, I spied a square sail and the rhythmic glint of light on a dozen oars that propelled a knarr up the Langon River. My inner vision showed a large number of people on the deck of the transport boat. It was hard to see the details, though. They were shielded, undoubtedly courtesy of Nana Magog, I thought wryly. I had sparred with Nana Magog for over a century.

Where were they going? Why so many? The *M'Ellara's* cargo manifest hadn't listed names. In fact, it hadn't said anything about women and stated only Livestock: Horses, Cattle, Sheep, and a list of ranches that had provided them. I could understand the misdirection if the women were escaping Lord Sengy's warrants for arrest of all Healers, and if they had no intention of traveling to Tokurat, as the manifest declared. Sam would want to protect his daughter and her friends. Margot would know who the Healers were on her father's ship, and if I could reach her, I could then have a way to locate them, and lure her mother to me as well. I watched the boat progress up the river a while longer, and finally returned to a conscious state.

From my trunk, I selected the clothing of a Scholars' Guild professor, and quickly dressed. I returned to the palace and entered Garrick's secret room beneath the building. Maps of the world lay on a gilded wooden table. I shuffled through the charts until I found one detailing the region where I had seen Margot. It appeared that she and her group would travel part of another day before the river became unnavigable. They would debark at a small town called Middenvale.

It had been decades since I passed through that part of the country. I needed an image, a landmark with which to imprint my traveling crystal. Back in my office, I thumbed through atlases and geography books, looking for a picture I could use. I dared not use Margot. I had learned, disastrously, that trying to create a portal to a moving destination, such as a ship, often left me drenched in the water. No, I had to journey to a place on land.

Finally, I found a picture of the burgh. Imprinting my crystal with the image, I commanded the air and drew the symbols. The space before me revealed a field, brightly illuminated by a setting gibbous moon. Barking dogs shattered the still night as I walked briskly to the village. It would be morning soon. Now I would wait for the travelers to arrive.

FIVE

ELLARA AND SAM

Sheldon

My pair'ti's double-masted merchant ship drifted closer to the pier. Men chanted as they tugged on thick ropes, pulling the vessel into position for unloading, and tied her off. Even in the dim light of the torches, I could make out the white letters on the bow. *M'Ellara*. Sam had named the ship after me when he became her master more than thirty-five years ago.

Heavy clouds with not a breath of wind enhanced the dread already forging a path through my being. Wrapping my heavy cloak more tightly around myself to keep away the early spring chill, I pulled the hood forward to hide my face. I shuffled from foot to foot and tugged nervously at the edge of my cloak. For the tenth time, I silenced the annoying little voice in my head that muttered, *You are putting yourself and Sam at risk by being here. You should have waited for him at home like he asked.* But Lord Sengy had posted guards at my house.

I probed at the flagstones with the toe of my boot, watching the dockworkers make fast the ship. Excitement to see my beloved, along with the imminent threat that Lord Sengy might sweep into town and capture me at any moment, tightened the knot in my belly. I hoped that the pre-dawn darkness would hide my presence.

Finally, Sam's tall, broad-shouldered form descended from the ship and strode purposefully towards the place I typically waited alongside the port warehouse. He collected me into his arms and passionately kissed me as he had done so often upon his return, during the many years we had been a pair'ti. "I'm glad you came."

"I wanted to see you before I leave for the Heartland."

He pulled me closer. "You took an unnecessary risk coming here." He leaned his cheek against my head. "I know you have to go, and I'm glad I could have some time with you."

Several crewmen ambled by us. They had come from the Harbormaster's office. Sam's helmsman commented, "Your pair'ti was antsy to get back to you, Ellara. I've never before seen him push the ship to her limits that way." He moved on with his shipmates. They stopped a short distance away, pulled out pipes, lit them, and leaned against the warehouse wall. Sam's first mate grumbled about the new taxes and all the useless forms that were required now. His companions grunted assent and watched the stevedores bustle to unload the cargo the *M'Ellara* had transported from Langon, a port town on the mainland about six hundred miles southeast. In the pre-dawn light, the dockworkers carefully lowered a massive stone miller's wheel from the ship onto a waiting wagon.

"How are Kian and Margot?" I asked. Sam had transported our son and daughter, along with one hundred twenty Albans escaping Lord Sengy's oppression, to Langon. Thirty of these had been handpicked by Nana Magog. She had instructed Margot to lead them across the Emerald Mountains to the lands of the Nogulus, a Goddess-oriented society of warriors. This undertaking had two purposes: learn the ways of the Nogulus and enlist their help defeating the latest cycle of Droc'ri conquest.

"Kian is at the Scholars' Guild in Langon by now. Margot wanted him to come with her, but he said he could do more good studying with the world's wisest and most creative minds. Kian said the Scholars' Guild has every manuscript and artifact on everything from ancient teachings, theurgy and elemental magical arts, and the latest in scientific wisdom. You know Kian. He hopes to find the answers to the Droc'ri problem there and learn more about his own abilities. Margot and her friends headed inland on the Langon River and will travel the river as far as they can, then proceed overland." He sighed. "It's a journey filled with danger for those Goddess-born youngsters and will be even more so if the Droc'ri sorcerers get wind of them. I pray they will be alright. Nana Magog gave them a daunting task."

"Nana says they must succeed. She assured me she would guide and instruct Margot every step of the way and keep them safe. For weeks before they left, Nana made Margot practice so they could communicate telepathically like you and I. Nana says those untrained Healers are our hope for the survival of the Goddess tradition. I hope both our children will be safe in the days to come."

Sam agreed. "Bruce the Terrible tried to attack us. However, with so many Healers on board, he didn't stand a chance." Sam laughed. "It was fantastic! Healers used their magic to call the wind for our sails and shift the currents to carry us away. When Bruce's ships fired a cannon at us, the Healers turned the balls around. His own canon fire swamped his ship and destroyed many others. Serves him right. He used a sorcerer to capture the *Sheila*." Sam chuckled and snuggled me closer. "Maybe I need to haul more Healers." His tone became serious. "I thought I was going to have to break you out of prison. I was afraid you'd be killed." Through our telepathic connection, Sam knew the details of what had happened as they had been happening. "Your death would have destroyed my will to live," he said softly. "I'm glad Cleric Paul was able to free you once more."

I tightened my arms around Sam's waist. "I wish I didn't have to leave, but Lord Sengy will be after me again. He's such a sanctimonious brute, claiming he is doing his God's will! Sara had just received a new shipment of gemstones for their shop. Sengy's soldiers captured Sara and her pair'ti and stole all the diamonds, emeralds, and rubies they use to make jewelry.

When Sara demanded Lord Sengy release them and return what was stolen, as they had done nothing illegal, he refused. In fact, he taunted her about how women should never be in business.

"Even though Sara has not been trained as a Healer, she has the talent. She called down the Goddess's wrath on Lord Sengy and all his brigands, cursing him and petitioning the Goddess to cast him out of Alba and into the Natuan Hell where he belongs! Sengy was furious, and afraid. He made Sara watch as his men tortured her pair'ti in an attempt to make her take back the curses."

I shook my head. "I would have joined the fight if Nana had let me. There was nothing I could do to help her." I took a deep breath. "Both of them are dead, now. Sara's not the only one to be persecuted. Other women have had their businesses raided, and their pair'ti killed while they watched. Many have died, like Sara and her pair'ti." I shuddered. "Sengy and his men have no right! Cleric Paul just told me that what that usurper is doing to us is illegal! He deserves the Goddess's fury for his barbaric actions!" I felt my anger rising and took a couple deep breaths to calm myself. I wanted to enjoy my last minutes with Sam.

"I'm sorry about Sara and Dan. She was a staunch supporter and friend. Her daughter is Margot's best friend. I'm glad the girls were gone when this happened." He sighed. "Bruce the Terrible is also getting bolder. I escaped this time only because of the Healers. I worry about what will happen to you if I am killed." He leaned against the building and held me at arm's length. "Those who want to destroy the Goddess have gathered their forces and are testing their might. The Goddess's protection is weakening. You must hurry to the Heartland, where you will be safe. I will join you as soon as I can. Nana Magog and the Gra'Bandian Council *must* find a way to stop the influx of darkness before the likes of Bruce the Terrible, Lord Sengy, and their Droc'ri masters destroy humankind." He cupped my face. "You, Margot, and Kian are the ones who have to fight this battle to protect what we value."

I groaned. "I'm good at healing and restoring people to health. But I can't command the spirits of the wind or sea or anything else."

"You are more capable than you think. The time has come for you to step into your legacy, and stop hiding from your true nature. The world needs you to overcome your fear and become an instrument of the Goddess. I'll help you every way I can."

I pressed against his muscular body, drawing upon his confidence. Sam, thirteen years older than me, had been in my life since before I was born. He was my best friend, lover, and rock-solid anchor. His feet were planted firmly on the ground, and I relied upon his steadfastness and practical perspective. Most of all, I enjoyed a profoundly intimate and telepathic connection with him that allowed us to sense each other no matter where we were. He was my Anam pair'ti, my soul-bonded mate.

One of the dockworkers drove the laden cart to where we stood by the Harbormaster's office and jumped down. "It's all loaded, Captain," he called over his shoulder as he hastened towards a waiting empty wagon.

Sam wrapped his arms around me and kissed me, his lips softly lingering against mine. "I'll always be there for you, Ellara." He caressed my cheek and gazed at me like he did when he left for one of his voyages. A breath of spring sea breeze lifted his straight brown hair from his forehead.

He glanced at the cart. "I need to get this to the miller." He noticed my horse standing in the shadows of the alley. "Leave while the soldiers are not around." He held me, and his loving brown eyes drank me in.

I brushed my fingers along his freshly shaven cheek, following the line of his jaw, and took in his kindly, tanned face. His handsome visage warmed my heart. Today, though, it did not chase away a sliver of silent dread. I had a distinct feeling that this was the last time I would see my beloved. I stretched to kiss him softly, sensually, and poured all the love I felt for him into the intimate touch. He responded in kind, and as our energies merged, we became one united being as we had done many times before.

I became aware of hot breath on my neck and an insistent nudge. I turned, and Boris, my horse, tossed his head and stomped a foot impatiently. I slowly drew away from Sam. "May the Goddess watch over you so that you return to me safely," I whispered.

70

A clatter of hooves shattered the still morning air. "Go!" Sam lifted me onto Boris's back, then quickly ran and climbed aboard the cart, urging the horses forward while I waited in the shadows. The soldiers would see me if I were to escape now.

A short distance from the port warehouse, the young lord and his guards surrounded the wagon. Sam wrapped his seaman's coat tightly around himself and lowered his head.

"What have we here, Captain Sam Ruark?"

"A grinding wheel for the miller, Lord Sengy," he said quietly.

"You owe duty on that stone."

"I already paid the Harbormaster the customs tax, sir."

"I say the tax on that stone is two hundred nobels."

I forced myself to take a deep breath, digging my fingernails into my palms. Confronting the young man would come with a price. Instead, I side-stepped the horse against the massive wooden structure to remain hidden in the shadows.

"I don't have that sort of money." Nobels were heavy coins minted from pure gold, and like their silver cousin, denars, were rarely seen even among wealthy merchants and craft-workers. "I paid the Harbormaster in accordance with the king's import decree. Go ask him." An edge crept into Sam's voice.

"*I* decide what the tax is, Captain." The young man spurred his chestnut stallion, and it leaped forward, circling the wagon. "Pay, or this chunk of granite goes to the bottom of the bay."

Sam pulled a small bag of coins from his coat. "Here. This is all I have." He tossed it to Lord Sengy, who caught it.

The self-appointed aristocrat circled the wagon again, dribbling Sam's coins onto the cobblestones. "Your coins are worthless to me. Give me the witch and her troublesome daughter, and I'll let you go. The miller can have his wheel."

Sam lowered his head and remained silent. Lord Sengy motioned for his men to overturn the cart, and with a lot of grunting, they did. Half a dozen men rolled the wheel across the wharf until it splashed into the bay's deep waters.

I clenched my fists. I knew I should take advantage of the distraction to escape, but every inch of my body burned to race out and confront the heartless man. The miller had paid for that stone to come from Langon. Sheldon needed it. *"No! Stay away. Go while you can!"* Sam sent telepathically.

I edged Boris along the warehouse wall, hoping the commotion would shield my departure along the far side of the wharf. I settled myself more firmly onto Boris's smooth back and prepared to dash away from the pier. As a Caretaker-raised horse, Boris could not be ridden with a saddle and bridle, like other domesticated steeds. Nana had said it was because he was Verndari and magical. I didn't know what that meant, but I had enjoyed riding him bareback, with just a rope halter. Because I had honored his needs, a camaraderie and close friendship had developed between us.

My full leather satchels, strapped together to form saddlebags, were slung over Boris's withers and cinched loosely around his girth. They provided a place for me to wedge my knees. I was ready to ride to the ancient forest known as the Heartland, after a quick stop at Nana Magog's cottage. She had said it was important.

"Hey!" one of the men called. He had heard the soft clop of Boris's unshod hooves. "Here she is!"

Men swarmed towards me. *"Run!"* I heard in my mind. Sam snatched up one of the boards that had supported the stone and started swinging. With formidable strength amplified by the plank's long reach, he knocked down those closest to him, clearing a swath towards me. Shipmates alerted by the ruckus on the docks swarmed to defend their captain, long daggers glinting in the lamplight. With angry shouts, Sam swung at the legs of Sengy's horse. The horse reared, dumping its master.

"Get to safety," I heard.

I kicked Boris's flanks. Boris refused to move. Instead, he waited for my assailants to approach, ears flattened and shifting from foot to foot, the tension in his body wound like a spring. Instinctively, I wrapped my legs around him and grabbed his mane with both hands. He leaped into the throng of oncoming men with the ferocity of a battle-hardened warhorse, ignoring the swords thrust at him. He bit at raised arms, slashed out with his front feet, and kicked at those behind him. Hands clawed at me. I spotted Sam fighting with

Lord Sengy and, for an instant, wished that our new provincial lord could be put in his place, just this once.

As if divining my desire, Boris angled his charge towards Lord Sengy and slammed into the soldier with his shoulder. Knocked off balance, the younger man fell against one of his guards, who shoved him upright. Boris spun around and let the self-important officer feel the wrath of the Sheldon province with some solidly placed kicks to his backside. I heard bones crack. The Natuan mercenary cried out and tumbled to the ground. A cheer went up, and the sailors pounced on their oppressors with renewed determination.

Sam paused in his fight and grinned at me. He pointed at Lord Sengy. "We'll pay the price for this, but it sure was fun to see him fall! May those who wish to suppress us likewise feel our fury." I bent down to kiss him one last time and galloped the few blocks to the street that led toward Nana Magog's cottage and the road to the southern portion of the province. More red-clothed soldiers raced towards the port from the direction of the garrison.

I stopped on the ridge that overlooked the port. Rays from the rising sun shone through a slit in the clouds, illuminating the raging battle below and the sea beyond. Below me, dock-workers and townsfolk flocked to join the skirmish. I saw friends, patrons, women, and men run to engage in the melee at the docks with whatever weapons could be brought to hand. Even bald-headed Cleric Paul wielded a staff and knocked soldiers down.

I sent my spirit to wrap around Sam, attempting to protect him from the mercenary reinforcements entering the fight. The blows that struck Sam's body felt as if his attackers were beating and stabbing me. Tears stung my eyes. I didn't want to see my friends, Sam's crew, or Sam killed because of me.

"The Goddess has blessed us with Her Light. We may die for rebelling, but at least you allowed us to die for what we believe in," I heard in my mind. *"Now go while you can. Get to safety. Let us concentrate on ridding our region of these interlopers."*

Tears streamed from my eyes. I lingered, unable to tear my gaze away from the scene below. Boris, though, turned and trotted up the hill. I looked back until my view of the docks was obscured. The clash of steel and yells echoed off the rocky cliffs that surrounded the town. Boris snorted, tossed his head, and picked up the pace. I became aware of a clatter of hooves behind us, and a glance over my shoulder revealed a dozen red-uniformed men galloping towards me from the port. We raced up the slope to the main road that led away from Sheldon.

Nana Magog's small stone cottage sat at the base of a rocky bluff where the vegetation shifted from coastal grasslands to forests of short evergreen, maple, and birch trees. She had a view of Sheldon, the harbor, approaching ships far out to sea, and the beaches and bluffs.

Instead of turning onto the narrow, brush-lined track leading to Nana's house, Boris bolted straight into a thicket. I bent low over his neck and hid my face in his mane to shield against branches beating against me as the horse dodged between the trees. He plunged through some shrubbery and then squeezed through a narrow opening in a rocky outcropping covered by ivy and other vines. It was pitch black in the cavern. A couple of minutes later, horse hooves thundered past on the main road.

I slid off Boris's back and sagged onto a rock. Using my Far Sight to survey the scene at the docks, I observed both soldiers and citizens lay dead or severely injured. Nana Magog was going to have a lot of wounded to tend. I noticed that none of the soldiers wore the blue and green uniforms of the Alban regimentals. The guards had all been from Sengy's squad. Lord Sengy's chestnut stallion stood aimlessly to the side. I looked for Sam. Blood streaked his face and soaked his clothes. He lay amid his shipmates, wounded. My heart sank.

I wrapped my spirit around him. *"I'm so sorry, Beloved,"* I sent. *"I didn't mean to start a rebellion. I didn't want you to be hurt."* I wept softly. *"Don't leave me, Sam. I'll come and heal you."*

He roused. *"No. Stay away. We didn't kill all of Sengy's men. There are patrols that will try to capture you. Stay hidden."*

I knew Sam was right, but I still wanted to help him. Through our link I could feel his life force ebbing. I sat in darkness. I closed my eyes and calmed myself the best I could, and called to the Goddess. I let Her essence fill me like She did when I worked with a client. Then I imagined Her Gra'yia surrounding Sam. Through our connection, I sensed his body relax and enough vitality return to sit up. I couldn't hold the vision any longer and the Goddess's Radiance departed from me. I slouched over, resting my head on my knees. My body burned. I pushed the pain aside and reached with my Far Sight for Sam. He stood shakily and tottered towards the Harbormaster's building, where he leaned against the wall. His clothes were soaked in blood. He needed proper healing.

Hope surged through me. *"Grab Sengy's horse and come with me, Sam. I can restore you."*

He chuckled. *"I can handle a pitching ship on a tumultuous sea any day, but I could never get used to a horse. They have minds of their own."*

I grinned. *"As if the M'Ellara is not willful? What will you do now? Do you have enough men to crew your ship and leave port? You'll be an outlaw."*

"No. Only a handful survived and they are wounded." There was a long pause. *"Do not wait for me. I must see to my men and my ship."*

The thud of hooves on the packed earthen roadway thundered back towards town. *"Hide, Sam. The patrol is returning."*

Using my Far Sight continuously drained me, and Nana cautioned against it, saying my spirit could become trapped by a sorcerer. Instead, I sat quietly and listened attentively, powerless to go to my beloved. Minutes lengthened. *No. I'm not powerless to help him!*

I stood and felt along Boris's body for the reins of the makeshift halter. I tugged on them, urging him to leave the cave. The horse refused to move. Suddenly, I clutched my belly, and dropped to my knees, crying out at the excruciating pain. "*Sam!*"

There was a long pause before he responded. "*Beloved, my love for you goes beyond time and this world. I am always with you. We will be together again,*" I heard in my mind. "*Do not let our deaths be for naught. Bring the change we need. Remember me.*"

Then emptiness replaced the familiar sense of Sam that had been with me most of my life. My Far Sight showed his broken, lifeless body lying on the cold stone of the wharf. My heart shattered. His presence wrapped around me like a warm blanket, then he was gone, and I was alone for the first time in my life.

SIX

ROKAN

Middenvale

The wharf at Middenvale bustled with villagers. As the last port of call ninety miles upriver from the seaport, Middenvale was the gathering point for the region's residents and merchants. Flocks of sheep and goats pushed against each other and milled around wooden barrels atop which rested bundles of woven wool blankets, coats, and cloaks wrapped in tanned sheepskins.

I stood in the shadows, watching the commotion, and listened to a dialect that I hadn't heard since the Religious Wars. Finally, with the boat tied up, Ellara's daughter, Margot, and a group of young men and women tramped across a wide plank to the shore. I had sensed Margot's presence the night before. Now, seeing her in person, a fire surged through me that I hadn't felt in years. I felt alive!

I became instantly enchanted with Margot. I had never sensed anyone with as much determination as she had packed into her lithe body. From what I could remember of Ellara when I had tried to steal her child, Margot looked like her mother. I could feel her mother's essence in her, yet she had her own very distinct persona. Margot had grown into a slender, athletic young woman. She dressed like a seaman and had cropped her flaxen hair very short. She didn't look like a Healer, yet I could feel raw, unharnessed power radiate from her. My blood stirred. Garrick will not have this one!

I directed my attention to the woman who stood protectively beside Margot. Unlike Margot, her energy was gentle, more like Ellara's. She appeared to be the calm, pragmatic one, yet alert and ready to defend her friend against any foe.

I could not read Margot's and her companion's auras. When I tried, it was like gazing through an opaque curtain. I sighed. I shouldn't have been surprised. Ellara, Sam, and probably Nana Magog, had placed a shield around these two.

I studied the rest of the group, reading their auras. Most of the travelers looked to be in their twenties, a few younger and a couple older. Their youthful optimism and vitality fascinated me. To the untrained eye, they looked ordinary, yet to my senses, they were all unschooled and inexperienced Healers and Mages! Only a handful, including Margot's protector, had the stocky, matronly build that I had associated with a typical Healer from the era of the Religious Wars. It appeared that the new generation of Healers didn't fit into the traditional

mold, partly because they did not wear the customary clothing, nor did they carry themselves with the haughty attitude of
the Healers I had experience with. I had not seen so many
Goddess-born gifted people in one place since the wars. In my
imagination, I harnessed these young people's powers like a
team of horses, ready to carry me to whatever I desired. Images
of weaving Garrick into a web so strong that he was powerless
flashed across my mind. I imagined feeding on the life force of
the young band, thereby making myself invincible to death.

They mingled together and joked with the playfulness of a
litter of puppies, demonstrating a complete lack of discipline
displayed by their elder counterparts. I should have restrained
them while they milled about in confusion. Garrick would
punish me for failing in my duties. But the energy of the
group sparked my curiosity. What were they up to? This had
to be Nana Magog's plan. What assignment had the old hag
given them?

Margot planted her feet firmly before a group of merchants
and waved her arms, making gestures to convey her desire for
horses and supplies to travel into the mountains. They obvi-
ously did not understand each other. I stepped forward.

"May I be of assistance?"

Margot assessed me from head to toe. Casting me a sidelong
glance, she drew away. Even more intriguing, she pulled in
her energy field. Margot's matronly companion shifted her
weight, ready to leap to her friend's defense. The rest of the

party gathered around behind her. It was evident that Margot was their leader.

"Do you want horses and supplies for yourself and your companions?" I asked.

She nodded.

I turned to the horse trader and spoke a few words in his dialect. Relieved to have someone to talk to besides Margot, he said he didn't have enough horses for so many. He could provide six pack animals, and that was it.

I knew there were more horses to be had. The merchant just didn't want to sell them. It was all part of the haggling process that formed a necessary component of making a bargain. I relayed his message to Margot, monitoring her reaction. She appeared to know he was deceiving her as well. She said she would buy all the horses she needed, if not from him, then from someone more agreeable.

"The merchant says there's no need to look elsewhere. He's sure he can find you the horses. How far do you plan to go into the mountains? He needs to know what kind of animals to bring you."

She appraised me and then replied, "They need to be mountain bred."

After more negotiating, I helped her get a reasonable price for the steeds, and then we waited while the horses were rounded up. Several of her companions gathered supplies, while I took Margot and her friend, Katarine, to an inn for a meal. I had asked members of her group where they were going. None appeared to know, and their auras confirmed the truth of their words. It seemed that not even Katarine knew the plan that Margot refused to reveal.

"Are you going to the monastery at Hidden Springs?" At her blank stare, I added, "Or the Temple of the Crescent Moon?"

"Perhaps."

She had another destination in mind, of that, I was sure. The less Margot revealed, the more curious I became.

Finally, the horses arrived, and were saddled and loaded with supplies. However, a commotion in the street drew us outside. Several horses struggled with their handlers as the men tried to saddle them. Katarine watched for a moment, then walked towards the men and the rearing mounts. Several paces from the animals, she halted and started humming. I had heard the melody when I was young. The horses pricked their ears toward the young woman. She approached them, stroked their necks, and continued humming. After a few minutes, they stood calmly, swished their tails once or twice, and lowered their heads. Katarine moved to the side of the closest mare, brushed her hand down her neck and along her back, then gently put the saddle in place, tightening the cinch slowly. She repeated the process with the other recalcitrant animals.

By now, the travelers had an audience. The horse trader had brought the untrained animals as a prank on the youngsters. Now he drew to the back of the crowd, murmuring among his friends. I heard claims of witchcraft, and the men argued about how much the reward would be for the capture of all thirty-three of them.

Finally, everyone mounted. Katarine had chosen to ride one of the wild horses, which now acted as if being ridden was ordinary.

I walked alongside Margot as she left the village. "You need a guide and someone to protect you from the villagers who would capture you for the reward."

She looked down at me. "Thank you for your help and your offer. We can manage on our own. You must have other tasks to attend to."

"As a matter of fact, I do not."

"We will be fine. Do not follow us."

I stopped and watched them disappear from sight. I should have captured Margot and her band before the local Droc'ri and the cleric got wind of them. But I wanted to find out what they were up to first. I would slip into their camp tonight, probe their minds while they slept, and get the answers I sought.

SEVEN

ELLARA ESCAPES

Sheldon

Nana Magog's melodious voice and bony arm around my shoulder consoled me. I brushed the tears from my eyes, slowly returning my awareness to the dark cave. She was saying, "Come back, Ellara. You can't follow Sam to the Mag Mell Otherworld."

Tears blurred the kindly, round face surrounded with a halo of short, curly white hair. A gnarled hand held mine. "Sam died so you could fulfill your destiny. Don't waste this opportunity."

The sobs returned. Nana left me to my tears and tended to the lacerations Boris had received in his charge through Sengy's men. Then she busied herself with stuffing more items she had brought into my saddlebags. She produced one of her tasty meat and vegetable pastries. "Eat." She shoved it into my hands, along with a bitter brew. "You must come back to this reality, Ellara, and ride to the Heartland. You can mourn Sam while you travel. I will see to his burial."

She urged me to eat, but my stomach resisted. I nibbled on the pie and drank most of the bitter-tasting herbal decoction she offered. While I ate and drank, she instructed, "Wait for me in the Heartland. Grieve Sam while you can. I'll come to you when I discover the date of the Council gathering at Cuilithe." She pulled a thin book from a pocket, waved it before my eyes, and stuffed it into one of the bags. "Read this. There are some things you need to know before you arrive at Cuilithe."

We waited in silence until the patrols had once again passed by on their way back toward Sheldon, then Nana blessed me, promised again to meet me in the Heartland in a few days, and sent us on our way.

I galloped along back trails and cart paths, through still woods, across meadows and farms. A brisk wind had picked up, swaying saplings and tugging on my cloak. As darkness fell, the clouds opened up, almost as if the sky shared my grief. Rain saturated the ground, overflowing rivers already swollen from the spring snow-melt. Gusts of wind tore at my cloak and drove drops of water against any exposed parts of my body. I wept for the loss of Sam and the emptiness in my heart where he had lived. When dawn came, I was miles from Sheldon.

For the next few days, I rode day and night, with only short rest periods so the horse and I could eat. Boris was one of the hardy equines native to the mountains of West Alba bred to endure endless miles running over rough terrain and to survive on whatever they found for forage. His unique coat bent light so that he blended into his surroundings, which was one of the reasons for riding bareback. I was grateful that Boris had chosen to be my friend and companion. His down-to-earth presence sometimes was the only thing that kept me sane.

Thankfully, the wind had died down, but the rain continued off and on. My cloak protected me from the showers, but my hands and feet were wet and numb. I wrapped the oiled canvas traveling garment tightly around myself, but even the thin woolen lining I had added was soaked. Boris's back was wet, too. I felt warm enough when I was astride him, but chill seeped into my bones from my wet woolen trousers the first time I got off. After that, I stayed astride while he grazed on the lush spring growth and leaned forward, resting my head on his mane to doze.

A fog clouded my mind. I could think of nothing but Sam. Only survival instinct, and Boris's uncanny horse sense, guided me to hiding places in woodlots, behind hedgerows, or in river gullies whenever the patrols thundered by. Boris seemed to know our destination and led me steadily towards the safety of the Heartland.

I replayed the scene at the wharf. I searched for what I could have done for Sam. An insistent inner voice reminded me I was responsible for Sam's death, the demise of his shipmates and many townsfolk, as well as the seizure of our precious ship. I should have left without seeing him. Then he would still be alive. Or perhaps I could have fought beside him, and we could have prevailed. Or at least died together.

Anger from somewhere deep inside raged through me. I forgot my training. The vows I had made to do no harm were long forgotten. I lusted for Lord Sengy's blood, though Sam or one of his mates had already dispatched him. In my madness, I railed at the perpetrators behind the destruction of our country. They had stolen my beloved and destroyed my family and life. I imagined wringing the Droc'ri Grand Master's neck, whoever he might be. I caressed my dagger as I visualized stabbing Lord Garth through the heart. *I killed once, many years ago, to protect Margot from the man who tried to steal her. This would be no different,* the irrational part of my mind argued. The fire of guilt for Sam's death burned through my body. In my sane moments, it seemed like my violent thoughts came from someone unknown to me, and that scared me. Was I possessed, and if so, by whom?

My heart hurt, broken into a thousand pieces. After four days, we reached the Heartland forest. My tears were spent. I let Boris fill his belly as I stared blankly at the wall of trees. The flames that had fueled my desire for revenge dulled to a few coals. Pain wracked my body. Fatigue and cold deadened my senses. It had finally stopped raining, though leaden clouds still blocked the sun. My zest for living had faded. I longed to join Sam in the Mag Mell and continue our life together in the Otherworld.

I slid off the horse and sat on the damp ground. I leaned against a tree, staring blankly ahead. I felt light-headed and barely aware of my body or surroundings. *It would be so easy to release my spirit and be with Sam.* I closed my eyes, emptied my mind, and relaxed my body. With each breath I exhaled, my body became heavier, dissolving into the earth.

Someone jostled me. I awoke groggily, annoyed at whoever was shoving my body from side to side. I opened my eyes and stared straight into the horse's unblinking gaze. Boris nudged me again.

"Why can't you leave me alone? I want to be with Sam," I whined. "He was right in front of me, in my dream, reaching for me."

Boris butted me again, pushing me away from the tree. He stared back the way we had come, ears pricked, listening intently. I climbed clumsily to my feet and peered in the direction the horse indicated. Boris snorted, turned back to me, and propelled me forward towards the forest. Soon my dulled senses caught the beat of hooves and the jingle of harnesses. Boris knelt so I could crawl onto his back. Before I was even settled, he bolted between the trees. We stopped behind a massive oak and watched as a group of soldiers milled about where I had rested moments before.

A nasal tenor voice said, "We're close. The manure is still warm and tracks fresh. She's in there. Let's catch her."

The air around me filled with whispered words. Some of them filtered through my grief. *"You are safe. This is your home now. We will protect you."* Even as the words entered my addled mind, a wind rose, and branches rustled. The patrol's mounts reared and bucked. As one, the horses pivoted and retreated, their riders clinging to their fleeing steeds.

Much as I longed to be with Sam, the soft embrace of the Goddess enfolded me, and Her Will seeped into my being. Boris tossed his head and trotted along a game trail further into the woods. Cool, damp air and the smell of decaying vegetation enveloped me. Invisible eyes watched our progress. As a Healer trained in the ancient wisdom, I was a welcome guest in the Heartland. The deeper we went into the forest, the more the fog enveloping my mind dissipated.

The Heartland was considered the sacred home of the Goddess and the heart of the island of Alba. The woodland comprised a vast expanse of trees thousands of years old, rumored to be the repositories of primeval earth wisdom. Legend had it that the Goddess rested in this forest from the exertions of creating this world, and it pleased Her so much that She often returned. The Sages said that it was one of the locations on the earth where the Goddess focused her benevolent blessings. In any case, the region was protected so that neither persons with dark hearts nor those serving the Tiarna Drocha could enter. It was said that only those with pure intentions and blessed by the Goddess were welcome. As a result, few people visited the Heartland. Even fewer saw the elusive and ephemeral Caretakers, who, legend said, were not of this world and effortlessly walked between the Heartland and their Verndari homeland. The Caretakers had vowed to serve the Goddess and to protect the wisdom of the Gra'bandia Healers. It was they who safeguarded me now.

We followed a river for two days, threading deeper into the shade cast by the massive deciduous and evergreen trees until we came to a brightly lit glen where Boris and I had ample feed to stay for an extended period. I made camp under a spruce, whose thick tangle of limbs drooped close to the ground and could deflect the showers that persisted. I built a small fire and made an herbal tea to help me sleep and restore my vitality. I missed Sam. I had known this time would come, but now that it was upon me, I didn't know what to do, where to turn, or whom to trust. I clung to the hope that Nana would arrive soon. I resolved to think about my future tomorrow. I wrapped myself in my cloak, curled up, and slept. I dreamed of Sam and his death and of luminous beings that sang ancient songs.

EIGHT

ROKAN IN MIDDENVALE FOREST

Middenvale

In the flicker of firelight, I saw Margot's companions stretched out side by side. Their camp was quiet, broken only by gentle snores and the occasional stomp of horse hooves. They didn't even have a sentry! How foolish, I thought.

Intending to glean from the sleeping youths what I wanted, I knelt beside a patch of brambles and probed the mind closest to me. Suddenly, a rope dropped over my head from behind and came tight around my chest, pinning my arms. A second rope snugged around my neck. I started to move but felt the prick of a dagger between my ribs from someone behind me. Margot stood before me.

"Why did you follow us?" she asked sternly. "Don't lie to me. I can tell even when you hide your aura."

These are just uninitiated children and... A force wrapped around me that ensnared me much more effectively than ropes. I couldn't help smiling.

"I admit I misjudged you."

Margot was not to be distracted. "Show me your forearm." She pointed to my left arm and drummed her fingers on the hilt of her dagger. When I didn't move to comply, her friends straightened. Katarine stood beside me, and another stood behind me. They focused their attention on me.

Margot noticed the small symbol I started to draw with my fingers. "Your magic will not work," she said flatly.

I raised an eyebrow. *What makes Margot think that?* But she was right. Even as I drew the symbol and said the words in my mind, the magic to entrap Margot dissolved. Finally, I slid up my sleeve and showed her the top of my forearm.

"Turn it over."

Margot didn't wait but grabbed my wrist and twisted it to reveal the dagger tattoo of the Droc'ri Order. "I knew it!" she exclaimed. "You're one of those infamous Droc'ri sorcerers. I suspected it the moment I saw you. How dare you try to infiltrate our ranks and ingratiate yourself with us!"

By now, the entire group had gathered around. The firelight illuminated hostile faces. Hands rested upon the hilts of their weapons. Margot still held my wrist in a vice grip.

"I wondered how long it would take you to figure it out. How did you know?"

She ignored me. "Show your aura."

"Or?"

She glanced at her friends. "We will kill you." Her expression reflected her determination.

Through her touch, I sensed an energy rise in her. I released the control I had over my aura. I had kept it close for so many years that I now felt naked and vulnerable. Margot dropped my arm and stepped back, frowning as she appraised me warily. *What does she see? Will she discover my secrets?*

"You are our sworn enemy. Did you intend to capture us?"

"I was sent to capture you and the other Healers aboard your father's ship." While I talked, in my mind I spoke the words that would free me. But the more I struggled, the more I felt my power fade. *How are they draining my magic? They are just children!* Behind Margot, her remaining companions who had been pretending to sleep stared intently at me. I sighed and relaxed. "It looks like you have outmaneuvered me. What are you going to do now that you have captured me?"

Margot and Katarine exchanged glances. But before she could speak, men emerged from the woods armed with bows and arrows, swords, pitchforks, and axes. They encircled us. Their ranks split apart to allow a squat man dressed in the black robes of a cleric to stomp towards the fire. He held a cross high and chanted prayers to the One God to cast down unholy souls. Behind him marched a corpulent, lavishly dressed man, who looked decidedly out of place in the middle of a forest. "Zarizo!" I murmured under my breath. "Of course, it would have to be you."

Margot glanced at me. "You know this man?"

I nodded. "Free me, and I will free you from Zarizo. He's no match for me, but he will kill you."

Margot acted as if she didn't hear me and instead focused on the newcomers.

Without breaking stride, Zarizo swept his hand in a circle, and an invisible barrier surrounded us. The man turned to one of the villagers. "Who is the witch? The one who can tame animals with only a song?" His deep clipped tone vibrated the air around us.

"Let me go, Margot," I said softly.

A villager pointed at Katarine, and the massive man moved to stand before her. So far, he had not seen me. That's just like him. Greed and his stomach dominate his senses. If I could get Margot to release her restricting hold on me...

"So, you're a witch." Zarizo looked Katarine up and down. "You don't look like one." His gaze strayed to Margot, who stood squarely in front of me. "Neither do you. Oh well. We'll

95

become rich on the reward for you lot." Zarizo started to turn away, then peered behind Margot. "Who are you hiding, Witch?"

Don't speak, Margot. Wisely, the woman didn't open her mouth. I was positive she would say something that would spark Zarizo's appetite for cruelty and bloodshed.

Zarizo pushed Margot and Katarine aside and stared at me, where I rested on my knees. The ropes still restrained me. He pointed at me and started laughing loudly, his ample belly jiggling. "Really? The all-powerful Rokan? Captured by a bunch of children!"

Suddenly the force that imprisoned me was gone. I laughed back. "What makes you think I am captured, Zarizo?" I stood slowly, letting the ropes slide to the ground. I placed a hand on Margot's shoulder and the other on Katarine's. "Why can't I just be having a bit of fun?" I pushed between the two women and stood eye to eye with Zarizo. I was taller, but he carried twice my weight. We glowered at each other. "What makes you think *I* didn't control those horses in the village?" I half-turned and swept an arm at the group of youths. "Look at them. They are just a bunch of aspiring academics out on an expedition from the Scholars' Guild. Would you accuse them of being witches? To get your reward, they have to be Healers."

Counting on Zarizo's avarice, I drew from my pocket a heavy bag of gold. "I know how much you hate leaving your comfortable domicile. Here is something to reward your trouble and that of all your village spies." I stepped back and shrugged. "Just pretend that you received the reward for a bunch of Healers, without soiling your hands." I scanned the faces of the villagers. The persuasion spell I had added to my words was having its effect.

Zarizo lifted the bag, calculating its value, and grunted. "Scholars' Guild. Humph! You're trying to cheat me, Rokan."

I opened my cloak to the sigil representing the illustrious Guild. "I am a professor in good standing with the Guild, Zarizo. Ask the headmaster if you don't believe me."

The big man pushed against me with his belly. He grasped my collar and dragged me closer. "If I find out you're deceiving me, Rokan, I will tear you limb from limb. The Grand Master will hear of this."

I jerked his hand away and grinned. I smelled his fear. "And if you, your cleric, or the villagers harass my students again..." I shook my head. "You know I have a fantastic imagination, Zarizo. Now go, before I change my mind." I waved my hand, and the force field around us evaporated. "By the way, Zarizo, the Grand Master will not take kindly to you meddling in his plans."

We watched the villagers disappear into the darkened woods. Zarizo and his cleric were not as easily cast out, and Zarizo flung one parting comment over his shoulder before the woods swallowed their forms. "You haven't seen the end of me, Rokan."

That should have been the end of it. But Zarizo had one last surprise for us. When the woods quieted, Katarine commented, "The horses are gone."

Sure enough, the lines where they had been tethered were vacant. I placed a hand on Katarine's shoulder. "Call them back."

She looked puzzled. "How do I do that?"

"The same way you calmed them this afternoon. I saw you make a connection with each horse. Imagine them in your mind, one at a time, and call them to come to you."

Katarine closed her eyes. Soon there were shouts, whinnies, and cursing. Hooves thundered towards us, crashing through the underbrush and snapping branches. The horses burst into our camp, stopping so abruptly, with heads down, that their riders toppled forward over their necks and hit the ground with a thud. The men struggled to their feet, cursing and shaking angry fists at the horses. The rest of the villagers ran into the clearing.

"Return to your homes," I commanded. "These horses were purchased honestly from the merchant, who paid you generously for your animals. I will not be so magnanimous if you attempt to steal them again." My words had their desired effect, and the villagers scattered. I smirked to myself—*master of persuasion.*

I met Margot's gaze. Surprisingly, she was not afraid of me. Neither were her friends. In fact, they jostled each other, whispering enthusiastically. She turned to the others. "What do we do with this Droc'ri sorcerer, who now claims he is our savior and teacher?"

Was there a hint of sarcasm in her tone?

With a measured stride, Margot came to stand before me. "It appears we owe you a debt of gratitude. However, you are not free to manipulate us as you did those villagers or Zarizo. Though you appear to be a sorcerer that others fear, we have proven you are not as invincible as you think. I, for one, do not trust you. It would be better for you to leave. Be warned that we will not allow ourselves to be captured by you, your brother sorcerers, or anyone else." Margot scanned the other members of her party. "However, I am but one voice. What should be done with him?" she asked the others.

The young women and men turned away from me. Fools! I would never turn my back on my enemy and carry on as if they were inconsequential. Once again, I thought about seizing them, but I hesitated. The more time I spent with these untutored Healers, the less I wanted to deliver them to Garrick, who would just torture them and consume their life force. They reminded me of what had been denied to me when I was their age. My worrisome youth had been spent not with a boisterous enthusiasm for life, but trying to survive Garrick's sadistic pranks. If Garrick's father, the previous Suzerain, had not sired me, and my parents had not been servants at the Suzerain's palace — and if I had grown up in the provinces or in Alba — perhaps I would have felt like these young people who were unafraid of danger because they didn't know enough to recognize it. I brought myself back to their discussion.

Someone was saying, "We can't let him leave. He will follow us or bring others to capture us."

"I say kill him and be done with it." This came from a young man. "It is our duty to prevent anything from interfering with Nana's objective." He pointed at me. "I know the Goddess teaches tolerance, but we also have to protect ourselves."

Smart boy. That's what I would do if I were in their position. Kill the enemy and have one less threat. Even though I could not read Margot's aura, I sensed she was not the murderous type, nor were her friends. Even the one who advocated for my death.

"What if we take him prisoner?" a slender woman asked.

"Who will watch him?"

Katarine spoke slowly. "He told the Droc'ri that we were his students, and he was a professor from the Scholars' Guild. We should have thought of that as our disguise. What if we make a bargain with him?" My ears pricked.

"What do you have in mind, Katarine?" Margot asked.

"I felt him assist me in calling back the horses. What if we let him remain alive with the understanding that he helps each of us learn about our special talents?"

"He's a Droc'ri!" Margot exploded. "We can't trust him! For all we know, he will try to bend us to his will and take our gifts to serve his own interests!"

I chuckled inwardly. *Yes, Margot. You have it exactly right.*

Margot cast a scathing glance at me. "We either have to kill him or keep him with us. If we keep him, it will be like having a pet scorpion!" She surveyed her companions' faces, then addressed me. "Why did you help us with Zarizo and the villagers?"

"I didn't want them to capture you."

Margot tilted her head to the side. "And the real reason?"

I felt an invisible pressure compelling me to answer. I exhaled and met Margot's stare. "Because... it would be a waste of your untapped talent to have you captured and taken to the Grand Master. I'm inclined to help you and your cause." *And I want to stay with you and discover how you steal my magic!*

She studied me for a long while. "What you say defies the vows you made to your Order. Who are you deceiving? Yourself? Or are you hoping to deceive us?"

I scanned her companions. "Nana Magog seems to have brought you together for a mission. You don't know who or what you are up against. You need my experience, my wisdom, and my abilities. I have studied the teachings of the Goddess extensively and know the protocols for training her initiates. I can teach you how to master your gifts to fight for the Goddess against the Dark Lords."

"And oppose your sworn brothers," Margot pointed out.

I nodded. "Yes, against the Droc'ri. Think of it this way. There is no pleasure in butchering a bunch of cubs. The real sport comes when one hunts a feline, such as a grimalkin of the Desert Lands. I have become bored of following the Grand Master's orders. It's all too easy for me. But if I train you, the battlefield would be leveled, and you stand a chance of defeating the Droc'ri. If I don't teach you, you will not survive." I let my words settle over those gathered.

"Your words imply we are defenseless against the sorcerers. You forget how easily we apprehended you. If you want to convince me, show your aura and prove to me your true intentions."

I frowned. In my confrontation with Zarizo, I had instinctively hidden it. In the Droc'ri world, revealing one's energy field meant certain death.

"You expect us to accept your word. Unlike the followers of the Goddess, the Droc'ri are not honor-bound to keep their promises. You must risk trusting us."

How does she know so much about the Droc'ri? After weighing the pros and cons, I released my aura. I felt exposed but stopped myself from hiding it. My skin tingled wherever Margot gazed. What a novel feeling. I regarded her approvingly. She was not one to be charmed easily. "Fate has brought us together. Perhaps we can work together for the benefit of all."

"Your words are like honey, but the blackness in your aura smothering a kind heart declares your deceit, Rokan."

I swallowed and silently cursed Ellara for her part in undermining the binding of my heart that defined me as Droc'ri. Could my Brothers see this weakness as easily as this child? I stood. "If you do not want me to remain with you, I will leave."

"How do we know you won't follow and spy upon us, or bring your friends to kill us?" Katarine said softly. She turned to Margot. "Perhaps it is better to keep our adversary where we can watch him and learn what he knows."

I nodded to the young woman. "You are truly wise beyond your years, Katarine."

"None of your silver-tongued words, Rokan. Katarine is right. You will stay with us and teach us about the Droc'ri. If you hide your aura or manipulate what it displays, I will know, and we will kill you." She pursed her lips. "I would imagine that as a sorcerer, normal restraints wouldn't work on you." She stretched her arm, and her forefinger touched my forehead. "The Goddess knows the best way to render you harmless."

I gasped at the fire that poured into my being, scouring evil desires and sinister intentions from me. I collapsed to the ground, panting, my body strangely alive like I had never before felt. I sat up. Colors appeared more vivid, and my senses attuned to the rhythmic energy patterns of the forest. Yet when I tried to summon even a simple binding spell, or fan the fire, nothing happened. My mind, however, was as sharp as ever. I fingered my traveling crystal and tried to open a portal, although I already knew that I could not. I moved to a nearby tree, and sat against it, watching the group and, in particular, Margot. I wasn't worried. She would not kill me. I was a strong man and could easily overpower her if I wanted. I was still in charge, even without my magic.

Margot addressed the others. "We need to get some sleep. You four keep watch for two hours." She pointed to four more. "You take the next watch. Tomorrow we will put some distance between Middenvale and us. And watch him, as well."

I exhaled. I had successfully maneuvered Margot into allowing me to stay with them. She was wise not to trust me. Now I could discover their mission and the identities of the Healers aboard Sam's ship.

NINE

ELLARA

The Heartland

Four honey cakes and a half-dozen scones lay on a log near the fire when I awoke. I held up each cake, offering thanks to the Goddess, who worked through her Caretakers to deliver them. Then I ate half of the cakes hungrily, shared one with Boris, and saved the last one for later. Sleep had cleared my mind, but I still moved aimlessly. Anguish tore at my heart.

I dumped out my soaked leather satchels to see what Nana had put into them and to see what had gotten wet. Thankfully, my herbs and medicine kit were undamaged by the downpours. Nana had supplied a collection of nuts, dried fruits, tubers, and root vegetables — heavy to carry, but dense in sustenance — as well as some salted, dried lamb and salmon. I turned Nana's book over in my hands, and picked up the tube containing Cleric Paul's research and inspected them for rain damage. Relieved to see that Paul's priceless translations were safe, I set them aside. Seeking the answers to Alba's and the Goddess's problems didn't interest me. My mind was still wrapped around the loss of my pair'ti.

My escape from Sheldon had been a blur of detours to avoid the patrols, and rivers swollen from the spring downpours that made crossings too dangerous. The clouds finally parted, and the prospect of being warmed by the sun lured me into the open meadow. Boris nickered and tossed his head as if inviting me to join him. Songbirds chirped and warbled. Hawks soared above, and the sweet scent of colorful wildflowers filled the warming air.

I shed my clothes and lay on the grass near a deep, clear pool in the center of the meadow, soaking in the warming rays. My mind drifted to the first time I had come to the Heartland. I had just turned seventeen. Sam, who had been a family friend my whole life, had asked my mother for her approval to hand-fast with me and to become my pair'ti. I had overheard Nana Magog and my mother arguing over the pairing.

Their words echoed in my mind. Nana had said, "Sam will protect Ellara and provide her with a business that would make use of her talents."

My mother had replied, "Sam is reliable, but he is gone most of the time. What protection can he give her? Besides, he is too old for her. The young wrangler who brings wild horses for Trevor to tame would be perfect for her."

Nana was determined that I become Sam's pair'ti, and in her championing me in my heart's desire, I reluctantly warmed to her. Maybe her brusque behavior towards me wasn't so bad, after all.

Finally, my mother had agreed to the pairing upon two conditions. She told me, "You have to spend a week in the Heartland alone, and you have to heal a debilitating injury Sam received from an accident ten years ago." I thought my mother had made the conditions so that I would fail. I had been determined to prove her wrong.

I smiled as I remembered how excited I had been to become the life mate of the man whom I adored and who cherished me. I had always felt close to him. He gave me the love and attention I had craved as a child but hadn't received from my perpetually ill and emotionally unavailable mother, or from Trevor, my step-father, who was often away.

Even though I enjoyed being on my own, I had been terrified about spending a week alone in the forest. My mother was too frail to make the journey, so Nana Magog had ridden to the border of the woods with me. We had said goodbye, and I walked alone into the shelter of the trees. I had been fine until nightfall, when the spirits of the night, as I called them, came out. I huddled around my fire, afraid to sleep, and peered into the darkness. I jumped at every rustle of leaves or snap of a twig. I never saw any people, animals, or ghosts, but I knew I was not alone, and I feared that the beings were not friendly. I reminded myself that I was safe and that no evil could lurk in the Heartland. I had wandered the woods for almost four days before I came upon the glen in which I now rested.

When I returned after the week, I had graduated from child-like dependence to self-sufficiency. After being immersed in the beauty around me, observing the purposeful habits of squirrels and rabbits, discerning the messages in the songs of the birds, and noticing how the meadow and forest glowed at sunset and under the full moon, I felt the Goddess awaken within me. Through repeated little miracles such as finding dry tinder to start a fire after it rained, or a rabbit allowing itself to be my dinner, or a deer leading me to find succulent greens, I had developed an understanding of the Divine Order of the Goddess and the interconnectedness of all life. Every-thing had a place and supported everything else, including me. I had become self-assured and trusted in a higher power that was always there for me. This experience had started me, unknowingly, on the path of my destiny. Nana Magog was pleased, although she didn't say anything, which was her way. I just knew.

When I recounted my adventures to Nana, the Elder had told me that the natural openings and meadows in the forest were vortices where the veil between worlds was thin, and the Goddess could speak directly to a person. They were neme-tons, sacred places of power. Maybe there was some truth to her words. Now, even with my diminished senses, my body tingled as life force filled me.

The next test in my youth had been to heal Sam. Shortly after he took over the merchant vessel from his father, his back had been injured while unloading a crate. It had fallen on him. He partly recovered from the injury after many sessions with Nana Magog, who was the prominent Healer in the region. He went to the finest minds at the Scholars' Guild in Langon, and their experiments gave him temporary relief from the pain but never fully restored him. For years, it was evident that he felt miserable, but he never talked about it.

Barely seven years old at the time, I had tried to ease the young captain's discomfort by placing my hands on his back and wishing the pain away. When he left to return to his ship, he gave me a warm hug and left smiling, walking more comfortably. Nana reassured me I was helping Sam to feel better.

Nana said the injury would shorten his life, and it would make it difficult to start and raise a family. She said I must restore his vitality. I never knew why she thought I could do it when she, as a seasoned Healer, couldn't. My mother was skeptical as well. However, I wanted to be pair'ti with Sam with all my heart, so I was willing to do whatever was required of me. To avoid arguments with my mother about this task, I learned how to heal Sam in secret.

With enhanced senses and a newfound confidence, Nana taught me how to invite the Goddess into my heart and allow Her to work through me to heal the man I loved. It had taken three months to complete the process. Sam regained his strength and functionality. He could then be the life-long pair'ti everyone expected, and who he wanted to be.

We also gained a level of intimacy that neither of us had ever known before. From our sessions together, I could sense Sam's every mood, thought, and desire. I felt his passionate love for me, even though he rarely spoke his feelings. He seemed to read my emotional state, fears, and wishes as if I were one of his navigation charts. I felt understood and appreciated. I didn't have to prove anything to receive his love. He had more faith in me than I had in myself and frequently told me so. With this deep connection, there were no secrets between us.

When I turned eighteen, I made my vows with him. My mother still did not approve, saying Sam was too old for me, but I was not concerned. In my eyes, the extra years made him someone wise and steadfast. Someone I could trust. We forged an unbreakable Goddess-bond linking us, no matter where we were in the world. This was the most valuable part of our unity. Tears slid along my cheeks. Now he was gone, and I didn't feel the thread that had always united us.

That night as I gazed into the fire, I poured out the love I felt for Sam and wished he was with me again. Movement in the corner of my eye caused me to look up, but I didn't see anything. I tensed, loosening my dagger in its sheath, but no one came out of the darkness.

I leaned back against the tree trunk, and then I saw it again. This time I heard Sam say, *"It's only me,"* in my mind.

I probed the darkness with my senses. Then I felt Sam's spirit wrap around me.

"Sam? You're here?"

Sam stood before me, youthful, clean-shaven, and handsome as ever. I jumped up to give him a hug, but my arms passed through him. The apparition disappeared.

I sat down and stared at the remaining honey cake, wondering if those I had eaten contained hallucinogenic herbs. I was not familiar with seeing or talking to ghosts and had ignored the beings I sensed years ago. However, Nana said she talked to spirits all of the time.

"Sam? Are you really there?"

The phantom appeared again. "It's tricky to stretch the veil enough for you to see me," he said. "And for me to touch you." He sat down beside me and put an etheric arm around my waist. "I'm here for you. Remember, I said I'd always be here for you."

Tears found their way back into my eyes. "I thought I only saw you because of the honey cakes."

He wrapped me in his filmy arms. "It's not the cakes that allow you to see me. It's your love. It thinned the boundary between our worlds so I can come to you."

"There seems to be more substance to you. I can actually feel you touching me. How did you do that?"

"I talked with some wizards in the Mag Mell. They told me how to make it possible for you to see and feel me, and to maintain this density for longer periods. At least while you are in the Heartland, where the veil between the worlds is naturally porous."

I nestled close to him. "I like it." I sighed. "I miss you."

"I'm more accessible to you now than when I was in my physical body. I am not constrained by time and space or the need to eat and sleep. I can watch out for you and our children and lead you away from danger. I've always wanted to keep you safe. You are precious." He chuckled at my dour expression and squeezed me. "I miss you, too, but we have to make the best of what we are given." He peered at me. "Can you accept this as a different way we can be together?"

I shook my head. "No. I feel so empty without you in my life. In my world," I amended. I wiped my eyes. "I don't know that I have a choice. I don't want to lose my connection to you. So, I'll learn and adapt."

"That's my Ellara." He leaned back against the tree.

Minutes passed. "This wasn't what I imagined when you said you would meet me in the Heartland. I was thinking of something more substantial."

Sam laughed. "I kept my word, didn't I?"

I grunted. "I know these last couple of years were hard on you. I wish I could have figured out how to stop the drain on your health. Since the new laws passed a few months ago, something happened to our country. A dark shadow stole your vitality and weakened the Goddess's protection."

"I wasn't the only one to get sick. Other sea captains were affected. I lost some of my best friends to the evil malady. You gave me your energy and kept me alive."

"I'd rather you were still alive." Tears streamed down my cheeks. "But I had to go ruin everything and get a lot of other people killed as well."

"I'm still here. Just not in the same way. I'm glad we got to say goodbye." After a long pause, he continued, "I prepared and protected you the best I could. I knew I was not destined for the battle you face with the Dark Lords. If I had remained alive, taking your life force, you would not have been able to follow the path of your destiny and do your part in protecting our way of life. I would have held you back. Now you are free to do what you need to do and go where you are needed without worrying about me."

I stared at him. "Are you saying you chose to die?"

He nodded. "I knew my time was soon. The Goddess gave me a choice. I chose this way to stir you into action so you would accept your birth-right."

I sat speechless, tears streaming down my cheeks and an ache in my heart. "Why did you hide this from me?" I croaked. Even though we had a telepathic connection, we didn't automatically know everything that the other thought or did.

"I'm sorry, Beloved. I wanted to spare you the anguish of knowing my fate. And I knew you would sacrifice yourself to protect me. I couldn't let you do that."

The next morning, I took a long walk in the forest, foraging for food and firewood. The knowledge that Sam had willingly chosen to die at the docks felt like a knife twisting in my heart.

I wept, feeling heart-broken and abandoned. However, I couldn't stay vexed with Sam, and after a purifying bath in the pool and nap in the sun, my perspective shifted to accept his act of love and sacrifice so that I could fulfill whatever I was supposed to do. He was right. As long as he lived, I would have done anything to keep him alive and would not have participated in the war between the representatives of the Goddess and the Dark Lords that had already started.

At night, when he appeared again, I asked, "What do I need to do next? Can you see the threads to unravel the shadow that crosses our lands?"

"I can't predict the future. All I know is that you were born to live out a certain destiny. Nana Magog knew that and tasked me with watching over and protecting you. I don't know what your mission is. Perhaps you will understand more when you go to Cuilithe."

We sat together in silence, basking in each other's company. "What did you discover about my mother when you were in Langon?"

"Did you know she was a Healer-priestess for her region in the Emerald Mountains?"

I shook my head. "She never said where she was from or what she did. She made it perfectly clear, though, that she didn't like me becoming a Healer. We argued often about the use of my talent."

"The woman I talked with was not very forthcoming, except to say that your mother was part of a Triune during the Religious Wars, and had escaped from a sorcerer who captured her but did not kill her because of her unborn child. You."

I squirmed on the log. I still carried resentments from growing up. Even though she was constantly infirm, she had vehemently refused to let me heal her. She died mysteriously when I was hiding at sea from Cleric Paul. I never had a chance to make peace with her in person. Sam had encouraged me to come to terms with my childhood and bless my mother for doing what she thought best for me, and I had. She had been a puzzle to me. "Why didn't she tell me? I would have understood."

"I think she was trying to protect you from her fate. What happened in the Emerald Mountains is happening now in Alba. You are not safe, no matter where you hide."

I sighed. "I know. I don't like it. I wish I could restore the world to harmony where we all get along and have the freedom to follow our natural calling."

"You can. You have the power within you." Sam stroked my back. It felt like the gentle wind created by a bumblebee's wings. "Know you are not alone. You are never alone. You have a lot of friends in your world and in other realms that want to serve you."

"Serve me? Why? How?"

"Do you remember many years ago I asked Matty to care for my family if something happened to me, as is customary for seafarers?"

I nodded uneasily. I remembered listening to Sam and the massive, friendly helmsman from the *Lovely Lady* swap tall tales at our home or at the local inn on the rare occasions when both ships were in port. He was one of Sam's best friends and adored our children and me almost as much as Sam did. Matty had wanted me to heal his crippled captain, but the young man always refused to come with Matty to our house.

"Seek Matty. We served together on my father's ship, and through the years of our friendship, I have known him to be an honest and Goddess-abiding man. If he could, he would part the seas for you."

I sat, silently peeling the bark from the stick I was about to throw on the fire. "I'm not ready to move on from you, Sam. No one can replace you."

"I know. Just be open to allowing him and others to help you." Sam hugged me and faded from view, leaving me to my thoughts.

I didn't know what I was going to do or where I was going after Cuilithe. I couldn't return to Sheldon. Nothing was there for me now. I poked the fire restlessly. I didn't want to think that far into the future. "When is Nana Magog going to show up?"

TEN

ELLARA

The Heartland

Something poked into my side. It jabbed again. I rolled over ready to chastise the horse, and instead, saw Nana Magog, armed with a cane, and behind her, the filmy form of Sam.

"Are you going to sleep away your life, Child?" Nana Magog jabbed again with the staff. "Come on. You have work to do."

I rubbed the sleep from my eyes. It was still dark, although songbirds announced the coming dawn. Nana stirred my campfire. I got up, smiled at Sam, and headed towards Nana.

"Come on, Child," Nana Magog said impatiently. "I don't have all day. Sit. I have a lot to tell you."

I slowly eased onto the log by the fire.

"Here. Eat this." Nana handed over a meat pie. She believed anything could be dealt with more effectively if you started the juices for digesting life with a full stomach. I inhaled deeply. The aroma of herbs and spices mixed with lamb and spring vegetables inside a simple oat crust made my mouth water.

"You might think you can hide out in the forest, but you have the work of the Goddess to do, and She is a stern taskmaster."

"But..."

"It's time you knew the Goddess's plan for you." She glanced at Sam, who moved behind me and placed his hands on my shoulders.

I squirmed on the log. The potpie in my hand shook slightly. Nana's presence reminded me of what Sam had revealed last night. "Why didn't you tell me I was from a long line of Healers? Why was I kept in the dark my whole life?"

"You were hunted long before you were born. A Droc'ri sorcerer captured your mother and let her live only because he vowed he would have her child when she was birthed. I sensed your potential in her womb. Your mother and I knew the Droc'ri would turn you into his pawn and use you to further his interests. We couldn't allow that. I helped your mother flee her home in the Emerald Mountains and hide in Alba, where we tried to make a safe life for you. We protected you the best we could, even when your natural abilities grew strong. We let you think you were just a talented Healer. It was for your safety that we revealed neither your mother's history nor your potential.

"We did everything we could to disguise your natural talent from the Natuan witch-hunters and the Droc'ri's interest in you. We used protection spells, but the best way to hide you would be to prevent you from doing magic or acting like a Healer. It is for this same reason that I didn't take you on as my apprentice and formally train you in the Gra'Bandia tradition or allow you to receive the Council's blessing. We could not let you know that you are from a Goddess-born lineage like me, and that if the Goddess chooses, She will transmit her radiant force through you, making you Her human host and Voice." Nana slowly spun her cane between her hands. "That sorcerer still watches you, and one day will return for you. He knows about Margot, who has as strong a connection to the Goddess. She has the potential to be as powerful, if not more. He wants both of you for what you are capable of, which will serve his cold-hearted ambitions. Already he pursues Margot to lure you into his trap."

I shuddered, hastily setting down the pasty. I rose and paced around the fire. I remembered the terror at almost losing my child long ago. I had worried about Margot and Kian ever since, even when I knew they were safe with their father.

"Why? What's so special about Margot and me?"

Nana Magog ticked off the reasons on her fingers. "You both are from an ancient line of Goddess-born Healers. You both have what it takes to become the Voice of the Goddess and harness the strong theurgy, the divine magic of the Goddess, used to form the Gra'bandia Triunes. You are a formidable threat to the Dark Lords of the Tiarna Drocha and their Droc'ri servants. Neither of you are seasoned in the use of the Goddess's theurgy other than for minor healing, and they believe you can be turned to serve the Dark Lords. And if not, you can be killed."

I held up my hands. "Why can't I just be an ordinary Healer? I'm grieving the loss of my pair'ti, and now you decide it is time for me to know my destiny. Why did you keep me uninformed until now?" I shifted uneasily.

"Sit down, Child," Nana Magog instructed. "It's time to start your training and prepare you for the Gra'Bandia Council's blessing. This is the first step in awaking your true potential."

Nana can be so bossy sometimes. I had developed a healthy respect, along with a measure of fear, for the old woman. "I don't have a good feeling about this." I glanced at Sam.

Nana chuckled. "You can't deny your life's mission. Your destiny will find you no matter how fast or far you run from it."

I scowled, but settled onto the log, picked up the meat pie, and inspected it. It didn't smell as enticing as it had earlier. I took a deep breath. "Alright, Nana. What do *you* think is my future?"

Nana pulled up a section of wood and sat across the flames from me. The light illuminated the front of her body. In the half-light, she didn't look as old and stooped as usual. Gnarled fingers folded firmly around her walking stick, holding it upright between her knees. The rest of her body, except for her pale face and curly white hair, seemed to dissolve into the inky sky at her back.

"Listen carefully, Child. You were born when the Goddess required Her Healers to restore the balance in our world." She shifted on the piece of wood.

"The Dark Lords of the Tiarna Drocha feed upon our world's fears and misery. Their agents, the Droc'ri sorcerers, do their best to create chaos, disrupting countries and people's lives to satisfy their shadowy masters. You already know the Grand Master means to destroy the Goddess, Her servants, and every Goddess-born they can find. He thinks he will then have unlimited power without anyone to stop him. In his ignorance, he thinks he will rule the world. In reality, Gea will become another domain of darkness upon which the Dark Lords feed. The Grand Master believes Alba is Her last stronghold. He has already started to undermine the Goddess's protection, and Alba is crumbling."

"How do I fit into this grand scheme?"

"The taint of the Tiarna Drocha has invaded Alba, destroying the harmony that has existed in our society for centuries. The source of it must be rooted out and touched by the Light of the Goddess."

I leaned back, shaking my head. "I don't see what I can do to solve this problem. The taint is like a shadow without form or location. How can one fight a shadow? Especially one from another realm, very unlike our world?"

"That's why it's time for you to receive the Gra'Bandia Council's blessing and step into your legacy."

"How will their blessing make things different? I already channel the Goddess for healing."

Nana snorted. "That's child's play. You have the talent and ability to become a human host to the Goddess. The Voice of the Goddess. You can become part of a Triune like your mother and I were. You *must* have the Council's blessing to do that. The blessing gives you the right to call yourself a Healer and bestows the triple crescent moon mark of the Healer over your heart, and upon your forehead, for all to see. You receive the full backing of the Gra'Bandia Healers, including the authority, protection, and responsibility that comes with the title."

"Why do I need a title when I am already called a Healer? Besides, considering our current political climate where Healers are arrested and killed, why would I want to announce to the clerics and the Droc'ri who I am?"

Nana laughed. "Now, do you understand why we kept you secluded your whole life, asked you not to draw attention to yourself, and encouraged you to pursue a profession that would keep you invisible?"

"You mean like Margot becoming an Advocate for Alban tradespeople and me handling all of the paperwork and orders for Sam's shipping business?"

Nana nodded. "Yes. We deliberately didn't train you about your strongest ability. Instead, I let Cleric Paul teach you about the philosophies and teachings of the Goddess — but not about how to *be* a Healer. Working with him afforded you immunity from the clerics. Besides, he was a wealth of information and educated you about the Goddess — far better than either your mother or I could have done on our own. You learned about the Natuan teachings and ecclesiastic law. And you were privileged to see more than one version of the same truth. You were not formally blessed by the Council, and therefore, not a Healer. Cleric Paul was able to use this technicality to free you many times from persecution. Especially after Lord Sengy came to Sheldon."

So that's how he did it. "Still, I wish I had known who I was." I peered at Nana. "You don't have a symbol on your forehead. Yet I have seen you teleport yourself wherever you want. You are a proficient Healer. Did the Council's blessing give you this ability?" I probed the ground with the toe of my boot. "If I am blessed by the Council, will I be able to do magic like you?"

I had asked Nana to teach me her magic. She had refused. I had watched her closely and tried to emulate what she did, without success. I had concluded I didn't have any magical abilities.

Nana ignored my question. "Now, before you are presented to the Council, you must learn some of the terms you will hear when you arrive. I realize that it would have been easier for you to learn over a longer period, but circumstances don't allow for it. Have you read the booklet I gave you? Or any of Cleric Paul's translations?"

I raised an eyebrow. How did she know about that document? And more importantly, why was Nana so intent on having the Council approve me now? I had been doing my work just fine without it, and it hadn't seemed important before. I didn't really care about a title. However, I wasn't going to argue with her. She knew something that I didn't, and I would never know until I deciphered her book and Cleric Paul's papers.

"Now I must go." Nana stood, and shook out her skirt. "By the way, the Council meets in two weeks in the Sacred Grove at Cuilithe. You'd better leave today so that you will arrive on time. Boris knows the way. I will meet you there. You need the time to prepare yourself for the Council evaluation. Study the book I gave you." She bowed her head in respect, touched her fingers to her heart, and muttered a couple of words.

"Nana." But she was gone, teleporting away as I had seen her do on other occasions. I'd have to tell her about Cleric Paul's ideas next time.

Alone again, I went to the pool, stripped, and poured cold water over myself. My mind was in chaos. I worried about Margot. I reached for her with my Far Sight, even though Nana had warned me against it, citing the sorcerer's ability to capture my spirit. I caught a glimpse of my daughter traveling along a narrow trail with a group of young women and men. An older man rode beside her. Margot leaned away from him and sat her mount stiffly.

She looked up when I touched her spirit and shook her head slightly as if warning me away. At least she was unharmed. Who was the man, dressed like a professor from the Scholars' Guild? Dare I ask Nana?

I sat at the edge of the pool, staring into the depths. Finally, I said, "Great Mother Goddess, I don't know how to surrender to your plan for me. I thought I had, when I opened my heart to receive your Gra'yia. But Nana and Sam seem to think there is a deeper, more powerful level that you can work through me. Change me so that I trust you completely and clearly hear your guidance. Show me how to use the talents you have given me and guide me gently on my path."

Movement among the trees on the far side of the meadow attracted my attention. The vague outline of a man appeared to be watching.

"Sam?" I reached with my senses. The man was a stranger, and the more he watched, the queasier I became. Hastily, I dressed, and then faced the apparition. Without thinking, I raised my hand, palm outward, and uttered the words, "Begone, unwelcome traveler." The image disappeared.

I returned to my campsite and gathered my things in preparation for my journey to Cuilithe. I didn't have a good feeling about the Council gathering. Was it merely my fear or a premonition?

Who was that man who was surrounded by darkness? *How long has he been watching me? Is this the sorcerer Nana warned me of?* I froze. *What if the Heartland is no longer a safe sanctuary?*

ELEVEN

ROKAN IN THE EASTERN PROVINCE

Emerald Mountains

T rue to Margot's word, my magic was bound. I could not summon even the smallest spell to move water, or earth, much less open a portal or send out my spirit to spy upon the world. I flexed my muscles. At least I still had unfettered use of my body and mind. I searched my memory of all the manuscripts I had studied to understand what she had done, but to no avail. I wasn't worried. *Why? What was it about Margot and her friends that allowed me to be comfortable without my magic?* Surprisingly, this unusual situation felt exhilarating. It reawakened long-lost dreams of being free to follow my passion for studying and exploring the natural mysteries of life, before I was forced to endure the Rith Bac'Croi and become a Droc'ri. *I did what was required to survive,* I thought sourly.

We rode into the flanks of the Emerald Mountains, following valleys, climbing over ridges, and entering other valleys, continually gaining in elevation. My mind drifted back to when I had traveled these same valleys with Garrick, Commander Garth, and his mercenary soldiers, hired by the Ethnarch to enforce the One God's commandments.

The trail followed along the base of a sheer cliff reaching hundreds of feet into the sky. We skirted the toe of a rockslide, bringing back a memory of how, fifty years ago, Zarizo, Sid, and a half-dozen Brothers had made yet another attempt to kill me. At that time, I was still content to be a Droc'ri.

Even after the Rith Bac'Croi ritual had created an indifference about others' lives, I hadn't given up my scholarly pursuits. Instead, I had turned my research towards how I could excel at everything I needed to survive. I became especially proficient at killing. It was with this hypervigilant awareness that I had detected a section of the rock face detaching, even before the first boulders crashed onto my unsuspecting companions and their horses.

The perpetrators had ridden up shortly afterward and were quite disappointed that I had survived. Zarizo and Sid, in particular, still coveted my authority and privilege as the Grand Master's Henchman. I smiled at the memory. I had acquired the talent to survive, no matter what attempts they made to destroy me. I had mastered what it took to be a Droc'ri and fulfilled the Droc'ri primary objective — kill the Healers.

My mind drifted to the Droc'ri Grand Master of that era, who had discovered that a Healer's vitality briefly made his body and magic more robust. Soon the rest of the Droc'ri followed our leader's example, which evolved into a practice of sadistically torturing Healers before consuming their life force.

During the Religious Wars, I had enjoyed playing cat and mouse with my victims, until I encountered one stalwart Healer. I offered to free her in exchange for her pledge of service to me. I fully intended to capture her after she had escaped and consume her life force.

The Healer had refused to leave, saying that I needed to learn a lesson about the Goddess. Her audacity piqued my curiosity. She was a Seer and foretold the coming of a fractured Healer who would take down our Order. She had told me the seeds of her prophecy came from our Book of Tornaad. She said we doomed our Order with our barbaric practices. She had added that the Healers and Droc'ri needed each other. This set me on a research project. I still killed Healers after I probed them for what they knew about the Seer's foretelling. The more I studied, the more I began to question if it was in the Droc'ri's best interest to kill all the Goddess-born. We needed them to keep the world alive. Garrick, however, never grasped this concept and still cruelly entertained himself with his prisoners.

Drawing my attention back to the trail, I scanned the long line of riders whose mounts picked their way along the tree-lined banks of a cascading creek. I didn't want Garrick to get his hands on these young Goddess-born and torture them before he devoured their vitality.

I recollected mercilessly assassinating many innocent lives. Senseless murder only served to satisfy some cruel injustice from my childhood. At least, that is how I rationalized my lust to kill.

During the first few years of the war, before the formation of the Gra'Bandia Triunes, I had captured the highest number of Healers, bringing them to the Grand Master for his pleasure. On one occasion, I brought the Grand Master the signet rings of twenty-five Healers. The Grand Master had proclaimed my prowess to the assembly and publicly bestowed lavish gifts of gold, land, and captured women. He renamed me Ravmavet, Master of Death. Even though I knew the display was to encourage the other sorcerers to capture more Healers, I had basked in the lofty status and the reverent fear with which my Brothers beheld me. They had always drawn a respectful distance away from me when I passed, often with murmurs praising my adroit talents. They never challenged me and many offered to serve me. Some Brothers still did, at my secret fortress in the desert. I smiled, remembering how jealous Zarizo and Sid had been. *They will never achieve what I have. Even now, they are second rate.*

Partway through the sixty-year campaign, I encountered a Triune composed of Nana Magog, Ellara's mother, Orva, and another Healer. By then, I had discovered that if we killed their mates, the women were weakened from grief and the loss of the supportive energetic framework their pair'ti supplied, which allowed the Healers to channel the Goddess's intense force.

This Triune and their Mages proved to be a very satisfying challenge. A group of Brothers tried the overt approach — a direct attack with knives, fireballs, earthen upheavals, and black lightning. The Healers and their pair'ti formed a protective shield around themselves and their village, easily diverting our attack. With my inner sight, I witnessed the three women draw from their respective Far'degan pair'ti, a power they should not have access to. Creating a dense column of energy, they focused it into a giant, invisible bat that instantaneously redirected our fireballs and lightning back to its source, mortally wounding most of our group. The image of their magic burned into my mind. They won that battle, but I was not about to give up.

Other attempts to separate these Healers and divide them from their pair'ti had failed. I chanced to capture a shepherdess from Orva's village. I placed a spell on her so I could control her. Wounding her, I placed her where one of the trio was bound to find her.

It was Orva who found the woman. When she opened her heart to heal the shepherdess, I surrounded Orva with my spirit, trapping her. She called for help. Jaleem Magog, and Esme Bean came to her rescue. I was prepared for them and, when Esme touched the shepherdess, I trapped her spirit as well. Nana Magog proved too cagey to capture and disappeared after she blasted me with a force that stripped me briefly of my magic.

I bound and gagged the Healers. Soon, their pair'tis came to the rescue. Shockingly, they were willing to exchange their lives for the lives of their mates. I would never have done that! Before Orva's mate, Josef, died, he had cursed me, saying, "Without love, you and all the Droc'ri will die." I didn't know what good love did. I killed him anyway, even without the use of my magic.

I didn't kill Magog's pair'ti, even though he offered his life for her freedom. Instead, I sent him into the place between worlds where she could not rescue him. She would have to come to me to save him. Then I could finally capture her.

I had no intention of honoring my promise to release the women. Just before I planned to kill Orva, I discovered the Healer was carrying a girl-child. Orva and her pair'ti had been formidable foes. Because the child had been bathed frequently by the Goddess's Gra'yia during her gestation, my study of Healers indicated the girl would be exceptionally powerful.

Word came that our assistance was needed in quelling a rebellion some distance away. Most of us went to support the Natuan soldiers. While I was away, Magog swooped into my camp, killed the sorcerers guarding the women, and helped Esme and Orva escape with the unborn child. The Healers had disappeared after that.

My gaze strayed to Margot, near the head of the line of travelers. I sensed the same potential in her as I had in her unborn mother. How could that be? I had read that only a fetus conceived and bathed in the Goddess's Gra'yia could wield that much power.

I had searched for Orva and her child. Several years later, I had finally found them in Sheldon. Posing as a rancher looking for breeding stock, I approached the cottage where she and Trevor, who had assumed the role of caretaker for the family, lived with her child. Trevor and the girl were not home. Her mother had recognized me, even in my disguise. I tried to blast her with black lightning, but only a tiny stream of gray light emerged from my fingers. I drew my dagger and attacked the frail woman.

"You cannot have the child," Orva had said and swept her hand to block me.

"Hah. You're weak, Orva. I'll kill you and take the child."

Out of the blue, Jaleem Magog arrived. At first, I couldn't move. Then my life force faded. I became weaker by the moment. Frantically, I tried to break away.

"Your magic doesn't work here, Rokan," Magog had said. "Now we have the upper hand." She came close and peered into my face. "Release my pair'ti."

I had laughed. She wouldn't kill me. Healers were forbidden from killing. "Never, Magog. He is my guarantee that you will serve me."

"I made no such agreement, Rokan." She had eyed me, then drew her hand into a fist and yanked on my spirit. "I will put you in the same place you sent my pair'ti."

I cried out in pain and my world went black. Sometime later, I awoke in the woods. I don't know how I had gotten there. Perhaps Magog has moved me to cover up my murder. Beside me, and softly singing a lullaby, sat a golden-haired little girl of about four. She noticed I was awake. She smiled at me. I slowly sat up, patting myself to see if I was still in the physical world.

She took my hand. "You were really sick. I had to bridge your blocked heart so that the Goddess's Radiance could heal you. You are alive, now."

I felt different — like I was somehow connected to her. Memory returned. I should take the child, but I hesitated. What would I do with an innocent girl who was so powerful at this young age that she could restore me from near death and an eternity in the Tiarna Drocha, and without any training?

I must bind this girl-child to me. Her power will make me invincible. I scanned my memory of all the spells I knew. Nothing felt appropriate. Instinctively, I touched her heart with a finger. "Take part of my heart," I said, sending my spirit into her. "In gratitude of what you have done for me. May we always be bound together."

What I had done out of greed and lust for glory almost forty years ago had backfired and become my bane. I saw the world and my actions through the compassionate eyes of the Goddess. Memories of my childhood had returned. Recollections of how I had felt safe and precious when my mother held me on her lap and told me stories of the demi-gods and other legends. Or the affectionate, although abrasive, grooming by my domesticated grimalkin cub.

My encounter with Ellara had awakened a longing for something different. Amassing enormous wealth, seducing lovely women, living a lavish lifestyle of expensive clothing, magnificent horses, or ultimate power and control over others had lost its charm and seemed empty now. I had started longing for what I could never again have: to feel love and be loved.

Every day, I could feel the child. I didn't want to kill anymore. But I lived in a brutal Droc'ri world. I shifted to a more subtle, sophisticated, and hence rewarding way to control people. When questioned, I told my Brothers this was the new way to be a Droc'ri. Of course, they didn't buy it. I became a target of ridicule and attack. It didn't matter. I liked how I could manipulate people without their even knowing it, as I had done to Margot. I paused in my train of thought. *Had I really influenced her, or did she just let me think I had?*

Margot's shriek startled me from my reverie. The young woman stood in the water, protesting her predicament while her horse struggled to his feet. Margot had been near the head of the line of riders who now crossed the raging creek single file. When our eyes met, she grabbed the reins of her soaked horse and carefully walked the rest of the way across the algae-covered, submerged, flat rocks. Once on land, her horse shook himself off vigorously, giving Margot another drenching. Her friends asked if she was hurt. She shook her head, and indicated that the rest of the group should cross upstream to avoid the treacherous stretch. She wrung out her clothes as best she could, and one of her friends offered her a dry coat, but I could see she was still soaked and shivering in the cold air. I could have dried her and the horse off in an instant, if I had access to my magic.

"We need to make a fire to warm you. Before chill sets in and weakens you." *In which case, you would be unable to release the Goddess's hold on me.*

"We have to keep going," she replied.

"You're not thinking clearly." I touched fingers to the side of her neck. Her skin felt cold. "You're freezing. Call the Goddess to warm yourself."

She pulled away from me.

While we talked, several women rummaged in their packs and extracted garments. They took Margot behind some shrubs and pulled her wet clothing off, briskly rubbed her skin to get the blood flowing, and dressed her in warm, dry sweaters and trousers. Katarine put Margot on her horse and rode behind, wrapping a cloak around her friend. A gentle glow surrounded the two women. Eventually, Margot stopped shivering, and a while later, the glow faded. I didn't realize I was tense until Margot threw open the cloak, proclaiming she was too hot. I felt a pang of jealousy. I had never had friends who would care for me like Katarine did for Margot.

As we rode, I surveyed those with me. The young Healers and Mages were enthusiastic and had good-naturedly accepted me as one of their entourage. They seemed to know the venom had been taken from my sting. I began to relax and enjoy myself. Their outlook on the challenges that faced the world was one of undaunted optimism. Even though every day was filled with danger, their spirits were free. I secretly longed to be free, as they were. *If I bind them to me, they can make me free.*

I pretended to surrender to Margot, following her commands. She seemed to take my submissiveness in stride, though Margot's cold and biting remarks, along with her deliberate avoidance of me, and wary watchfulness, made it very clear that I was an unwelcome member of their party. In contrast, her friends often sought my company and chatted easily with me, and even shared their food with me. Margot seemed to know that I was no longer a threat to her or the others. *What went on in her mind?* It frustrated me that I couldn't read her as effortlessly as she seemed to understand me.

Every now and then, I sensed Garrick, and the more days that passed, the stronger became the feeling. Instead of apprehension for failing to bring him Healers, I felt strangely liberated. After all, I *was* doing his bidding and I was powerless to return just yet. I grinned. Maybe Margot taking my magic wasn't so bad after all. I settled deeper into my saddle. I liked it here. I was in no hurry to return to Garrick. I decided to fulfill my bargain with Margot and teach her friends about their powers.

Each of her friends had a particular talent that they took for granted. Katarine demonstrated her natural talent with the animals. She communicated with them in such a way that they followed her willingly. She also had healing abilities and tended to cuts and overstretched tendons on injured animals. One young woman had a gift with plants, finding and growing enough edible greens to feed the group. One was a hunter, consistently bringing game for meals by inviting her prey to allow itself to be sacrificed, and another could build a fire with a spark from her fingertip and her breath. Yet another could stop the rain.

It was apparent to me that these men and women were untaught and had no clue about the vast potential that lay within them. Even Margot, who had used her healing talent alongside Katarine with the horses, and for cuts, sprains, and even wasp stings, had a limited view of herself and lacked the discipline to focus her energy. She had an uncanny ability to read people, matching my own. *If I teach them, they will serve me, as is traditional between master and apprentice.* The idea excited me.

I relished my time with the travelers. I knew I could easily take control of these inexperienced Goddess-born at any time, if not by sorcery, then with my ability to twist words and circumstances that would allow me to entrap them. Or I could physically restrain them or even kill them. However, the natural trust and camaraderie between the young people intrigued me. Their auras indicated they had been strangers before Nana Magog had brought them together. Yet, they willingly worked cooperatively for the benefit of the whole.

That was not the Droc'ri way. I imagined myself and my Brothers on a similar undertaking. To gain cooperation, there would have to be promises of reward, as well as a lot of coercion. Even then, each Brother would be watching for an opportunity to take command and subjugate or kill his companions. This group exhibited no threatening undercurrents, which allowed them to focus on the task at hand without the need to watch their back. I wanted to be part of what they offered.

On the fourth evening, we had entered the foothills, and the nights were getting cold. I listened to the stories and jokes swapped between companions. A topic finally came up about which I was particularly interested.

A man asked, "Margot, where are we going, and why?"

Margot darted a stern look at me, then said, "Didn't Nana tell you?"

Heads shook.

She scowled at me before replying, "I'm not sure. Nana said to head east into the Emerald Mountains. She would show me where to go."

What I could see of her energy field showed she was telling the truth. I puzzled over this. I was sure she knew more than she was saying.

The conversation turned to the scourge of the Droc'ri and their machinations to destroy the Goddess. One of the women said, "The Goddess has survived for eons. She will continue to survive."

"But how?" someone asked. "The Droc'ri kill our kind. We have to learn how to defeat them and the Dark Lords."

"Mother said that the Droc'ri cannot sustain their evil ways and have doomed themselves." Margot's stare was a challenge.

"What if the Droc'ri are getting weak and are blaming the Goddess? And that is why they attack Her Healers," I suggested.

All heads turned to me. "Why do you say that?"

"I've been studying the Goddess's teachings and the Droc'ri code for a very long time. There are flaws in the Droc'ri ways, and one who knows about them could exploit them."

Now I had everyone's attention.

"Go on," Margot said. "Give us an example."

"The Droc'ri Code requires a Brother to use his magic as much as possible. Now this works for a young Droc'ri, who builds his capacity for magic, but for a mature sorcerer, it wastes vital life force and weakens him."

Margot studied me. "Are most of the members of the Droc'ri Order 'mature'?"

I nodded. "Most have lived over one hundred eighty years."

"Does that make them weak?"

I laughed. "Never make the mistake of thinking a Droc'ri is weak! If one is clever enough to get a sorcerer to expend his resources in futile pursuits, the sorcerer can be weakened. However, the older a Droc'ri gets, the wiser he becomes, and it is, therefore, harder to fool him."

Margot snorted. "You talk in circles, Rokan." But I had captured her attention. "Why don't you have new members joining your Order?"

I shrugged. "No one has been recruiting. After all, we are a secret organization, and not everyone knows about us, at least directly. A candidate has to go through a rigorous series of tests. Then there is the training, which takes decades. Many don't have what it takes."

"Which makes the Droc'ri an elite organization. Greedy gombeens. Don't think there is enough of the pie to go around, right?" She leaned toward me. "There is never enough for the Droc'ri. Do they cling to what they have, and grasp for more just to make sure they have enough? Or try to manipulate people to support their point of view even if it is harmful to the populace? Are the Droc'ri afraid they will become invisible if they allow the Goddess's children to thrive? Is a Droc'ri Brother perpetually cursed to clawing his way up? Zarizo fears you. Why? Have you tromped on him in your rise to power?"

I thought a moment before answering her. "No. I have earned my position by performing my duties effectively. I have not trodden on toes to get where I am." I looked away. *I haven't had to kill to get to my lofty rank, like others, because...Garrick has helped me.* I hated Garrick. Admitting he contributed to my position in the Order was not something I wanted to do.

As the days progressed, we climbed higher into the Emerald Mountains. Spring was slow to come in the snow-covered, summer grazing valleys. Rivers gushed with snowmelt, making crossing hazardous. As we journeyed and opportunities arose, I pointed out to individuals what unique talent they were using. Soon, I noticed they were deliberately calling on their extraordinary gifts and, like children, were delighted to see what they were capable of. They practiced calming the water enough so we could cross, finding food and game for meals, preparing comfortable campsites, and magically lighting fires.

With my magic entrapped, I had not been able to monitor world events and was decidedly at a disadvantage. One evening, I overheard Margot and Katarine passionately talking about Sam's brutal death and how Ellara was hiding in the Heartland, having escaped from Lord Sengy's men. Margot had tugged on her horse's reins, preparing to return to Alba to help her mother. But Katarine convinced her it was more important to complete Nana's mission. How did Margot know about events in Sheldon? The young woman never ceased to surprise me. *I must find out what Nana has tasked them with!*

I decided that Margot's sharp tongue came partly from despair about her father's death. Even though I wanted to spend as much time with her as possible, she generally avoided me, and when our paths did cross, what little she said was filled with barbs. She tolerated nothing less than honesty from me and seemed to know when my words were not wholly truthful. *Did she suspect me of causing her father's death?*

Eventually, Margot asked, "Why were you looking for us?"

"Garrick sent me."

"He's the Grand Master?"

"Yes. How did you know I was a Droc'ri?"

She shot me a glance. "No aura. And the tattoo. I recognized it from the man who tried to steal me when I was little."

I controlled my surprise. "And you think I was that person?"

"I don't think. I *know* you are. Why did you try to take me?"

"Your talent. I wanted to train you."

"So, I could be your slave? Don't think I am not aware of what you haven't said."

I chuckled. I liked Margot. "Somehow, I don't think you'll ever be anyone's slave. It's true, I wanted you to serve me. Now, I want your help."

She shook her head. "Same difference."

I nodded to the line of men and women. "Unlike you, they are so trusting."

She shrugged. "We were raised in the loving benevolence of the Goddess. Something you have never known."

"You're wrong about that. I was once like you. I didn't want to become a Droc'ri. I was happily studying the history of our civilizations. I wanted to be a scholar, and I studied at the Scholars' Guild. A hundred fifty-some years ago, Garrick, in one of his cruel pranks, had convinced the old Grand Master I had to join or die. The former Grand Master could sense power in me and said if I didn't join, my family would be killed. Looking back, I think he was afraid I would choose to follow the path of the Goddess and became a Mage like your grandfather."

Margot harrumphed. "It was still your choice."

I sighed. "Sometimes I wonder what would have happened if I had made a different choice."

Margot smiled. Finally, she said. "Mother says that we often can't see the bigger picture and to trust everything happens for a reason."

"You believe that?"

"You said fate has brought us together. The Goddess has rendered you harmless to us. Perhaps you are part of Her plan."

"So, you trust me, then?"

"Not at all, Rokan. But I trust the Goddess." She looked at me speculatively, reading my aura.

"What do you see?"

"That you are not the threat you want us to think. And you will help in the tasks ahead."

I frowned. "What makes you say that?"

She pointed. "There. In your aura. The darkness that smothers your heart is thinning. Haven't you noticed it?" She smiled to herself, kicking her horse to catch up with Katarine. "I have an idea how to break the Droc'ri threat," I overheard her tell her friend.

TWELVE

ELLARA

The Heartland

As I proceeded towards Cuilithe, I saw for myself how the isle of Alba was truly blessed by the Goddess. From the maps I had studied with Cleric Paul, I remembered how the island's main body stretched roughly eight hundred miles long and about six hundred miles wide. A smattering of smaller islands formed two archipelagos that curved seawards from the northwestern and southeastern corners of the island, almost as if the Goddess had spun the land like a top and bits had flown off before it came to a stop. These smaller isles stretched for miles into the sea. If one were to shove Alba southeasterly, the island would tuck nicely into the curve created by the mainland and the Weyverin peninsula.

Alba enjoyed a latitude where the northern regions were temperate, had adequate rainfall and ample water to support vegetation, pastures, forests, fruit orchards, and vineyards. The semi-tropical southern portion included the capital city of Araval. A network of rivers filled with nutrients flowed from the Heartland Mountains. This allowed for year-round production of vegetables, animal fodder, and grains, along with nut and fruit orchards. The citizens of the northern portion of Alba raised livestock, while the southerners marketed a plethora of crops. Most of the island's population lived on the gently rolling hills and plains that formed the eastern flanks of the untamed mountains of central and western Alba. The Heartland wilderness dominated the center of the island, occupying approximately nine hundred square miles.

I thought Nana Magog was exaggerating when she said it would take two weeks to get to Cuilithe. When I entered the Heartland from the northeast, the terrain and the animal trails had been easily traveled. Oak, maple, birch, and a few ever-green trees dotted low hills, and waterways carved shallow grooves in the terrain.

As Boris and I worked our way south and westerly towards Cuilithe, we started climbing in elevation, and a dense mix of evergreen and deciduous trees dominated the landscape. We followed meandering animal tracks and crossed rivers that cut deep gorges. Under the tree canopies, the air was crisp and damp, and I could not see the sun. After a few hours in which I thought we were going in circles, we came to a clearing. The sun slid behind the trees to the west, and I knew we had made some progress. I was grateful that Boris appeared to know the way.

The murky apparition I had seen before I left the meadow disturbed me. I had been raised to believe that the Heartland was protected from anything and anyone evil. That the Heartland's sanctity had been violated alarmed me. As we traveled, I imagined I was being watched. It rattled my sense of safety and amplified the realization that I had no idea how to combat the ignoble forces polarizing our people and provoking fear in their hearts or the evil Kurat spirits Cleric Paul had referred to.

I had grown up as a sheltered child. We had lived some distance from Sheldon on ranch land, and raised sheep, goats, and horses. My step-father, Trevor, had a talent for understanding animals. He regaled me with stories of how, when I was little, almost before I could walk, I would slip away while Mother slept and go with him to the pastures and lay my hands on the sick animals. He had said I "wished them to be well." He described how the horses had watched over me and showed me a secret hideout in the forest where I went to be alone. He didn't know why I stopped healing his flocks after the stranger passed through. I had simply lost interest and he dismissed it as the whimsical nature of children. However, my strong desire to help Sam feel better after his accident reawakened my talent. That time seemed a lifetime ago, now.

My overly protective mother had never let me have friends, so I made friends with the animals. I could only go to Sheldon if it was with her friend, Nana Magog, or herself. I had sensed there was something between them, but my mother told me we were not blood-related. Against my mother's wishes, Nana tutored me in my healing talent just enough to use physical techniques or herbs to restore the vitality of a person. I practiced on Sam. Later, Nana showed me how to channel the Goddess to heal him. I discovered how to address physical and emotional issues on my own by experimenting with my clients. My only experience of darkness had been working with the shadow sides of a person, such as fear, lack of self-worth or confidence, the need to prove oneself, or feeling unloved. I had experienced all of these shadows myself and understood how they could play out in others. But pure evil like the apparition in the forest was beyond my training.

Strangely, even after I started helping Nana Magog in her ministrations, she didn't want me associating with other Healers. She forbade me to call myself a Healer, even though that was a title Sam's crew had bestowed upon me after they witnessed the restoration of Sam and the abatement of a storm that threatened our ship. The label caught on and soon other clients started calling me Healer. Nana didn't explain her reasons for avoiding the title, or her reluctance to teach me how to master my talent or do the magic she could. I honored her warnings about the title, but in the privacy of my mind, I thought of myself as a Healer.

That night, Boris and I ate one of the travel cakes Nana had given me. Edible greens foraged from the meadows we traversed supplemented the fatty biscuits made from grains, nuts, salt, lard, and Nana's tonic herbal formula. I tossed wood on the fire to get more light, pulled out the book Nana had given me, and turned it over. The cover was a strip of animal hide, and embossed into the leather was the word *One*. I thought about putting it back in my bag like I had done several times before, but I needed to know what I was up against. With Sam looking over my shoulder, I opened to a faded page of brittle parchment. Surprisingly, the ink was still crisp and the writing legible. A tight script filled the gaps between detailed drawings. I squinted at the text, finally muttering, "It's in Leonini."

I had learned a few words of the Leonini language from Cleric Paul when he showed me some of the ancient texts. I quickly grasped that the dialect was complex and the words filled with multiple meanings, which made translation and comprehension difficult. Cleric Paul had said that to understand the old tongue, one had to put oneself back into the era in which it was written and let one's inner guidance convey the intended meaning. Translations could not be based on rote word meanings alone. Context determined the message. Hence, he had said that many of the transcriptions made were not correct. I had marveled at his abilities, and he had helped me understand a few of the concepts. I had used these principles to guide my life as a servant of the Goddess. But to read a book in the Leonini language was beyond me.

I put the book aside and carefully removed Cleric Paul's life work from the leather tube. There were three hundred eighteen pages of tight, precise printing. Typical of the old scholar, he numbered each page and notated the document from which it was rendered at the bottom of each sheet. He wrote the full title of the manuscript, the estimated era during which it was written, where he had found it, who else had interpreted it, and what it referenced. After thumbing through the pages, I sincerely appreciated his efforts and vowed I'd protect this work the best I could.

His treatise started with the creation stories. I read some of them, then decided to skip to the section where it talked about the Droc'ri's conflicts with the Goddess. One part caught my eye. It spoke of the history of the Goddess tradition and of the priests who had split from the matriarchal society, and later became the Droc'ri. *The Droc'ri are descendants of the Goddess-born lineage. They are no different from Healers, except by the choices they make. I wonder if there is a way to undo the Rith Bac'Croi that cuts them off from the Goddess?*

Nana appeared the next night. Sam joined us. Nana was not pleased when I told her about the figure I had seen. She shook her head, muttering, "It is worse than I thought."

I shoved aside the anxiety her words stirred and showed her Cleric Paul's document. Nana scanned the text, then pulled out some pages and placed them on top. "Study these. You must be prepared to receive the blessing of the Gra'Bandia Council."

Before she departed, Nana pointed to Cleric Paul's document. "I don't always agree with the cleric's interpretation of the Goddess's teachings. This work is a composite summary of all of the Goddess's traditional, somewhat controversial, lost and forbidden teachings. Don't show it to anyone, especially anyone at the Council. Some would want to destroy it. Guard it with your life."

Each day we traveled, I read the pages to Boris, trying to comprehend the nuances in the multiple ways one phrase could be interpreted. Thankfully, the wise scholar had noted alternate interpretations in footnotes. Besides learning what Nana had indicated, top on my list was to learn to protect myself from the dark entities.

The next night, I brought up Cleric Paul's concerns. "Cleric Paul believes that the Triunes were a failure because they were not formed correctly."

"Why does he believe this, Child?"

I held up a sheet. "The Triunes were to be formed from the unity of the masculine and feminine qualities. The masculine grounds the spiritual energy of the Healer and discharges excess energies from the Goddess, so that the Healer is not harmed by the Goddess's Radiance.

"I understand that the Triunes created during the Religious Wars had been formed from three Healers united by a special form of the Ceangal Bandia or Goddess bonding, which the High Council conferred upon the chosen trio. This sheet says that their pair'ti became Far'degan, the supportive protector for their soul-bonded mate, allowing her to survive the immense force of the Goddess. Without their Far'degans, the Triune cannot function. The Droc'ri killed off the Far'degans, and that was how they were able to defeat the Gra'Bandia Triunes. It seems like this was a fatal flaw."

"That is true." Nana didn't elaborate.

"What if the Triunes were formed differently?"

"What do you mean?"

I glanced at Sam before addressing Nana. "What if the Triunes were formed of two women and a man, or some combination thereof. Or three pairs of Healers *and* their pair'ti?"

Nana gasped. "Never!"

"Why not? You were weakened because you lost your pair'ti. What if your pair'ti were part of the unit? There would be no separation and no way to split the Triune apart. The Far'degan could strengthen the Healer's ability to embody the Goddess's Light and discharge any excess energy, thereby protecting her."

"Child, you are too young to understand. Men would over-power their partners and use the Triunes for their own greed and glory. It was decided long ago that men could not host the Goddess, and Healers have never been allowed to host Her *with* their pair'ti."

"But... Sam wouldn't overpower me. And Mages do magic."

Nana snorted. "Mages use Elemental magic, not the Goddess's Divine Radiance. Put this notion out of your mind. It will not work." Nana rose and, after a brief nod and a few words, vanished.

The next night, I asked Nana, "How exactly does a Far'degan support his pair'ti Healer?"

Nana settled on a raised root near the fire. "The energetic framework of a woman is very different from a man's. Women have a network of threads that interconnect and form a delicate latticework that permeates their being. If the matrix is not robust, this web of energies can easily be overwhelmed when a Healer calls in the Divine Loving Radiance. The Light of the Goddess purges, purifies, and destroys. It can incapacitate an unprotected Healer. Her nervous system could be destroyed and she could die. Divine Love creates, builds, heals, and nurtures. Remember that basic principle." She pointed at me. "You have been using the Goddess's Divine Love, Her Gra'yia, to accomplish your restorative work. You have not used Her Divine Light, Her Lig'yia, which is the primary energy used by the Triunes." She pursed her lips, appearing to be lost in thought.

"The masculine energy is composed of heavy filaments and forms an impervious band around the perimeter of his aura, much like a shell. By combining these two vibrational shapes, both pair'ti receive the protective shell of the masculine and the complex weaving and wisdom of the feminine. This allows the Healer to transmit the Goddess's energies without harm."

She leaned toward me. "Sam provided you the support you needed to be able to channel the Goddess for the healing work you did. Now that Sam is gone, you need to find a replacement Far'degan."

I drew back. "No one can replace Sam! Why can't I continue doing what I did without Sam?"

Nana shrugged. "You might be able to. Getting the Council's blessing will help to solidify the framework Sam gave you. Ultimately, to face the darkness in the world, you will need a strong Far'degan. You have barely touched the ability within you."

I was silent. I didn't want another protector. I had read that to receive the benefits of the masculine energy, I would need to share my heart with him. Sam's death was still too fresh for me to consider carrying on my healing work, much less going up against the Droc'ri.

Nana continued kindly. "No one can replace Sam. But perhaps there is one who can give you the support you need. Just keep an open mind."

One week moved into the next. I read more of Cleric Paul's pages to Boris. I asked the horse what specific terms meant, told him my worries, and cried into his mane. For his part, Boris unwaveringly carried me towards our destination with steadfastness and confidence that I found comforting. The concept of the Triunes fascinated me, and my mind explored the different possible formations. I shared my ideas with Boris and Sam, but not Nana. Sam was likewise intrigued at what we could have done together if we had merged our energies into one unit in defense of our homeland. Maybe he would have prevailed in Sheldon and he would still be alive.

It took two weeks of travel before I spotted the massive, extinct volcano, known as Cuilithe, home to the Sacred Grove. After a day of following narrow ridge tops, descending into canyons, crossing raging rivers, and scrambling up the steep slope to the crater top, I could finally look into the caldera. Massive trees with sweeping canopies and slender, above-ground roots like many-legged creatures covered the broad plain. Varieties of trees that I didn't recognize reached for the heavens alongside tall evergreens.

The sun slipped below the horizon as I descended onto the flat land. In the twilight, a woman blocked my way, demanding, "Who are you? Who is your mentor?"

"Nana Magog."

At the mention of Nana Magog, the woman groaned. She studied me with flinty eyes and said flatly, "The horse may not enter."

I patted Boris's neck. "He is my travel companion."

"No animals are allowed on the sacred ground at Cuilithe." Her tone said there would be no discussion. "He stays outside the Sacred Grove where he can forage. It is the rules of the gathering." She motioned for me to dismount. "Come on. It will be dark soon."

I slid from Boris's back and pulled the makeshift rope halter over his ears. "Thank you, Boris," I whispered to him. Reluctant to leave, I hugged him, then shouldered my satchel and followed the Healer.

We walked a short distance, and the air around us abruptly became still and venerable. I looked back to where Boris watched me with head held high. Tossing his head, he nickered, then shook himself. I followed the stern woman as we threaded through the massive trees, tripping over raised roots. From the distance came the sound of chanting and the smoke from cook fires. My guide didn't say a word, but I sensed her displeasure that she had been given the task of fetching me.

I discerned the somber attitude of the gathering even before it came into sight. Crowds congregated around the central fire, and cook fires dotted the border of the broad clearing. The smell of food and aromatic wood smoke filled the air. As we approached, everyone stopped talking and inspected me.

My guide introduced me. "This is Ellara Ruark, Magog's uninitiated."

I heard whispers among those closest to me. "She and her pair'ti started the Sheldon rebellion." Another said, "Let's see if Magog has atoned by training her properly." Others turned away, muttering. A stiff-backed, hawk-faced woman moved through the gathering and stood ten paces from me. She appraised me. An aura of command surrounded her, and I guessed she was the one I'd have to appease to receive the Council's blessing. Without a word, she sniffed and returned to her place by the central fire.

Nervously, I asked, "Where's Nana Magog?"

"She's not here." My escort pointed into the darkness. "You may sleep with the uninitiated."

With an ever-growing knot in my stomach, I gritted my teeth, straightened, and walked stiffly in the direction indicated, tripping over stones and roots. I didn't have a good feeling about this.

THIRTEEN

ROKAN IN THE EMERALD MOUNTAINS

The Temple of the Crescent Moon

After almost two weeks, we entered a narrow, snow-covered valley that rose to a sheer rock outcropping. I studied the snow for footprints. I knew people lived in the mountains, but we had not seen a soul on our journey. Grazing was sparse for the horses in these high, snow-covered pastures.

I pointed at the mountaintop in the distance. "That's the Temple of the Crescent Moon. The temple was once formed out of the solid rock. It was a sanctuary for Healers and Mages. The inhabitants and Guardians of the temple were killed during the Religious Wars, and the temple demolished."

Margot said nothing, but I perceived her anger. I was getting good at reading her, just as I suspected she had become of me.

As we drew closer to the mountain, the air warmed, and lush spring grass pushed through a thin crust of snow. I inhaled deeply. "This is one of the Goddess's places of power, just like the Heartland is in Alba."

I had been one of the sorcerers who had desecrated the sanctuary. I watched warily for the Verndari Guardians, who undoubtedly would not welcome me.

Margot noticed the shift in my composure. "You look worried. Are you suspecting an attack?"

I shook my head. "I don't know."

She gave me a sharp look. "In the short time I've known you, you have never been unsure. What makes you uncomfortable?" She scanned the area carefully.

We rode further into the valley, which had been the site of many skirmishes between the Droc'ri and the Healers. I stopped my horse. "Something's not right. This time of year, these pastures should be filled with wildlife. Where are the animals?"

The answer to my question came in the form of a black lightning bolt directed at me. It knocked me from my horse. Immediately I rose and put out a hand to block the next assault, and realized too late that my ability was bound and I had no access to it.

"Margot, you must free me, or these Droc'ri will capture you."

But Margot was busy giving instructions to her companions, and they scattered in twos and threes. She stayed with me, pulling me behind a giant boulder.

I grabbed her arms and tried to bend her to my will. "Free the Goddess's hold on me before it's too late."

"Use your head, Rokan," she said calmly. "Not every problem is solved by using brute force."

I stared at her, imagining I had just heard Nana Magog speak. I ducked as another assault of black lightning crackled around us. I shook her. "Free me."

"I don't know how. The Goddess constrained you. I don't know what She did. *I* can't undo it."

"You channeled the Goddess once; you can do it again."

"Instead of arguing about whether I can or can't free you, let's find an alternative." She appraised me. "My guess is that they want to kill you, because with you out of the way, we'll become easy prey. Am I right?"

I nodded.

She smiled. She peeked over the edge of the rock and scanned the valley. Then she stood up and called loudly, "Do you want Rokan? He's right here with me. We've captured him." She waited for a few seconds. "Don't believe me? Come see for yourself."

"What are you doing?" I hissed. "They'll kill me and then you for sure!"

She looked down at me as I huddled behind the rock. "Do I detect fear, Rokan?"

I clamped my mouth shut. Between gritted teeth, I growled, "I have something to do before I can die."

She patted my shoulder. "No worries. You're more useful to us alive right now."

I wished I could read her aura. She was better at the game of bluff than I was! I heard footsteps approach and voices speaking the Tokurian dialect. I peered over the rock and saw six brown-robed Droc'ri. Garrick's men. I struggled to find just a little bit of magic to defend myself.

"That's far enough, boys."

"Show us the captured sorcerer," one of the Droc'ri said.

With a broad smile, Margot hoisted me to my feet. She kept a hand on my arm, and her aura surrounded me. I lifted my chin and grinned at them. Maybe I could bluff my way out of this. These were the men who had tried to kill me just a few days ago in Tokurat.

The men laughed. "So, we can't kill you, but a woman can steal your magic?" They jostled each other. "Why didn't we think of that? He has a weakness for young women."

"Be careful. I might steal your powers as well." Margot lifted a hand, palm outward.

The Droc'ri reacted, hurling bolts of black lightning at us. I started to duck, but she pulled me back to stand beside her.

The energy dissipated around us, shattering into a million sparks. The sorcerers grumbled in surprise and hurled more magical destruction at us. Their lightning and balls of fire simply evaporated as it touched Margot's shield, emboldening me. I didn't know what Margot or her Goddess were doing, but I was pleased. I laughed and taunted the men who wanted to kill me. I started to move, but Margot held me firmly in place.

"Don't move," she hissed at me.

I glanced at her, puzzled. Outwardly relaxed, she was keenly attuned to what was happening all around her.

Out of nowhere, the rest of the youths appeared. I felt their unified force press on me, restricting my ability to move, and draining away any malice. They formed a circle around the half-dozen Droc'ri. Still holding my arm, Margot dragged me to stand before the men. "You see? He is our captive. And now, so are you." She turned to me. "Shall we do to them what we did to you, Rokan?"

I paused, quickly calculating the best response. "I don't think they would like it." I looked at my Brothers. "Look what she has done to me. She has consumed all of my magic. I am powerless against her. Just like you are." I leaned forward. "She'll do the same to you."

The sorcerers glanced at each other and edged backward. A ring of daggers halted their retreat.

Twenty or thirty brown-robed men emerged from the forest and dashed towards us, hurling fireballs and black lightning. The force field the youths had created stopped the first few salvos and then collapsed. The freed Droc'ri lunged at Margot's companions, knives ready to slit their throats. Instead of killing the youths, the sorcerers rounded the uninitiated Healers up into a tight group and secured them together in a magical force field, much like what the youngsters had just placed on the Droc'ri.

Zarizo waddled towards us. "So Rokan, you lied to me. These are Healers, after all. Now I'll get my reward, *and* you will be drawn and quartered." He rubbed his hands together. "I do hope you cry out for mercy."

I groaned. I should have suspected this was too good of an opportunity for Zarizo to pass up. He would have lured supporters with the promise of a share in the reward for killing me — and the heightened status. Capturing the Healers was the icing on the cake.

Margot's presence had become a distraction. My mind raced. *How can I save myself?*

FOURTEEN

ELLARA AT CUILITHE

The Heartland

I looked longingly at the central fire, set in the open space surrounded by stone monoliths. The chill night air at this elevation penetrated through my clothes and permeated the damp bed I had made from moss. On my journey, I had made a fire, and had the companionship of Boris, Sam, and often Nana Magog. At the coldest part of the night, Boris would lie down beside me and share his warmth. While I journeyed to Cuilithe, I had imagined that I would encounter other Healers who would welcome me as a sister. I anticipated sharing ideas and learning new ways of healing. I wasn't so sure now.

I wanted to build a fire, but I wasn't sure if it was allowed to collect and burn wood in the Sacred Grove. Six cook fires adjacent to the central one, were the only fires I saw. It appeared that Nana Magog had neglected to tell me the rules of Cuilithe.

The aroma of savory stews drew me towards the cook fires. I watched the initiates bringing bowls and cups to the matronly woman tending a cauldron. She spooned stew into the vessels. I fetched my dish, but when I offered it to be filled, I was waved away from each campfire.

I overheard remarks about Nana Magog that led me to believe that she was not welcome here and, by association, neither was I. Disheartened, I asked the woman tending the kettle furthest from the central fire if I could have something to eat. At first, she waved me away. I started to leave when she called me back. She glanced quickly around, then ladled a thick mixture of vegetables, lentils, and wild rice into my bowl, then immediately motioned me on. I withdrew to a safe distance and slowly ate.

I lingered around the fires, observing the movements of the Healers and their uninitiated apprentices. The latter appeared to fill the role of servants to their Healer mentors. Not only did they fetch food and water for their mistresses, but they also used magic to create globes of light to illuminate their way under the broad-canopied trees, dry off rain-soaked logs, and enhance the comfort of their mossy beds. I marveled as Healers made holes in the air, coming and going through these openings. I could do none of that. However, I didn't see anyone pop in or out of the grove like Nana could do.

I sat at my dark, meager campsite, and contemplated leaving, but I didn't know where I would go. In the wee hours, Nana Magog arrived, attended by a young man carrying her supplies. She was her usual cheery self and poked me, "Get to sleep, Child." She noticed my gaze stray to the hardy man. She bent down and whispered. "Don't you recognize him? He has been your traveling companion for weeks."

"Boris?"

She laughed at my surprise. "He's the horse — in disguise." She tapped my leg with her stick. "We're in the Heartland, Child. This is the Goddess's playground. Anything is possible."

I smiled to myself, pleased that my sour-faced escort had been out-maneuvered. *There is a way around the rules. Simply turn the animal into a man.*

Before dawn, I arose to relieve myself and noticed Boris sitting against a tree. He was dressed only in tunic and trousers, and despite his air of vitality, he shivered. When I put my hand on his shoulder, he looked up with wide-spaced, large brown eyes. Black hair fell across his forehead and partly covered his eyes, strands reaching down his long, narrow face. He felt familiar. He felt like Boris, the horse. I thought about giving him my cloak, but I was cold, even with all the clothes I wore. Instead, I asked if I could sit beside him.

Wordlessly, Boris made room for me, and I draped my cloak over us. In a short time, he stopped shivering. I fell asleep, warm at last. I awoke to Nana's chuckle.

"Don't sleep away your life, Child. The Council will deliberate today."

"Nana, I don't belong here."

"Nonsense, Child. You can out-Heal anyone here if put to the test."

In the daylight, the gathered women and their pair'ti didn't look so unfriendly. Plus, I had Nana by my side and Boris following behind.

I stood beside Nana outside the inner circle of the High Council of Elder Healers, along with many other women of all ages. "The oldest Healers are on the High Council," Nana commented. "The senior elder becomes the Doyen and is the Council spokeswoman."

An aura of competent mastery surrounded the Council members. Though they were long-lived, they appeared to be robust women in their fifties or sixties, with smooth skin and sturdily built, supple bodies, and blonde, copper, or brown hair, with only an occasional streak of gray or white. In fact, as I surveyed the gathering, most of the Healers looked similarly youthful. In contrast, Nana Magog was stooped, white-haired, her face a mass of wrinkles. Yet, she had a devilish twinkle in her eye and a bounce in her step. She gripped her walking stick firmly and leaned heavily on it.

"Why aren't you on the Council?" I whispered to Nana.

She laughed. "I used to be, but I was kicked off." Before I could ask why, she continued, "Most of them are over two hundred years old except for those two, who are about one hundred eighty-something. Camila is the oldest Healer alive. She is almost three hundred years old."

My jaw dropped. I closed my mouth quickly. "How old are you, Nana?"

"I'll be two hundred twenty-eight in a few months."

I positioned myself so I could survey my fellow uninitiated. Some looked to be about my age. A few were younger, and others appeared older. Eagerness shone in their faces. One woman resembled me, except she was slightly taller and more curvaceous. She had a pleasant smile, but it vanished when she spotted me. *Who is she?* She stood beside the sour-faced Healer, Leisel, who had escorted me into the Sacred Grove. *Was she that Healer's apprentice?* However, the apprentice wasn't the only one who watched Nana and me with aversion.

"If they pass the tests and the High Council finds them fit, they will be blessed by the Goddess and bear the title of Healer. Only then can they learn how to summon the Goddess. Uninitiated women with healing talent, like you, cannot call themselves Gra'Bandia Healers."

I stared at the elder. "But I can already summon the Goddess. You taught me how years ago. Have I been breaking the code all this time?"

"That's why you are here. To make it official and to receive the blessing of the Council."

The day's rituals began by calling the sisters of the Gra'Bandia and their pair'ti together to pledge service to the Goddess and to uphold Her traditions and teachings to the best of each person's ability. I was encouraged by the opening ceremonies. The prayers were ones I had heard before, and uplifted the overall atmosphere of the gathering.

Afterward, I wandered throughout the assembly. Healers distinguished themselves from their apprentices by a triple crescent moon symbol on their forehead and a long tunic with the triple crescent moon emblazoned over the heart. The robe was cinched at the waist with a broad belt. Their apprentices dressed plainly, like I did.

Some Healers had come alone. One such lady caught my attention. Actually, it was Boris who brought my attention to her. He fixed his gaze upon her and extended his neck slightly as if trying to get a better view. Something didn't feel right about her. I pointed out a dark thread trailing behind her to Nana. Without hesitation, Nana Magog boldly approached the Healer, greeted her, and encased her in a brilliant light, which severed the thread. This caused an uproar.

Within seconds, Camila, the hawk-faced Doyen and Council Spokeswoman, stormed up to Nana Magog. "What have you done, Jaleem Magog? Do you attack your fellow Healers now? Haven't you learned your lesson about abuse of power yet?"

Nana smiled sweetly at Camila. "I wouldn't dream of harming any of our sisters. But Anya from Inyua carries a Droc'ri stowaway." She chuckled. "He thinks he is clever and can spy upon us. What shall we do with him?"

Camila held her palm facing outward and muttered a few words. The white light vanished, and the Healer sagged to the ground. The darkness I had sensed around her was gone. When I glanced at Boris, he had lost interest in the woman.

When the outraged voices quieted, and those around Anya wandered off, I knelt down, supported her to rise, and guided her back to her sleeping area. She didn't look at me and frowned while we walked, muttering, "That gombeen. Tricking me like that. I should have known better."

"Who? How did he trick you?"

Finally, she turned her attention to me. "Rokan. A scholar from the Guild." She pulled a scroll of vellum from her tunic. "He gave me these to bring to the gathering."

I inspected them. "They are not tainted."

"Of course not." She sank onto a log.

Through the translucent material, I could see writing. "What do the pages say?"

"They are some of the lost teachings. They talk about a different way of forming Triunes. I was going to argue for a change in how the Triunes are formed, but Camila won't listen to me now. That ructabund has discredited me."

"Do the papers tell about forming the Triunes with a man as one of the members?"

Anya looked sharply at me. "No, but that could be one possibility, as long as the man was carefully chosen. Sit down, Child." She studied me. "You are Magog's untrained initiate, aren't you? You're not like the others."

I shrugged.

"You are too young to know about the failure of the Triunes of the Religious Wars. Perhaps that is for the best." Anya appeared to reach a decision. She lifted the scroll. "These pages prove that the current thinking about how a Triune is formed won't work. It suggests an alternative."

"Cleric Paul had a similar theory. He said that the interpretations were incorrect."

Anya's eyes lit up. "You know Cleric Paul? We have been friends for decades. How is he?"

"Sadly, he died in the uprising in Sheldon."

"The one you started?"

I lowered my head. Just then, the sour-faced Healer, Leisel, spotted me as she walked to her sleeping area. She pointed an imperious finger at me. "Go. It is not allowed for an uninitiated to talk with other Healers, and especially with Anya, who is tainted!"

I bristled at her overbearing attitude but decided it would be wiser to follow instructions than resist her. Was Anya also an unwanted guest at the assembly? Again, I wished Nana had instructed me in the gathering's protocols and about some of those attending.

But I didn't go directly back to my little corner of the woods. This was the first time I had been around Healers, and I wanted to understand more about my heritage. Mealtime approached, and apprentices prepared meals for themselves and their mistresses in the big cauldrons near the ceremonial fire. I wandered among those gathered. Many of the uninitiated watched me warily as if I might contaminate them so that they might be denied the coveted Healer status. Didn't their mentors explain that a title didn't automatically bestow magical powers? You had the gift and wanted to serve the Goddess, or you didn't.

A stout Healer beckoned to me and patted the log beside her. She brushed her thick plaits of auburn hair over her shoulder and rested her hands on her ample bosom. In a husky voice, she commented, "I didn't know Magog had taken on an apprentice."

I nodded. "I have known Nana since I was a child."

The elder inspected me. "How was she as your mentor?"

The question caught me off guard. "What do you mean?"

"Magog was always the rebel. That's why she was not allowed to become Doyen for the Council. I just wondered how you were trained."

"I have no one to compare her to. She has guided me to understand my talent." Impulsively, I asked, "Why do you call Nana a rebel? What did she do?"

The woman smiled. She seemed to have been waiting for this question. "Jaleem Magog broke her vow to the Goddess." At my surprised look, she continued, "She used the Goddess's power for revenge, which is forbidden." She smiled. "Camila stripped her powers and dissolved her Triune. I wondered how well she could teach you since she was missing what you would need to receive the Council's blessing."

"What was she supposed to give me?" *Nana seems powerful enough. What was taken away from her?* I glanced at the woman beside me. *Other than respect by this group.*

"Her competency will be revealed at the initiate evaluation." She patted my hand in a motherly fashion. "How well the initiate performs during the trials reflects upon the quality of the training by her mentor. How well do you think you will do? Will Nana's punishment continue because you fail the tests?"

Her barely disguised insinuations angered me. I rose abruptly and politely took my leave, biting my lip to stop myself from saying something that would bring Nana Magog any more trouble.

I had not seen Nana Magog since the morning ceremonies. Was she even at Cuilithe? I returned to my campsite and made a small fire in the usual way, with kindling and flint. I reasoned that if the other initiates could make the big cook fires, so could I. That it was not in the clearing with the other fires was beside the point. Somehow, manual labor, rather than pointing a finger and calling forth the flames to ignite damp wood, felt more satisfying. Even though I had often been frustrated with Nana, I felt protective of her. It appeared that receiving the blessing of the Council was going to be based upon Nana's competency as my mentor, as well as my own merit.

Cuilithe felt like a foreign land, and I had only a vague idea of what the residents would interpret as offensive and unacceptable. I reflected on what I had seen and heard so far. I had observed a strict dress code among the Healers, and protocols for what was and was not allowed between initiates and non-mentor Healers. Moreover, I had not seen initiates wandering around the gathering like I did, unless they were on a specific errand. I understood the need for ritual, but the strict adherence to tradition seemed too confining.

I rummaged in Nana's sacks for what she had brought to eat. "These Healers are all a bunch of stuffed shirts," I muttered to Boris as I chopped tubers and put them in a pot. "I don't need their title to do what I do. Maybe Nana has the right idea. Be the rebel. Do I really want to limit myself so I can fit into an outdated organization?" I shook my head, tossing greens, herbs, and spices into the pot to make a savory, meatless stew. Nana had warned me that consuming meat or animal products while in Cuilithe was forbidden.

After dinner we assembled. Doyen Camila stood proudly erect. The flickering firelight cast her already imposing presence into a greater-than-life illusion. She spoke clearly.

"We have gathered when the new Moon is in the Great Mother's arms; a time to create anew. The Dark Lords of the Tiarna Drocha and their servants, the Droc'ri, have tipped the balance of power between the light of the Goddess and the darkness of the Tiarna Drocha. Their minions, the Droc'ri sorcerers, attack the Goddess tradition, killing her Healers and their Mage pair'ti. The isle of Alba is under attack with an evil spell that has tainted Alba's mines and which spreads across the land, destroying the connection to the Goddess in human hearts. This attack must be stopped and balance restored to our world. We are at war with the Dark Lords and their servants. We have gathered together to combine our wisdom and determine a response to this attack. Even now, the Droc'ri seek to invade the Sacred Grove and our Council to uncover new ways to destroy us and what we represent. Bring the Healer, Anya, before this Council."

The Healer was brought before Camila. "Anya of Inyua. You have carried a Droc'ri spell into our midst, compromising our assembly and the safety of us all. It is lucky the spell was discovered before we formed any plans." Camila's cold gaze lingered on Nana Magog, then settled solidly on me. "It appears one of our uninitiated recognized the taint about you. This raises the question: if one can recognize the taint in another, perhaps that one is also tainted."

Camila's accusatory stare drew others' attention to me. I inhaled sharply. I didn't like the implications.

"Be that as it may. Who put this spell upon you? Who have you seen recently?" Camila's hawk-like expression bored into the old Healer.

Anya shook her head. "A professor from the Langon Scholars' Guild visited me not long ago. He has been researching the Goddess tradition for decades and found some of the lost teachings, which I brought to show the Council." She twisted her hands. "I haven't had any other visitors for a very long time."

"Anya, you know the penalty for consorting with the Droc'ri, whether intentional or not. You will be punished, and your title of Healer removed." The Doyen stretched out her hand and beckoned. A tendril of gold escaped from Anya's body. Camila inhaled deeply, and the golden thread disappeared. The symbol of the Goddess on Anya's forehead dissolved as well. Anya slumped, and friends supported her. Her face aged, hair silvered, and soon she looked similar to Nana Magog. She was taken away.

I tightened my jaw. This didn't make sense. Camila had just said we were at war with the Dark Lords, yet she stripped the abilities of one who had the wisdom needed to defend the Goddess. Nana gripped my elbow firmly, in a warning. I made myself breathe, then eased myself from the meeting, edged my way to the back of those assembled, then circled around in the direction that Anya had been taken.

When I came upon the woman, she was weeping. I knelt down, pulled her into my arms, and pillowed her head upon my shoulder. Finally, her sobbing stopped. "I'm sorry," I said softly. "I didn't know you would be stripped of the Goddess's blessing."

"I've been a Healer my whole life. I survived the wars. I'm too old for this fight. I'm glad the Goddess has seen fit to take me out of it."

"I don't know whether the Goddess had anything to do with it." *This seems like Camila's doing.*

She lifted her head. Pale eyes studied me. "The prophecy talked about a Healer who is not a Healer, who will restore the balance."

"Are you referring to the prophecy Cleric Paul talked about?"

She hesitated. "When the Beast of Evil roams the land and the Leonini rise to fight it, a fractured Healer, who is not a Healer, will unite with a mate from the sea and her counterpart, and invade the Dark Lords in their realm, restoring the balance. In the process, she will destroy the old Goddess tradition, uniting the world into a new form of existence. At least that's the gist of it. There's more, something about the Great Seal and Radiant Lady, but I don't remember it." She picked at her fingernails. "The Beast of Evil has not yet been released but will be. Very soon." She looked into my eyes. "Already, the Verndari Guardians, descendants of the Leonini, rise."

"Do you know what the prophecy means?"

Anya shook her head. "Your guess is as good as mine. The Council has talked about it since Nana Magog discovered its existence from Cleric Paul, who heard about it during the Religious Wars. A fractured Healer who is not a Healer. No one really knows who that might be. And her counterpart. Does that mean her pair'ti? Or her opposite, meaning a Droc'ri who is not a Droc'ri?" She took a sip of water. Very quietly, she added. "Camila, as Doyen of the Council, wants to find and capture her. I think she means to destroy her. While the Council wants to restore the balance between the Goddess and the Dark Lords of the Tiarna Drocha, Camila doesn't want the Goddess tradition, as she has administered it, toppled." She chuckled. "Maybe it's time for a new Order. The old ways stopped working long ago." She picked up the scroll. "Here. Keep this safe until you can get it back to the Scholars' Guild archives. I should not have brought it."

I tucked the papers inside my tunic. "What were the old ways that used to work?"

"You should be with your mentor, Ellara," a harsh voice said out of the darkness. "Your mentor is supposed to have taught you about the old ways." Leisel and her apprentice, Felicity, came into view. "This woman is not allowed to have visitors. Now go." She waved imperiously.

As I walked back to my sleeping area, I thought, *for Healers who are supposed to be trained to be tolerant, compassionate, and caring, I haven't seen much of that yet.* I carefully stowed the lost teachings with Cleric Paul's document.

The next day, everyone gathered around the High Council seated on tall-backed stone chairs within a circle of massive monoliths. Doyen Camila directed the discussion. "We all know the problem facing our world. This threat surpasses the Religious Wars in the Emerald Mountains, in which many of our Healer sisters and brothers were lost. How many remain of the original Gra'Bandia Triunes, and what new ones can be formed?"

"Not enough," someone behind me said.

One of the Councilors pointed at the forty or fifty uninitiated. "From these can be formed new Triunes."

"But it takes years to train them. We don't have time," another Council member argued. "They must have the strong protection afforded by a soul-bonded mate, an Anam pair'ti, to safely host the Goddess. Look at them. Do you see strong Far'degan among their pair'ti?"

Nana nudged me. "You and Sam had a soul bond. That made you Anam pair'ti. He was your Far'degan."

"Shhh!" someone said beside me.

I felt Camila's cold stare sweep across me. "Do you have something to say, Jaleem? Do not disrupt this Council by explaining to your untrained apprentice what she should already know."

I bowed my head and kept silent for the rest of the day. Try as I might to keep an open mind about Camila and the Council, I found myself disliking the woman and what she represented.

Terms like *Triune*, *Ceangal Bandia*, *Voice of the Goddess*, *Far'degan*, and *Droc'ri* were bantered back and forth throughout the day. I had read Cleric Paul's descriptions and listened to Nana explain the terminology. I understood the terms, as I had experienced them with Sam. Yet, I sensed a deep, intricate connectivity that the other Healers didn't appear to grasp. The wisdom seemed just out of my grasp. I wanted to discuss my perceptions with Nana, but she was called away for a private meeting with several Council members. When Nana returned much later, she was not in a good mood.

"You will be tested tomorrow, Ellara. Sleep well. You will need to have all your wits about you."

FIFTEEN

ROKAN IN THE EMERALD MOUNTAINS

The Temple of the Crescent Moon

"Seize them." Zarizo pointed at Margot and me.

"Are you all here now?" Margot asked. She grinned and appeared at ease.

The sorcerers looked at her in shock. What was she doing? What did she know that I didn't? A memory came to mind. Margot's actions mimicked a prank Nana Magog had played upon us many years ago. Was she in communication with the old hag? Was that how she knew so much about the Droc'ri and me? Was that where she got the power to incapacitate my magic? Only the members of a Triune could communicate telepathically. I studied the young woman, but sensed nothing of Nana's presence around her.

Almost imperceptibly, the rocks and trees began to move. The Guardians! They were back. Forest animals raced towards the Droc'ri. The boulder that we hid behind creaked and groaned to life, along with many others. The Guardians would kill those who had destroyed their home. I pulled back, hoping to avoid notice.

Margot continued to hold my arm, muttering sternly, "Stand still!"

The other Droc'ri's fear mirrored my own. They scattered, but animals, birds, rocks, or trees pursued them. Screams of pain from the sorcerers filled the air. I froze, hoping I wouldn't be noticed, and watched in horror as rocks crushed my fellow Droc'ri or tree limbs scooped them up and tossed them high into the sky where the hawks and eagles tore at their flesh. Wild cats and wolves brought down those who were fleeter of foot. Only a few escaped through a portal, including Zarizo. In minutes, the carnage was over, and the Guardians returned to their resting places. Margot's friends joined us and stared at the massacre. With a dull rumbling, the ground opened and swallowed the ravaged bodies. Soon the meadow appeared pristine as if no battle had taken place.

Finally, Margot released my arm, and blood rushed back to where her fingers had dug into my flesh. I rubbed my arm. It vexed me that I had been powerless during the contest, and not in command. "Why didn't you free the Goddess's hold on me so I could protect you?"

"Did you want to die like your Brothers?"

I had seriously underestimated Margot and her friends. I would not make that mistake again. "Why did you keep me alive?"

She ignored my question, instead placing her hand on the rock, which had settled back into its position in the earth, and concentrated. Her friends followed suit. I guessed they were thanking or honoring the Guardians. Had Nana told her about them?

After collecting the horses and taking time for a meal, we continued up the valley. I analyzed the possible ways that Nana could be communicating with Margot, giving her instructions, and possibly even providing the force Margot used to restrict me. I took every opportunity to probe Margot for talismans or magical spells. The protection in her aura had the energetic signature of her parents, her brother, and Katarine. How were Nana and Margot connected?

We followed the narrow trail up the mountain to a broad tabletop of smooth rock. The once beautiful temple of white stone was now just a pile of rubble with a few broken columns still standing. The Goddess's essence swirled in the wind, welcoming, purifying, and revitalizing us. My companions opened their arms and spun in circles, laughing and singing.

A force gripped my insides. I collapsed to my knees, gasping for air as my past deeds paraded before my inner sight. I had been one of the sorcerers who had desecrated the temple, and now the Goddess would extract her retribution. I fell to the ground, barely breathing.

Margot and Katarine stared down at me.

"You must do something, Margot. He's dying."

"Maybe he needs to die for what he has done."

"Margot! You vowed to serve the Goddess. The Goddess has chosen him to help us," Katarine pressed. "You can't let him die."

By now, the rest of the group had gathered. I heard murmurs of agreement.

Reluctantly, Margot knelt beside me. "If the Goddess wishes that he live, then so be it." She looked at Katarine. "I don't know what to do. This is the kind of work Mother does."

"Do what you did to bind his magic."

"I didn't do anything. The Goddess did it." She passed her hand over me. My energy field tingled wherever her hand moved. She placed her hand over my heart, and warmth flowed around me. Suddenly she snatched her hand from me and sat back on her haunches, looking horrified. She scrambled back. "I can't."

I breathed more deeply. Margot had given me enough vitality to overcome my distress. Slowly, I drew myself to sitting, feeling my magic flood back into my body. Many pairs of eyes stared at me. Margot had withdrawn and was nowhere to be seen. I sighed. Margot had seen my secrets — the ones that would get me terminated by my Brothers. I'd have to kill her, after all.

SIXTEEN

ELLARA AT CUILITHE

The Heartland

T he following day, the apprentices came one by one for examination by the Council. They were questioned about the Gra'Bandian history, and the significance of certain rituals. Then they were asked to demonstrate their magical abilities, and their knowledge of herbs, of wound tending, and of the physical body. Lastly, the members of the Council read the applicant's aura. Nana had said it was to see the purity of their heart. Then the woman was dismissed to return to her mentor, who stood nearby watching the proceedings.

I observed the apprentices come and go with rising dread. I had only skimmed the creation stories in the Goddess's teachings that Cleric Paul had translated and gleaned a superficial understanding of the terms that were bandied about. I barely knew the names of rituals. I listened carefully to the questions and the women's replies. Annoyingly, Felicity, Leisel's apprentice and the woman who openly displayed her dislike for me, sailed through the trials smoothly. Nana frowned and pursed her lips but didn't say anything.

Darkness was falling by the time my turn came. I was the last uninitiated. Nana urged me forward. I struggled to remain calm under the scrutiny of the thirteen Council members. The dispassionate authority that radiated from the hawk-faced Doyen intimidated me. Doyen Camila asked me different questions than she had my predecessors. I made my best guess to some of her queries and to others, I shrugged and said I didn't know. After the third time I said that, Camila addressed Nana Magog sternly. "You've failed once again, Jaleem. The Goddess is displeased. This initiate is not worthy of receiving the Goddess's blessing."

"Don't dismiss her so quickly, Camila. She may not have had traditional schooling, but Ellara deserves the blessing of the Council and title of Gra'Bandia Healer. She has a gift."

"She's not trained. She's already turned our homeland into chaos by starting a rebellion in Sheldon. Now provinces all over the island are attacking the Natuan guards and defying the decrees. We cannot have an undisciplined Healer running loose. We already have one. You. She doesn't understand the reasons and the responsibility of the title, nor can she do any magic."

"She understands more than you give her credit for. Theurgy, the Goddess's divine magic, is vastly more than igniting fires or lighting one's way. It comes in many forms. You know that, Camila." Nana lowered her voice. "Don't judge Ellara based upon your feelings about me."

Camila turned her back on Nana.

Nana addressed the Council. "There are two kinds of Healer. One has a talent that must be coaxed and nurtured over many years. In the other, the gift is already awakened and active. She requires very little training. At this time, we need strong Healers who don't require years of mentoring. See for yourself the talents of my pupil and what she has accomplished. She is descended from a lineage of fearsome Healers and comes by the gift naturally. The Goddess has smiled upon her, even in her special circumstances. She deserves the blessing of the Council." Nana lifted her chin defiantly and drew herself up to her full, yet stooped, height. "I claim the Rite of the Dushlan."

I had no idea what that meant, but judging by the way Camila's face turned crimson and the two women faced off, it must be a challenge. *Why is Nana so anxious for me to gain the title of Gra'Bandia Healer? I haven't seen her so adamant about something in a long time. There must be more at stake here than just a title.*

Camila's lips twisted derisively. "Do you think you can get back your connection to the Goddess and use of Her power so easily, Jaleem?" She flicked a speck from her robes. "Very well. You can claim the Rite of the Dushlan, but if she fails, your punishment will double."

I glanced from one to the other. Camila beckoned to me and pointed to the ground before her.

Before the Doyen could commence, a voice declared, "She is a Droc'ri spy, sent to disrupt the Council. She should not be considered for the blessing of the Goddess. In fact, she should be killed!"

I turned to stare at my accuser, as did all the others.

Camila shot Nana a superior look, then asked, "Felicity Tubbs, on what grounds do you make this accusation?"

"I know first-hand that she has misused the Goddess's Gra'yia and has proclaimed herself to be a Healer without the Council's blessing. She has cast a spell on a crippled sea captain, who is also an agent of the Droc'ri, to hide his demonic deformity. He tried to seduce me and draw me into his unholy schemes. Of course, I rejected him and his offer."

I straightened and opened my mouth to protest. *Was she referring to Matty's captain? He is the only crippled captain I know.* Nana clamped her hand on my wrist and shook her head once.

"Is that all?" Camila asked.

"I have on good authority other incidents where she has falsely used the Goddess's power to serve her Droc'ri master, but I cannot swear to them like I can about Captain Thaddeus."

Thaddeus? I've never even met the man, much less healed him!

Camila turned an icy gaze to Nana and me.

Nana smiled as if nothing out of the ordinary had happened. "Now that Felicity has said her piece, let the Rite of Dushlan disprove her accusations. Ellara has served the Goddess with a pure heart." She pushed me to stand before Camila.

Camila glared at Nana. Wordlessly, she pushed her finger against my forehead between my eyes. I winced in pain. As if sucked through a straw, images raced past my inner sight. Instinctively, I threw up a protective wall, but not before I had relived the scenes at the docks and Sam's death. I pulled away sharply, tears welling from my eyes, and growled, "What gives you the right to probe my mind without my consent and to bring up memories I have been trying to reconcile and heal?"

Camila lowered her hand and glowered at Nana. "She blocks me. I cannot read her past. She has failed."

Words flew from my mouth before I could stop them. "Nana has been a good teacher in her own way, yet you treat her with contempt. She has taught me the principles of the Healer's code, something you seem to have forgotten. She has taught me how to call the Goddess so She can work through me." I stopped at a shriek from Camila.

"Child, have you no respect for your elders?" Camila rounded on Nana. "You know it is forbidden to teach an uninitiated how to host the Goddess. You breached the Gra'Bandia Healer's protocol in training this apprentice in what she cannot be acquainted with until *after* she is blessed by the Council! You carelessly put her life in danger without the proper protection from a strong Far'degan and made her an aid to the Droc'ri because she does not have the wisdom to handle the Goddess's power wisely. Furthermore, you have not taught her proper respect. There is no place in our Order for her kind, or you!"

"Not so fast, Camila. You break the Dushlan ritual by deciding before it is over. Ellara, you must allow Camila to show your memories to the Council. The Rite of the Dushlan requires it."

I stepped forward again, sullenly apologized to the elder, and waited for Camila to recompose herself. *She thinks she is superior, but she is no different from Nana or me or Sam*, I thought. *Where is the humility, respect, and understanding that are forefront in the Goddess's teachings?*

Camila placed her finger on my forehead, and I allowed the images to flow. There were joyful segments with Sam. Tears slipped down my cheeks, knowing those times would never be again. Many scenes where I had assisted in childbirth or restored to health many of my clients and guided others to the afterlife in the Mag Mell, passed before me. Anger surged through me at the scene where the stranger tried to steal Margot. Images of my children's births, Sam's healing, my time in the forest, and protecting my mother from someone who wanted to kill her flowed from me. There were depictions of giving Sam healing energies in my childhood, restoring to life a dying man in the woods, and of Trevor, my step-father, healing goats, sheep, and horses as a toddler. The images didn't stop there. I saw myself surrounded by a golden light as a growing fetus in my mother's womb, and watched her become captured by the man I had healed in the forest and escape from her homeland. Finally, the regression ended, and Camila withdrew her fingers.

The Doyen didn't speak for a very long time. Finally, she said quietly, "As the Council and I have just witnessed, you have the gift and have been truly blessed by the Goddess. Your expertise in understanding the deeper imbalances that contribute to ill health or injury far exceeds that of the average initiate. You handle the Goddess's radiant energies naturally and without all the rigorous training that a formally blessed initiate must go through. Your capacity to host Her energies is already that of an experienced Healer. In fact, the Council's blessing would not give you any more than you already possess. Your talent lies not in simple earth magic, but in using the highest theurgy to purge the darkness from, and transform, souls."

She paused and took a breath.

"However, you are cursed, Child. You have given a piece of your soul to a Droc'ri sorcerer, and he has given you part of his. You carry a taint and are unfit to become the Goddess's representative, much less a host of the Goddess."

What does she mean? I gave a piece of my soul to someone? How did I do that?

The Doyen gazed at me with pity in her eyes. "We could use your special talents. You would make a powerful host to the Goddess and a strong member of a Triune, Child. But we cannot risk having one who has been touched by the Dark Lords in our midst."

She loomed over my mentor. "Jaleem, you should never have trained the child. Furthermore, Ellara's son and daughter are unfit to be trained because of the Droc'ri taint. You knew she had been touched by the Droc'ri, yet you willfully taught her how to host the Goddess. You have failed miserably in your duties, and your punishment is extended another fifty years." Camila stretched her hand towards me. "As the Council is my witness, you are forbidden from practicing your healing skills, summoning the Goddess, or calling yourself a Healer. You shall never again touch another person, as you convey the taint to everyone you touch. It is why your pair'ti died."

I felt a drawing upon my essence and hastily stepped back, throwing up my hands and blocking the force that tugged upon my spirit. "I will not allow you to take what the Goddess has given me!" I declared. "I do not agree with your pronouncement. I have benefited those around me, and I have fought against the shadow that lives within me. No person has a heart that does not hold at least one shadow. Not even you! From what I have studied, the Goddess would not have allowed me to accomplish what I have if it was harmful to others. And if I have shared a piece of my soul with a sorcerer, She has willed it!"

"Insolent child!" She thrust her hand towards me, and I felt a force yank my spirit. Fire rose inside me and surrounded me like a luminous shield. I glared at Camila through a gold-white veil. It would have been so easy to crush her, yet I resisted, instinctively knowing love was the more potent force. Camila fell back, wide-eyed, and put her hand over her mouth.

She addressed Nana. "What manner of monster have you created, Jaleem? She must be stripped of her talent so she can do no further harm. She's your student. Gut her ability, or I will!"

I drew myself up and faced the Council. Words flowed through me. "I do not share your perspectives of what it means to be a Healer or of what is required to contain this Droc'ri threat. I have not been trained traditionally, and for that, I am grateful. The Triunes of the Religious Wars were a horrible failure, and if you consider forming them again, you will be signing all of our death warrants. You must merge the masculine with the feminine into a new configuration. If three or more people are bound together in the Ceangal Bandia, male and female alike, the Droc'ri will not be able to kill her Far'degan and then capture the Healer."

Murmurs of protest and shock ran through the crowd.

"You don't have to take my word for it. The Healer, Anya, whom you have stripped of authority, has studied the ancient texts, and recently, a lost teaching that outlines Triune creation. She can tell you about another way to form Triunes that will make them stronger and more impenetrable. Go back to the time-worn manuscripts and reread them, this time from the point of view that the Triunes created for the Religious Wars have proved defective. Hosting the Goddess requires the merging of the masculine and feminine energies. You must be open to a different way of interpreting the teachings if we are to outsmart the Droc'ri and survive."

The energy speaking through me dwindled. I took a deep breath and glanced at the mixture of emotions expressed by those around me.

"She's a Droc'ri's pawn. See how she disrupts the Council," someone nearby called out.

Felicity had moved to where I stood. She addressed the gathering. "She failed the initiate's examination and the Rite of Dushlan. Doyen Camila has pronounced her cursed, yet she, trained by a discredited mentor, claims to know the solution to our dilemma. Are you going to believe the one with an affiliation with the Droc'ri, or those," she indicated the thirteen Council members, "who have experience?"

I took a deep breath and waited for words of rebuff to come, but they didn't. Instead, I felt myself connect solidly to the earth, almost as if I had deep roots anchoring me firmly to the truth of my being. I allowed myself to relax, and the ground to nurture me. In a sudden insight, I realized I would receive no help from this close-minded Council. I had done the task with which Cleric Paul had charged me. It was time to leave and do what I could on my own.

With dignity, I bowed my head to the Council, touched my heart with my fingertips, then opened my hand in the traditional salutation and turned away, striding purposefully towards my campsite.

It was a few minutes before a cacophony of voices filled the Sacred Grove. When Nana finally joined me, her step had a spring in it. "You've stirred the pot, Child."

I gathered my few possessions and stuffed them into my satchel. "Who does that woman think she is to steal what the Goddess has given me? And who is that initiate, Felicity? She cheated on the examination. Even I could see her talent is weak and her heart impure. She is not the true apprentice of Leisel. Someone else has been training her." I thought for a moment. "It's puzzling. Could a sorcerer have trained her and made Leisel bring her for the Council's blessing?"

Nana patted my cheek. "You are perceptive, Child. You're the best apprentice I've ever had. As far as I'm concerned, you passed the Council's tests with flying colors." She noticed my dour expression. "I had to see if you had the strength to follow the truth in your heart. This test was easy compared to what you will face with the Droc'ri. Don't complain. It could have been worse. You could have let Camila take your gift from you." She gathered food and placed it into my satchel. "I'll accompany you outside the Grove. I'm sure you can figure out how to pass through the protective shield, but it will be quicker if I show you. And I have something to tell you."

SEVENTEEN

ROKAN IN THE EMERALD MOUNTAINS

The Temple of the Crescent Moon

Margot did not eat with us, nor did she join us afterward to swap stories. I finally found her sitting on a fallen stone overlooking the valley below in the direction of the sea and Alba. She sobbed quietly. Her aura revealed she was intensely sad. I had initially thought she had identified my longing to be free of my pledge to the Dark Lords by using Ellara's soul fragment, but now I wasn't so sure. I was aware that Katarine had followed me and was watching over her friend.

"May I join you?" I asked, and waited for Margot to invite me to sit.

After a while, she grunted.

I sat beside her and waited. *What has she done to me to make me wait upon her? I've never acted this way before. She has a talent for enchantment that I never suspected.* "What's wrong?"

Margot roused and, in a swift movement, held a pair of daggers to my throat. "You killed Father," she accused. "I'd kill Lord Sengy with my bare hands, except Father already did, and lost his life for it. And now Bruce the Terrible has commandeered our ship, no doubt also at your command." She sobbed again and the daggers wavered.

"I did not kill your father. Lord Sengy did. And Bruce is an opportunist. With your father out of the way, it was no doubt easy to take his ship."

"You think you can hide behind words. You are as involved in this murder as if you had done the deed yourself! You may not have directly ordered Lord Sengy to kill my father, but you organized the Alban attack. You sent the mercenaries to Alba to force their barbaric beliefs upon us and destroy the ways of the Goddess. You have no respect for life or regret for the pain and suffering your vile actions cause to innocent lives."

I grabbed her arms and slowly pushed them away. *I am not responsible for Sam's death. He had to die,* I kept reminding myself. *Garrick would have killed me if I didn't follow his orders. I don't want to die.* However, the heartbreak driving her words rattled my conviction. I released my hold on her.

The force of her ire surrounded me. She lifted the knives again menacingly. "Know this, Rokan. You and the Droc'ri will *never* succeed. As you destroy the Goddess's theurgy, so too, do you destroy the Droc'ri existence. You need the Goddess as much as we do."

Does she know of the prophecy? "I'm sorry about your father, Margot. I truly am."

"You don't know what sorry means. You are devoid of emotion. You don't deserve forgiveness after all the pain and suffering you have caused."

Sitting in front of this distraught young woman gave me a pang of guilt. I had been trying to kill her father for a long time. I had never thought about the consequences of my actions before, of the heartbreak and destruction I brought upon people. *I'm going soft!* How many times had I been ordered to assassinate Droc'ri who had started to care? The lucky ones were turned into imps to serve living sorcerers.

I had to get away from her before she corrupted me completely. Yet try as I might to harden myself to her suffering, every time she glared at me, I felt her anger like invisible spears hurled at me.

I could handle her wrath a lot easier than her sadness. "The Goddess works in strange ways, Margot. There is a prophecy about the Droc'ri Order being destroyed. At least that is the general consensus. The last few days I have spent with you and your companions have shown me how we lack joy for life and the vital force it brings. The Droc'ri are weakening."

"And what do you want, Rokan?" She glared at me with tear-filled eyes. "Are you trying to save the Droc'ri, no matter who you have to destroy, including me, Father, Mother, and all of my friends?" She swept her hand in the direction of our camp.

I shook my head. "I want to find a different solution. I cannot kill your mother or you."

"Why? You had no reservations about killing my father."

I picked at the bark of the log on which I sat. *Should I tell Margot? Do I trust her with this secret that could get me instantly killed by my Brothers?* I stole a glance at her, and then at Katarine, who stood several paces away. Something about Margot's presence caused me to take the leap of faith. "Your mother gave me a piece of her soul long ago."

"What! What would possess her to do that?"

I shook my head. "She was only four or five and didn't know any better." I remembered the golden-haired little girl sitting beside me when I awoke in the forest after trying to kill Nana Magog and Orva. "She saved my life. I don't know how, but in the process, I received a piece of her soul. It changed me. I see the flaws in the Droc'ri way of existence and..." I lowered my voice to barely audible. "I want a different life."

"Give her soul back."

"I wish I could. It's not that easy."

"You have it. Give it back."

"She holds a piece of my soul, as well. It appears that when she restored me, we exchanged soul pieces."

"What does that mean? Is that why you said you were not ready to die? Because your soul is not whole, and without that missing piece, you cannot travel to the Tiarna Drocha?"

"I will go to the Tiarna Drocha, but I don't know what will happen to your mother if I take a piece of her soul with me. And the Dark Lords will come looking for the rest of my soul." *Because the piece she holds will keep me from becoming a permanent resident of the Tiarna Drocha.*

Margot gaped at me, and her brows drew down. For an instant, I thought she might kill me where I sat. Instead, she shot to her feet. I'd rattled her, I could see it. "Enough of your deceptions, Rokan." She moved off. "Stay away from me. I need to think."

I stared out over the mountain ridges. I felt Margot's words and the force of her emotion, and it disturbed me. I bit my lip. The ritual that made me a servant of the Dark Lords encased my heart to prevent me from feeling the pain and suffering I left in my wake. It is what made the Droc'ri strong. But possessing Ellara's soul piece had weakened the bindings of the Rith Bac'Croi, and the more time I spent with Margot, the more awareness I had of my feelings and suppressed desires. She appeared to have a power over me like the innocent child who had willingly shared her soul so I could live. *I should have given Ellara's piece back. Then my life would not be so conflicted.*

I began to pace. I was only doing my job, I rationalized. I hadn't wanted to become a Droc'ri. I was forced to do what I have done to survive. But I could hear Margot's words repeating over and over in my mind. I had a choice. I had made a choice. Would I continue down that path? Could I give it up? I shook my head. The only way a Droc'ri sorcerer quit was when he died. I wasn't ready for that. I had to leave Margot's camp.

Now that I had regained control of my magic, I fingered the traveling crystal, fully intending to depart immediately. Then I felt someone grip my arm.

"As much as I dislike you," Margot said, "it appears we are tied together in a strange fate. I fully expect you to make it right with Mother and atone for all the heartbreak and despair you have caused. I will not have you dragging Mother into the realm of the Dark Lords."

Truth was, I didn't know how to "make it right." The past could not be undone. As a high ranking Droc'ri, I didn't believe I had a choice to do anything but what I had done. To Margot, I said, "I will do what I can. Now, I must return to Tokurat. The Droc'ri know you are here. They will be back. You will be safe from the Droc'ri as long as you stay on the temple grounds. I know you don't trust me, and you are wise not to. However, I will not reveal your presence and will protect you in the best way I know." I picked up a white stone from the rubble and spoke a word. I handed it to her. "Keep this with you at all times. It will make your magic invisible to the sorcerers and keep all of you safe."

She didn't say anything, but her anger and grief washed around me. I walked a few paces down the escarpment where I would be out of sight of the others, imprinted my traveling crystal, and opened a portal to the Desert Lands. I became aware of Margot's gaze on my back, and a quick glance behind showed she had come to the brink and watched.

She hurled the pebble I had imprinted to shield her through the opening, narrowly missing me. "Take your talisman, Rokan. We don't need the kind of protection you would give us."

She pivoted and departed. Anger surged through me. "I try to do something nice, and she spurns me! You will regret this, Margot," I growled under my breath as I stepped through the gateway.

EIGHTEEN
ELLARA AT CUILITHE

The Heartland

Nana Magog and I walked towards the Sacred Grove border. Boris, in his human form, trailed behind. I mulled over the events since my arrival. Finally, I had to ask. "Nana, it's obvious that Camila doesn't like you. What happened that you were ousted from the Council in disgrace? Why did Camila extend your punishment?"

We continued along the path. I thought Nana wasn't going to answer. "Camila and I go way back. She has been Doyen since before the Religious Wars. Prior to that, we had a falling out over a person."

"Your pair'ti?" When Nana refused to say more, I asked, "What are you punished for?"

"Abuse of the Goddess's power."

"You said something about giving up your ability to summon the Goddess to save my mother and me. That doesn't sound like an abuse of power. What did you do?"

"Child, never act when the intention is for revenge."

"You mean like my wanting to kill those who orchestrated Sam's death and are making life miserable in our country?" I knew very little of Nana's past, but I thought her pair'ti had died long ago. "Did you use the Goddess's Lig'yia to kill the sorcerers who captured my mother and avenge your pair'ti?"

Nana shot me a stern look. That was Nana's maddening way. Drop a few tidbits and let me figure out what it meant. I sighed. Experience had taught me that when Nana did not want to elaborate, she wouldn't. I changed the subject. "If I am to believe Camila, I am forbidden to use my Goddess-given talents. She says a Droc'ri sorcerer, the same one you were trying to protect me from, has cursed me. What did she mean when she said I gave him a piece of my soul, and he has given me a piece of his? Am I really cursed?"

Nana laughed. "No, Child. Exchanging soul fragments is more common than you might think. I just wish it hadn't been with a Droc'ri. You are bound to him until the day you can retrieve your soul piece. Some might think this makes you impure of heart."

"How do I get it back? Has his bit of soul tainted the restorations I have done on all of my patrons? Was it why Sam died, as Camila claims?"

"The sorcerer is involved in Sam's death and a lot of other things you will discover. But Sam's decline does not have anything to do with a debasing of you or your healing talent. Even though Rokan has pledged his soul to the Dark Lords of the Tiarna Drocha, you carry a piece of his spirit. That piece belongs to the Goddess. If he were to die, all but the piece of his soul that lives in you would go to the Tiarna Drocha. At that point, the Dark Lords would come for that fragment, so as to cement his service to them. Until that time, don't worry."

"But... what about the piece of *my* soul he holds? If Rokan goes to the Tiarna Drocha, won't he take my soul with him? Will I become trapped there or compromised somehow?"

Nana laughed. "The Goddess has a sense of humor. Now that he has a piece of your soul, how can he be truly evil? He will be constantly reminded of his connection with the Goddess." She shook her head. "I don't envy that man. You have made his Droc'ri life miserable. If he still possesses your fragment when he dies..." Nana drifted off in thought. "Is that what the prophecy foretells?" she muttered to herself. We had reached the invisible energetic barrier. Nana motioned me forward. "Go on. Go through."

I touched the shield with my fingertips. Energy sparked and knocked me back. I searched my memory for what my guide had done when we passed through. Nana watched patiently as I tried one thing after the other, each time getting shocked. Each time, she nodded encouragement.

Finally, I gave up, frustrated. I turned to Nana. "I don't know how."

"Yes, you do. The solution just may not be what you expect. Maybe you don't have to *do* anything. Remember what I've taught you. Try *being*."

I took a few deep breaths, walked forward and through the veil. Nana and Boris followed. Nana motioned for the man to drop the gunnysack of food and supplies he carried. Boris disappeared into the darkness. The night was moonless. I would wait until first light before attempting the rigorous descent.

The air felt alive and fresh after the Sacred Grove. Already the heaviness I had felt from the gathering lifted. Camila's worrisome words still occupied my mind and awakened old doubts and fears, though. "I thought the Sacred Grove was a place filled with the Goddess's loving energy. Instead, I found it oppressive," I commented. "Is that because I didn't belong there?"

Nana placed twigs in a pile to start a fire. "You needed to come. I was surprised at how many Healers and uninitiated were at this meeting." She lit the tinder with a flame from her finger and bent to blow on the embers. "This is a small gathering compared to years ago. It's nice to see so many uninitiated. There is hope yet."

"Is your punishment really extended another fifty years because I failed the Rite of Dushlan?"

Nana puffed vigorously. "Ellara, you didn't fail the Rite of Dushlan. If anything, you proved to the Council that you are worthy of being the Voice of the Goddess. Camila knows better, but since you hold a piece of a Droc'ri soul, that creates doubt, which was exactly what Felicity came to seed."

"That woman blatantly lied! She dishonors herself. There will be consequences for her actions." I went back through the barrier and fetched an armload of wood for the fire, letting my anger cool. When I returned, I said, "Camila declared I was cursed and unfit to be a Healer. I have spent my life trying to prove I am worthy of the Goddess. Was it all for naught?"

"Are you going to believe everything you hear?"

"Her words were powerful," I said softly. "She radiates authority. It's hard not to take them seriously."

"Then hear these equally authoritative words, Child." She leaned closer to me. "The Gra'Bandia Healers and the Council are no longer the pure-hearted Order they once were. The Religious Wars not only reduced our numbers but also have allowed the Droc'ri to infiltrate our tradition. Many of the Healers and their apprentices have been in hiding on the mainland or in Alba. Until recently, they could practice their art freely, like you could. However, some were allowed to live only if they gave up their ability to host the Goddess and became spies for the Droc'ri Grand Master."

I gasped. My vision of the highest ethical and honorable sister-hood of the Gra'Bandia Healers, which I had aspired to emulate, crumbled with each word Nana uttered. "If the

Goddess's Healers are no longer pure of heart, then the world is indeed doomed," I said.

"Don't wear such a long face, Ellara. Not everyone has lost his or her integrity. But it only takes a few to ruin it for everyone."

"Is Camila one of the compromised Healers?"

"Camila has a secret, and I know it." Nana piled more branches on the fire. "She has tried to silence me." Nana grinned. "The Doyen is constrained by the same rules with which she has punished me, and Camila would rather die than surrender the Goddess's blessing and the power she wields."

Nana's words disturbed me more than Camila's accusations. "I don't want to leave the Heartland, but I know I can't stay here for the rest of my life. With Camila running the Council, nothing will change, and the Droc'ri will kill us all." I stared into the fire, allowing the dancing flames to mesmerize and draw me deeper into another realm. Tongues of fire coalesced into the faces of Sam, and other unfamiliar people, whose mouths moved as if speaking to me. I was startled from my contemplation by voices coming from the Grove.

Out of the darkness appeared a dozen women and men. They came towards us. I leaped to my feet, hand on my dagger. In the light of the fire, I recognized one of the Council members.

"I am called Valkyrie. This is my pair'ti, and these are my apprentices and their pair'ti. We are sorry about today's events and want you to know that not all of us agree with the Doyen's pronouncements. We witnessed your memories in the Rite of the Dushlan, and recognize you have the true spirit of the Goddess. We feel the Doyen mistreated you. I speak for all of us when I commend you on your courage in standing up for what you believe in — what *we* believe in — against those in authority who would restrict us. You give us hope that perhaps we can win this battle with the Dark Lords, despite the odds. The Gra'Bandia Council needs a fresh outlook, brought forward by an untrained natural Healer."

The elder handed me a small disc with a symbol engraved upon it. "This is our signet. Call upon me and my clan when you are ready to take command of this Council or start your own. If we are able, we will answer your summons." She bowed her head and touched her heart in salutation. "I wish we could have met under friendlier circumstances." They retreated into the gloom of the night.

Three more groups of Healers arrived, two of which included Council members, expressing similar sentiments. They said the Council had gotten stale and needed a leader who remembered and practiced the principles of the Goddess. They added that Camila had forbidden anyone from associating with Nana Magog or me. Each Healer gave me a signet ring and promised to serve me.

Nana nodded. "Already, you gather your warriors."

I turned over the gold and silver emblems in my hand. "Do they really want me to depose Camila? I don't see how that will help our problems. Camila won't go down without a fight, and I don't want to kill her. I'm sure she has loyal followers. I'm an outcast, and apparently cursed. I'd be creating a division within the very organization that is supposed to defend the Goddess, allowing the Droc'ri to continue their conquest unhindered."

Nana laughed softly. "Coming to this gathering has helped you cast aside the sorcerer's curse, Ellara. Instead of assassinating you years ago, he cast into your mind the belief that you were unworthy and weak. You have doubted yourself ever since.

"If you look back on your life, you will see how you have driven yourself to excel. You have never let anything stop you. You gather the information and resources needed to pursue a solution relentlessly like you did to heal Sam. You are not afraid to experiment, which is how you gained experience. Your caution makes you wisely stop and think before you act.

"Most of all, you have learned to trust yourself and the Goddess. This is what has made you an effective healer and unafraid to tackle even the most daunting maladies. The sorcerer's spell was meant to keep you small and unnoticed. You have turned Rokan's curse into a blessing." She chuckled. "In a way, Rokan has made you strong. Now, look at you. Highly respected Healers want you to lead them against the Droc'ri."

Nana Magog tossed a chunk of wood on the fire and made herself comfortable on the ground. She closed her eyes. After a time, she spoke. "Know that you have significant leverage over this Droc'ri that holds your soul piece. He thinks he can use your fragment to force you to obey him. You can use the bit you hold to do the same and bend him to your goals."

I looked up sharply. "Leverage? You mean I can convince him to stop this conquest of Alba? How do I do that?" I asked eagerly.

She chuckled. "Rokan will resist, but I have faith in you, Child. Now get some sleep."

NINETEEN
ROKAN

The Desert Lands

I stood on a plateau and scanned the horizon. Before me stretched a dry gorge and the boulder-strewn path that led to the Gauntlet Sea a half-day's ride away. In every direction were the tawny shades of desert sands, and deeper shades of sandstone formed into low hills and ridges. Behind me rose a red rocky bluff, riddled with a network of natural caves. I inhaled. On the breeze, warmed from the day's heat, came the faint scents of hot earth and aromatic resins from the shrubs that grew in gullies. I inhaled again, letting the dry desert air cleanse me of the Emerald Mountains and Margot's influence. I was glad I hadn't returned directly to Tokurat.

"Master." A man with pale hair and tanned skin climbed to where I stood. "How may we serve you?"

I took another deep breath, then followed Achmed. The cool air inside the fortress was refreshing. The caverns were extensive, housing sleeping quarters for both men and desert-bred horses, a cooking area, holding cells, and storage. I held court over the fifty or so Droc'ri in the largest cavern.

I settled onto the massive stone throne, carved into the cavern wall, sinking my forearms into grooves worn into the stony armrests. The Droc'ri gathered before me, renewing their pledge to serve me.

These Brothers were my private army — my henchmen, proficient at assassination. I delegated all the lethal work to them. They loved their job and I rewarded them with gold, women, horses, jewels, manor houses. And freedom.

Independent-minded like me, they wanted to taste freedom without the Grand Master's oversight or the aggressive ambitions that surrounded Garrick in Tokurat. This was the greatest prize I gave to them. The Brothers had to obey my orders, but in between missions, they were free to do what they wanted.

The throne was hard and it was not long before my backside became numb. It seemed like it took an eternity for each black-robed man to repeat the lengthy pledge. I made myself remain erect, resisting the urge to ease the growing discomfort. I could show no weakness to my band of cut-throats. Their cold-hearted lust for blood is what made them powerful, and if I did not measure up, I would be assassinated without a second thought.

I handed Achmed a list of Healers. "Take some men. Capture these women and bring them here. I will take them to the Grand Master."

Achmed dipped his head. "Yes, Master." His long black robes swished as he strode the short distance to where the rest of the Brothers gathered. Mingling with them, he delivered instructions.

After the Brothers filed out, I sat, drumming my fingers on the hard surface. I had gleaned the names and faces of the Healers who had been aboard the *M'Ellara* from Margot's friends' minds. Of the one hundred twenty-three people that Sam had transported, thirty were active Healers. Another ten were Healers whom I had forced to give up their abilities to channel the Goddess if they wanted to continue living. Fifty were women who owned businesses or were advocates, and their mates. Margot and her friends accounted for the last of the escapees. I had ferreted out the locations of the Healers with my Far Sight, then compiled a list and sent Achmed and his companions to capture and bring them to me.

By the end of the next day, I had collected twenty Healers, five of whom Camila had stripped of the Goddess's blessing, making them no longer a threat to the Order. I wasn't too concerned about the rest. I'd find them later. *How ironic. These were the same women who had brought me a private moment of pleasure when they had destroyed some of Bruce the Terrible's ships.*

Thanks to Margot and her unwelcome voice in my head, instead of stripping the Healers of their magic as I had done in the past, I only had the will to block them so that they couldn't defend themselves or escape. It was not permanent and could be easily undone by someone with Margot's abilities. I cursed, blasting a boulder to rubble with a ball of fire. *That woman has hexed me, just like her mother!* Achmed and his Brothers kept their distance, eying me warily.

I rounded up the women and held my traveling crystal, intending to make a portal to the Suzerain's palace. I hesitated, Margot's accusations nagging in my mind. If I took them to Garrick, he would torture and eventually kill them. He would not be satisfied. I knew the Healer he sought was not among them.

Garrick had set up a sanctuary, more like a gilded prison, for the refugees from Alba, called the Chaste Palace. It was a magnificent marble fortress with a large courtyard, expansive gardens growing a variety of fruit trees and vines, and a stone building to house its guests. Most impressive was the gleaming, unscalable, white marble wall that surrounded the villa, effectively entrapping any who entered. Women were the sole residents. No men were allowed.

I scowled at the women. I couldn't let Achmed see my apprehension about performing this task. Better to get it over with.

I opened a gateway to the Chaste Palace. Two of Achmed's men went through to communicate with the guards. One came back into view and beckoned. Irritably, I shoved the women through the opening and strode through behind them. *I'm losing control. Margot and her Goddess are interfering with me!*

After depositing the Healers at the Chaste Palace, I gritted my teeth and started towards the Suzerain's palace. I dreaded facing Garrick in my present state of mind to report I had rounded up fewer than half the Healers on board Sam's ship. He had an uncanny ability to read me, no matter how much I tried to hide my secrets. I detoured through the market, thinking I would bring Sophia a new necklace. I munched on a pocket bread filled with spiced lamb and goat cheese. The juices ran over my fingers. I was about to enter my private sanctuary under the palace, when I paused. Licking my fingers, I turned into an alley leading away. I found my Katz-paw, one of my many spies, in a seedier district of Tokurat.

"Jack."

The lanky young man looked up from the half-carved rose in his hands. He shot to his feet, spilling wood shavings from his lap onto the circle of chips already formed around his stool.

"Rokan! I've been waiting for you! Do you have a task for me?"

I put a calming hand on the young man. "Yes, I do have a mission for you. One you'll like, I think."

"Where? Who? When?" he asked enthusiastically. His light brown curls fluttered with his excited movements.

"Come with me, Jack. I must prepare you."

We threaded through narrow streets that led to the oldest area of Tokurat, where I had my small hut.

I had discovered Jack as a rangy, tattered boy growing up in Tokurat. The boy's father was killed in a gambling hall for cheating. Thinking Jack's mother was dead as well, the crippled, half-man captain, Thaddeus, had delivered the youth to relatives that lived in the western reaches of the Desert Lands. His mother, Cerise, had followed the boy to the Desert Lands shortly after. Neither mother nor son was satisfied with eking out an existence from the sea, so they journeyed to the region's thriving city. As it was the Desert Lands' custom for a woman to have the protection of a man to survive, Cerise had sought out the strongest man she could find. Me. She had pleaded with me to shelter her and her son and provide a means to earn a living. I agreed, for a price.

"You're going to Alba," I said.

"Why? I don't like that place. You won't be there." He frowned. "Do I have to go on a boat?"

I laughed. "No. You'll be there in no time." I patted Jack's back. "I'll be with you and help you, Jack, just like I have always done. I have an important task for you. I'd do it myself, but I can't get away right now. Besides, I'll make sure you have plenty of wine and women and whatever else you want."

His schoolboy features brightened. "Whatever I want? What do I have to do?

"Find someone."

"Who?"

We had arrived at the small building and entered. "I need you to listen carefully. Here is a bag of coin. When you are following my instruction, there will always be coins for you to spend. If you get distracted and forget about the mission, you will not have any coins, and that will remind you to get back on task. Understand?"

The young man nodded. "You'll take care of me while I do your bidding."

"Exactly. When you get to Alba, make your way to Araval. Meet with the queen, help her to assassinate the king and overthrow the Alban monarchy." *That will satisfy Garrick.* "You will also be looking for a particular woman. I'll guide you in finding her. You will keep her safe until I get to Alba." I embedded in Jack a desire for Ellara that would awaken when he met her. If he was in love with her, he'd be more likely to want to protect her. And I needed her alive.

I touched Jack's temple, and he slumped into my arms. I picked up a silver double tetrahedron talisman from the shelf above the trunk and said a few words. The wall of the cottage shimmered, revealing a wooded area far from Tokur. I carried the young man through the gateway and deposited him on the sun-warmed fir needles. I retreated to stand inside my hut, said a few words, drew the appropriate symbol, and closed the doorway. I closed my eyes, watching with my inner sight until Jack woke a minute later, stood up groggily, and sauntered off.

TWENTY

ELLARA

The Heartland

Boris, in his horse form, had returned to our camp outside the Sacred Grove while I slept. Now, as I left Cuilithe, we moved slowly through the Heartland forest. The massive trees gave me a sense of safety. Nana had given me a map of the landmarks in the Heartland, making it easier for me to pick a less demanding route southward toward Araval. Boris became more protective of me. He didn't stray far when he grazed and stood close or lay down beside me at night. I was grateful for his company. That he could become a man intrigued me. Could he talk? What else could he do?

Nana said she would continue to monitor the decisions of the Council and report to me. It frustrated me that Nana Magog wasn't more forthcoming about the Council, its members, the other Healers she knew, or her suspicions. Even though the other Healers treated her as an outcast, I suspected she had her own goals and knew a lot more than she let on. Finally, I decided that perhaps she did me a service by letting me figure out whom to trust, or not, on my own.

Nana had never allowed me to take the easy route. She prodded me to figure things out for myself, then tested me to see if my conclusions actually were valid. I often wished she had been more supportive and informative with me like she had been with Margot. Long ago, frustrated by Nana's deaf ear to my questions, I had decided to learn on my own. Margot shared with me what Nana taught her, which gave me threads to explore.

The first night after leaving Cuilithe, Sam visited me like usual. With him was a regal woman who appeared happy and radiant. Long pale hair flowed around her shoulders and down her back, catching the crescent moonlight like a field of ripe grain in the wind. Sky-blue eyes looked lovingly at me. She wore a white linen robe with golden ribbons that crisscrossed her bodice and wrapped around her waist. She looked like a picture of a priestess I had seen in one of Nana's old manuscripts. A smile lit up her face.

"Mother?!" I exclaimed. Shortly after I had hand-fasted with Sam, she had died mysteriously.

My mother, Orva, stepped forward and reached towards me. "I'm very proud of you, Ellara. You have grown into a talented Healer."

Beside her floated a tall, stately man with black, shoulder-length hair and a bushy mustache. He dressed in formal attire with a frilled shirt, vest, and a coat that came to his knees. Instead of boots, the apparition wore shoes under his long trousers. Immediately, I liked him.

Orva lovingly touched his arm. "You never knew your father. He was killed during the wars in the Emerald Mountains. Meet Josef."

His brilliant aura enshrouded all of us. Josef radiated calm confidence. His dark eyes gazed approvingly at me.

I nodded acknowledgment. "Father."

"We have come to awaken you to your heritage," Josef said.

Over the next few nights, my parents came with Sam and proceeded to teach me the ancient language so that I could read from the book Nana had given me, and learn a spell that made me invisible. Nana popped in on several occasions and, together with my mother, guided me in mastering it. Nana said it was one of the simplest for conjuring and would be very useful for me. My parents and Nana urged me to practice it over and over until I could do it without any effort. It would prepare me for more complicated incantations.

Each night, before they left, my mother and father blessed me. They touched different points on my head and body and guided the energy of the Goddess into those centers. After the first time, I was violently sick, purging the contents of bowels, stomach, and kidneys. The following day, I felt lighter, could see more clearly, and my senses became fine-tuned. The next time they anointed me, my body welcomed the blessing.

When I asked what they were doing, my mother replied, "Camila would never admit it, nor does she realize that even as she cursed you and tried to steal your natural gifts for herself, she actually conferred upon you the Council's blessing by naming your strongest talent. We are cleansing your auric field and awakening and strengthening the centers in your body to hold more of the Goddess's energies. It requires the blending of the masculine and feminine aspects, which is why we are both here, to activate the next level of your abilities and prepare you so that you can host the Goddess." A soft smile curved her lips. "We break with tradition, yet again, Daughter, giving you the masculine as well as the feminine theurgy of the Goddess. If you were trained as Camila expected, you would be missing the masculine part, only to rely upon what your Far'degan pair'ti could supply."

Josef patted my shoulder. "When Nana taught you how to channel the Goddess to heal Sam and many others, you were given a shortcut to the many years of traditional training a novice typically undergoes. Trust in yourself. You are much more than you think you are."

I thought about what I had witnessed at the Cuilithe gathering. "I am grateful you broke with tradition and didn't force me into an outdated structure. And I'm grateful for the way I was trained, since I was left to explore other ideologies without censorship."

Josef nodded. "With the recent blessings your mother and I have bestowed upon you, you are ready to host the Goddess."

"What do you mean by 'hosting?' She already works through me."

"Yes. She does. You allow Her Radiance to flow *through* you to the person you are working with. You retain a clear sense of yourself, and a sense of separateness, even as you merge into Her energies." Josef glanced at his pair'ti. "Hosting the Goddess means the Goddess takes on your physical form and works through you as if She were human. You and the Goddess become one. That is why you need training and a powerful Far'degan, to be able to embody Her intense Gra'yia and become Her. It is not written in the doctrine, but the stronger the Far'degan, the more of the Goddess's power you can access. You will understand once you experience it."

"How do I embody the Goddess?"

Orva smiled. "It takes time and practice, Daughter. Practice these spells. The more you draw upon the Goddess's Loving Radiance, the more your body will adapt to Her high state of Being."

"What can I do with this power?"

"Anything you want, Ellara. You must remember that there are consequences for every action you take. If you use the Goddess's power wrongly, you will pay the price, and many people will be hurt or die."

I was excited to have access to a potent tool I could use to change the darkness afflicting our country. On the other hand, I feared what I could do with the unlimited power of the Goddess, especially if a Droc'ri were to capture me. Caution curbed my optimism.

One night, Nana reported on the Council meeting. "Camila refuses to acknowledge that this escalation of the Dark Lords needs to be handled differently," Nana grumbled.

I wasn't surprised. "I believe the Droc'ri strategy is to bring as much disruption and chaos into the Alban citizens' daily lives as possible, including the Council. Their goal is to destroy the harmony of our traditions and splinter our people, setting us against each other. What better way to sow discord into the spiritual foundation of Alba than by dividing the Council, pitting those who are determined to maintain the status quo against those who share a bigger vision."

Nana agreed with my assessment.

On my last night in the Heartland, Nana, Sam, Orva, and Josef gathered. It was goodbye for the formless ones, as I would not be able to see them outside the enchanted forest.

I commented to no one in particular, "I don't think Camila meant to encourage me by identifying the nature of my talent so precisely. But I can't shake Camila's words about how I am unworthy of using the Goddess's Gra'yia for healing. It is creating an inner conundrum for me. I want to do the Goddess's work, yet I fear inadvertently harming others. I worry that I had something to do with Sam's illness and death."

Nana chuckled. "There is great power in words. You use words to command the elements when you do magic. Think of Camila's words as pronouncing a spell on you, just like you do when you call forth the elements to create your invisibility shield."

"Could she have really taken my talent?"

"Only if you had given it to her. No one, not even the strongest sorcerer or most powerful Healer, can take what you are unwilling to give. They can *never* strip you of who you are. But through the power of their words, they can trick and manipulate you into giving them what they want. You must remember this, Ellara, with whomever you encounter. Many want to steal your abilities, like Camila's attempt. She took Anya's." At my surprised look, Nana added, "Didn't you notice?"

I nodded my head. "I saw her inhale the gossamer thread. I thought that was part of the ritual. What would she do with my theurgy?"

Nana sliced a sweet turnip and handed me a piece. Boris begged from her, and she gave him a slice as well. "Camila is getting old. Years ago, Rokan made a bargain with her to remove the blessing of the Goddess from the Healers he captured in exchange for supporting her as Doyen."

"Can Healers like Anya be blessed again?"

"The Goddess confers her blessing only once. If a Healer abuses Her power or loses it, it is lost forever. Rokan showed Camila how to consume the Goddess's gift, making it permanently unavailable to reclaim, even if the Healer had the will to do so."

"That doesn't make sense. Do you believe that, Nana?"

Nana ignored my question. "Camila's practice of stealing the Goddess's essence revitalized her for years. She knows her position as Doyen is fragile and fears you will displace her as leader of the High Council, even though you are not nearly old enough. Camila has fought to keep her position for decades and will not allow you to overthrow her. You must be ever watchful when you arrive in Araval."

"At least she is occupied at Cuilithe."

"Camila has many friends who support her in Araval and on the mainland. She would steal your essence and annihilate you, much like the sorcerer and Grand Master would do. Lord Garth has many spies and a Droc'ri who serves him. He is angry that you slipped out of his grasp in Sheldon, which placed him in disfavor with his master. However, he is secretly pleased by the rebellion, which gave him a license to further harass the citizens of Alba." She peered at me and handed me another piece of the root to chew on. "You will not have much time in Araval before you are discovered by one of these factions. Do you have a plan?"

I squirmed on my stump. I exhaled. "I want to convince the king to change the laws and restore the harmony that existed before all of this started. Then I want to reunite the people of Alba with the heritage that has allowed us to thrive for centuries in peace and happiness and strengthen the Goddess's protection of Alba." I paused. Hearing my plan spoken aloud made it sound simple. I continued, "I know there are many moving parts to this situation, the biggest being the shadow invading the Albans' hearts. The challenge becomes harder when Albans forget their roots and adopt the patriarchal and self-gratifying practices of the natives in the Desert Lands and the Natuans, when they believe wealth means pillaging the earth and enslaving its peoples to amass material things. I want to halt the erosion of the principles of respect and equality upon which our lifestyle is founded, and restore them."

"That is an ambitious plan. I trust in your resourcefulness." She tossed the peelings into the fire and shook off her skirt. "What are you going to do first?"

"See the king."

"Ellara, you have always been sheltered: by myself, your mother, and Sam. We are no longer available to protect you. You are alone, now. Sam is no longer your pair'ti and Far'degan. It will be months before Margot will be back to support you." She paused, looking into the forest. "By the way, all of the initiates were blessed by the Council. Even Felicity."

"What! How could the Council approve her? Even I could see she was not qualified." My faith in the Gra'Bandia Council dwindled, yet again. "Didn't anyone contest the appointment?"

Nana chuckled. "Camila controls the Council."

"And the Droc'ri control Camila," I interrupted bitterly.

"Those that opposed were overruled." Nana leaned forward. "Camila has taken an interest in Felicity. For what purpose, I am not certain. Do nothing to attract Camila's attention, and she will leave you alone. Otherwise..." Boris nosed in Nana's skirt, looking for more of the root. She scratched his forehead and said, "I believe in you. This is the path of your destiny. You must learn to discern who is a friend and who pretends to be one for their own agenda. Your life depends upon it."

"Won't you still come to visit?" I asked worriedly.

Nana shook her head. "I will support you in the best ways I can, but I am not welcome in Araval." She paused, and I thought she wouldn't say more. "Araval is Camila's home. Be wary, Child."

TWENTY-ONE

ROKAN IN TOKURAT

The Desert Lands

I delayed my audience with Garrick. I was certain he would see I was not myself. How could I play this so that he didn't kill me on the spot, as I had seen him do to others who had failed him?

I strode into the refreshing coolness of the marble palace, relieved to be out of the sweltering desert sun. I paused in my errand to stare at the backside of a young servant hurrying along the passageway, admiring her curves and graceful movement. "Sophia?"

The woman turned. "Rokan!" She glanced along the corridor, then hastened to me. She dipped her head deferentially, as was befitting of a servant in the Suzerain's palace. "How are you?" Her affection wrapped me in an invisible embrace.

I lifted her chin so I could look into her face. *I've missed you.* Aloud, I said, "I've been away on business."

"Something's different about you, Rokan." She lowered her eyes, listening with another sense. "You're more — alive."

I laughed. "I will come to you as soon as I can, Sophia." I caressed the flawless skin of her cheek, lingering longer than I normally would have. I reluctantly brought myself back to my task. I nudged her away. "Go." I watched Sophia's lithe form disappear around a corner. I turned away abruptly. *Margot! She's ruined me!*

I proceeded toward the garden where the Grand Master spent most of his time. Outside the entry I took a deep breath, relaxed my facial muscles, and then entered. The best deception was honesty.

The scent of roses dominated the air. A large tiled, spring-fed pool filled the space. Fruit-laden trees, manicured low shrubs, and ornate grasses lined paved paths. Garrick lounged on a golden velvet settee in the shade near the water.

"You've been gone for days. What do you have to report?"

"I captured twenty Healers. Here is a list. They await your pleasure at the Chaste Palace."

Garrick studied me. "What happened to you? You aren't your usual cocky self."

I hung my head. "No, Master. I have failed you." I had never, in all my years of service to Garrick, admitted I had failed him. I had no doubt that he had heard about the fight at the Temple of the Crescent Moon. Perhaps Margot could save me once again.

Garrick stroked his chin in contemplation.

I shuffled my feet, waiting for the killing blow.

After an inordinate amount of time calculated to unnerve me, Garrick said, "My sources say you were captured by a bunch of children. How is it that you, the most powerful sorcerer second only to me, could have been captured?"

I glanced at Garrick. He wore a genuine smile. I relaxed a little. "Master, you commanded me to find and capture the Healers that escaped. I came across a group of young men and women who had been on the ship with the Healers. They were heading into the mountains for a reason I still haven't determined. I let them capture me so I could get close to them and identify and find the Healers on board the *M'Ellara*. It turns out they were a group of untrained Healers. Once they figured out I was a Droc'ri, they made me their prisoner and took away my magic. When the Droc'ri Brothers attacked in the valley of the Crescent Moon, I had no access to my sorcery. I was hopelessly trapped."

"Hmm. How could a group of untrained initiates restrain you?"

"They used a different sort of witchcraft. I studied them while they held me captive. Their magic is like nothing we have encountered before. And it is powerful." I looked up. "This could be how the Goddess plans to destroy the Droc'ri Order." I dropped my head submissively.

Garrick studied me. "You're changed, Rokan. What did they do to you?"

"Master, I have failed the Order. They changed me somehow. I'm not the man I used to be." I shook my head. "I never want to encounter them again. They weakened my magic somehow. I'm struggling to regain who I am."

Garrick stood and walked towards me. He ran a bejeweled-fingered hand down my back. "For the first time in all of our years together, you have been humbled. By a group of children!" He laughed and laughed. Then he became serious. "How did you escape?"

"They have a weakness. Compassion. The Goddess sought revenge for my part in the temple's desecration and struck me down. Without my magic, I could not defend myself. The group restored me, and in the process, some of my powers returned."

"You must learn what magic they are using, then destroy them."

"Master, please don't send me back to them. They will steal the rest of my sorcery and I will not be able to serve you."

Garrick peered at me. "You are really frightened of them, aren't you?" He smiled. "Confronting them will be your punishment for failing me. Get me the information I want, then annihilate them." He flicked his fingers. "Now go and attend to the conquest of Alba. A Healer has done us a great service. The rebellion she started in Sheldon has spread throughout the island. The country is in chaos, giving Lord Garth just what he needs to take control."

"Yes, Master." I nodded in deference to him and quickly departed. The truth was that my magic was actually stronger after my experience with the young uninitiated, and my strength and endurance from my younger years had returned. What had weakened was my desire to do the tasks Garrick commanded me to do. Ellara's influence had been subtle. It had influenced me to moderate needless cruelty. But it had not stopped me. In contrast, Margot's voice invaded my mind continually, reminding me I had a choice. It was a hex meant to drive me mad.

TWENTY-TWO

ELLARA

Araval, Alba

It took over a week to travel to the capital of Alba after I left the sanctuary of the Heartland. I left Boris at the outskirts of the city and told him to not wander far. Slinging my saddlebags over my shoulder, I went in search of lodging.

I arrived in Araval wearing the guise of a young man, the tunic bearing an insignia designating the wearer as a messenger from one of the midland manor houses. I hoped that I could blend in, as well as enjoy some of the respect and authority that men still retained. I knew that as a woman recently arrived in the town, someone would certainly notice me. I definitely didn't want to look like a Healer.

The Healers at Cuilithe had worn a turquoise or deep blue, knee-length tunic, embroidered with the triple crescent representing the Goddess, over ankle-length skirts. They braided their hip-length hair into distinctive plaits that took time and another set of hands to weave. I gathered that long, thick hair indicated the degree of the Goddess's vitality and clout one was said to possess and cutting one's tresses blatantly disrespected the Goddess. The garb was beautiful and set Healers apart. I wished I could have had an outfit like theirs. But as I watched the Healers at Cuilithe, I quickly adjudged the garments to be cumbersome for practical matters, especially for climbing the rigging on board a ship, or for horseback riding. Nana Magog and my mother had dressed like native Albans in a hip-length work tunic and loose trousers or a split skirt. That worked for me, too.

Partly to rebel against Camila and what she upheld, and as a matter of disguise, I had cropped my waist-length hair to just below my shoulders, hoping to make my gender less easily determined. I stuffed the outer, lighter strands under a gray felt cap and pulled the darker hairs into a ponytail, as was the fashion for youths. At my waist, I belted a dagger, my coin purse, and a small pouch for sundries.

The early morning sun cast long shadows as it crept over the orchards covering the rolling hills surrounding the city. I gawked at the houses several stories high painted in a colorful array of blue, pink, yellow, and ochre. Trees lined the wide brick-paved avenues, and flowers grew between the trunks. The white crenelated walls of the castle glinted in the sun and overlooked the city from atop a hill.

Main Street in Araval was not much different from the one in Sheldon, with metal and wood-working shops, greengrocers, boutiques with handmade clothing and jewelry, butchers, and bookstores. Most of the businesses had living space above or behind their shops. Even at this early hour, the streets swarmed with customers and hawkers. The air was filled with the scents of fresh baked pastries, roasting meats, cheeses, porridge, stewed cabbage, and herbed teas.

As I walked through Old Araval, I noticed a willowy, semi-blind baker. Gray hair curled around her face, and the rest of her thick salt and pepper locks formed a loose braid that stretched down her back. In a cheerful voice, she enthusiastically greeted each of her customers by name.

The delicious aroma of her bread broadcast the nature of her establishment far more effectively than the small wooden sign that swung above her lintel, and reminded me I had eaten only foraged greens and Nana Magog's travel cakes for days. A group of patrons gathered around her doorway, where baskets of steaming bread cooled on a couple of wooden barrels. She collected copper coins from her customers.

As I approached, I noticed two men standing in the street, watching the commotion around the barrels displaying the bread. The taller man flicked a glance from side to side, and moved behind two nanas who chatted with the baker. He crouched, sliding his hand between the women. He extracted two loaves of bread and retreated to his friend. They sauntered down the street without the elder appearing to notice. I glanced at her and at them as they made their carefree way down the street chatting and munching. Unable to curb the fire that surged through me, I dropped my travel satchels by her door and raced down the street after them. I reached between them, grabbed their coat sleeves, and swung them around. They stared at me in surprise.

I met the sky-blue eyes of the dark-haired man and caught my breath. He was the man who had entered my dreams ever since I had left the Heartland. His presence had chased away the threatening creatures that pursued me. But I had seen him somewhere else. *Where?* Straight, chocolate brown hair fell over his forehead, partially hiding long eyebrows. A thin mustache and small goatee framed sensuous lips. A wide scar crossed sunken cheeks and deep lines etched his otherwise handsome face. A cloth wrapped around his head partly hid a small gold circlet in one ear which gleamed in the sun. He wore the oiled long coat of a seaman.

He drew away, attempting to free himself, growling, "Let go, boy." He tugged against my grip.

I tightened my fingers on his forearm and turned my attention to the taller man, who also yanked against my restraint.

The smells of sweat, stale urine, and ale assaulted my keen senses, and I wrinkled my nose. Above an unkempt plain shirt, dirty trousers, and stained long coat which came to mid fore-arms and mid thighs, was a smooth boyish face. Light brown hair fluttered in the breeze above pale skin. He had a rosy blush on his cheeks and a narrow mouth. A shadow encased each man's aura.

"I notice you didn't pay for the bread," I said firmly to the younger man. "I believe that's two copper pence each, and two gold hektes each for the collection fee."

"She sells her bread for a copper coin!" the leggy man protested.

"That's if you paid at the time you picked it up. You didn't pay, and I had to chase you down and confront you about your oversight." I tipped my head slightly and glared at each of them intently.

The shorter man laughed tensely, displaying a pearly set of teeth. "Collection fee. Jack, I can use that on certain people I know. Thanks for the idea, lad." He moved his arm, testing my grip.

The timbre of his voice stirred my memory.

"You're just a boy. We don't pay boys collection fees or anything else." Jack turned to leave, jerking to free himself. I gripped his wrist firmly and dug in my heels. Petulantly, Jack swung at me with his other hand. I ducked, but not before the bread he held dislodged my cap, and my hair spilled around my shoulders. I tossed my head to get it out of my eyes.

"He's a woman. I don't need to pay *you!*" Jack said condescendingly.

"It doesn't matter who or what I am," I snapped. "You stole from the elderly nana. Where's your respect?"

The lanky man lifted the edge of his soiled, undersized coat. "We don't have the money to pay."

I scrutinized him. "Why not? You look young and able-bodied. What do you do?"

"I'm a carpenter by trade."

"And what's stopping you from working?"

Jack shrugged and looked away. The young man left a disgusting taste in my mouth. I turned to the dark-haired man who stood stonily. Irritably, I demanded, "And you? You look like a smuggler captain."

He shook his head vigorously but didn't speak. His arm shook where I held it. A closer inspection revealed his ashen face and sweat forming on his brow. "Let me go," he wheezed.

I released my hold and faced Jack. "I know both of you can pay for your food. Just because Lord Garth interprets the new decrees as giving him the right to punish and persecute the common folk, and especially women, does not justify your larcenous behavior. Pay up!" I demanded. I held out my palm. Reluctantly, Jack fished a couple of copper coins from a pocket in his coat. "And the gold pieces?"

"I don't have them. This is all you are ever going to get, woman!" His tone was bitter. He wrenched hard, freeing himself, and stomped a short distance away. "Come on, Thaddeus."

Annoyed by Jack's attitude, I fixed his companion with a glare. *Thaddeus? Captain of the* Lovely Lady? Color had returned to the captain's face, and he breathed normally again. He inched away from me. I held out my hand. "I know you have the coins, Captain."

The mariner scowled and started to follow his friend. I darted in front of him, barring his path, and reached for his arm. He recoiled, hissing, "Don't touch me!" He flicked a glance at Jack behind me.

I planted myself in front of him and waited. I had never come face to face with the crippled captain. I remembered his voice, though, as he had called commands to his crew. I had caught distant glimpses of him hiding in the shadows on his ship or in a quiet corner of a pub, many years ago when I traveled with Sam to avoid Cleric Paul. He had leaned heavily on a cane and limped when he walked. A beard had disguised the scars on his pinched, youthful face. I had sensed his pain then. Now he walked without a cane, but his discomfort was still palpable. Had he finally sought healing?

Eying me as if weighing the odds for a favorable bargain, his fingers strayed to a pocket and hesitated. Finally, he pulled out two copper coins and dropped them into my outstretched palm. I stood my ground while he continued to contemplate me. Appearing to reach a decision, he rummaged in another pocket. Plucking out four small gold coins, he moved close. "There are those who would kill you, if they found you, Witch!" He fixed me in the eye and deliberately took my hand.

The moment he touched my flesh, the Goddess's Lig'yia ripped through me and into the captain. For an instant, he glowed white. He gasped, and his face contorted. Excruciating pain gripped my body. I opened my mouth to cry out, but no sound came. I clutched his sleeve with my free hand to keep from falling. The agony drew tears to my eyes. I tried to free my hand, but he held it firmly. "Let go," I croaked. "Please, let go." I dared not summon the Goddess's Gra'yia to purge the suffering I had empathically drawn from him.

He ignored my plea and slowly pressed the small gold coins, one by one, into my palm, all the while watching me endure my distress with cold indifference. Abruptly, he released my hand, pivoted out of my grasp, and strode towards his companion.

I sank to my hands and knees, panting. The gold coins burned my hand, and wave after wave of the man's torment passed through my body. I struggled to regain my sense of self and breathe. I heard someone calling to me, from a great distance, then felt a hand on my shoulder. Finally, I was able to look into the kindly face of an elderly woman.

"Are you alright? Did that man hurt you?"

I wiped my eyes and sniffed. The spasms were passing, and I breathed more easily. "I haven't eaten in a long while," I said weakly, not wanting to reveal to the onlookers what had really happened.

The nana helped me to stand. My fingers slowly curled around the coins and I bent down to retrieve my cap. My head cleared and my balance returned. "I'm fine, now. Thank you." *So much for not being noticed,* I thought as I nodded to the crowd that had gathered around me. Then I worried. *Did anyone see the Goddess's Light?* I stared after the man whose pain I had absorbed and whose purifying could get me captured.

I heard Jack laugh. "Looks like you brought her to her knees. You'll have to show me that trick." He nudged his companion, who studied his palm. "Serves her right. What a vixen!"

"Huh? Yes, she deserved it."

"What did she do to you? Burn you or something?" Jack pointed to the captain's hand and clapped him on the back. "Let's go to the Red Rose and forget about it."

I watched them saunter away. Before they rounded the corner, the captain stopped and gazed back along the street to where I stood.

I trudged back to the bakery, staring at the golden hektes I had collected. I had typically been the one to collect payment for the goods Sam brought to Sheldon, but I didn't remember being so forceful or determined. I didn't know what had come over me to accost the strangers so aggressively.

"Bless you, Child," the aged baker said as I gave her the coins. "I've been short every day for weeks."

I handed her two gold hektes. "Maybe this will make up for all the loaves they didn't pay for."

She pointed towards my haversack. "Newly in town? I could use some help in the bakery, and it looks like you need a safe place to stay."

"Thank you. Yes, I'd love to help you." The woman reminded me of Nana Magog. "Do you know who those two men are that have been stealing from you?"

She laughed. "The captain has a ship. The *Lovely Lady*, I think it is. The boy is a bottom-feeder. He has no qualms about helping himself to whatever he wants, whether he has a right to it or not." She peered at me. "Don't worry, Child. You'll be safe here."

I entered the small cottage that was Nana Bean's bakery. Half of the room housed a large table upon which rested lumps of dough to be formed into loaves. To one side was a large stone oven from which came the aroma of baking bread. A hearth with a pot hanger supported a small, steaming cauldron. To my left was a smaller space that formed the sleeping area, containing a bed and a sleeping mat on the floor. Intersecting the main room was a passageway that led to a garden at the back of the house and a storage room that shared a wall with the sleeping area.

I dropped my bags on the sleeping mat and sat in the soft chair at the end of the bed. I didn't feel well. My legs felt like rubber, my back ached, and my head swam. My body burned, especially the arm and hand that had touched the captain's. For better or worse, the recent encounter left me keenly aware of the crippled captain, Thaddeus Finn, who Matty and Sam had wanted me to heal for decades. My heart went out to the captain and the intense suffering he lived with.

Nana Bean handed me a bowl of stew. "This will make you feel better after taking on that young man's misery."

I stared at her. *Was it that obvious?* I worried. The food cleared my mind and chased away the rest of the malaise. I assisted Nana with the loaves and customers the rest of the day. Busyness kept my mind from straying to the captain who didn't look so crippled now, and to Sam.

As twilight stole through the city, Nana Bean commented, "You look tired and heart-sore, Child. How about a hot bath? The Red Rose has the best bathhouse in Araval."

"I'm fine, Nana." I hesitated. "Did your customers say they saw anything unusual when I collected the coins from your two thieves?"

"I don't see so well anymore. No one said anything if they did notice." She winked at me. "But I felt it."

Was Nana Bean a Healer in hiding? Then I remembered Nana Magog's warning about Camila having friends in Araval. I watched Nana move about her kitchen, then shook my head. *She's not Camila's friend,* I decided. Still, I needed to be careful.

After dinner, as Nana Bean started a fresh batch of dough for the morning patrons, she again urged me to go to the Red Rose. "Let the Goddess wash away your troubles and then you will feel better and ready for Araval."

245

"I'm fine," I muttered and settled onto my sleeping mat. But I couldn't fall asleep. Snippets of conversation from Nana's patrons rolled through my mind, and my muscles burned from my encounter with the captain.

The more I thought about the comforting hot water, the more I believed it might cleanse me from my brush with the two bread thieves, and give me the quiet I needed to sort out what had happened. I could talk to the Goddess — and maybe even Sam. It was nearly midnight when I decided to go to the Red Rose. I hoped that at this late hour, I would be able to have a bath to myself.

I gathered a change of clothes, stuffed them into a flour sack that Nana used to carry produce from the market, and stepped out into the moonlit night. Lanterns placed atop lampposts cast dim patches of light along the street.

I walked towards the Red Rose, darting into darkened doorways when I heard footsteps or oncoming voices. After several blocks and corners, I spotted a big brick building with patrons entering and leaving. Above the door swung a sign painted with a brilliant red rose. A soft golden glow from a high lamp cast a circle of light onto the smooth flagstones around the stairs leading to the entry. I climbed the three steps to the main door. My hand was on the latch when the door burst open.

A man stood silhouetted by the light in the establishment. He pursed his lips as he diligently struggled to maintain an upright posture. In one hand, he held an almost empty bottle of rum. Taking a deep breath, he swayed as he thrust out his chest, and looked up.

"You!" The captain braced a hand against the doorjamb and grabbed a handful of my coat at the throat, pulling me toward him. "You've jinxed my life, Witch! And ruined my night!"

The captain's face was inches from mine and his breath reeked of liquor. I leaned back and glanced at the bottle. "I think you've done a good job of that all on your own." I grabbed his hand to detach it, yelping as searing pain coursed through my body. I withdrew my hand instantly. My legs gave way, and I half fell down the steps, clutching the railing. The captain reeled. Still grasping my coat, he plunged down the steps with me. He would have fallen if I had not caught him.

I had often felt the ache from Sam in my body when I worked with him. It had taken me years to understand that what I felt from another was not mine and that one of my gifts was to transmute another's suffering as part of the restorative work I did. I had learned that the quickest way to release it from my body was to not fight it, and instead, open my heart to the Goddess and let Her energy transmute and purge it from me. Even though I didn't see the shadow around Thaddeus any longer, I instinctively knew to not call the Goddess.

The captain rested against me. I collected myself and shoved him off, steadying him as he attempted to get his feet under him. He made a valiant effort to stand upright, unsupported, and stared down at me. He leaned back to inspect me, balancing himself against the railing. His words were bitter, each syllable enunciated slowly and loudly. "He didn't tell me you were a harpy and had turned into another Nana Magog!" His voice carried in the still night. "What did you do to me?" he growled. "You've befuddled my mind, Witch." He appeared oblivious to approaching footsteps. He stabbed a finger at me. "You are the reason for the Kurat spirit — Rokan's curse. My life has been miserable as a result."

I kept my voice low. "How can that be? I don't know you, yet you blame me for your suffering. I am not responsible for your life. You could have come to me anytime for healing and I would have done my best to restore you. Even as you are now freed of the curse and of much of your pain, the imprint of the evil creature clouds your mind. I have done all I can do for you." I stepped around him. "You now have a choice for how you will live your life."

I started up the steps.

Thaddeus grabbed my hand. "Wait." Shoving the rum bottle into a pocket, he pulled me towards him while he pawed through his coat pockets until he produced a gold and silver pendant. He placed it reverently into my palm. "Sam wanted me to give this to you." He grimaced. "I almost died attempting to use it to cast out the black creature that sucks the life from me. I haven't been able to touch it until now."

My fingers caressed the amulet. I had given Sam the Goddess knot formed into overlapping hearts — so that they created a third, united heart — when we were hand-fasted. It repre-sented our connection and love. He wore it ever-after, saying he felt protected by my love. The cloth sack I carried slipped from my grasp. Leaning against the railing and squeezing my eyes shut, I held the pendant to my heart with both hands. Sam's essence washed over me. Tears slid silently down my cheeks. *I wish you hadn't died, Sam.*

Voices from the latest arrivals brought me back to the present. The captain had shifted so that his arms braced against the railing to either side of me. He leaned close and used his body to block the newcomers' view of me. Lord Garth's mercenaries glanced sidelong as they walked around us and climbed the stairs. Thaddeus lifted his bottle to them in a drunken greeting. Patrons leaving the Red Rose stood at the doorway, gawking. He waved them past us. When they were gone, he drew me into the shadows across the street, and away from the constant flow of clientele. Surprisingly stable on his feet for one who appeared to be quite intoxicated, he rested against the wall and held me at arm's length.

"I was coming to find you. Sam made me promise to keep you safe." He placed the hand that held the bottle over his heart and dipped his head. Solemnly he declared, "Sam was a good man. He believed in me when no one else did. He'll be sorely missed. I will keep my pledge to him." He leaned so that his face was inches from mine and whispered loudly, "I'll be your new Anam pair'ti, if you'll have me."

I choked, appalled. *A heartless drunk, who believes I have ruined his life, to replace Sam?* I closed my eyes and took a deep breath. "You must be mistaken. Sam asked Matty to be his successor. I don't know you." I shook my head, wordlessly

249

lifted the sack with my clothes, and pivoted towards the Red Rose's entrance.

"Don't forsake me," Thaddeus pleaded. His fingers brushed my back. "Give me a chance..."

But I wasn't listening. An invisible pressure on my back alerted me to danger. I glanced around, probing the darkness with my senses. Movement within the shadows gave away the presence of someone who had been watching us. I eased against the wall and stared into the darkness. *I could make a run for the Red Rose. But then I'll never know who is stalking me.*

Thaddeus mistook my movement and drunkenly pulled me close. "Changed your mind about me, have you?"

I pointed with my chin. "There's someone over there."

Before he could reply, a man's voice commanded, "Captain, I require your services and your vessel immediately."

A medium-built, plainly dressed man with a travel cloak tossed over his shoulder emerged from the shadows and approached us. The figure moved with the graceful silence of an assassin. He dismissed me with a toss of his head in my direction. An invisible hand pushed at me, and I took an involuntary step to the side. The captain's fingers dug into my arm, stopping me.

"Can't you see I'm busy, Hadlan?" Thaddeus slurred, and he crushed me against his body.

The assassin stepped directly in front of the captain. "I have business to conduct. I command your services. Now." He leaned closer. "You don't want me to repeat myself." The stranger assessed me. My insides turned to ice. "Let the whore go. She is not wanted," he commanded.

I bristled. I had been called a lot of things, but never a whore. Instantly, I disliked the man and resented how he bullied the captain and me.

A retired assassin had trained Margot and me in the art of self-defense. He had taught us to listen with our senses and not to rely solely upon our eyes. The man standing before us was no ordinary assassin. Even though I had never met a Droc'ri face to face, Cleric Paul had told me about their air of superiority and how they were not afraid to use magic to back up their demands. I suspected this man was from that nefarious guild. *Was he Lord Garth's Droc'ri?*

I fastened my gaze to one side of Hadlan and became very still. I pulled my aura close to my body. The captain tightened his arm around me. I detected his fear. "I have to go, Luv. Duty calls." He straightened, weaved from side to side, and released his hold. The Droc'ri assassin watched me.

"Come on, Hadlan. Let's go out to sea so you can talk to your master," he mumbled. "It's a shame your magic doesn't work in Alba." He nodded to me. "But it's good for my business." He pushed away from the wall, took a step, and would have collapsed if I had not ducked under his arm. He stifled a smile and leaned heavily on me. He shrugged at the

Droc'ri and turned to me. "Do you mind helping a drunk sea captain find his ship?" He gave me his most winning smile.

I looked toward the Red Rose and lifted my sack. "I was going to take a bath."

The assassin moved in front of the captain and grabbed him by the neck. The captain thrashed, releasing his hold on me. "Stop playing games, Captain Thaddeus." He glared at me. "Shoo! Go." He waved his fingers and an invisible hand pushed weakly at me. He turned back to the captain. "You're wasting time. Let's go."

Thaddeus stood unsteadily and nodded to me. "Go do your ablutions. I can manage on my own." He pressed his lips together and stiffly took a short step, then another. On the third one, he toppled against the wall, and leaned there, breathing heavily. He lifted the bottle to his face and inspected it. "I drank all of that? No wonder I can't walk." He threw the bottle at the feet of the sorcerer. It shattered, splattering liquid on the man's boots. The Droc'ri scowled at his soiled footwear.

Sam's pendant warmed in my hand. Sam had trusted Matty, and Matty cared deeply for his crippled captain. Reluctantly, I eased under the captain's arm. "Alright," I sighed. "I'll help you. Promise me you will stop hiding from yourself through drink."

"I promise I won't drink another drop tonight," he declared. He planted his hand on mine and pulled my arm firmly around his body. "Ah!" He started forward, leaning heavily on me. The Droc'ri followed.

We walked about ten paces before I stopped. Thaddeus had stepped on my feet several times and his longer stride threatened to pull us apart. Wordlessly, I pushed up on the arm that was draped around me and levered Thaddeus to straighten and take most of his weight off me.

Progress was halting and fraught with missteps and more trodden toes. Thaddeus lurched following a blow from behind by the sorcerer, and we almost crashed to the cobblestones. "Stop delaying if you want your plaything to live."

I stiffened. Thaddeus smiled to himself. The smile vanished when I slid my hand inside his coat and midway up his spine. His back grew hot where my palm rested. My other hand sought the hand resting over my shoulder. "What are you doing?" he whispered in alarm as my fingers grazed his.

I glanced at him, then deliberately grabbed his hand and held it firmly. He stumbled and I steadied him. Life force flowed through me and into him. I sensed his mind clear and his footsteps became more certain, although he continued with his drunken charade. After a few more paces, I levered him up so that he walked mostly on his own.

I wasn't afraid of the sinister assassin, although Hadlan was not the sort with whom I would want to go for a stroll. By the same token, I didn't want to press my luck and provoke him, either. I debated about whether to abandon the captain to the sorcerer and let them make their way to the moorage without me, but after a sneak peek at the annoyance on Hadlan's face, I opted to play along. Besides, if the sorcerer realized that Thaddeus was cleared of the effects of drink, he might wonder about Thaddeus's "plaything" and report it to his master.

As we walked, I allowed myself to receive an impression of Thaddeus. Years of longing, sadness, fear, and physical pain dominated the tapestry of the captain's life. However, the man had more mettle than he let be known. He yearned to become free from a bondage that sucked the life from him. His life contrasted drastically with the happiness and contentment I had known with Sam, and I couldn't help feeling melancholy that he had suffered while I had experienced what he desired most: love, companionship, children, and satisfaction with life.

I continued to receive from him and at one point saw an image of his master. I halted abruptly. The Droc'ri was the same man I had seen riding beside Margot in the mountains. What was he doing with her? Was he bending Margot to his will as he had done to Thaddeus?

Disregarding Nana Magog's warnings about using the Far Sight, especially in the presence of a Droc'ri, I risked taking a quick peek at Margot. My daughter slept in a camp with her friends, with no sign of the sorcerer. I exhaled and relaxed. Thaddeus watched me, concern intensifying the lines on his face.

"Get moving." Something hard jabbed into my back.

We tramped along dusty, silent streets. The captain's spirits lifted, and as I relaxed and allowed myself to move with him, a natural ease developed between us. It took another block for us to get in step with each other. However, for the benefit of the sorcerer, he continued his drunken performance, masterfully appearing to lean unsteadily on me, without actually doing so.

"We make a great team, don't we? Call me Thaddeus, by the way." He darted a glance at me. Our steady pace inspired him to start singing sea ditties. He had a resonant baritone voice, and it pleased him that I listened.

It was some distance to where his ship was tied up in a quiet recess beyond the main docks, and Thaddeus guided me the longest way he could imagine. As we progressed, he sang one sea ballad after another. Then he started on an old favorite that Sam had sung to me and our children many times, about the sea queen and her captain pair'ti, who traveled the seas and was lost. The queen searched for him so they could be reunited again.

My pace slowed. I dashed away the tears gliding down my cheeks.

He launched into another of Sam's favorites, about Lorelei, the mermaid who loved a human and pleaded with the Goddess so that she could become mortal to be with him, only to have pirates kill her beloved. It had a sad ending and a haunting melody.

By the time we reached the *Lovely Lady*, Thaddeus was steady on his feet and elated. A big man called from on board. "That you, Cap'm?"

"Make ready for departure, Matty. We have a passenger." He motioned to Hadlan. "Get on board. We leave immediately."

The sorcerer gave us a scathing look, then strode up the plank. Thaddeus turned to me, blocking the assassin's view with his back to the ship. He asked softly, "Are you alright?" He brushed the tears from my cheeks.

I turned my head, pressing my lips together, stifling a sob. The songs had reminded me that I'd never hear Sam's voice again, nor would he come back to me like in the Ballad of the Sea Queen.

Thaddeus wrapped his arms around me, pulling me against him. He was about the same height and build as Sam, and he smelled of the sea. I resisted, wedging my arms against his chest. He cradled the back of my head and stroked his other hand down my back, like Sam used to do. My heart ached. After a few minutes, I shifted so I could rest against him.

"We're ready, Cap'm."

Reluctantly Thaddeus pushed away and held my shoulders. He lifted my chin. Finally, I met his clear-eyed gaze. "Come with me."

Tight-lipped, I shook my head.

"Will you wait for me?"

I bit my lip and again shook my head.

"I'll be back for you," he promised, caressing my cheek with his thumb, like Sam often did. "Will you be alright until then?"

Thaddeus handed me the sack with my clothes, then backed away, and finally released his hold. On impulse, I pressed Sam's amulet into his palm, curling his fingers around it. "May the Goddess protect you, Captain, as She did for Sam," I murmured.

Thaddeus gazed longingly at me, then leapt to the deck, all vestiges of prior years of deformity gone. He called to his crew to shove off.

Occasionally, I was granted the ability to see auras, and now, the brilliant luminescence surrounding Thaddeus sparkled. He stared into the shadows where I lingered. Gratitude for taking away his pain and joy at being freed from Rokan's curse wrapped around me. Still, deep loneliness surrounded him, as well as trepidation that the recent turn in his fortune would be discovered, and the resultant punishment he would receive. As the vessel drifted into the current, and the smaller sails were let out, his yearning for a different life touched my heart.

TWENTY-THREE

ROKAN AND THE SKELD

Tokurat, The Desert Lands

Therem Skeld hovered impassively before me, relaying the most recent events of Ellara. I slammed my fist onto the desk, upsetting the contents resting atop it, and growled. *That imbecile! The half-man was not supposed meet her and take her to his ship so she could meet with Matty!* My fingernails dug into the wooden surface. I hadn't trusted Jack to complete his task, especially after he started philandering with Captain Thaddeus several weeks ago. As a precaution, I had assigned Lord Garth's sorcerer to Ellara's care.

Is Hadlan really so stupid that he can't recognize a Healer and thought she was just a common harlot? Didn't he notice how she cleared Thaddeus of drink even while he pretended to be drunk? Lord Garth's fool didn't get Thaddeus away while Ellara despised the captain. *He will pay for his incompetence!*

I leaned back in my chair, steepled my fingers, and tapped my lips. *Ah*. I shaped a small piece of paper into a symbol, spoke a few words, exhaled sharply upon the instrument, and handed it to the Skeld. "Take this to Jack. You know what to do."

The Skeld faded, leaving a faint musty residue in the small room.

The Skeld was my secret and most treasured spy. I not only had an imp who delivered messages, but years ago I had secretly conjured a Skeld who served as my invisible eyes. It recorded everything it witnessed, except for sounds or conversations. Not limited by time or space, and invisible to all but me, the Skeld spied upon people of interest, such as Garrick, Garrick's sister, Qadira, Thaddeus, Ellara, and provincial leaders. As soon as I became aware that Ellara had departed the Heartland, I had assigned the Skeld to monitor her progress towards Araval.

Sam and Matty had been bosom buddies even before Ellara was born. Through my spy portals on the *Lovely Lady*, I had overheard Sam ask Matty to protect her if he died. I wasn't certain just how receptive Ellara would be to Matty. But since I had Matty's pair'ti and family killed a few years ago, and knowing how much the helmsman adored Ellara, I couldn't risk Ellara becoming Matty's pair'ti. Certain she would seek out Matty, I didn't want the *Lovely Lady* in port when she arrived in Araval.

When Ellara was two days from Araval, I instructed Hadlan to give the *Lovely Lady* a cargo to haul to the mainland. The vessel was supposed to be at sea when she arrived, and Ellara would not encounter Matty.

When I discovered the ship had not departed, I sent a message with my imp to Hadlan to get the *Lovely Lady* out of port immediately. Hadlan had been too slow to act and now, not only had Ellara met Thaddeus, but she had expelled the Kurat spirit so that I could no longer control him.

Was Thaddeus going to become a problem? Orphaned when he was ten, Thaddeus had dreamed of having a family and a pair'ti. I could never allow him this pleasure. It would interfere with his ability to serve me, and he was the best captain in my clandestine fleet. To protect my interests, I had derailed all of Thaddeus's attempts to find a mate, sometimes even killing the unlucky woman.

I paced around my small space. Thaddeus had never expressed an interest in Ellara, and to my knowledge, they had never met. Now that he was free of the Kurat curse that kept him from seeking a mate, I surmised that if Thaddeus encountered Ellara again, he would attempt to win her heart.

The captain had served me since he was fifteen years old, after I restored him from a paralyzing accident. I healed him just enough so he could limp around and have some control over his bowels. I had promised to heal him the rest of the way if he served me willingly. But he was headstrong, and I had had to take more drastic measures — including the Kurat spirit that drained his life force — to control him.

I didn't know what transpired at the *Lovely Lady* before Thaddeus left. Did she meet with Matty? Reflecting upon the misty images from the Skeld, I thought that Ellara didn't recognize Thaddeus and was just being kind. In fact, she appeared to be put off by the captain. It was obvious that she still missed Sam. I shook my head. *Love is such a waste of time. It makes people weak and vulnerable.* I was pleased to see that Thaddeus had treated Ellara the way I had taught him to engage with the ladies at the brothels. *I have to make him afraid of her.*

I passed my hand before the marble wall, to spy by scrying. Ellara lounged in the water of a tiled bath at the Red Rose. As before, the vision of Ellara was vague, and I could only guess at her expression and what she was thinking. I expanded the scene, and spotted the *Lovely Lady* at the mouth of the Slant River. Thaddeus stood at the helm, apparently lost in thought while Matty called orders to the crew. I wove a spell, intending to cast fear of Healers, and especially Ellara, into the captain's aura. Alarmingly, unlike my previous spells, it did not penetrate, and the magic dissolved.

I pushed against my desk, rocking my chair precariously backward. *What happened between them?* That I still couldn't see Ellara clearly annoyed me. With Sam out of the picture, she didn't have his protection. Just yesterday, Ellara had been slightly more discernible.

I stood abruptly, the chair crashing to the floor. *Thaddeus! It has to be! Did she heal him? The Skeld would have seen if she had.* But the Skeld had limitations and couldn't record ener-getic exchanges. I glided my finger along a row of books, but the titles were a blur. *Ellara is mine! She will not escape me, and whoever gets in my way will be eliminated, even if it means the half-man, Matty, and anyone else!*

Since before Ellara was born, I had sensed her power and declared she would serve me. I had gone to Sheldon to steal the girl, intending to raise her as my own. However, her mother and Nana Magog had protected the child with the ferocity of a mother bear protecting her cub. After experiencing the Goddess's Radiance that the child wielded, including the exchange of soul parts, I realized I had no safe place for her. My duties kept me perpetually on the move. I trusted no one to watch over her, especially if they discovered what she was. I determined the best course of action was to suppress her magic and cast doubt of her abilities into her unconscious mind. I'd let Nana Magog and her mother raise and train her.

At first, having a bit of Ellara's soul made my magic strong, especially in Alba, where the Droc'ri sorcery barely worked, if at all. In time, it became harder to execute the Grand Master's commands, and I became a target for the other Droc'ri. I scoured every manuscript I could find, looking for a way to get rid of her soul piece. Quite unexpectedly, I discovered that I could use Ellara's soul fragment to break my contract with the Dark Lords. For the first time in decades, I had a glimmer of hope that I could become ordinary and go to the Mag Mell after I died, instead of the Tiarna Drocha, from which my soul could never return.

Worried that someone else would discover my secret, I had taken Ellara's soul fragment from my energy field and placed it into an etheric container. Requiring a safe place to store Ellara's soul piece where Garrick wouldn't find it, I went in search of my mother. She was the only one who would understand. I found her in the Mag Mell. She had not chosen to reincarnate yet.

My mother had greeted me affectionately. I remembered her promise. "My beloved son, you know I'd do anything for you. What do you need, Loran?"

I hadn't heard my birth name spoken for decades. It was a practice in the Desert Lands to take on a public name, the reasoning being that speaking a person's birth name gave one power over the other. I handed my mother the energetic package. "Keep this. It protects me from eternal death."

"I will guard this faithfully, Loran." She had chuckled. "I'd say 'with my life,' but that phrase has a different meaning here in the Mag Mell."

I had returned periodically over the last thirty-five years to check on my prize. My mother had assured me she had no visitors and the fragment was safe. Even after years of study, I still wasn't sure just how I could use Ellara's bit of soul to break my contract with the Dark Lords.

In the meantime, I dreamed of awakening and harnessing the seeds of darkness that lay deep within Ellara and to use her Goddess powers to further my own interests. Paradoxically, I didn't want to be Grand Master. I wanted freedom. These desires were not congruent with the Droc'ri ambition, and if my Brothers found out, I would be punished and most likely sent prematurely to the Tiarna Drocha to serve my sentence. No one must know.

With the aid of my Skeld, I had been watching Ellara for some time and knew her behaviors quite well. I knew she was emotionally fragile right now after losing her beloved mate. I grimaced. What is the benefit of having such a deep connection with another if the one is almost destroyed when the other willingly sacrifices himself? *I'd never sacrifice myself for anyone!*

Finally, I found the journal and flipped it open to a book-marked page. Pacing around my small room, I read, "After the death of her Far'degan pair'ti, the Healer must soon surrender her heart to the Goddess in healing another or she will die. If the Goddess wills it, the person she heals has a potent force on her affections and can become her next Anam pair'ti."

Thoughtfully, I closed the book and re-shelved it. I wanted to be the one who replaced Sam in her heart. Not Matty or that half-man! I must make her heal me. How, when I'm stuck here in Tokurat and she's in Alba? I could make a portal to Araval, but my magic wasn't strong enough in Alba to make a portal back, *unless I had access to her magic...*

I righted my chair slowly, weighing the odds. *It will take too long. Judging by how easily she cast out the Kurat spirit, she's stronger than she looks.* It would take two weeks to get back to Tokurat if I was unsuccessful, and Garrick was sure to investigate. *I can't let Garrick know how important Ellara is, and I can't get away right now.* I would have to rely upon Jack, Camila's hex, and perhaps Felicity. I hadn't heard from Felicity on how the events at the Council had proceeded. I'd be meeting with her soon.

I sat and drummed my fingers on the arms of my chair. *What do I do about the* Lovely Lady?

I had never liked Matty. From the beginning, he was politely hostile towards me and overly protective of the crippled boy. Matty seemed to know I manipulated Thaddeus and argued against the bargain I made with the youth that bestowed upon him a measure of functionality and the captaincy of the *Lovely Lady* — in exchange for his lifelong service. I had overheard Matty and Sam regularly urging Thaddeus to seek healing with Ellara. Even if Thaddeus had wanted, he was deathly afraid of the consequences if he ever attempted it. I had made sure of that. I shook my head. Sam was out of the picture, but Matty was still a threat. He had too much influence over the captain and Ellara.

I rocked onto the back legs of my chair, musing: the sea is a dangerous place, claiming many a ship and lives. How about a nice long journey to the treacherous waters of the northern lands of the Inyua, and maybe an encounter with Thaddeus's nemesis, Bruce the Terrible? That should give me time to complete my tasks here, steal Felicity's meager Goddess magic so I can go to Alba and get Ellara to heal me and entrap her spirit. I stroked my chin. *I wonder how well his little ship can weather a massive storm at sea?* I smiled, summoned my imp, and gave him instructions for Lord Garth's Droc'ri on board the *Lovely Lady*.

TWENTY-FOUR

ELLARA AND JACK

Araval, Alba

L it sconces in the corners of the bathing chamber at the Red Rose cast a soft glow on the mosaic-tiled walls. Immersed in warm water scented with rose oil, I let the peaceful atmosphere settle about me. I leaned against the sloped wall of the tub, stretching out my legs. I closed my eyes, sweeping my fingers back and forth, creating soft currents to caress my body. I could almost imagine myself in the womb of the Goddess.

I struggled to reclaim the certainty with which I had entered Araval just hours ago. I felt ungrounded and off-kilter. My rocky meeting with Thaddeus, along with the encounter with the sorcerer, reminded me I was very alone, now that Sam was gone. The captain had stolen into my awareness. Even now, as he sailed out to sea, his presence clung to me as if I were a lifeline that kept him afloat. I wanted to help him, but I also knew he would distract me from my mission in Araval.

What about Matty? The sound of his voice had reminded me of when Sam and I had stood on the *M'Ellara's* deck and watched him call orders to his crew to tie up or cast off. What made Thaddeus think he could replace Sam? Or Matty? I barely knew the man. Yet, I felt strangely drawn to the captain. What he longed for reminded me of what I had lost with Sam.

Camila's accusations stole into my mind. I had to admit, when it came to using my talent, Camila had rattled my confidence. Her destructive words, uttered from her position of power, made me feel sorely inadequate. I had mostly put her jinx aside, but now I questioned if I had it in me to do what Thaddeus needed to be fully restored, not only in his body, but to clear the effects of the sorcerer's cruel indoctrination.

I was glad they were out to sea, since that delayed any decision I'd have to make regarding either Matty or Thaddeus. I asked the Goddess to bless the captain. His fate lay in what he chose next.

The bath refreshed my body and calmed my mind. The parlor was empty when I crossed. As I neared the entrance, a tall, lean young man with light-brown curly hair fell in beside me. I would have ignored him, but he caught my hand. When he spoke, his voice was smooth and kindly.

"Let me apologize for my behavior earlier today. It was very disrespectful."

I gaped at him, recognizing the unkempt bread thief. "Jack?" He wore an expensive woolen jacket over a white shirt with frilled cuffs and collar. He smelled of cologne. The pitch of his voice had lowered, and there was a measured cadence and deliberate choice to his words.

He dug into a coat pocket. "Here are the two gold hektes you asked for." He lifted my hand and held it while he dropped them, one by one, into my palm. I stared at the coins in the hand that he still held, then at him. In a trick of light, his appearance shifted to become a magnificent, auburn-haired man, who smiled invitingly at me through the visage of the adoring face before me. I squeezed my eyes shut, certain I was hallucinating from lack of sleep.

"Thank you, Jack," I muttered, pulling my hand away. "I'm really tired and must get back to Nana's."

"I'll escort you, and protect you from the soldiers."

I shook my head. My return from the port via a shorter route had included several detours to avoid Lord Garth's mercenaries. I could slip between the shadows. I didn't want some lanky oaf to slow me down. "I am fine, Jack. It's late. You need to sleep."

"I insist. It's not safe for a woman alone at night."

As we traversed the blocks back to Nana's bakery, Jack tried to engage me in conversation. I responded with monosyllables. He rambled on about times when he had lived in the Desert Lands. The more he talked, the more I craved silence. His behavior had changed, but he still had the black shadow that smothered his aura. And he didn't seem genuine.

"You are in great danger. Let me protect you." When I shook my head, he continued, "Araval is filled with dangerous people who would capture and kill you for who you are. Like that captain you met earlier today. I know. I've been looking for you for weeks and so has he, although he tried to disguise it. He works for the Droc'ri Grand Master and aims to capture you for a generous reward. But before he turns you over to the Grand Master, he wants to take you away on his ship to his private hideout where he can torture you and force you to give him your special powers." He gripped my arm. "I know. The captain is a master of illusion and his victims open their hearts to him." He stopped and stood before me. "I will be your bodyguard. As a trained assassin, I will prevent the captain or any like him from harming you."

I frowned. "What do you know about me or the captain?"

"I know everything about you! Like I said, I've been looking for you for a very long time. That captain means to do you harm."

His groomed words repelled me, and I wanted to be away from him. I politely wished him a good night and slipped into Nana's warm cottage. Dropping the cloth sack on the floor, I settled onto the mat. I hoped a good night's sleep would clear my head and let me sort out what to do with Jack and Thaddeus.

But I couldn't sleep. Jack's words made me angry. *Who does he think he is, claiming he knows everything about me and who or what's good for me?* I don't know much about Thaddeus, except for Sam's kind words about the crippled captain. I had trusted Sam's judgment, even when I didn't know his reasoning. The Goddess had cleared the shadow from the captain. She didn't choose to clear the darkness from Jack. *There is another presence around Jack. If anything, he is the agent of the Droc'ri.* But Thaddeus had been controlled by a sorcerer... Rokan, Thaddeus had called the Droc'ri.

Sam had confided that he would never have made the bargain Thaddeus did with a Droc'ri. Getting limited mobility, making the ship profitable, and its captain wealthy was not worth the price of his soul. Sam said the younger captain was a good man at heart, and a victim of tragic circumstances. There was a lot I didn't know about the captain. I needed to talk with Matty. I respected the old helmsman.

My desires and fears warred with each other. I had to find my way through the jumbled forces that tugged me in multiple directions. Reestablishing my connection with the Goddess would guide me to the truth. But sadness still filled the empty spaces in my heart, making me reluctant to heal anyone. Sam was gone. I was alone. I had to rely upon my wits and find my own rock in a stormy sea.

Finally, I fell asleep, to dreams filled with ugly creatures chasing me. Towards morning, I dreamed of Thaddeus. In the dream, he paced the small confines of his cabin, holding a picture of me. I could hear his thoughts. *She's unlocked feel-*

ings I had long buried. I want to fulfill my promise to Sam and be worthy of her so she will choose me for her pair'ti. I can't let Jack know. He'll relay it to his master. How can I break free of the contract with Rokan so I can be with Ellara, without him finding out and punishing me? The farther out to sea we go, the chances of getting her cooperation get slimmer. I should have let Matty make the run without me. But I don't know what Rokan would do to my ship and crew or me.

The scene in the dream changed. His ship sailed in the middle of the ocean and a massive storm bore down upon it. Waves washed over the sides, rolling the vessel precariously. Thaddeus called to Matty, "The Droc'ri has cursed me. We have to hide from the storm."

Matty called back, "Deadman's Reef." Darkness closed around the ship and its crew. Not the darkness of night, but an evil shadow that took the form of a giant hand reaching for the *Lovely Lady* to crush between its fingers.

I awoke panting and shivering from the icy water that had threatened to drown me. A glow from the banked coals in the hearth faintly illuminated the room. The aroma of dough penetrated my awareness and I sighed, lying back onto my mat. I stared at the ceiling, still caught in the residue of the dream. I typically dreamed a lot, and occasionally had dreams that felt so real that when I awoke, I thought I had actually been there. After one about Sam being attacked by pirates, and the next day having a close encounter with Bruce the Terrible, I realized these dreams were warnings.

Tentatively, I reached with my Far Sight for a glimpse of Thaddeus. He sat at his chart table, alternately staring between a bottle of rum, a drawing of me, and navigation charts. Resting on top of the maps was the chain and pendant that Sam had worn ever since we had become a couple. A Heartland smith, who was a Mage strong in earth magic, had formed the Goddess knot. Nana and I had imprinted it with the Goddess's protection. Before I gave it to Sam, I had summoned the Goddess's Gra'yia and poured all the love I felt for him into the amulet. It was my heartfelt gift to Sam. It did more than protect him. It had given him the strength to endure.

Tears stung my eyes. Sam knew he was returning to Sheldon to die. That was the only possible explanation for why he would have given it and the picture of me he carried over his heart to Matty. Or had he chosen Thaddeus without telling me? I wished I had known. Was this the Goddess's idea of a change of the watch, with Sam handing over the tiller to his successor? Sam may have chosen to die, but I didn't want that fate for Thaddeus, even if he was a stranger. Not if I could help it.

I reached again with my Far Sight. When Thaddeus felt my spirit touch him, he looked toward me. *"A storm's coming that will destroy you and your ship."* I sent him the image. *"Seek shelter."* I didn't know if he heard my message or not. We did not share a telepathic connection, as I had had with Sam. However, he grabbed his navigation instruments and headed on deck.

Next morning, as we set out the first loaves for the waiting customers, Jack arrived, impeccably dressed and bearing gifts. I watched from the doorway as he helped Nana's patrons pack their purchases into baskets and even offered to carry them back to their homes.

After one such departure, I questioned Nana, "Is this the same man that was so rude to me and stole from you yesterday?"

She shook her head. "He seems the same, but this is a novel one for me, Child." She winked at me. "Maybe he is trying to woo you. After all, you are quite enchanting, even if you disguise your feminine charms by wearing men's clothing."

I grimaced. "People don't transform overnight, at least not in my experience. Not unless they have undergone a healing or some sort of divine intervention."

"You'd be the one to know about that, Child. Maybe you have inspired him to turn over a new leaf. Just like the young captain has."

"Huh? I don't have that sort of power to transform people. If I did, I'd get rid of these laws and restore peace and harmony in Alba."

Nana shoved loaves into the oven, laughing. "The Goddess radiates from you, even when you have not called Her. People are affected simply by being in your presence. You are more influential than you give yourself credit for. Be chary about how you choose to use your talent and with whom you choose to share it."

I gave her a puzzled look. "What is that supposed to mean?" But Nana acted as if she had not heard me. I returned to kneading, muttering, "He wants something from me. I know it."

Jack returned with a roasted leg of lamb and a clay bowl filled with a fresh vegetable stew. From a basket, he pulled something wrapped in baker's cloth. "Here. I thought you might like a proper meal after your long journey from Sheldon, and a pasty to remind you of Nana Magog."

I stiffened. Had I said anything about where I was from? However, the lamb and vegetable pasty in an oat crust smelled delicious.

"Thank you, Jack. What makes you think I'm from Sheldon? And how do you know of Nana Magog's pasties?" I watched him closely. Head forward, his mannerisms were buoyant and quick, and he spoke in a high, tenor voice. At the moment, I determined he was Jack, the thief.

"I've been following your progress for years."

"For what purpose?"

Jack faltered. "I don't know. I just have been."

I cleared a place at the edge of our bread-making table and invited Jack to join us. It seemed the right thing to do, since he had produced the meal. After we had eaten, he drew from inside his coat a carved wooden rose and handed it to me.

"I made this for you."

Each thin petal was perfectly formed. Even the stem was slightly curved and had tiny thorns. If it had been painted, it would have looked like a real rose. "It's beautiful, Jack! The craftsmanship is exquisite!"

"You like it?"

"Yes. But I can't accept this from you. I am not able to return your favor. You have paid Nana for all the bread you stole and brought us food and helped her customers. You've already done a lot for us. We are in your debt."

He beamed and looked at me ardently. His voice dropped an octave and his back straightened. "I've been waiting for you for a long time. You are in great danger. I want to protect you and win your heart. I want you for my pair'ti."

My jaw dropped at this bold admission.

"I'm sorry, Jack, but my heart is in no condition to be had by anyone. Please don't pursue me. I will just disappoint you."

For an instant, a murky cloud passed over his visage. It lifted immediately and his charm was back. "I'll help you any way I can until you are ready to be my mate. And remember the words I spoke last night, of protecting you from those that would harm you. I am your protector. You are safe with me."

I tightened my jaw, keeping my thoughts to myself for the time being. I set the rose carving down at the edge of the table, and threw myself into making a new batch of loaves for the afternoon customers. Jack stayed all afternoon, regaling us with stories of his travels. I listened for clues to his claims about knowing me. It became obvious that Jack, the thief, knew very little about Sheldon, what I actually did, or who my pair'ti had been. But the alter personality, who spoke through Jack, was well versed in my history. To have someone spying upon me my whole life left an unpalatable taste in my mouth. Was this the sorcerer that Nana Magog and my mother had warned me of? What was the sorcerer's agenda?

Jack finally made ready to depart that evening. The wind rustled papers and awnings. A spring storm was coming. He grabbed my hand and lifted it to brush my fingers with his lips. For an instant, Jack's appearance shifted and an older man stood before me, then the image was gone.

I closed the door and leaned against it, squeezing my eyes closed, and took a few deep breaths. *A sorcerer has to be using Jack. He must be very powerful, indeed, to be able to speak and show himself through Jack's form.*

TWENTY-FIVE

ROKAN AND FELICITY

Tokurat, The Desert Lands

I yawned and stretched. I concentrated on the sounds of Tokurat outside my small abode, waiting for the disorientation to pass.

Merging with Jack exhausted me. Even though the man had learned to emulate many of my behaviors, he was still the lazy, undisciplined youth who had failed the Assassins' Guild. It took single-minded effort to see through his eyes and speak with his voice. However, it had been worth it. For the first time in years, I was actually able to see Ellara. Like her daughter, her aura was protected and I couldn't read it.

It irked me that Ellara had rejected the rose I had Jack carve for her. Like I had done with other women, I had hoped to entrap her with an attraction spell that would draw her to me.

But she had sold it to one of Nana's customers when Jack wasn't looking!

Nonetheless, I rose from my cot, feeling satisfied with myself. I had not undertaken a possession of this magnitude before. Now, I needed to feed and replenish myself. I sat on the edge of my bed and contemplated my options. Sophia could not supply what I needed. I could harvest the life force from random citizens, but that seemed too crude. *I'm not a vampire!* My mind strayed to Margot and her friends. I smiled. Now there was a meal! — albeit risky. I imagined what the untrained Healers' vitality would do for me, then settled on using Jack again. He would be a willing agent in this activity.

I lay back and, through the energetic implant I had placed in Jack's unconscious mind, nudged him to hire a half-dozen robust women for his pleasure. While he engaged in sexual pursuits, I fed from each woman, taking more of their vitality than I would have from Sophia. One by one, the ladies collapsed on the bed in Jack's room, asleep. Finally, Jack slept. Now I was free to meet with Felicity.

I paced impatiently along the bluff north of the Langon harbor, tugging my cloak more tightly around me to keep out the chill wind. *She's late. Again.*

I had tasked Felicity with making a list of all the Healers who had gathered and notations of where they were from. The last time Felicity had come with her mentor, Leisel, she had confided that she had not completed it yet. At least I had gotten to feed on Felicity's life force, so the clandestine encounter had not been completely fruitless. I hoped Felicity would come tonight. If they ever showed up!

A whiff of cedar smoke from the Sacred Grove fires alerted me to Leisel's arrival. She marched up to me and said tersely, "I have fulfilled my obligation to you, Rokan. Do not ask me to do any more of your unholy tasks." She turned away, immediately forming a doorway in the air to return to the Sacred Grove. Before she stepped through, Felicity dodged past her and ran to me. Leisel scowled at the younger woman, then addressed me. "I no longer accept Felicity as my apprentice. Find another to mentor her." She disappeared through the portal and it snapped shut behind her.

I shrugged. Leisel had dragged her feet when I asked her to sponsor Felicity at the Council assemblage so the initiate could receive the Council's blessing of Healer. But the old Healer had played her part, and I didn't need her anymore.

Felicity threw her arms around me, kissing me passionately. "I received the Goddess's blessing from the Council. Now you can finish training me."

"That's excellent news, Felicity." No other Droc'ri had trained an apprentice to pass the rigorous tests of the Council and receive the Council's blessing. Of course, Camila had something to do with that. What I did was extremely risky and forbidden by the Droc'ri Code. However, Felicity foolishly loved me and that clouded any ethical or moral considerations about her use of the Goddess's Gra'yia. With her new title of Healer, she would make an excellent spy.

"The Council said I need a strong Far'degan. Will you be my pair'ti?"

I laughed. "Don't you want someone more your age to become your mate?"

"No! I love you. You are the most influential Mage I know. You will make me strong, and I can channel the Goddess's energy to do whatever you want."

"I don't think love has to be part of the process of channeling the Goddess's force safely."

She clasped me tightly. "Oh yes, it does. It's what makes the potent magic that the Goddess uses." She pointed to the space where Leisel had walked through the portal. "Will you show me how to make those?"

I held the woman and wondered the best way I could use her. Felicity came from a Goddess-born lineage and had a natural talent, though not nearly as strong as Ellara's. As a merchant's daughter, she had been raised in a strict Natuan religious family and came to the way of the Goddess later in life. Twenty years ago, when Felicity turned twenty, she had tried to seduce Thaddeus to become her pair'ti so as to circumvent becoming the mate of an old merchant her father had picked. Thaddeus had actually considered her invitation. She was that persuasive.

Luckily, I had intervened and warned her about Thaddeus's deformity, reminding her about the Natuan teachings of the devil and his evil creatures. She hadn't believed me.

The memory of Thaddeus's disgrace still delighted me. I had been visiting Felicity's father when Thaddeus anchored in the cove offshore of their village. The crew and the merchant's men unloaded an illegal cargo of Heartland-forged weapons and an array of handmade cabinets and quality jewelry for Felicity's father. As the broker for the contraband, I split the extra profit created by avoiding the steep import taxes. I also took a modest commission for locating buyers, again, adding to my wealth.

Thaddeus had come ashore to see Felicity, who took him to an unused corner of her father's warehouse. A short while later, we heard a scream and Felicity burst from the building, hastily buttoning her bodice.

She ran into my arms, screaming incoherently. She exclaimed, "Thaddeus is the spawn of the devil! He tried to cast his evil upon me! He tried to steal my soul and impregnate me with evil beasts."

"Where is the creature?" her father growled, picking up a stout staff.

Felicity pointed. "In the warehouse."

Her father had stormed out of his office. Felicity clung to me as she relayed what happened.

She had said, "When I first saw the captain, I could see he wanted someone to love. I thought he would serve me better as a mate than the antiquated merchant my father had picked. Yet he held back. I thought I would convince him with a passionate tryst. When I saw his torso completely covered with scars, I remembered your warning." She had flushed. In a whisper, she said, "When he revealed his manhood... It was horrible!" She patted herself and looked pleadingly at me. "I'm not cursed, am I?"

I shook my head. "You got away before he could do anything to you."

She leaned against me. "You were right, Rokan. I should have listened to you."

Shouts and curses passed by the office windows as Thaddeus beat a hasty retreat to his ship. With shirt half-buttoned, and coat billowing behind, he had commandeered two long staves. Wedging them under his arms, he used them like crutches to propel himself forward in giant leaps, touching down only to launch himself onward. Every time I thought of the scene, I chuckled inwardly. Felicity had shamed Thaddeus, renewing my control over him. And she had become a loyal lover ever after.

Out of favor with her father, Felicity had been sent from her home near Langon to Zambril, to become the mate of her father's friend. After five years and two children, her mate met with a fatal accident. She returned to her father's home with her children and helped him in his business.

It was only a few years ago that I hit upon the idea of training Felicity to be a Healer. I had awakened the inner gates within her so that she could access her magical abilities. I sent Felicity to study with Leisel, a local Healer who didn't want known some very personal secrets. Leisel had never approved, but she reluctantly complied. She took on Felicity as an apprentice and sponsored her at the Council gathering.

I ran my hand along the silky strands of Felicity's hair. I could give the woman the protection she needed without becoming her pair'ti. On the other hand, if I went through the ritual, I would have access to what little ability she wielded and I could use it to freely come and go in Alba. But she would know I wasn't a Mage of the Goddess, like I led her to believe. And she would discover my secrets. I had systematically killed anyone who learned of them.

"Let me give you what you need so that you can get started on your training. Then we can plan the ritual needed to formalize our arrangement."

"Will you show me how to do what you do?"

"Yes. I will teach you my magic as well as how to summon the Goddess."

She kissed me again. "We'll make such a great team, won't we?"

"I hope so," I said. I removed her arms and placed a hand on her back. We walked toward the small village near Langon that she called home. "Tell me about the Council meeting. Do you have the list?"

She laughed, pulling a scrap of paper from her bosom. "Those old crones argue all day and never get anything accomplished. They want to recreate the Triunes. If I have a strong pair'ti, I can be in a Triune." She turned to me, handing me the list, which I scanned quickly and tucked safely away. "Have I pleased you, Rokan?" she asked enthusiastically.

"Yes, Felicity. I am very pleased." That she wanted me to return her love was annoying. I'd have to create another spell to make her think I loved her. I pulled from my pocket one of the thin books on the Goddess's teachings. "Here. Read this. When I return, we will discuss the wisdom it contains. How did you do with the other task I assigned you?"

Felicity leaped astride me, kissing me passionately. "Nana Magog's untrained apprentice is a disgrace to the Healers! Nana Magog called for the Rite of Dushlan. What is that? Is it some sort of contest?"

I laughed. "That sounds like something Nana Magog would do." *What was the old witch up to?* "It challenges the Doyen's decision, and the person in question must play out their life memories for the Council to witness. The challenger hopes for a more favorable outcome."

Felicity sniggered. "She failed miserably. In fact, not only was Ellara denied the Council's blessing, Doyen Camila said she was cursed and forbade her from using magic, and especially from healing anyone. Camila tried to strip Ellara of her powers, but Ellara fought back. Camila was furious and banned her. Then the woman had the audacity to claim she knew how to solve the Droc'ri incursion."

Camila had done just as I expected. "You performed masterfully, Felicity." *I wish I had been training Ellara instead of this witless, love-struck woman. I wish Ellara would serve me as willingly as this one does.*

"Doyen Camila said Ellara held a piece of a Droc'ri sorcerer's soul. That's bad, isn't it?"

I frowned. "Yes. Did she say whose?"

Felicity shook her head. "If she knew, she wasn't saying, and I couldn't see the memories that the Council witnessed. Who do you think it is?"

Was Nana trying to expose me to the Council? I can't let anyone know I am the one Ellara exchanged soul pieces with. If Garrick found out... My mind raced. Camila answered to Garrick as well as to me. What if she revealed this knowledge to him as a way to settle a score with me? Garrick would kill me — and Ellara for sure.

I pretended to enjoy Felicity's company as I escorted her to the rooms above her father's warehouse. After getting her settled and feeding from her, I quickly returned to Tokurat. It would be morning soon. Felicity's life force would be enough to get me through the coming day without the need to sleep. I rushed to my underground sanctuary, already shifting my thoughts to Ellara and how to capture her before Garrick discovered my secret. Jack could gather the information I needed about what she liked and where she was vulnerable. I sat in contemplation. Who would protect Ellara until I could get to Alba? How could I trap her? Could Jack win her affection? If she heals him, I can capture her spirit...

TWENTY-SIX

ELLARA AT THE BAKERY

Araval, Alba

The next day Jack came to attend me. That's what Nana Bean laughingly called the way he hovered around me. His charm was as tailored as the fine clothes he wore. Now that I had attuned my awareness to him, I saw not only a lanky young man, but the vaporous image of a strapping gentleman. He seemed vaguely familiar, but I was not about to reach out with my inner sight to get a clearer look. The invisible one watched me with keen interest. Most of the words that flowed from Jack's mouth were those of the older man. I pretended not to notice Jack's dual personalities.

After a couple of hours of Jack and his master trying to convince me of the danger I was in, of how I needed his protection from people like the captain or his helmsman, as well as the dangerous Natuan clerics, I had had enough.

"Leave, Jack. I have work to do." I turned my back on him and focused on the task of creating edible works of art from the sourdough.

Jack, or rather, his master, was not so easily dismissed. Jack stood beside me where I worked. "Come with me. I know of a place of safety in the mountains east of Langon. A Temple that your daughter and her friends have rebuilt. There is plenty of food and the place is sacred to the Goddess." He touched my arm. "Let's find a ship and leave now."

The pressure of the master's will, veiled by carefully chosen words, enhanced the discordant energy that swirled around Jack and, by association, me. I figured the unspoken intention was to put me off of Thaddeus or of seeking Matty. The more he pressed, the more I resisted and, quite unintentionally, found myself championing Thaddeus in my mind.

"It is unsafe for you to use your healing talents in your current state of grieving."

I rounded on him. "You don't have any right to tell me what I can and cannot do. You continually warn me of strangers who want to charm me, kidnap me, and take me away. You use your captain friend as an example. Why should I trust you when you twist your words so that I am deceived and confused? You are a complete stranger to me. Moreover, you have no respect when I ask you to leave." I planted a hand on his chest and pushed, marching him backwards out of the bakery. Hastily, I closed the door after him. I leaned against the door, panting. *I absolutely will not become the pair'ti to that man or the man who speaks through him! I can't stand either of them!*

Jack did not leave. Instead, he talked with Nana and her customers. The sound of his voice was like an unrelenting mosquito. I finished what I had started and retreated to the back garden. I sat amid the herbs, trying to collect myself. But the dissonance from Jack and the fear-laced thought forms he had woven around me would not allow me to find peace. Whoever said the Droc'ri magic didn't work in Alba had overlooked the subtler forms of mind manipulation!

Frustrated, I climbed over the back wall and trotted down the alley, made several turns, and came to an apothecary owned by one of Nana Bean's friends. I looked over my shoulder and ducked into the shop. The woman who had assisted me on the street after taking on Thaddeus's pain came from a back room and greeted me. Without a word, she beckoned me through the curtain and into her living quarters. She motioned for me to sit, then rummaged among an array of bottles sitting upon a table.

"I just made this."

She handed me a vial. I removed the stopper and sniffed. It had an earthy-sweet smell. Immediately, my head cleared. "What is it?"

"Vetiver. It will remind you of your roots, so when people like Camila or Jack or others wrap their distorting beliefs around you, you can find your way back to your true self and the Goddess's truth."

I took another sniff. "I could sure use that. How do you know about Camila or Jack?"

The nana laughed. "If one knows how to see, one can see all."

I peered at her. Though the tell-tale triple crescent moons on her forehead were absent, I asked, "You're a retired Healer, aren't you?"

She ignored my question. "This infusion is most effective if you rub it on your feet." She rummaged among bottles on a counter and extracted three more. "Here. Some lavender to restore the harmony between you and the Goddess. Place it on the point of your second sight. And jasmine and rose to heal the grief in your heart."

I took the bottles, inhaled from each one and carefully re-corked them. "Thank you, Nana. What can I give you in exchange?"

The elder shook her head. "Stay alive and fulfill your destiny. That is worth far more to me and the rest of us than a few coins."

The shop doorbell tinkled. A minute later Jack thrust his head through the curtain. "There you are. I've been looking all over for you." Jack lifted his head, sniffing the air. "Ah. It smells good in here. Very herby."

I grimaced as I concealed the vials of herbal oils. I nodded thanks to the nana, pushed past Jack, and exited the shop. *I need to ask the nana for a decoction to get rid of unwanted people in my life,* I thought irritably.

Twilight settled over the city and the rain had stopped. The oils from Nana Bean's friend helped to anchor me amidst the inharmonious whirlwind that Jack and his master tried to create around me. They allowed me to remember that my purpose in coming to Araval was to see the king.

Nana Bean indicated to me that my services were needed for a birthing. Impatiently, I urged Jack and his invisible double to leave, but he lingered at the door. Jack reached for my hand. I snatched it away. "Go entertain yourself at the Red Rose, Jack. I've had a long day and cannot listen to another of your stories. I need to be alone."

"Promise me you won't go out." He leaned towards me.

"Go on, Jack. I will be fine. I don't need your services."

Finally, he left. He glanced back, then walked away, a spring in his step. I scowled after him.

I closed the door and performed a quick purification ritual before grabbing my medicine kit. After cracking open the door and scanning up and down the street, I slipped out. I ran lightly down the damp cobblestones and around the corner, trotted a couple of blocks, and stopped at a house. I knocked and was immediately admitted.

It took several hours for the birthing and all went seamlessly. I was relieved that I didn't need to call upon the Goddess for Her assistance. Jack had warned me over and over how dangerous it was for Healers in Araval. This was one area where I heeded his warning. I emerged onto the quiet street, waited for my eyes to adjust to the dim light, and started back towards the bakery.

"Ellara."

I stopped.

"It's me." Thaddeus caught my hand, pulling me towards him.

"Thaddeus? I thought you had to take the Droc'ri somewhere and would be gone for a long while."

"I did. I was supposed to take him far north to the lands of the Inyua. It would have been weeks before I could have returned. Then the storm came up and I decided to return to you." He shook his head. "I must be mad to have braved such a wild sea," he muttered to himself.

I quieted, receiving from the man who leaned against the wall holding my hand, and felt his pain in my body. "You're injured."

Thaddeus grinned crookedly. "It wasn't easy to return to you."

"Come." I drew his arm across my shoulder and supported him to the bakery, where I deposited him in a straight-backed wooden chair. Lamplight revealed the full extent of his battered head and hands, which explained what I had felt in my body.

Deftly, I untied the strip of cloth around his head that showed several fresh bloodied cuts and ran my fingers lightly across his skull, gently peeling the matted hair from the gashes in his scalp. I lightly dragged my fingers down his neck, across his shoulders, down his arms and to his hands, which I turned over and inspected. I moved to where I could scan his back and chest, then continued down his legs. Images of his return to Araval flowed through my inner vision as I scanned him. I noticed he wore Sam's protective pendant, which I believed is what had allowed him to survive.

I stood back and asked, "What made you risk your life against the rocks in a storm-driven surf, to swim ashore and almost die from chill, then slog through the squalls all the way to Araval? You can't possibly care so much about me after our brief encounter at the Red Rose to disregard the spells and bindings that the sorcerer has imprinted into your nervous system. They will return you to a crippled state or worse, kill you, if you seek healing with me." I rummaged in my bag for a jar of salve.

Thaddeus blushed. "You're in great danger. I want to take you somewhere where you will be safe."

I eyed him. "There is nowhere safe in our current world. However, Jack said it was too dangerous for me in Araval as well. He wanted to whisk me away to safety somewhere in the Emerald Mountains. What is so important that you risk your life to get back here?"

"Has Jack been around?"

I nodded and continued with my task.

"What did he want?"

"To become my protector, pair'ti, and who knows what else. And generally, be a nuisance."

Thaddeus winced as I applied ointment to the lacerations on his forehead. "Jack is not who he pretends to be."

"What makes you say that?"

Thaddeus considered before he answered. "He is a Droc'ri Katz-paw."

"What is a Katz-paw?"

"He is an agent, a spy, for a sorcerer."

"I suspected something like that. What's he doing in Alba?"

"That is what I was trying to find out." Thaddeus frowned and looked into my face. "You are in great danger. So am I."

"What is this great danger to which Jack and you allude?"

Thaddeus remained quiet while I applied ointment to cuts on his hands and forearms. Finally, he continued softly, "It's a gut feeling. You have enemies here in Araval."

"Who?" When he didn't answer, I continued testily, "And where is it safe for me?" Why were both men so vague? What were the real reasons behind their concern?

Thaddeus shook his head, worry deepening the lines on his face. "There is nowhere safe for you, Ellara."

I finished tending Thaddeus's wounds, and with my hand resting on his shoulder, paused to listen with my inner awareness. Thaddeus drank in the vitality that flowed through me as if it was balm for his soul. With my second sight, I witnessed life force cascade throughout his body and purge his pain. I started to remove my hand, but he set his over mine, holding it in place. I let him draw more energy through me.

He shuffled his feet, scanned the room nervously, and lowered his voice. "When we first met... the Kurat entity made... your touch excruciatingly painful. I regret treating you so cruelly. Will you forgive my actions? Can we start over?"

I cocked my head. "What do you want to start?"

Thaddeus looked away. Color stole onto his cheeks. "I trusted Sam. He was an honorable man and never have I known him to cheat or deceive anyone in any of his dealings. Sam bestowed upon me a great honor when he asked me to protect you. He said you could free me from the Droc'ri curse. He was right. You have. I mean to fulfill my pledge to the best of my abilities, despite the sorcerer who would kill both of us, if he found out." He looked as if he wanted to say more, but he held back.

I regarded Thaddeus, as he did me. Even though the shadow had been removed from his energy field, the remnants of the hex and attendant fear of me lingered about him.

I stood back, surveying my handiwork. I wrapped the cloth around his head and wiped my hands. His back had been injured and his vitality was severely depleted. He needed more restorative work, but I was reluctant to invite him to ask for it. I suspected that if I summoned the Goddess's healing grace, Thaddeus would risk all to regain full health, despite the consequences he would face from Rokan.

"Matty and Sam invited you to come to me many times. I would have done what I could for you. Why didn't you?"

Thaddeus glanced away. "Rokan said if I sought healing, I would revert to the paralyzed state I was in before he gave me some mobility. I didn't want that. So I stayed away."

I nodded slowly. "That's why you refused to join Sam, Matty, and me in the pub in Langon after we salvaged your lost crates? And why you always stayed in the shadows on your ship?"

Thaddeus nodded. "Just being near you awakened his jinx and my legs would turn to oakum."

"When I saw you last, you hobbled around with a cane. Who healed you?"

Thaddeus blushed. "Sam. And you. Indirectly." He stared at the floor. Quietly, he continued, "Sam told Matty how you massaged his back so he could walk easier. He gave me your picture and his amulet, saying they are what kept him alive and healthy. At first, I couldn't touch them — when I did, the Kurat spirit drained me." He sighed. "I was determined to honor Sam's request, and Matty massaged my back every day, morning and night." He smiled. "It worked. Here I am."

"How did you get the role Sam had asked of Matty?"

"Before Sam died a few weeks ago, I was commissioned by Lord Sengy to transport a witch to Araval. I didn't know it was you until I met Sam outside Sheldon. He was frantic. He asked me to become his replacement. He... knew I — cared about you."

I sighed. "That sounds like something Sam would do." I bit my lip, holding back the sadness that welled up in my heart. "I miss Sam terribly."

He touched my hand. "I know. I'm not Sam but let me do what I can for you."

I turned away, hiding my tears and the lump in my throat. I replaced the lid on my jar of ointment and stowed it in my medicine kit. "What's done is done. I am sure the Goddess has Her reasons for Sam asking you." My mind turned to the Droc'ri I had seen in Thaddeus's aura and who had been with Margot. That the sorcerer pursued Margot unsettled me and I worried about her safety. "I do not know this sorcerer that controls you, hunts me, and pursues Margot. There is much to discover about how to thwart him."

"Perhaps we can work together to defeat him?" He watched me hopefully.

I chewed my lip. I had no idea how to gain the upper hand over any Droc'ri, and especially this one, despite Nana Magog's hints. Silence settled over the room, disturbed only by Nana Bean's soft snore.

"It's late. I should go." Thaddeus struggled to his feet, holding the chair until his legs steadied under him. He shuffled stiffly towards the door, looked longingly at the empty sleeping mat, and back at me with the ghost of a smile.

"Just a minute." I reached behind my neck to unclasp a chain threaded through a golden disc, inlaid with multicolored gemstones shaped into a spiral. Protective glyphs were engraved around the edge. "I found this in my pocket after you left with Hadlan. It's lovely, but I cannot accept this from you. It obligates me to you and I cannot be indebted to anyone right now."

His hands stopped my fingers. "It's a gift to atone for my uncivilized behavior. The talisman will protect you. No strings attached. I promise."

I tilted my head to meet his gaze, keenly aware of his arms around my shoulders and the heat of his desire. Longing warred with trepidation of what would befall him if he succumbed to it. "Thank you for tending my wounds." He quickly removed his hands from mine and slipped out the door.

TWENTY-SEVEN

ROKAN AND GARRICK

Tokurat, The Desert Lands

I halted abruptly at the entrance to my private study beneath the Suzerain's palace. To an ordinary onlooker, the room appeared untouched. My desk remained as I had left it, bare except for a stack of newly acquired books lining one side. The bookshelf appeared the same, as did the row of talismans that I used for various magical purposes. But someone had penetrated my protective barrier and had been in the room. *Garrick!* I thought sourly. *He's the only one who would know how to break my wards.*

I moved to the center of the room and stood still, assessing what was missing or had been disturbed. At a movement behind me, I spun around, hand raised ready to defend myself. "Master!" I lowered my hand. "What brings you here?"

The shorter man surveyed the room. "I just wanted to see if you had any new instruments or talismans." He presented himself as a picture of friendliness.

I tensed. I had grown up with Garrick, and we had had an ongoing, very one-sided rivalry, always ending in Garrick's favor. Since he had become Grand Master of the Droc'ri five years ago, I had been careful not to engage in any displays that could be interpreted as threatening by the Grand Master.

Garrick moved around the small room, stopping to stroke my arm.

I pretended to like his advances and smiled at the wiry man.

"You look so youthful for being over two hundred years old," Garrick said. He leaned closer. "You *must* tell me your secret."

"You don't look so bad yourself, Master," I lied. Fine lines etched Garrick's pallid skin. I moved to my desk. "It must be our good life that keeps us young and vigorous, Master."

Garrick gave a reedy laugh. "I think it's the food we eat." His fingers drifted along my back. "You still like the ladies?"

"Of course, Master. And the men." I smiled invitingly at the Grand Master. I would not mind stealing some of Garrick's life force, for a change. "Women are more satiating, though." *What does he really want?*

"I don't waste my time with mating anymore. When I partake of pleasure, I harvest the vitality from a young servant." His thin lips curved into a cruel smile. "You waste too much time with the ladies and don't tend to your duties like you should."

"Where have I been remiss, Master?"

"Where are the Gra'bandia Healers you promised me?" His friendly voice turned cold. "I'm running out of time and patience."

"I brought you some Healers recently. You know we can only find them when they use their magic. They are in hiding and it takes time to flush them out."

Garrick snorted. "None of them are who I am looking for. There is a large gathering at Cuilithe. Why haven't you captured them and delivered them to me?"

"You know we can't just storm the Heartland."

"We may not. But what of those that have pledged to serve us?" Garrick jabbed a finger at me. "See, you have been remiss in your duties. You should be plotting a way to capture these Goddess worshippers."

I bowed my head. "I am not nearly as clever as you, Master. I have people gathering the Healers' names as we speak. What else do you want me to do?" This wasn't the real reason he was here.

The slender man shrugged and sauntered around the small space. "You're my Henchman. Think of something. By the way." The Grand Master dipped his hand into a fold in his robe and pulled out two thin books. He held them up for me to see. "What's this? Why do you have books on the teachings of the Goddess?" His tone returned to its former silky, silent menace. "You disappoint me, Rokan. You have betrayed your oath to our Order. You, of all people." His words trailed off.

I reached for the books. The Grand Master lifted them out of reach. "Master, I'm trying to be cunning like you. I thought that if I knew what the Healers were taught, I could find them more easily, and learn how to capture them."

Our gazes locked. After a minute, I looked down. "I am trying to discover the kind of magic that the untrained Healers used to capture me. Their form of harnessing the Goddess's power still eludes me. I'm sorry if I displeased you, Master. I will prove my loyalty to you."

Garrick smoothed a hand over his bald head. Eventually, he said, "It's not a bad idea. What have you learned?"

"Master, did you know that Healers need to join energies with a mate so that they can harness the intense powers of the Goddess?"

"What of it?"

"The Healer whose mate has been killed will need to choose another Anam pair'ti to Goddess-bond with if she is to continue as a Healer and Voice of the Goddess. Otherwise, she will lose her powers and die."

Garrick waved his arm impatiently. "Why is this important?"

I lowered my voice. "What if you were to become the Healer's next pair'ti?" I hastened on. "The book says that the mate has access to all of the Healer's powers. How would you like to have her powers at your beck and call and, in addition, be able to command her to do whatever you wanted? Think of the weapon she can become for you!"

The Grand Master paused and stroked his chin. "I've thought about binding a Healer to me for just that reason, but they have all been so cantankerous. It was simpler to take their life force." Garrick made a sour face. "Isn't there another way to harness her powers?"

"I'm still researching that, Master."

Garrick waved a hand dismissively. "Find one who can be controlled and bring this Healer to me." He tossed the fragile manuscripts on my desk and exited the small study. "Tame one of those at the Chaste Palace."

"Yes, Master."

I watched him go and, after the swish of Garrick's robes silenced, released my pent-up breath and relaxed. Automatically, I spoke a few words and traced symbols with my fingers to form a protective shield where I could work in private and away from prying eyes. I retrieved the small books and carefully inspected them. They appeared intact and undamaged.

I sat in my comfortable chair and opened one titled, *A Tradition of Love: Teachings of the Goddess*, and started reading. I paused after a few minutes and thoughtfully closed the book. I set it on a side table, and rose.

I summoned my Skeld for my nightly review. It displayed the images it had recorded since the last time I had called it. I wasn't interested in what the leaders of other countries were doing. I carefully watched the scenes the Skeld replayed of Margot and her friends, but I could not make sense of their actions. They descended the mountain of the Crescent Moon to the valley where we had had our skirmish with the Droc'ri, then returned, but didn't appear to be carrying anything. They repeated this over and over. I needed to go to the Temple of the Crescent Moon and see what they were doing.

I studied the images of Ellara and Jack. She had attended a birthing, then she met with Thaddeus and took him back to the bakery where she treated his wounds. At least she appeared to treat him coolly. He had looked cautiously hopeful. From what I could tell, she had not summoned the Goddess to heal him. Not for the first time, I wished I could hear the conversation.

Anger surged through me. *I sent him north. How did he get back? He has to be punished. I must keep her away from the half-man captain who, despite my best efforts, still searches for love.*

I sought out Jack, who was engaged in satisfying his carnal desires. That he ignored my commands further vexed me. I blasted Jack with my rage through the link to him, then watched in satisfaction as Jack finally went in search of Thaddeus with murder in his heart.

Satisfied that Thaddeus would no longer be a thorn in my side, I turned my mind to Cuilithe. Certain members of the gathering were beholden to me. I smiled. Unwittingly, Anya had served me perfectly. So had Felicity. I scanned my talismans, picking up the one that would summon my agent at the Council gathering to meet with me. It was time.

TWENTY-EIGHT

ELLARA AND THADDEUS

Araval

Nana bustled to get the bread in the big brick oven for the first morning patrons. Thaddeus slumped in a chair while I assessed him. Images of a violent fight flowed to me as I scanned him. "What happened? Why were you and Jack fighting?"

"How did you know?"

I raised an eyebrow. "It's in your aura. You were in no condition to be fighting after your ordeal in the storm." A big lump had formed under a laceration on the side of his head. I cleaned the wound. Using my inner sight, I skimmed my fingers across his scalp. Then I slid my hands along his body, arms, and legs to assess other injuries. I positioned myself in front of him and gently held his cranial bones with my fingertips. I would need the help of the Goddess to restore him.

I hesitated. The clerics tolerated a Healer if she dressed wounds, set bones, relaxed tight muscles, or delivered babies. She was allowed to use herbs. But anything that suggested divine intervention, which is what Thaddeus needed, was construed as the work of the devil. It meant certain death to the Healer, after an unpleasant period of imprisonment and torture.

In Sheldon, my patients didn't worry about how I relieved their pain. I knew all my clients, and the new proclamations didn't stop them from summoning me when needed. In Araval, though, I didn't know who was friendly to the Goddess and who wasn't. I had seen clerics strutting down the streets with Lord Garth's soldiers. Nana Bean even had clerics for patrons.

For simple wound tending, I preferred to work with a hand-picked spirit healing team that I invoked to do the restoration work. These spirits had agreed to rebalance the energy fields of my clients, thus aiding in their speedy recovery. For life-threatening injuries or illnesses, I called upon the Goddess and allowed her to work through me. I became a channel of Her Radiant Gra'yia in the healing process. I had frequently directed the Goddess's Love and Light to Sam, and it became effortless.

Nana's warning before we had parted in the Heartland popped into my mind. She had said, "It is your presence as much as your technique that brings results. You glow when you work with a client. And this is what will get you killed if the wrong people witness it. Be selective with whom you do this work."

Each level of healing held a corresponding level of intimacy and exchange of energies with the patient. To heal Thaddeus's wounds, I would have to open my heart to him and the Goddess. Could I do so safely without becoming overwhelmed when his despair merged with my sadness? Would I unwittingly create an avenue for darkness to enter and control me as he had been?

Thaddeus searched my face. "Can you fix the hole from the brick?" He tentatively touched the bloodied gash in his head.

I studied him in turn. He needed the help of the Goddess or he would die. I risked capture if I called the Goddess. I resented being placed in this position, but Nana had taught me a powerful lesson when, as a fledgling Healer, I had refused to tend a cleric because I didn't like his god.

She had refused to let me work with anyone for a month, and when I complained, told me sternly, "We are all creatures of the Goddess. Even the god of the clerics is Her creation, and if you can't honor that simple truth, you have no business being a Healer." I could still hear her biting words in my mind. I sighed. There was no reason to deny Thaddeus access to my talent. But what of the darkness that had been part of him for so long?

I rested a hand on his shoulder. "I need to summon the Goddess to heal your injury. The wound is deep and has put pressure on your brain. If it is not addressed, you could die."

He tried to shake his head, but instead, cried out in pain.

"The creature that entrapped you is gone and your energy field is pure. However, you have been imprinted with a plethora of beliefs that have kept you fearful for many years. I cannot say what will happen when I call the Goddess to heal you. However, your chances of survival are not good, if I do not."

Thaddeus squirmed in the chair, his face blanching as I talked. "He said if I was healed with the Goddess's Gra'yia, I would die," he whispered. "He said his healing and the Goddess's were incompatible."

I stood calmly, patiently awaiting his decision.

He took my hand. "It seems I'll die no matter what I choose. Go ahead."

I closed my eyes, whispered a protective prayer, then drew my hands from in front of my heart to above my head, capturing the essence of the Divine. I swept my arms out and collected the essence of the Earth Mother who governed the physical body and brought the blended energy back to my heart.

I breathed into my heart and it expanded, creating the sacred space for my healing team to work their magic. Then I petitioned the Goddess to restore Thaddeus in the best way to fulfill his highest purpose. I welcomed the embrace of Her

Divine Love and Light, Her Gra'yia, into my being, which then radiated from me, and merged with his energy field. Under my hands, the tension in Thaddeus's body dissolved. The Goddess guided my fingers. In my mind's eye, I saw his fractured skull mend and cranial bones realign, allowing the brain the space it needed to breathe. He drew in a breath and exhaled slowly.

"How do you feel?" I released my hold on his head and let my hands drop.

"My head doesn't hurt." He reached up and felt where a brick had hit him. "It's like it never happened!" He smiled.

I wrapped the cloth over his wound, even though it was completely healed. "I don't want Jack to know what I've done."

"Don't trust him?"

I shook my head.

"So you trust me?"

"You're in the business of secrets. Now let's get to your fractured ribs. This next part won't be so easy. Take off your coat."

He balked. I helped him reluctantly slip out of his overcoat. It was surprisingly heavy. I hefted it and quirked an eyebrow. He started to shrug, wearing an innocent smile, and winced instead. We removed his vest, items in its pockets making it equally weighty, and I pointed to his shirt. "This too."

Coaxing Thaddeus like a skittish foal, he hesitantly allowed me to unbutton his shirt. I paused at Sam's amulet, brushing my fingers across the triple heart. My heart swelled at the memories, and I was grateful that Thaddeus had chosen to accept what protection it afforded. Perhaps that was why he was still alive, now. On another gold chain, a talisman that looked like a silver lightning bolt winked at me.

As I worked down the line of buttons, he sat rigidly, mouth pressed firmly closed. He cringed from the brush of my fingers on his skin. About halfway down, he caught my hand. "Leave the shirt on." His eyes were wide. If he hadn't been suffering, he would have bolted.

"That's fine, Thaddeus. Come." I guided him to Nana's bed, laying him on it so that I could easily reach the injured side when I knelt on the floor. He groaned when the ribs stretched as his spine straightened. I covered him with a blanket. I made him as comfortable as he could be under the circumstances, then slid my hands under the covering, positioning them above and below the injured ribs. I petitioned the Goddess again. The warm embrace of Divine Gra'yia flowed through me. He moaned and writhed, squeezing his eyes shut. I imagined the ribs solid and aligned. I slid my hands under his back and let my fingertips press against the contracted muscles along his spine. In a few minutes, the large muscles released, and the rib connections to the vertebrae gently aligned. "Breathe, Thaddeus. Take deep breaths."

His first breaths were short and ragged. As the muscles lengthened and bones aligned, he drew in full breaths without
restriction.

I sat on the edge of the bed and gazed upon him through the
compassionate eyes of the Goddess. The taut expression on
his face was gone. He stretched, reaching over his head.

"How do you feel?"

"Tender but functional." He sat up and picked up my hand,
brought it to his lips, and kissed my palm. "I survived Rokan's
jinx! I don't know how to thank you."

"You'll think of something, I'm sure. For now, you need to rest.
Let your body catch up with the Goddess's work and allow
your bones time to finish mending." I settled him back down
onto the bed and regarded him. "Rest now." I drew a symbol
on his forehead to sedate him, and he drifted to sleep. I sat
beside him, watching the steady rise and fall of his chest.
When our energies had merged in the Goddess's Gra'yia, I
sensed the essence of the man and his history, filled with guilt,
rejection, pain, and despair. He longed for what I had had
with Sam — and would never have again — a family, a loving
companion, and acceptance. Tears stole into my eyes.

Nana Bean knocked on the closed bakery door before she
opened it and peeked in. I quickly rose from the bed where
Thaddeus lay sleeping, brushing tears from my cheeks as I
moved into the kitchen.

Jack stood in the doorway. He had a few cuts on his face and hands. I tightened my jaw and waved him to the chair Thaddeus had recently occupied. "Looks like you fared better than Thaddeus."

"Thaddeus? He started it!" Jack protested.

"You should not be fighting over me. I am not interested in either of you!" I pressed my lips together, holding back expressing what I really felt. Coolly, I dabbed a little salve on the lacerations.

"Thaddeus beat me soundly. My whole body hurts. Will you use the Goddess's Gra'yia to heal me?"

I stepped back, put my hands on my hips, and glowered at him. "I will *not* heal you. You started the fight and therefore should pay the consequences. You almost killed Thaddeus."

Jack spied the chain from the golden disc tucked inside my shirt. "You still wear that pendant! Thaddeus has entrapped you with that device and you don't even know it!" His hand arced toward the jewelry. I stepped back.

Thaddeus moved restlessly on the bed, attracting Jack's attention. Jack's tone turned surly. "So this is where he came. I looked all over for him!"

He grabbed my arms. "Did you call the Goddess to heal him?" He shook me. "Tell me!"

I attempted to pull free. "Why did you try to kill the captain?"

For a second, I saw desperation in Jack's eyes, then he shoved me aside and lunged at Thaddeus. I jumped between them. Thaddeus became agitated and groaned.

"Leave, Jack," I commanded.

Jack tried to reach around me to the sleeping man. "You shouldn't defend the captain. He answers to a powerful master who would not take kindly to your interfering with his agents."

"Thaddeus is free to choose his own life — whatever that is — and whoever this arrogant master is, he has no right to control Thaddeus or what Thaddeus chooses!" With a strength I didn't know I possessed, I shoved Jack towards the door. "You are not welcome here. You are causing distress to my patient. Go."

Jack twisted, clawing at me in an attempt to drag me with him. I kicked him in the shins and bit the hand that restrained me.

His voice deepened. "You belong to me, Ellara! I will not let anyone come between us, even if it means killing the captain. Your rightful place is with me!"

"I belong to no man. I will *never* be *yours*," I snapped. "You and your master get out of my life." I shoved Jack out the door and shut it firmly behind him. I leaned against the door and listened to the sounds of Jack cursing.

From a crack in the door jamb, I watched Jack progress down the street, kicking over a mother's basket, scattering fruits and vegetables. He pounded his fist into a post, almost knocking it over, and snarled at anyone who came close. He slapped the rumps of two carthorses so hard that the horses squealed and bolted, spilling the cart's contents as it bounced down the street. He ignored the shouts hurled at him.

Thaddeus stared at me, wide-eyed. He cowered the closer I drew to him, pressing against the wall. I reached out to comfort him, but stopped at his unmistakable dread of me. His body trembled and pain pinched his face.

I worried that all of the healing work had been undone. Deciding nothing I could say or do would soothe him right now, I turned my back on him, and sat on the edge of the bed at his feet. As I had often done as a child with the wild horses Trevor tamed, I started humming the calming song I learned from Nana Magog. I allowed myself to receive from Thaddeus. Once I realized that his injuries had not reopened, I surrounded myself with love.

Time stood still. Tentative fingers brushed my back. I ignored them until his hand came to rest. I turned halfway, and we regarded each other. I answered the worry foremost in his mind. "Your body is still restored. I will *not* let you become deformed again. You must make a choice whether you want to listen to the wisdom in your heart or to the voices in your head. Whichever you choose will determine whether you regain your health or lose it."

Thaddeus closed his eyes, wearing a pained look. I touched his temple with my fingertips. He twisted away, then stopped, placed his hand on mine, and pressed my hand against the side of his face. The taut features softened. He took a deep breath and tried to sit up.

"I must go. You have angered the sorcerer. I am a danger to you, and you are a danger to me."

I shook my head. "You're still recovering from near-fatal injuries. You need rest and more sessions before you are recovered.

"He will kill you," he whispered. "He kills anyone who gets in his way. And he'll kill me, too."

"Will you at least rest until nightfall? You'll be safe here."

He looked dubious but lay back on the bed. I touched his forehead, but he grabbed my hand to stop it from drawing the symbol for sleep.

I nodded reassuringly at him. "I will watch over you. I will not let any harm come to you while you sleep. When you awake, you can decide what you must do." He withdrew his hand and allowed me to encourage sleep. The marks of his suffering faded and his visage relaxed into that of a much younger man.

I moved to Nana's comfortable chair. Why was the Droc'ri going to all the effort to trap me instead of just killing me as he had done with so many other Healers? He must want me alive for some reason. That means he won't kill me. However, he would kill Thaddeus without hesitation. He already had tried, through Jack. He would do so again.

My eyes drifted closed and I slipped into the memory of a time on Sam's ship when I had first encountered the captain of the *Lovely Lady*.

The sea had calmed after a massive storm, and the sun warmed my back. I had been very pregnant with Margot. With an arm around me, Sam and I stood at the railing, as we came alongside the *Lovely Lady*. Matty greeted Sam heartily.

"Did you lose some crates?" Sam had asked.

Matty replied, "Yes. Did you find them?" Matty had addressed me. "We have wounded from that wild storm. Can you attend to them?"

I nodded. "I'd be happy to."

While the *M'Ellara* deckhands hoisted the dozen salvaged wooden crates and barrels over to the *Lovely Lady*, I tended her crewmen. One by one, they boarded Sam's ship. They had mostly cuts and bruises, and one had a broken forearm. After the last man, I leaned against the railing, watching the sailors lash the salvaged cargo to cleats in the decking near the scuppers.

I had noticed a young man, about my age, watching from the shadows of his cabin door. He leaned against the bulkhead, propping his broken body upright with a cane. Matty indicated that he was their captain.

"Would he like some healing work, too?"

"He needs your ministrations. He damaged his shoulder." He nudged me. "He could use restoration, like you did for Sam." Matty climbed down the rope ladder to his ship and crossed the deck to the captain. They had talked. The young man shook his head vigorously. Promptly, he disappeared inside the cabin, but not without a long look at me. I had felt his pain and hopelessness. His presence had lingered around me for days afterward. I had thought it was just my imagination.

His actions didn't make sense to me at the time, especially since I had felt his longing as he watched me tend his crew, and as he observed Sam and me together. I heard bits and pieces about him over the years from Sam and caught a glimpse of him when Matty brought one of their mariners for restoration.

Now, I understood why Sam had asked him to watch over me and gave him his pendant, before he sailed into Sheldon and to his death. Sam knew that Thaddeus was more than willing to take on the responsibility for our family. Additionally, he had a hidden strength I had never before felt in anyone I had encountered.

I must have drifted off to sleep. A pot clattered on the stone floor, startling me awake. I sat up abruptly, gasping for air. I gazed around blankly, not knowing where I was. My gaze fell on Thaddeus, who rested on an elbow, studying me.

"Bad dream?"

I nodded slowly as awareness returned. Nana came in from the garden at the back of the cottage and I saw it was getting dark. I got up to help her. "You're fine, Child. I have it all under control. Go tend to your patient."

I sat beside Thaddeus, and passed my hand through his aura, assessing him, and nodded my head. "You look rested."

He sat up. "I feel great." He picked up my hand and pressed it to his lips. "I owe you my life, Ellara." He sat on the edge of the bed. "Now I must go, so I don't put you in peril."

"You must eat first, Son," Nana Bean ordered. She handed him a bowl of stew. "You'll need your strength to be able to run and hide." She peered at him. "It would be better if you stayed off the streets for a few days and let yourself heal. You will be safe here."

Thaddeus smiled at Nana Bean. "I'd love to stay, but I bring death to whomever I care about."

"The sorcerer will not kill me," I said flatly. I didn't want him to go, either. I knew he was not fit for defending himself from Jack or Jack's master. "The sorcerer cannot kill you while you are with me."

Thaddeus looked quizzically at me. "Why do you say that?"

"If Jack's master is the same sorcerer as your master, and is the one that has been hunting me, then he wants me for something besides simply eliminating another Healer. And for him to have twisted your mind so, yet not have been able to successfully kill you, must mean that you are somehow too mighty for him, and are a part of the Goddess's plan."

"The Goddess and I — we don't get along so well." Thaddeus grimaced and stood. "All the more reason why I need to leave." He groaned as he carefully shrugged into his vest and coat.

"Where will you go? Is your ship back in port?"

Thaddeus lifted his head, and like a dog testing the wind, nodded. "The *Lovely Lady* is back." He started towards the door.

"May the Goddess bless your journey and keep you safe, Thaddeus." A knot tightened in my belly. I touched his hand. I wondered if he sensed it, too. "Don't go, Thaddeus."

He hesitated. Hunger showed in his eyes. "I don't want to leave you. Harm will come if I stay. You don't know this Droc'ri like I do." He reached for the latch.

I caught his hand, listening to the rhythmic tromp of soldiers' boots drawing closer and stopping outside our door. He heard it too. In one swift movement, he caressed my cheek with a thumb, then dashed out the back door of the cottage and over the garden wall just as a heavy fist pummeled the door.

A gruff voice demanded, "King's Guard. Open up."

TWENTY-NINE

ROKAN AND FELICITY

Mainland

W hy did I always have to hold my covert meetings in this inhospitable country? I grimaced, pulling my cloak tighter around me to block Inyua's penetrating cold. *Probably since no one in their right mind comes here.* I wore the disguise of a Scholars' Guild professor. It was easier to extract information from people if they thought I was doing research.

Snow crunched. A short, round man, shrouded in a thick woolen cloak, emerged from the forest and came to where I sat on the trunk of a fallen tree in the small clearing.

I stood. "Ben. What news do you have for me?"

Ben rubbed his hands briskly, blowing on them. "The Council asked Anya about the lost teachings," my agent reported. As the pair'ti to one of the Council members, he was privy to more information than most. "The teachings sparked a heated debate and effectively divided the Council. My pair'ti sided with Camila in keeping with the traditional Triune formation. Other members were more sympathetic to Nana Magog's upstart, Ellara, and asked to review the Gra'Bandia practices in search of a more effective way to deal with the Droc'ri."

"I will be interested to see which opinion prevails. What else interesting has happened? What of Nana Magog's apprentice?"

Ben laughed and shoved his hood back to reveal a pock-marked face and balding head. "After she failed the Rite of Dushlan, and Camila cursed her, my pair'ti and a group of us met with her outside the Sacred Grove. My pair'ti told her to call upon us when she wanted to depose Camila." He chuck-led. "She is young and gullible. She believed us. And we can track her movements through our signet ring now."

I patted him on the back. "Excellent, Ben. Do you have the attendance list?"

Ben thrust pudgy fingers into a pocket and extracted a wrin-kled piece of paper with a list of names. Handing it to me, he said, "This is a complete list of all of the Healers who have shown up. Some have returned home. I've tried to notate which ones come and go, like you asked."

I glanced at the entries, noticing that Camila had not left Cuilithe. I wanted to know one more thing before we separated. "Did your pair'ti say anything about who Ellara shared her soul with?"

Ben shook his head. "She is a staunch supporter of Camila, but she thinks Camila made up the bit about Ellara holding a piece of a Droc'ri soul." He shrugged. "She said she didn't see anything in the untrained initiate's memories that would cause Camila to come to that conclusion."

I heaved an inner sigh of relief. "Interesting. I wonder why Camila cursed the woman. The Council needs all the experienced Healers they can find."

"I think it's Nana Magog. The Doyen detests her and she used Magog's uninitiated for a bit of revenge." He smiled and winked. "Healers are not as perfect as they want their believers to think."

I laughed. "You're right there, Ben. If you hear of anything else, let me know." I pressed a small bag of gold into his hand. "The Guild appreciates your diligence in reporting events accurately."

I watched him leave, replaying his words in my mind. Did Camila really see something in Ellara's memories, or did she make it up? Or did she know from another source? Who? My stomach tightened. Camila was a sly one. I'd have to keep a watch on her. I could only hope she didn't communicate my involvement to the Council. I would need to contact each member privately to ensure her ignorance.

I froze. When have I started to "hope?" Where was the certainty that had been with me so long? I was losing control. *By the Goddess's fingernails, Magog will pay for her meddling!*

Angrily, I spoke the words that would allow me to instantly travel back to Tokurat, my initial satisfaction with my Katz-paw's report souring. At least he had delivered a detailed list of the attendees and their current locations. Instead of returning to my study, I went to my abode in Old Tokurat and lay on my bed. I had a task for Jack.

It would be dawn soon in Araval. I prodded Jack awake. Still hung over, he stumbled to the back entrance of the castle. The guard at the postern gate recognized and admitted him. Once inside the castle, Jack made his way along high-ceilinged corridors to the east wing where Queen Qadira resided. He tapped lightly on the ornate door. It cracked open and a slender, almond-eyed woman peeked out. It shut immediately. In a moment, the door swung open and Jack was ushered before the queen, who lounged amid pillows piled high on her bed. She tugged the silk comforter higher around her chest.

"What do you want, Jack?" Her voice was terse. "Did you bring me more of my special cream from Langon?"

"Your brother, the Suzerain of Tokur, wants..." I started.

She waved her hand dismissively. "Forget the formalities, Rokan. I know what Garrick wants. He can't have Alba until I'm good and ready to let him have it!" She glared defiantly at me. "He can just wait!"

"I just want you to know that you can use this young man to do your tasks. He is at your service."

Qadira snorted. "This half-baked assassin is only good for one thing. Wood carving. He is worthless as an assassin and pitiful as a lover." She pointed at the body I shared. "Tell me how I can use him."

"I will help you kill the king and take over the country."

"For my brother to take from me." She shook her head. "I don't need your help, Rokan. I am more capable of assassinating the worthless man who calls himself king of this God-forsaken country than that lout you control."

I studied her. A web of faint lines marred her youthful beauty. "What's wrong, Qadira. Are you running short on your supply of youth cream? Why don't you have a Healer to keep up your vitality?"

She sat straighter in her bed. "I am just fine, Rokan. Now stop wasting my time and leave."

Outside the door I paused, listening. A moment later, she cursed in the Tokurian dialect, then summoned her women. "Bring me the Healer who just arrived."

Smiling, I, in Jack's body, strode jauntily to the gate he had entered. I, through Jack, would help Qadira ensnare Ellara. The queen would ferociously protect the Healer from harm in exchange for the rejuvenation Ellara could provide her. However, Jack must convince Ellara to cooperate with the queen. With Ellara in the queen's custody, she would be safe and out of reach of Thaddeus or Matty until I could arrive in Alba.

I stretched and rose from my bed. Could I manipulate the queen *and* Ellara? Was I skilled enough at possession to make Jack do my bidding? The prospect excited me.

Now, to enlist Felicity into my plan.

The crisp air had just started to warm when I stepped through my portal onto the coastal plain near Felicity's village. A short walk brought me to Felicity's rooms adjacent to her father's mercantile shop and warehouse. Her living space was small, warm, and cozy. She lived alone now that her children had grown old enough to be apprenticed to local tradespeople. I knocked softly on her door. Immediately it burst open. Without a word, she grabbed my hand and pulled me through the entry, quickly shutting the door behind me.

"I don't want Father to know you are here. He doesn't approve of my becoming a Healer and has threatened to turn me over to the clerics." She darted to a desk near her bed and picked up the booklet I had given her. "I read the whole thing. Can we try some of the spells?"

"First, I need to give you an attunement so that you can handle the Goddess's force. Then I will show you how to perform some simple magic."

She bounced in excitement and threw her arms around me. After kissing me, she asked, "What do I do?"

She sat, and I directed a part of my essence into her energy field, spoke a few words, and drew figure eights and other mystical symbols in her aura. In my mind's eye, I saw filaments crisscross in her energy field and strengthen as I continued to direct my will into her aura.

When I was satisfied that she would not be harmed by the Goddess's force, I stood before her. "To summon the Goddess, you command her to work through you. Let's try a small thing." I picked up a vase that held some flowers that had begun to wilt. "Restore these flowers to their freshly picked state by commanding the Goddess's vitality to flow through you and into the flowers."

Felicity tried, but nothing happened. She tried again and again, with similar results. I hid my impatience. She had to figure out how to call the Goddess. I asked, "What are you thinking when you try to restore these flowers?"

"I want them to become perfect again."

"The Goddess works with the vibration of Love. Perhaps if you try thinking differently about the flowers. Try thinking how beautiful they are. Or something else that activates and expands your heart."

She looked at me, then smiled. She stretched out her hand and touched the vase. Almost instantly, the wilted flowers perked up. "I did it! I did it!" She turned to me. "I thought about how much I love you and that did it."

I nodded encouragement. We practiced other simple tasks a while longer. "Practice simple things with the Goddess energy and you can move to bigger things. I have a mission for you as soon as you are ready."

She put her arms around my neck. "Anything for you, Rokan. Just tell me what you want."

I grinned. *Why couldn't other Healers be so agreeable?*

She drew me to the bed and pulled me down beside her. "Rokan, let's do something different this time. I want to give you a gift for training me."

"What's that?"

"I want to give you a child."

Mentally, I recoiled, although I kept my arms around her and my voice curious. "A child? Why? They are a lot of work. You know that. You've had two."

"I thought that since you are my pair'ti and Far'degan, I want to have your child. And your child will be special."

I pulled her closer so she could not witness my aversion to the idea.

"I know that you have not been actually mating with me. Why not?"

"What makes you say that?"

"I have had children and I know how they are created, and the mess that is often the result of mating. I never have that with you."

I laughed, thinking quickly. "You are clever. Did it ever occur to you that I wanted to protect you from getting pregnant?"

She lifted her head and looked into my eyes. "I appreciate that, Rokan, but now I want to bear you a son or daughter. Let's do it for real this time." She slipped off her robe and sat astride me, slid up my tunic, unbuttoned my trousers, and started kissing my bared skin. I found my manhood responding to her Goddess-enhanced touch. I drew in a deep breath and forced myself to relax, struggling to keep my mind on reviewing my options.

When I was a young man, I had enjoyed the pleasures of physical, sensuous lovemaking, especially with a willing partner. Then I learned that a man became weakened if he spilled his seed too often, and I shifted my practices to pleasuring my companion and holding back from sharing my life force with them. I discovered that in the moments that led to erotic ecstasy, my partner's aura merged with mine, and that energy supercharged me. It was not long before I found it less exhausting to simply give my lovers erotic dreams and harvest the energy they radiated to replenish my vitality. I had not engaged in physical mating for at least one hundred years.

Was Felicity worth it? I had already invested a lot of time and effort in getting her to be blessed by the Council as a Healer. I wanted to use her magic to gain the freedom to come and go in

Alba. That was all. What would that cost me? A committed relationship with her was not part of my plan. She would try to control me with the child. As far as I was concerned, she was just another of my exploitable and expendable tools that looked a lot like Ellara.

"If you want to use my magic to travel easily to Alba, you will need to mate with me and unite as a pair'ti. Then you will have access to my talents, and I will have access to yours. That's what the book said."

I groaned inwardly. She was right. I had just been reading about that in regards to Ellara. *Can I share just enough of my energies with her without her learning my secrets?*

I lifted her head and stopped her hands. "Felicity, there is a lot you don't know about me. If we do the merging that is required to bond us together, you will learn about me. I have done a lot of things that I am not proud of but were required of me as a Mage during the Religious Wars. I would not wish those memories upon anyone, especially you." I sat up and cupped her face in my hands. "I care about you too much to thrust this darkness on you. It is not wise for us to join as a pair'ti right now. Perhaps in the future, when you have worked with the Goddess enough so that my past will not destroy you. Until that time, I will continue to help you build your magical muscles."

Felicity's lips formed into a pout and a tear slid from the corner of her eyes. "I thought you loved me, Rokan. I really did. My love for you is what makes my magic work. If you loved me, think about how much more powerful I could make you."

I stood, placed a hand on her shoulder, and said as kindly as I could, "Do not give up hope for us, Felicity. I want to spare you the pain of my past. Let me think on the best time for us to become united." I bent down and kissed her. "Now I have to attend to another task for my master."

I left quickly, relieved to escape the trap Felicity had lain for me. Even though she had been raised as a devout Natuan, she could be as manipulative as me. I'd get what I wanted from her and she would need to die. If only Ellara would be so willing....

I imprinted my traveling crystal with a location near Araval, said the words, and traced the symbols. An opening appeared, then collapsed almost immediately. I smiled. Another session or two with Felicity and I would have enough of her magic to travel to and from Alba. Then I wouldn't need her, and the Healer I would direct her to in Araval, or Lord Garth, would kill her. *Love. It makes one weak, self-sacrificing, and very easy to manipulate.*

I returned to Tokurat. Would Felicity's desire to mate further cloud her judgment? Would she be willing to work with Jack and help Qadira take over the Alban monarchy? My inner sense warned me that she could be as unpredictable as Jack had become. I'd hold off using her until I needed her.

THIRTY

ELLARA AND THADDEUS

Araval

Fearing the soldiers had come for me because of healing Thaddeus, I darted into the garden and made myself invisible. The pounding continued.

Nana called cheerily, "Coming."

She swung open the door. A massive man wearing an authoritarian expression peered in, gaze sweeping the open space that served as kitchen and sleeping area.

"Commander, what brings you to my door at this time of night? Does your wife need more bread? A special order?" The old woman tilted her head to the side to peek up at him.

"No, Nana." His stern expression softened. "We are looking for a criminal who was last seen here."

Nana stepped back, putting a hand to her mouth. "Commander! Are we safe here? We bolt the doors at night because my customers tell me there are dangerous people around. We are just two women, one old and one who wears her age gracefully. Lord Garth's soldiers prey on women like us." She trailed off.

"Don't worry, Nana. Don't go out at night and keep your doors barred, and you will be alright." He stepped inside. "Forgive me, Nana, but I must search your house to make sure the culprit is not still here."

"Who are you looking for?"

"A rogue sea captain by the name of Thaddeus Finn."

"Heavens!" She put a hand to her chest. "He has been one of my best customers. What has he done to have you hunt him down?"

The commander shook his head. "Don't know. I have orders to bring him in and impound his ship. Do you mind?" The bulky man turned from Nana and poked his head into the cool storeroom, then took a lantern and went into the garden. I pressed against the wall, barely breathing and praying that my magic worked.

Thankfully, he didn't linger, and I released my pent breath after he returned to stand beside Nana. "Where's your assistant?" His gaze swept the room again.

"She went out. Maybe to the Red Rose?"

He leaned close to Nana Bean and lowered his voice. "I hear she is a Healer newly arrived in Araval, and her gift is forceful enough to break the curse of a Kurat spirit. Will you send her to me when she returns?"

After the guards left, I returned inside. "What does the commander want with me?"

"The king is cursed. It will take someone strong in the Goddess's Gra'yia to dissolve it. Someone like you." She hummed to herself while her sinewy hands kneaded dough.

"But you're a Healer and so are your friends. Why can't you do it?" I asked.

"We gave up our ability to channel the Goddess's Radiance when we went into hiding."

"Is it gone forever? It seems to me that once you learn a talent, you always have it. It might get rusty from lack of use, and you may not be as potent in your abilities as you once were, but it is still there. The Goddess wouldn't take it away from you just because you retire, or surrender it to please the Natuan Ethnarch."

Nana chuckled. "Didn't you witness a Healer's powers stripped from her?"

I nodded. "But I still don't believe the memory of the Goddess is removed from your body."

Nana smiled to herself and murmured, "That's why you are the one to break the king's curse." She busied herself with cleaning the table for the next day's labors. "But be wary. This invitation comes with danger."

She started humming a tune that was hauntingly familiar. Then I remembered. I had heard it at the Council meeting the very first day during the opening ceremonies. It was a chant and there were words that went with it. "What do the words mean, Nana?"

"Hm? Oh, the words. The Goddess's Light purifies. The Goddess's Love creates."

"Do you think it's a trap?" I asked as I straightened the blankets where Thaddeus had rested.

"Commander Fabian was raised in the Goddess's tradition. He is an honest man. He won't let his guards mistreat citizens. I believe he would not deceive me. But he answers to someone higher up. The question is, who gave him the order to ask about you?"

A flash of light drew my attention to a silver lightning-shaped pendant hidden in the blankets. I picked it up, feeling the purifying force of it course through my body. It also contained an overpowering imprint of its owner. I held it up, saying, "Thaddeus lost this."

Nana Bean became very quiet, then turned her blurry eyes to mine and said matter-of-factly, "The young captain goes to his death. You must not let that happen. You must protect him since he does not have this safeguarding talisman." She pointed at the silver pendant.

I moved to the door.

"No. He'll be dead by the time you reach him. Use the Goddess's power."

I searched for Thaddeus with my Far Sight. Surprisingly, the captain was only a few blocks from the back entrance to the bakery. He walked quickly towards the river. My senses expanded and I saw a shadowy figure lurking behind a building that Thaddeus had just passed. Quickly, I wrapped my spirit around him, impressing upon him the vision of his danger. He stopped, slipped his long mariner's knife from his belt, and spun around, just as Hadlan sprang into the street and raced towards him. I pulled my spirit back, wary of the sorcerer and any attempt to capture me.

Nana Bean rested her hand on my back. "Summon the Goddess." At my hesitation, she urged, "He is in no condition to withstand a trained assassin. You must hurry."

"I don't know how."

"Do what you do to channel Her essence to someone, only direct that force to protect the young man."

I wasn't sure just what she meant, but I clenched Thaddeus's talisman in both hands. It provided a solid link to him. I opened my heart to the Goddess and imagined Thaddeus wrapped in Her protective presence. The talisman burned in my hand, and for an instant, I stood on the street with him. White lightning lanced from the silver pendant and surrounded Hadlan, making his movements sluggish.

Without delay, Thaddeus dispatched the incapacitated sorcerer. "Serves you right, Hadlan. I never did like you or your Droc'ri masters," Thaddeus muttered as he cleaned his knife on the sorcerer's shirt and re-sheathed it. He turned to see where the brilliant light had come from and started towards me. My body burned. I fell to the ground, gasping.

Someone lifted me and held me. Pain from being jostled washed through me in waves. The burning in my body engulfed me. I surrendered to it.

I hovered outside my body. Sam floated beside me, but his attention was on another. I reached for him. He took my hand, shaking his head at me. "It's not your time." He returned to observing the man holding me. "Hurry up!" He glanced at me. "He must restore you to fully break free of the Droc'ri curse." His words didn't make sense, but nothing mattered now. I shifted to see what interested Sam.

Thaddeus sat on Nana Bean's bed and had pulled my body onto his lap. Devastated, he hunched over me, pleading with the elder to heal me.

Nana Bean shook her head. "I gave up that ability when I went into hiding. You are the only one who can save her. She doesn't have much time. Her spirit has already left her body."

Thaddeus clutched me. "No! Ellara, don't leave me," he pleaded. "Nana, can't you do something?"

Nana placed a hand on my physical form and shook her head. "When her body cools, and breathing becomes shallow, she will be beyond saving. You must act now, Thaddeus." Nana read his reluctance and leaned forward, saying softly. "She did not hesitate to risk her life to save you from the sorcerer-assassin. The Droc'ri who declares he is your master will kill you if you save her. You can let her die and remain forever his minion. What will you tell her daughter and son, or Sam, when you finally join him in the Mag Mell? It's your choice. You alone will bear the consequences of your decision." Nana returned to the bread table and started working a lump of dough, leaving Thaddeus to sort out this dilemma on his own.

Thaddeus brushed stray hairs from my face. Finally he muttered, "If I let her die, life won't be worth living. If I do as you ask, Rokan will kill me. Either way, she'll be the death of me." He sighed. "What do I do?"

"Welcome the Goddess into your heart."

Thaddeus shot the elder a surprised look.

"You have to summon the Goddess to help her. To do that, you have to surrender who you think you are, your identity, and unbarricade your heart so that the Goddess can work through you."

"You ask the impossible," he muttered. He closed his eyes and concentrated. "I can't. I don't know how she does it."

Nana laughed. "You deceive yourself. Think about how you feel when your energies entangle in the Goddess's Gra'yia."

Thaddeus closed his eyes again. His aura expanded a little. "It's not working."

"Do you remember how you felt when you first saw Ellara? You dreamed of having her by your side and her children being yours. You would have given your life for her. Use those feelings."

Thaddeus blushed. "This wasn't part of the plan," he muttered. But his aura expanded and blended with my fading life force.

"Now ask the Goddess to restore Ellara."

Thaddeus glowed with a golden light tinged with rose and the field of energy around him intensified. It wrapped around me, penetrating my physical form so that my body also glowed in the loving Radiance of the Goddess. Thaddeus held me tenderly. I could hear his thoughts and feel his worries. He bent to kiss me. "I've wanted to do that from the first time I saw you, Ellara."

Sam drew me into an ephemeral embrace. He kissed me gently. "Beloved, go back and fulfill your destiny." He nudged me towards my body.

Coolness touched my skin and penetrated slowly inward to soothe my burning nerves. Finally, the fire subsided and I opened my eyes to the concerned face of Thaddeus. He held me tightly, even after the flow of the Goddess's Gra'yia had stopped. I blinked. There was something different about him.

"It worked? You are alive? I healed you?"

I smiled weakly at him and squirmed. He released his hold, but kept a hand on my back as I slid off his lap, sat up on the edge of the bed, and leaned against him. My limbs felt like dead wood and it took effort to keep myself sitting upright. "I didn't know that men could be Healers," I addressed Nana.

The baker was beaming. "You're lucky the captain has the gift, Ellara."

I nodded, smiling crookedly at Thaddeus. "Thank you. It appears that now I owe you a debt."

Thaddeus wasn't listening. He glowered at something across the room. I softened my gaze and saw a vaporous form floating near the far wall. Thaddeus grabbed the hand that still held his pendant and pointed it at the creature. White lightning flowed through me and shot towards the entity. It dissolved, making an unearthly squeal and leaving a horrible stench. I sagged against Thaddeus. "That evil beast must be the spy that reports to Rokan," he growled. "Good riddance!"

He faced me, grinning. His whole presence had transformed, and he had a twinkle in his eye. Instead of sadness and despair, hope emanated from him. His hands cupped my face. "We make quite a team!"

I nodded, then closed my eyes and let myself drift into the restorative realm of sleep.

I awoke on the sleeping mat. Thaddeus rested in Nana's comfortable chair. The pendant around his neck glinted in the firelight. He sat proudly, like a man with a purpose. I stretched and yawned. Immediately, he was beside me. "How are you feeling?"

The corner of my mouth lifted. That was what I usually asked my patients. I got up and stretched. "Sore, tired, but alive." I took in his confident countenance, lightly tracing the scar on his cheek.

After breakfast, I started making loaves. Thaddeus came to stand close behind me, waiting quietly. Finally, I turned to face him. "Is there something on your mind?"

He didn't answer immediately, his gentle gaze resting on me. Finally, he said, "Will you show me how to do what you do?"

"Make bread?"

He shook his head. "The magic that you do."

I pursed my lips. I had taught Margot and Kian everything I knew, half of which had been gained through experimentation with my clients and Kian. Then I had discovered at the Council that I hadn't been properly trained. Even with Cleric Paul's pages, I was aware of how little I knew of the Goddess tradition. Was it wise to show Thaddeus? "Why do you want to know?"

He hesitated. "I sensed your forewarning of the storm. It saved my ship and crew. I saw the image of Hadlan and felt your spirit protect me." He shifted. "Then you.... almost died. I want to repay you for what you have done for me in a way that will benefit you." He remained confident under my scrutiny, then grinned. "For the first time in my life, I feel powerful, useful, and worthy. Healing you and destroying the evil creature of the sorcerer liberated something inside me. I want to do more of that. I want to defeat the sorcerer who has manipulated me my whole life." He cradled my face. "I need your help to do this."

His enthusiasm was infectious. I held back. The Goddess's power in the wrong hands or used with malicious intent would only add to the world's problems, not help. "Are you saying you want to join the cause of restoring the balance in our world?"

His delight dimmed. "I don't know if I'd go that far. But I want to be free of the sorcerer and together we can do it." He tried to draw me closer, giving me his most charming smile. "Besides, it will be such a pleasure working with you."

I stepped back. "My, haven't you gotten bold all of a sudden. What happened to your fear of me and the curse?"

He blushed. "I... I made a mistake." He contemplated me. "When Nana Magog first healed me after my accident, she told me that I had a great destiny." His tone became earnest. "She said I came from a long line of Mages and had powers that others either wanted to suppress or to steal. The first part is true. Certain people have done very well at making me doubt myself and feel unworthy. Restoring you and destroying the Droc'ri spy has shown me that I have misjudged and shortchanged myself. You have awakened parts of me I didn't know I had."

I listened to his words and read his emotions. "Let me think on this. Now, if you want to help make bread, go wash your hands."

THIRTY-ONE

ROKAN AND GARRICK

Tokurat, The Desert Lands

I flung the pages that Garrick had given me on my desk. That idiot had delayed me with pointless chatter. I had to endure him gloating about Alba and his becoming Master of the world. He had me make sure that each country's leader was beholden to him. It could have been done in a few minutes, but no, it had to take half the night, sending me to fetch the documents from the archives that designated him Suzerain of each country, one at a time. He could have sent an underling. I could have brought all of them at once, saving countless trips up and down stairs and along corridors that led deep into the rock that formed the back of the palace. Why was he wasting my time?

I shoved my chair and it crashed to the floor. *Had that gombeen deliberately delayed me so that I could not monitor*

Ellara through Jack? Jack was supposed to kill the captain. Yet the half-man had somehow survived and made his way to Ellara. Jack had arrived at the bakery too late to be of any use to me, especially since Ellara had cast him out. Why did she protect the worthless half-man? I had to know if Ellara had summoned the Goddess to restore him.

Impatiently, I picked up the flat black disk that I used to summon my Skeld and commanded it to appear. The creature had always appeared promptly. I checked all my tell-tale alerts and protective spells before summoning it again. Finally, I called Numbskull, an imp I had created from a Droc'ri who had betrayed the Order and had been spared death. "Find Skeld," I commanded. I rapped fingers on my desk, impatiently awaiting a response. In seconds, Numbskull returned, along with Hadlan's imp.

"What's this?" I demanded. "Why aren't you with Hadlan?"

"Hadlan's been murdered!" the creature whined. "Take me on as your servant, Master," he pleaded. "I can serve you better than I could Hadlan."

I scowled at the twisted features of the imp. I knew that if another sorcerer didn't accept the services of an imp after its master had been killed, the imp would die as well and follow the Droc'ri sorcerers' fate of perpetual service in the realm of the Tiarna Drocha.

I plucked the small form from where he stood on my desk and held him by the scruff of his neck. "What happened to Hadlan?" I growled.

"The sea captain killed him."

"Thaddeus!?"

"Yes, Master." I pinched my fingers tighter around the little creature's neck. "Ouch, Master. He had help."

"Who?" My face was inches from the imp.

"I don't know, Master." The imp struggled. "He was surrounded with a bright light and my master couldn't move."

"Where's my Skeld?"

"It was destroyed, too, Master." The little creature cringed. "I don't know how or who did it."

Thunderclouds gathered around me. "My Skeld, destroyed!? Someone will pay for this!" I raged.

I flung the little man-like demon onto the desk and pointed a finger. Black lightning burned him to a crisp. I hurled lightning bolts at the marble stone, and the ceiling shifted dangerously. Swinging around, I caught Numbskull in a crushing grip, and squeezed. I dropped the nearly dead creature, angrily muttered a few words that formed a protective bubble, and stepped into the Otherworld. In an instant, I arrived at the bakery. Through the filmy veil of the Mag Mell, I watched Ellara sleeping on a mat. I spied Thaddeus resting in a broad, soft chair with high arms. I would have killed the captain with my bare hands, if I could pass through the veil of the Mag Mell.

A tattle-tale spell in my study warned me I had a visitor. Back in my private study, I veiled my annoyance at Garrick's unwelcome visit with a cool smile.

"I came to see if everything is alright." Garrick's silky voice grated on my nerves. When I didn't respond, Garrick continued, "I felt a disturbance." Garrick noticed the cracks in the wall and pile of rock dust on the floor. "What is going on?" Garrick's voice took on the edge of command. "Tell me, Rokan."

I sighed and collapsed into my chair. "I've lost my best spy in Alba, Master. Now I'm blind. You know our usual methods are blocked by the Alban magic. Let me go there to see what happened and make sure that its downfall is proceeding according to plan."

Garrick shook his head. "I need you here."

"But..."

Garrick stared fiercely at me. "I said, you stay here and serve me. I'll send another Droc'ri to spy for you in Alba."

I sagged in my chair and looked down submissively. "Yes, Master. What do you want me to do?"

"I want you to take a package. A present," he amended, "to the Healers in the Chaste Palace. Then monitor who has the talent to thwart its magic."

"I am at your service, Master. What is the present you want me to deliver?"

The wiry man pulled a golden box not much bigger than his fist from a fold in his robes. Geometric shapes covered all six sides so that one could not detect the seam where the lid rested. "It's a puzzle box. Let's see how well they do with it. Whoever opens it will find a most unexpected reward." He suppressed a grin.

I took the gift and slipped it into a pocket in my tunic. "Very well, Master. I'll take it now."

"Don't help them, Rokan. I know how you are with the ladies."

"I won't. This will be a good test to see how clever they are."

Garrick hummed as he departed.

I watched him go sourly. *What a waste of my time. I have more important things to do.* It rankled that Garrick constantly kept me under his thumb. I begrudgingly submitted to his dominion because I had to protect my secret. While it wasn't forbidden to steal another's soul as a way to weaken those one wanted to control, it was forbidden to possess the soul of a Healer. It was said a Healer's soul would weaken the Droc'ri who held it. Would Camila or Nana Magog expose me? As if that wasn't bad enough, if Garrick discovered I wanted to use Ellara and Margot to break my contract with the Dark Lords and free my soul, I would be disgraced before the whole Order, then ritualistically killed as a traitor. No. I couldn't let him know how important Ellara and Margot were to me.

I couldn't even return to Margot and her companions. My Far Sight showed that they had transformed the decimated mountain top, and again, the white marble stones formed the ancient temple to the Goddess. How had they done that in such a short time? They must be utilizing an unknown form of magic. If I could harness it, imagine what I could do. I wanted to find out, but Garrick did not send me back, and I could not ask, or he would wonder at my interest. Perhaps it was for the best, judging by the effect Margot had had on me.

I pulled the case out and studied it. I knew the deadly surprise that the Healers would find if one figured out how to open it. I hoped that they wouldn't be able to.

This time of night would be ideal for delivering the packet without being noticed. Tomorrow I'd return to the Chaste Palace and see what had transpired. After I helped Jack kill Thaddeus.

A veiled form waited in the shadows near my customary exit. As I approached, a woman blocked the way. "Rokan. I need your help."

"Sophia?" I lifted the veil to peer at the young woman's worried features. "What has happened?"

"Garrick has killed my friend, who was his servant, this past week. Now I have been assigned to replace her. I..."

"I'll take care of it. Come with me, Sophia. You can stay at the Chaste Palace until I can hide you properly."

THIRTY-TWO

ELLARA AND THE KING

Araval

The morning rush of patrons had barely subsided when we heard Nana talking with Jack. Jack and his invisible master burst into the kitchen where Thaddeus and I worked together, forming dough into loaves. Without even a greeting, Jack launched himself at Thaddeus, homicidal intent written on his face.

The two men grappled, knocking over pans and chairs. Jack grabbed Thaddeus by the neck and held his dagger in the other. Thaddeus struggled to keep the dagger at bay and break free from the chokehold.

"Release him, Jack, or this blade will slip between your ribs. You'll die quickly."

Jack ignored me. I let the sharp tip prick the skin, drawing blood. Jack froze, but he still held Thaddeus by the throat. "Let him go. Now." I dug a little deeper with my dagger. "Are you willing to die for your master? Is he worth it?"

Jack slacked off slightly, yet he still kept Thaddeus pinned against the wall. "You wouldn't kill me. Healers don't kill." He leaned into Thaddeus.

"I killed before. It was the right thing to do. I will kill again, if I need to."

The man controlling Jack snorted and renewed his efforts to defeat Thaddeus. I kicked at the side of Jack's knee and, taking the hilt of my dagger, knocked just under the base of his skull. Jack staggered and released his hold on Thaddeus, who gasped for air.

In a flash, Thaddeus had his mariner's long knife at Jack's neck. "Killing you will remove your master and his agent." His tone was menacing. I had not seen this side of Thaddeus before. He drew vitality from me, using it to fortify his own.

"You wouldn't kill me, Thaddeus." Jack's nasal voice whined. "When you took me to the Desert Lands, you said you cared about me and felt responsible for my mother's death. You won't kill me."

"I did like you as a boy, but you embraced the Droc'ri way and tainted what was good in you. I will not allow your master to intimidate or control me any longer."

"He's your master, too, Thaddeus. Don't forget it." The deep voice of Jack's master returned. "Remember what happened the last time you rebelled against my dominion."

Thaddeus didn't say anything.

Jack's gaze darted to me and back to Thaddeus. "You think because you have her help, you are invincible? He'll never allow her to become your pair'ti! Hah! Rokan will make mincemeat of both of you! He will kill you, Thaddeus." The master within Jack turned to me. "You are mine. I will have you for my mate, Ellara."

I bristled.

Thaddeus held his weapon easily. "You Droc'ri think relationships are about taking what you want, and what you can get from someone through control, intimidation, and coercion. When you don't get what you want, you blame the Goddess for your lack. Your Droc'ri traditions limit you and will be your undoing."

I stood beside Thaddeus. "You have been warned. We will not be cowed by you."

Jack pointed at Thaddeus. "He serves the Droc'ri just like I do. Thaddeus manipulates you. Why do you choose him over me?"

"Perhaps he does. Now go. We have work to do." I took Thaddeus's hand and imagined we were pillars of light. Jack cringed. Together we walked forward, driving the Katz-paw and his master from the cottage.

After Jack left, Thaddeus asked, "Would you have killed him?"

I shrugged. "Would you?"

Not too long afterward, the King's Guard stopped outside the bakery. The commander's gruff voice asked if I was there. Nana paused, then said she thought I might be. She tapped lightly on the closed door of her cottage, then opened it to the commander.

I ushered Thaddeus into the storeroom and, when I returned to the kitchen, came face to face with the huge man.

"You healed a certain Captain Thaddeus Finn yesterday?"

I nodded cautiously. "He was near death."

"Do you know his whereabouts?"

"You came last night looking for him for an unspecified reason. What is that reason?"

"He is charged with murder."

I stared at the commander. "I can tell you he was in no shape to be fighting, much less killing anyone."

"A man was found dead this morning and a witness identified the killer as the captain."

I harrumphed, and returned to the table where dough rested and continued forming loaves.

"This is no light matter, Madam."

"No it isn't. Why is it that Lord Garth's mercenaries can ravage the town and go undisciplined, yet when someone is killed, an innocent man is blamed?"

The commander leaned over me. "How do you know he's innocent?"

"Because, Jack, the man outside, has tried to kill the captain at least three times that I know of, and twice while he recovered here. The captain had a fractured skull and several broken ribs. Now tell me, Commander, how fit would a man like that be to kill someone?"

"The captain must be brought before the Peers to hear the evidence for and against him. I only administer the laws; I don't make them."

"Do you have a writ with this accusation against the captain and for impounding his ship?"

The commander gripped the handle of his sword. "No," he admitted slowly.

"Then who ordered his arrest?"

"The Queen."

I studied the soldier. "Don't you answer to the king?"

He nodded.

I poured him a cup of tea, shoved a fresh loaf of bread and a dish of butter towards him. "Sit down, Commander. We need to talk." I noticed that Nana had given his men bread upon which they contentedly ate as they watched the cottage from across the street. I closed the door to Jack's probing countenance, and went back to my work.

"I understand you were asking about me in regard to a curse on the king. Who asked you to make this inquiry?"

He picked up the small cup with thick fingers, and scanned the room hastily. "I came on my own," he rumbled softly. He surveyed the room again. "I served under old King Theodopolis as his Commander of the Alban Guard. I watched Prince Leopold grow up. I know he's a good man, but..." He lowered his voice even more. "Since his marriage to the queen, and coronation, the young king's sovereignty has been usurped by a non-Alban authority. Our country is under attack from this same foreigner. I risk my career and that of my garrison, as well as your life, in asking you for your help." The old soldier set his empty cup down.

"Who stands in your way of righting this wrong?"

"Lord Garth has spies everywhere. He has bribed or manipulated most of the King's Council to serve his directives, as given to him by his master. The man who was killed was Lord Garth's Droc'ri. Whoever eliminated him has done Alba a service. I will not pursue the murder of this man, but rest assured, Lord Garth will not let any stone go unturned until he finds the perpetrator."

"What recourse do you have against Lord Garth?"

Commander Fabian leaned back in his chair and sighed. "Alas, very little. King Leopold's predecessor was not in sound mind in his later years. King Theodopolis, Leo's father, was forced to accept Commander Garth and his soldiers by the Natuan Ethnarch, as punishment for not participating in the Emerald Mountain Religious Wars. To satisfy an alliance with the Ethnarch, King Theodopolis was to grant Garth lands and title. King Theo dragged his feet on this condition, but it became part of the marriage contract with the Suzerain of Tokur's sister." He shook his head. "As long as King Leopold is married to the Tokurian woman, our hands are tied. We are stuck with the agreements, and Lord Garth gets bolder by the day. He thinks he runs the kingdom, now!"

"There must be something we can do." I placed the last loaf on the shelf to rise. Ridding the country of Lord Garth and his mercenaries would dramatically help Alba. "Can you take me to the king?"

"Yes, but he is drugged. As if a curse was not enough!"

"Do you know what herbs he was given?"

The commander shook his head. "He is listless. He sleeps a lot and is very pale."

I rummaged in my medicine kit and pulled out a couple of tincture bottles and slipped them into my pocket.

As I draped a light cloak around my shoulders, a disheveled Thaddeus burst into the kitchen. He walked with a limp and leaned to one side, holding his ribs. He grabbed my arm. "Don't go. It's a trap. Lord Garth will capture you."

Thaddeus sagged into the vacated chair, and addressed the commander. "Don't let anything happen to her. She's saved my life and saved me from that vicious man outside who has tried to kill me several times while I recuperate. He is cruel and serves a ruthless foreign master." He slumped as if the exertion of so many words exhausted him.

"You're the captain that I'm supposed to arrest."

I stood between them. "Not without a proper writ, signed by the king."

The guard nodded and smiled slightly. "You should be an Advocate. Still, you are not safe, Captain. Others hunt you that are not so law-abiding."

Thaddeus took my hand. I pointed to the bed and dipped my head slightly. "I'll be back. The Alban Commander will not let me be harmed or detained. Rest and let your body heal from your injuries."

Thaddeus sighed, "May the Goddess protect you," and let go of my hand. In that brief encounter, he had shared with me some of his essence. Self-assuredly, I opened the door and said, "Let's go."

We walked through the busy streets. The Alban commander slowed his pace so I could keep up without running. The guards fell in behind us. I noticed that Jack trailed us. *What part has he played in this? At least if he follows me, then he won't try to kill Thaddeus.* Strangely, I wasn't worried about myself or my safety. I had my own secret tools. And when Thaddeus had restored me last night, the flow of energy from the Goddess through him had imprinted much of his essence and natural talents into me. *Is that what happens when I work with people? Does my spirit organize their energetic structure?* The thought sobered me. No wonder I instinctively labored to keep my state of being as pure as possible.

The commander took me to a side gate and the gatekeeper immediately unbarred the door for us. The majority of his guards remained in the small courtyard, sitting and chatting among themselves. They were mostly younger men with kindly, serious faces. Two guardsmen trailed behind the commander and me as we threaded through corridors until we came to a tall, wood-carved door. The commander pushed on the wide door and we entered the private study of the king.

The room was empty except for a manservant, who bustled about, straightening papers on the desk, arranging the ink stand and pens in a neat row and dusting the impressive velvet-covered chair. He looked up sharply.

"Where's the king, Ralph?"

The servant appraised me before responding. He nodded towards a door concealed in the wall behind the broad desk and scurried to knock softly, then opened the door for us. He followed us in and went to stand protectively by his master.

A young man in his mid-twenties lounged on a sofa. He appeared to be dozing. The servant shook him gently and whispered, "Commander Fabian is here to see you, Sire." He repeated this several times before the king opened his eyes and gazed blankly at us. "Commander Fabian, Sire."

The king lifted a limp hand and waved haphazardly. The manservant stepped back a pace. The commander came closer.

He pushed me forward. "Sire, I have brought a visitor for you."

"Has she come to assassinate me?" he slurred.

"No, Sire. To help you feel more like yourself."

I scanned the room. On a small table rested a decanter of water and a goblet. A sheer veil covered a porcelain dish filled with crackers, cheese, a small bowl of shelled almonds, a handful of strawberries, and four plump apricots.

I moved to the table and sniffed each item, and passed my hand over them to discern their energies. Determining they were wholesome, I ambled around the room, scanning with my inner sight for anomalies, or anything out of the ordinary.

Finding nothing that appeared to be harmful, I returned to the king, who had been half-heartedly watching me. I sat, perching on the edge of the sofa, and studied the man. A plain band of gold shaped into a crown rested on his silver-haired head. Fused into the metal were raised symbols representing the Natuan religion. As I observed it, my head tingled and began to numb. I quickly turned my attention to the rest of the man and assessed him by feeling what I felt in my body. Other than an overwhelming fatigue, he was healthy and robust.

The king watched me. "Who are you?" he finally asked.

"I'm called Ellara."

The commander started to say, "She's a H..."

The door burst open and a short, wiry man limped in. A ragged scar stretched from his temple down one side of his face. He scowled at the commander, spotted me, and brutishly dragged me away from the king. "She's an assassin, Sire. Thank the One God I got here in time!" He motioned for his subordinates to restrain me. "Commander, you are a traitor and will be punished for allowing this woman to make an attempt on the king's life."

The commander widened his stance and faced the slender man, who drew himself more erect.

"May I make the assumption that you are the famous Lord Garth?" I asked innocently.

The old soldier rounded on me. "And who are you?"

Meeting his gaze, I took the measure of the man. He didn't know who or what I was. I dipped my head submissively. "I am a humble servant who wanted to see if I could bring comfort to the king. The commander took pity on my pleading and brought me here. I am no assassin." I spread my hands. "Truly, I appreciate that you protect our king with such vigilance and determination. He is the father to our people and I don't want any harm to befall him."

Lord Garth grunted, looked me up and down again, then motioned his men to release me and the commander. "Get out of here, both of you. Don't you ever come back, wench." He glowered at the commander. "You should know better. Now get back to your post."

Commander Fabian flexed his fingers, as if they itched to put the arrogant man in his place. Garth had clearly overstepped his position. After all, this was Fabian's castle and his king. Instead, he grunted. "The king is my overlord, Garth. You have no business interfering with my duties."

Garth's face flushed and his hand grasped the hilt of his sword. "You think bringing some strumpet to sit by the king is doing your duties? Hah! You Albans don't know the meaning of being a soldier or protecting your country."

The commander puffed out his chest. It looked as if they would come to blows. I dipped my head to Lord Garth and the king, who languidly watched the whole exchange. I started to back away, intending to beat a hasty retreat.

The king made a feeble sound and beckoned to me. "Come here. Sit by me while these two argue."

Both commanders stopped and stared at the king. Commander Fabian growled to Garth, "Would you deprive the king of a little pleasure?" He faced the smaller man.

"Now, get out and let the king have fun for a change!" The Alban took a step towards the mercenary.

"You'll regret this, Fabian," Garth hurled as he swept out of the room, but not without one more appraising look at me.

The king reached weakly for my hand and guided me to sit beside him. He studied me. I met his gaze, calmed myself, and let myself feel the Goddess's presence. Certain that Lord Garth watched, I dared not invite the Goddess to work through me. Instead, I calmed myself and projected serenity to the king. The crown on his head repeatedly drew my attention. Finally, I broke eye contact and asked, "Do you wear your crown all of the time?"

He nodded. "I'm supposed to."

"Who says?"

"Lord Garth says that to show I'm the king, I need to wear my crown."

I nodded slowly. "Can I try an experiment? Can I remove your crown?"

The king sat up, shocked. "No!"

I laughed. "Can we see what happens when you take it off, just for a few minutes?"

The king lay back, pondered the question for a while, then said, "If it would please you."

I nodded.

He reached up and removed the crown, setting it on the back of the sofa. One hand still held it. I held out both hands, inviting him to take mine. Reluctantly, he did. I closed my eyes and noticed what I felt. With each passing minute, the dizziness and sluggish mental function cleared. I asked my invisible healing team of spirit helpers to clear from him the residue of the dark magic. Finally, I opened my eyes and asked him, "Do you notice anything different?"

Color had returned to his face. His eyes brightened. He appeared more cognizant of his surroundings. "I can think more clearly. Did anyone tell you how lovely you are?"

I rolled my eyes and glanced at the commander. "I'd say he's feeling better, but still not thinking clearly."

I pointed at the crown. I couldn't just say the crown was hexed and the source of his malaise. Nor could I tell him to stop wearing it. "This may sound strange to you, but your crown fits too tightly and that's why you feel tired and can't think straight. May I suggest that you have your goldsmith make the crown bigger?"

"But then it won't stay on my head!"

"You're right. Line the inside of your crown with a band of Heartland silver and cover the silver with a thin piece of leather so that it rests softly on your head. The leather will keep it from slipping. Perhaps you can delegate this task to your commander? I believe you will feel much better." I held his hands a little longer, then set them gently in his lap and rose to leave.

My Far Sight showed an agitated Lord Garth pacing the hallway outside the king's private office. The King's Guards blocked the doorway, determined to not allow the mercenary entry. "Is there another way out of this room?" I asked the commander.

He glanced at the king, who nodded. "Ralph, show them out." He looked at me. "Will you come back?"

I smiled at him. "I will be back." *And return your sovereignty.*

THIRTY-THREE

ROKAN AND KIAN

Tokurat, The Desert Lands

The sun peeked above the desert sands east of the city. Other than wanting to make sure Sophia was fine, going to the Chaste Palace was a waste of my time. I wanted to get it over with so I could pursue my other agendas. As I expected, I arrived to wailing. Women clustered around five of their lifeless companions. A quick scan revealed Sophia was not one of the victims. And none of the dead were the Healers I had captured. I scowled. This was another of Garrick's cruel games. What would he do to Ellara or Margot if they fell into his hands? I had to make sure Garrick didn't find them. This meant spying upon the Droc'ri that he used as his agents. I sighed. My life had gotten complicated.

"Where's the woman who arrived last night?"

The crowd parted. Someone said, "She captured and killed the venomous spiders before they could bite any more of us."

I beckoned to Sophia. She came towards me, head bowed as befitted a servant in the Desert Lands.

"Are you harmed?" I picked up her hands and inspected them. Two puncture marks darkened the creamy skin in the web between thumb and forefinger of one hand. "You were bitten, yet you did not die? What magic is this?" I probed her with my inner sight. She appeared in vibrant health.

Sophia shook her head. "I don't know, Master. My hand hurts, but I live, while my sisters do not."

I decided to drop the inquiry. I didn't want to draw attention to Sophia. That she was immune to Garrick's magic intrigued me. Was she an untrained Healer? But even a Healer would succumb to the magically enhanced poison from the spiders. Was she...? I searched my memory of ancient texts. Was she a Bandrio'deirvi, a mythical enchantress of old, said to be immune to the magic of the Goddess and the Dark Lords? There was more to this woman than I realized. I must protect her from Garrick while I figured out how I could make use of her. I turned to the others. Indicating the corpses, I instructed, "Prepare them for burial."

While the women proceeded with preparations, I singled out the Healers I had captured. One by one, I persuaded each Healer to support Margot, promising that she would restore their powers. While skeptical, each one was wise enough to realize that working with me was the lesser evil than the

Grand Master. Now I had to get Margot to lead them where I wanted, and that depended upon Garrick's next move.

Finally, I was free to go in search of Kian. Then I'd see if Felicity was ready to go to Araval and work with Jack.

Before departing from the Chaste Palace, I drew Sophia to the main entrance. "Come with me. I will take you to the Scholars' Guild in Langon. You will be safe there."

Sophia bowed her head. "Thank you for your kindness, Rokan. I appreciate your caring. However, I would like to remain here with the refugees."

"It's not safe for you here. You saw what Garrick is capable of. You will be safe in Langon."

She shook her head. "The Grand Master will find me, no matter where you hide me. Will you let me remain here? I am among friends."

I stared at her. Who was this woman? Finally, I nodded. "It's not safe, Sophia. But if you insist, you may remain until I return and find a more suitable hiding place for you." Warmth enfolded me. Automatically, I responded to her unspoken invitation and moved closer to gather her into an embrace. At the last minute, I stopped myself. Instead, I gazed at her, stroking her cheek. I held back the words of kindness I longed to say. Quickly, I turned away from her, exiting the compound. *She has an unusual power over me. Like Margot. She* must *be an enchantress.*

The Scholars' Guild resided in a sheltered valley about thirty miles inland from Langon. I arrived in the late afternoon and the day's warmth radiated from the stone pavement. Walking in the long shadows cast by the westerly sun, I made my way past ivy-covered, antiquated stone buildings. Only a few students lounged in the shade, most being in the dining hall. I entered one such venerable building. Carved into the lintel were the words, "May ye who enter, find the answers ye seek," in the Leonini dialect. The building was quiet. I traversed wood-paneled passageways, climbed a set of stairs, and walked down a long corridor to the last room on the left. I opened the door.

At first, I thought the room was empty, but after a moment, a voice called, "Who is it?" A short man emerged from a closet, tucking his shirt into his trousers. He smoothed his fringe of graying hair as he hurried towards me.

I smiled and pretended not to notice the rouge on the man's cheeks.

The headmaster cleared his throat and straightened the cuffs on his shirt. "Rokan Daniels. What brings you?"

"Headmaster Philips." I glanced around the room, hoping to catch a glimpse of his new paramour. "I hope I wasn't interrupting anything?"

The portly man shrugged. "Nothing that can't wait. What do you want?"

"I'm inquiring about a new student. He would have arrived about a month or two ago. The name is Kian Ruark. I'm looking for recruits for my latest research and his name came up. Where might I find him?"

The headmaster rubbed his hands together and rummaged on his desk. He extracted a sheet. "Looks like the boy just arrived. He has been assigned to Professor Sanders in Mystical Arts. You'll have to talk with Mina." Philips came back around the desk and glanced longingly at the closet. "Is that all?" he asked brusquely.

I smiled. "My apologies for interrupting, Headmaster. I'll let you get back to reading your book." That's what Philips always said he was doing, when I interrupted his romantic liaisons. As I left, I smirked. With my Far Sight, I spied a lovely, semi-naked woman waiting in the large closet. *I wonder who she is? A new student?*

The building that housed the Mystical Arts was furthest from the complex that formed the Guild. For good reason. That building had been rebuilt a number of times from magic gone awry. The walk was pleasant and gave me time to reminisce about the time I had spent at the Scholars' Guild. Those were the happiest days of my life, as long as Garrick was elsewhere. I had loved every branch of study at the Guild, from the Mystical Arts to the latest in scientific research, to philosophies, theologies, and the healing arts.

I arrived at the stone edifice all too soon. Unlike the other buildings of the school, this building was not encased in ivy.

Quite the contrary. Its creamy granite walls gleamed in the sun and protective spells kept the magic within.

It was cool inside. The air tingled with the vital forces of the cosmos. We had called it orgone energy. I closed my eyes and inhaled deeply, letting the atmosphere bring back memories of conjuring. And of the girl I had loved. She had made my studies beyond magical. Garrick had killed her when he found out about her. I tightened my jaw. Anger from losing her still festered.

The door to the library was ajar. I peered in and spotted a young man with head bent over a thick manual. Intent upon what he was reading, he made notes in a journal.

"Not hungry?"

Startled, the student looked up. He could have been a younger version of Ellara, except that he was as tall as me, and skinny as a bean pole. Intelligent blue eyes appraised me curiously. He shook his head.

"What are you reading?" I moved closer and sat at the table opposite him.

"About the interplay of elements in nature."

I leaned back. "That was one of my favorite topics." At his inquiring look, I added, "That was a long time ago. Now I'm a professor of theological philosophies. Goddess studies. I am often traveling the world, seeking new information. What's your name?"

"Kian."

I leaned forward. "I could use a young mind like yours to help me with my research. Ever thought of traveling the world and learning new things?"

Kian leaned back. "Where do you travel and what are you researching?"

"I specialize in the Goddess's teachings. Recently I discovered some of her lost teachings and shared them with a colleague."

"What are you looking for now?"

"I understand there is a new magic that the Goddess uses, but have not been able to discover anything about it. I don't even know where to start." I laced my words with persuasion. "I could use a scholar like you who is not afraid to dig for the deeper meaning. Will you join me?"

Kian appeared to entertain my proposition. "Thank you for your kind offer. At present I would not even know what to look for. A solid foundation in the Goddess teachings would make me of more assistance to you."

I couldn't help but smile. Wise lad. "I can teach you as we go." Casually, I said, "I hear a group of young Healers is using a new kind of magic to restore the Goddess's temples that were destroyed during the Religious Wars. That's where I want to go next. Would you like to join me in this venture?"

Kian set his pencil down and leaned back. I had his attention. Certain he knew more than he let on, I pressed on.

"This is an opportunity for you to get some firsthand experience with magic." I glanced around the room. "You will learn about the elements far better than from a book."

Kian nodded his head. "I'm sure you are right, Professor." He paused. "I appreciate your offer, but I want to get a foundational understanding, then what I experience in the world will make more sense." He picked up his pencil as an unspoken, yet polite way to dismiss me.

He reminded me of when I was his age and the passion I had for doing everything to perfection. Oh, the innocence of youth. I felt a pang of regret for the life I had chosen. What if I had chosen the path of the Goddess? I could have remained at the Scholars' Guild. And my family would not have died. But they did anyway. Garrick had killed them after I endured the Rith Bac'croi. He had said it was a reward for my decision.

Surprised my persuasion didn't work on him, I rose and leaned on the edge of the table, scanning his aura. *Of course. He has protection woven into it, just like Margot and Ellara.*

I should take the youth with me. But where? Dare I leave him with Achmed in my fortress? No. I know where he is, now. And he's safe for the moment. He will come with me when I need him. "If you change your mind, just ask Mina Sanders or the Headmaster for me. My name is Rokan Daniels."

Halfway down the hall, I stopped, retraced my steps and re-entered the library. Kian looked up. "Kian, I have a legend I want to research, but I don't have the time right now. Would you be willing to do it?"

"What is it?"

"May I?" I indicated his notebook. He turned to a blank page. I took his pencil and wrote one word. Bandrio'deirvi. "Legend has it that she is an enchantress and uses a different magic than the Healers, or the Droc'ri. None of my research has indicated whether the Bandrio'deirvi is real. I'd like to know if she is, and just what she can do." I swept my hand around the expansive room filled with manuscripts, scrolls, sheets of parchment, and magical treatises. "I'm sure the answers are here."

Silently, Kian pulled the book closer to study the word.

"Will you look into this?" I waited impatiently.

Finally, he nodded. "I'll look into this when I have time."

"Much appreciated, Kian. I'll be back for a report."

Outside the Guild complex I smiled. Kian had unwittingly accepted my spell. Now I could spy on him far more effectively than with my scrying wall, and without his knowing. And he would find answers about Sophia for me.

I had one last stop before leaving the academic guild. I entered another ivy-covered building. The Hall of Ancestral Records. It was a long shot, since I didn't know Sophia's real name, but I had heard her mother's name was Adeline Ross, from the Emerald Mountain borderlands.

The archive was quiet. Lamps set into the walls cast light on row after row of journals containing birth records. They were organized by region. I searched along the walls until I came to the Emerald Mountain region north of Langon, near the border of Inyua. I pulled the most recent records and flipped through the pages, looking for Sophia's mother's name. I wished I had something of Sophia's to use to energetically narrow the field. I stopped after I had scanned ten volumes and four centuries without any mention of an Adeline or receiving an intuitive nudge. I sighed. I needed to get more information about Sophia's family. I would unravel Sophia's secrets.

As I walked beyond the Guild complex, I couldn't help but compare Felicity's children, now in their late teens, to Ellara's children. I had to admit that Kian left me with the same awe and enthusiasm about life and the wondrous world we live in as Margot and her friends. By comparison, Felicity's children were dull, and unhappy with the life forced upon them. Was it the religious beliefs that made the difference? Or the parents? This generation of Goddess-born had mutated. They appeared impervious to my magic. I would discover their technique.

I sighed and made a gateway to Felicity's village. She wasn't home when I knocked on her door. Discreet inquiries directed me to the home of a seamstress. I knocked and, after a long delay, Felicity's daughter opened the door. She recognized me and led me through a narrow hallway to the seamstress's workroom. I paused to caress a sensuously soft, blue silk fabric spread across a broad table.

Felicity and the seamstress emerged from behind a screen. When the younger woman saw me, she ran to me. "Rokan!" She pointed at the bolt of material. "Sally's going to make me a gown like the Healers at Cuilithe wore! What do you think?"

"It's lovely, Felicity, and you will look stunning when you wear it." I smiled, as I groaned inwardly. "Felicity, can we talk, alone?"

She followed me out of the shop to a darkened corner. She threw her arms around me.

"I have a task for you. It's very important, but I am reluctant to send you into danger." I paused.

"What do you want me to do, Rokan? Will it be like what you wanted me to do at Cuilithe?"

"No. You will work with the Alban queen and one of her servants to complete a task. You will have a chance to use the magic I've taught you, and deepen your abilities."

She clung to me. "Will I see you?"

"I'll come to Araval as soon as I can get away from my other duties."

"When do you want me to go?"

"I can help you make a portal now. Otherwise, you'll have to take a ship, and that may take a week or two. That will be too long. I need you in Araval now."

She brightened. "If it will please you, I will go." She detached herself. "Can you wait a few minutes while I let Sally know I'll be gone for a while? How long will I be away?"

I shook my head. "A week, two? It's hard to say. It depends upon how long the queen needs you."

An hour later, she was finally ready, with a change of clothes and personal sundries in a travel bag slung over her shoulder, and a medicine kit and pouch of coins I had given her belted at her waist. Before I made a portal to Araval, I handed her a jar of magical cream and a letter. "Give this to Queen Qadira. Tell her it's from me. She will receive you."

I placed my hand upon her shoulder. Together, we said the words and drew the symbols that commanded my traveling crystal. The air split to a grove at the outskirts of Araval.

"You don't know how much I wish I could come with you, Felicity." I kissed her lightly on the forehead. "I will come as soon as I can."

I watched her step through the portal. She turned back and waved to me. I located Jack with my Far Sight and urged him to find Felicity. He could help her get an audience with the queen.

THIRTY-FOUR

ELLARA AND THADDEUS

Araval

W hen I returned to the bakery, Thaddeus was particularly anxious for a healing session. He appeared to know about the encounter with Lord Garth.

I was willing enough to work with him. I could use the recharging that channeling the Goddess energy gave me. I often received inspiration as well.

Typically, in the healing work I performed, I was the active party, delivering the Goddess's Loving Radiance to my client. The recipient simply surrendered and received. It was their spirit's interaction with the Goddess that actually did the healing. Even though my essence mingled with the flow of Goddess Gra'yia, I typically did not engage in actively sharing my spirit or emotions with my clients. I was just a doorway, a hollow bone.

Shortly after we started, Thaddeus merged his spirit with mine. Other than Sam and my children, my patients had never joined their spirit with me. I wasn't sure whether I wanted Thaddeus to unite with me or not. I stopped the session.

Nana noticed. "Let him meld with you, Child. It will strengthen you so you can handle more of the Goddess's Light energy, the Lig'yia. Do you want to be burned again?"

I frowned at Thaddeus, who nodded in agreement with Nana. "She knows best, Ellara." Thaddeus continued holding my hands. "I was worried that you would be captured, and I want to learn how to protect you, like you do for me."

Cautiously, I welcomed the Goddess into my being, and let Thaddeus unite his spirit with mine. However, I was not willing to share all of myself with him, and held back. During our exchange, we basked in the Goddess's Gra'yia. It revital- ized me as well as Thaddeus. Through the exchange, I perceived his thoughts and feelings, and he knew mine. He hungered for more.

When we finished, Thaddeus said. "I didn't mean for my behavior to make you uneasy when I addressed Jack today, or to steal your life force. I need to learn how to draw upon the Goddess's radiant energies and not drain yours. I want to master working together. When I'm with you, I feel alive and valued. We can beat the sorcerer's hold over both of us." He paused, touching my arm tentatively. "Every time you work with the Goddess, you risk capture. You almost died protecting me. Why do you risk your life for me?"

"I've been wondering that myself," I replied wryly. I fidgeted with the edge of the pocket in my trousers. I didn't want to admit the restoration work I had performed on him had softened my heart, and I was developing an affection for him. It felt like that was betraying Sam. The weight of his scrutiny pressed on me. I knew I could not deceive him, not after combining our spirits. Finally, I said, "In these times, a Healer risks capture every time she practices her art. I care about you, both as my patient and as a friend of Sam's." I met his gaze. "With what I have to do, it would be handy to have someone around who can restore me to health when needed." I smiled slightly at his puzzled expression.

"I didn't say I was going to help you with straightening out the chaos in the world."

"No, you didn't. I'm hoping you will want to. Perhaps the talents you feel awakening are the tools that will aid in this needed transformation, which will also rid us of the sorcerer. In exchange, I offer you and your ship the best protection I know how to give."

He grinned mischievously, went to my travel bags, and pulled out one of Nana Magog's thin books. He shrugged innocently at my frown. "I read these while you were gone with the commander. I wanted to find out if there was anything I could do for you." He flipped it open to a page displaying the image of a couple intertwined in lovemaking. Encircling them was a protective dome of tightly interwoven strands. The words were in the ancient Leonini script, but the meaning was obvious. He pointed. "This tells how to make a protective shield." Thaddeus chuckled at my reaction. "You know about this?"

"Not exactly. Sam and I figured this out on our own. It's what kept him safe from Bruce the Terrible. He could either outrun Bruce's pirates or the *M'Ellara* would be unharmed in an attack." I pointed to the book. "You can read this?"

Thaddeus laughed. "My mother taught me. She read me the legends of Baldaran, Shane and Delfina, and many more."

"Leonini legends? I hadn't heard of them." *What else did my mother or Nana Magog forget to tell me?*

Thaddeus indicated Cleric Paul's papers. "Some of the stories of the demigods are in these translations. You will enjoy reading them." He nudged me. "Some apply to us." He returned his attention to the booklet with the protection ritual. "Can we make this?"

My face burned. Sam and I had merged with the Goddess's Gra'yia in spirit and with our physical bodies. Two of those out-of-this-world encounters had produced Margot and Kian. The little booklet called this coalescing of body, heart, and spirit with the Goddess the Ceangal Bandia.

"No!" I swallowed several times. I shook my head rapidly, the flush draining away from my face. I edged away. The memories cruelly reminded me that Sam was no longer with me.

I retreated into the garden to be alone with my grief, and sat on the bench with my back next to the warm bricks of the oven. Pulling my knees to my chest and sobbing quietly, I despaired that I would never again feel the bliss of mating with Sam.

Roused by a rustle of clothing, I watched as Thaddeus crossed the garden and climbed the wall. He sat looking in the direction of the Red Rose. From what I could see of his expression, he looked dejected. I exhaled. If he went to seek solace in drink, it would mean he was not ready for the responsibility that came with the Goddess's theurgy, and I would not teach him. I waited.

He jumped down, retraced his steps, and came to sit beside me. He put an arm around my shoulders. "I know you love me, even if you won't admit it. I feel it when we unite. I... have not had good experiences with women and love."

I sighed. "It's not you, Thaddeus. I love Sam with all my heart. I am not ready to say goodbye to him yet. Engaging in the Ceangal Bandia with you, even as a practical matter, would feel like a betrayal of what Sam and I had together."

He didn't say anything. He bent so that his cheek rested lightly on my head. *"One day, I hope you will love me with the loyalty and passion with which you love Sam,"* I heard in my mind.

My thoughts drifted along their own inner currents. One of the benefits of the Ceangal Bandia was a durable connection that had allowed Sam to have access to my abilities. I had never felt him draw upon them like Thaddeus had earlier today. Sam had commented how my senses had expanded his ability to read the sea, giving him a foreknowledge of storms or a shift in currents beyond his natural seaman's talent. Although he was adept at understanding people, by tapping into his enhanced intuition he could immediately discern who was trying to cheat him in a bargain. He had said he bene-fitted the most by the companionship between us, knowing he was not alone in whatever he did.

Why did I care about Thaddeus? Through the exchange of spirit in the Gra'yia, I discovered that Thaddeus had secretly loved me for years. This love was the reason for the Kurat spirit, although Thaddeus had kept his heart's desire hidden from Rokan. It was true the strength of his love had restored me to health. But I didn't return his passion. I still viewed him as a stranger, even if we had shared our energies. By the same token, a buried potential within him attracted me. He may have cracked the wall around his heart and professed his love for me, but he had had years of indoctrination by the sorcerer. What if I taught him the ways of the Goddess's Gra'yia and he used them for harmful purposes, or the Droc'ri regained control over him, and used Thaddeus for his own evil purposes?

My muscles ached, reminding me that only a few hours ago, I had briefly visited Sam in the Mag Mell. That Sam had not welcomed me to stay with him stung. Was this his way of telling me to get on with my life? Why had he been so intent upon Thaddeus healing me? I shifted to get more comfortable. My thoughts returned to the Ceangal Bandia. I didn't want to see Thaddeus come to harm. Could we do a modified version of it that would afford Thaddeus some protection?

Hunger drove me inside. After consuming a bowl of stew, I grabbed a light cloak one of Nana's patrons had left for me, tossed it around my body, and headed towards the door.

"Wait. Where are you going? I'll come with you!" Thaddeus slid his arms into his coat and was right behind me.

"I thought you were reluctant to get involved in solving the world's problems."

"Doesn't a person have the right to test the winds?" He slipped his arm through mine. "Where are we going?"

"To the castle. I want to see the king. I have an idea."

Thaddeus planted his feet. "You barely escaped today. How do you expect to get in there undetected? Last time you had the commander to escort you."

I smiled at him. "You don't have to come. Besides, it's too dangerous for you."

Thaddeus sputtered, "You don't know your way around the castle. You need me to be your guide."

We ducked into doorways and between buildings to avoid notice. At one such interval, I spotted a lanky man heading towards the side entrance of the fortress. He appeared to be escorting a young woman. A hooded cloak concealed her features. Thaddeus urged me forward. "Let's see what Jack's up to."

We stole after them. Jack appeared to be completely unaware of us. At the postern gate, he told the guard that the queen expected him. The guard rattled a bunch of keys, then the squeaky lock clicked. Hastily, I made Thaddeus and myself invisible and tugged him to stand behind Jack and the woman. They looked around, then stepped into the small courtyard. *Felicity! What's she doing here? And with Jack?*

We followed on their heels. Thaddeus pulled me into the first cross corridor and leaned against the wall.

"What did you do? Why didn't Jack, the woman with him, or the guard notice us?"

"Invisibility," I whispered.

Thaddeus grinned in delight.

"I can't hold it for long. It really drains my vitality. I dare not call upon the Goddess's power like I do for healing."

"Maybe I can help you." He took my elbow. "Let's go this way."

We traveled the same corridors that the commander and I had earlier, and came to the hallway that led to a formidable guard planted in front of an imposing door leading to the king's private office. The guard stood with his back almost touching the door, and he monitored the hallway vigilantly.

Thaddeus plucked a gold coin from his pocket. Flipping the coin in his hand, he sauntered toward the guard. He stopped before the man, smiled winningly, and asked, "I think I'm lost. I'm looking for the galley. Oh, no. I mean the kitchen. No, I mean the place where the servants eat."

The sentry inspected Thaddeus, but his eyes strayed to the coin twinkling in the lamplight as it rose and fell rhythmically from Thaddeus's palm. Imperceptibly, Thaddeus edged backward, drawing the guard forward just enough so I could conjure invisibility and squeeze behind him.

I opened the massive door and ducked into the private office, but the king was not there. I looked into his private chamber to no avail. I raced back to the door and cracked it open. Luckily, the guard had inched slightly farther away from the door, and I was able to glide past him without notice.

Thaddeus caught the coin. "Which way did you say?"

The soldier pointed down a corridor.

Thaddeus thanked the man and sauntered off. I walked beside him, struggling to remain hidden. Once out of sight, I leaned against the wall and caught my breath. I whispered, "He wasn't there."

"Let's go."

"Wait. I hear voices."

"They're coming from the Great Hall," Thaddeus supplied.

We crept along the walls, following the rise and fall of voices, alert for servants or guards. We came to an intersection of corridors that poured into a large room with wide double doors. Only one door was open. I made us invisible again and peeked inside. At this late hour, the room was in deep shadows except for the circle of light from bronze lamps illuminating a group of men standing before the king's throne. I tugged on Thaddeus's arm. We edged around the door and hid behind tall, cushioned chairs lining the walls. As Thaddeus took my hand, refreshing life force flowed into me.

Lord Garth and some of the councilors argued. The king sat placidly on his throne, seemingly off in his own world, picking at his fingernails or at an invisible thread along the hem of his tunic. He wore the Natuan crown. I strained to hear the conversation about a new tax. The argument was about how much the tax should be. Nothing was said about the effect upon those who would be taxed.

We crouched lower when we heard footsteps and the swish of silk. Jack and Queen Qadira entered. Jack stopped near the doorway. He could have seen us if we moved. The queen glided regally to Lord Garth, who bowed to her, and handed her a document.

"These are the laws you requested, My Queen."

I perked up. Was the queen going to help the people?

The queen scanned the ordinance and nodded her approval. "This will help our cause." She turned to the king. "Sign this, Leo." A clerk slipped a pen into the king's hand and closed his fingers around it. "Sign," the queen commanded.

Wearing a lackluster expression, the young monarch did as instructed. The queen graced Lord Garth with a hint of a nod, ignored the other councilors, and swept out of the room, followed by Jack. What was the relationship between Jack and the queen?

Dismissed by Lord Garth, the councilors filed from the Great Hall. A servant systematically moved about the room, dousing the lamps. The king remained on his throne, alone and forlorn. He rubbed the fingers that had held the pen.

Not wanting to miss an opportunity to see the king, I cautiously approached him. He didn't notice me. I assessed him with my inner sight and saw a cloud of darkness around him that radiated from the crown.

I placed my hand on his, stopping his fingers, and let the Goddess energy flow into him, asking my invisible healing team of spirit helpers to clear the darkness from the crown and the king. He lifted his head and fixed his eyes upon mine.

Hurried footsteps approached. Thaddeus pulled me into the gloom behind the throne, just as Lord Garth and several of his men entered. One man carried a silver goblet. The aroma of the herbal tinctures mixed in his wine alerted me to the nature of the sedative that controlled him. Lord Garth offered the goblet to the king. King Leo slowly reached out to grasp the cup and held it, staring blankly at its contents.

"Drink, Sire," Lord Garth ordered.

The king lifted his gaze to meet Lord Garth's. He slowly tipped the wine cup so that the contents spilled onto the floor at Lord Garth's feet. The man jumped back to avoid soiling his exquisitely tooled leather boots. He stared in shock at the young man, then raised a hand to strike him.

I caught my breath. *How dare he!* Thaddeus tightened his hold on me.

With surprising speed, King Leo grabbed the hand arcing towards him and clamped it in a vise grip. His brows drew together. *"Never* do that again, Garth," his deep voice commanded.

Thaddeus and I exchanged glances. Had the Goddess been able to clear some of the malaise from the young man in just those few minutes?

Lord Garth lowered his hand and his tone shifted. "You need to rest, Sire." He nodded to his men, who supported the monarch to rise from his throne. Garth's retainers surrounded the king and guided him through a concealed door behind the throne. As the last one closed the door, he looked back into the chamber, and happened to notice us. He shouted, "Assassins!"

Thaddeus dragged me towards the entrance as I muttered the words to make us invisible again. I managed to get us out of the room and partly down the corridor before my magic flagged. We huddled in a dim nook. The alarm had been sounded. The corridors bustled with running servants and guards.

"I've got to ask Nana how to sustain concealment," I muttered. Making a stationary dome to hide my campsites hadn't drained my vitality. Trying to maintain a disguise for active people required a lot more concentration. I must be missing something. "How do we get out of here? I don't know if I can make or maintain our disguise long enough to reach the castle gates."

"I know a short cut. If you can make us unnoticeable for a little longer..." From behind me, Thaddeus encircled me with his arms, pressing his palms over my heart. "Let me assist you."

Together we spoke the ancient words and I guided his hand in tracing the symbols. I felt a surge of energy from him and sensed a strong shield surrounding us.

Thaddeus grabbed my hand, and we joined the bustle of servants in the corridors. Soon we exited at a quiet corner of the castle that had no gatekeeper.

"How do you know so much about the castle?"

He smiled at me. "Smugglers know all the secrets of a place." He took a breath.

Before he could chastise me for another brush with Lord Garth, I threw my arms around his neck. "Thank you, Thaddeus. I couldn't have done this without you." I stretched to lightly kiss him on the cheek.

As if the thunder had been stolen from the lecture he had been preparing, he paused, speechless. His fingers touched his cheek and a grin spread across his face. He started to collect me into his arms for what I guessed would be a proper kiss. I slipped away. "Let's get back to the bakery." *I must learn how to sustain my energy when I command the elements. Thaddeus makes me stronger, but he won't always be around to help me.*

"What makes you think that?" he asked, putting an arm around my shoulder.

We were almost to the bakery when a thought struck me. "Do you realize that all the years you endured Rokan's magic and his curses, he was actually teaching you how to use your own theurgy?"

Thaddeus halted, staring at me in horror. "How can you say that? I struggled to keep my sanity. I was forced to perform illicit tasks. I smuggled dangerous contraband, despicable personages, and priceless Heartland blades. All so he and his greedy Brothers could prosper as merchants." He shook his head. "I hate how he debased me and killed anyone I cared about. Rokan embarrassed and humiliated me so that I believed I was unworthy of love. There is nothing good about that man." He faced me. "Sam and Matty were the only ones in my life who treated me with respect." He hesitated. "And now you. Sam said you'd accept me." He added softly, "I was afraid you would reject me like all the other women."

"I know. It hasn't been easy for you. When we merged, I gained a deep understanding of you and your history. What you underwent makes you strong. It has given you the tools you need to move forward."

We started walking again. "It is for the best that we did not meet earlier. If Rokan knew, he would have killed you. It was my way of protecting you." Thaddeus became quiet. Our steps echoed in the narrow alley. "I suppose you are right. Rokan, in his evilness, actually did me a service. He has made me capable and, in so doing, also revealed his weaknesses." Thaddeus stopped before me. "Are you willing to help me break his hold over me?"

I met his gaze but said nothing as I weighed the consequences of aligning with him.

"Rokan is at the root of the challenges you face in restoring balance in our world. And he hunts you as well. Together we can defeat him." He looked hopeful.

I sighed. "He is a nemesis for both of us and has to be dealt with."

"You'll help me?"

"Yes."

Thaddeus pulled me into his arms and leaned his cheek on my head. It was as if a great weight had lifted from him.

"Together, we can face the old Droc'ri and succeed. I know it."

"Or die trying," I heard in my mind.

I let his desire envelop me, then slid out of his embrace. "Well, we have to figure out how to use the Goddess's energies before we can be any sort of a match for him."

As we neared the bakery, I caught a glint of steel from a darkened food stall across the street from Nana Bean's cottage. I tensed. "As long as Jack is the instrument for Rokan, Rokan will always be a threat to your safety."

Thaddeus grunted.

Jack emerged from the shadows across from the bakery, holding his dagger as if it were a natural extension of his hand. He headed towards Thaddeus. I stepped between them and faced Jack, confident he would not harm me.

Jack glowered at Thaddeus, then turned his attention to me. "Where have you been? I've been looking all over for you, Ellara."

"What I do is my business, Jack." I didn't sense the master. "Put your knife away. You will not be using it here." I lifted my hand, palm out, and slowly swept it downward.

Jack shuffled his feet, glanced at Thaddeus, then slowly sheathed his dagger.

"Now go, Jack." We turned towards the bakery entry.

"Wait, Ellara! Before you send me away, I bear a message for you from the queen."

I stopped and eyed him suspiciously. "What does the queen want?"

"She wants to meet with you."

THIRTY-FIVE
ROKAN

Tokurat, The Desert Lands

I entered Garrick's favorite garden, carrying a small, ornate wooden box, the right size for a pendant or ring.

"What do you have for me, Rokan?" Garrick lounged on his settee, holding a goblet of rose water in one hand and a sheaf of papers in the other. He set the papers down and reached for the box, opened it, and exclaimed, "Magnificent! No one will suspect these priceless diamonds are talismans that will break down the Albans' Goddess tradition, and, dare I say, even Natuan ethical codes." He caressed the large diamond that appeared flawless to the unaware, yet was imprinted with a spell that activated the shadow nature in people. He looked at me. "Once again, you surprise me, Rokan."

I bowed my head in humility. "The diamonds have a potent destructive power, Master. Most of the crew on the ship that delivered these gems from the Alban mines were either dead, dying, or behaving violently. I hid the evil residue with an illusion. The diamonds' taint will spread like a plague — a disease not of the body, but an invisible one that will destroy the heart of Alba."

"Splendid! Start distributing these in Alba and then to the leaders and important people in the world." He flicked an invisible speck of dust from his robe. "Send one to the Ethnarch." He waved idly. "I know just the person for this task. You'll oversee this, won't you?"

"Yes, Master. Who am I working with?"

"Sophia, of course." His lips curved up at the corners. "The woman you frequent for gratification."

I struggled to remain impassive and lowered my gaze. I knew this day would come. Garrick always destroyed anything or anyone with whom I found pleasure.

Garrick continued. "You know she is a Healer who is not a Healer." He watched me intently. "She survived my venomous pets." He shook his head in mock sadness. "Unlike her sisters."

"She wasn't trained as a Healer, nor did she display any of their characteristics."

Garrick chuckled. "You're going soft, Rokan. You should have discerned who she was. Her magic is so subtle that she has you enchanted, and you don't even know it. You can't see her for who she really is." He shook his head sadly. "You were always the best for locating Healers. You can thank me. I keep an eye on you to protect you from going astray."

I tightened my jaw. "What assignment have you given her?" *He won't take her from me this time!*

"I just told you. Deliver the tainted diamonds and seed the world with discord."

"The task will kill her."

Garrick smiled. "It might at that. But she appears to be immune to the Dark Lords' energies. Why is that, do you think?" He leaned forward. "Perhaps it is because she is the Healer of the prophecy?"

I swallowed, shaking my head. "She can't be. She's just someone Bruce the Terrible captured."

Garrick leaned back, looking quite pleased with himself. "Rokan, for my Henchman, you've been remiss. But perhaps that was part of her magic — to distract you from your duties. My spies discovered she was mated to a sea captain from Langon. She is from a Goddess-born lineage, a sea-faring people, perhaps even a part of your family."

"You killed my family," I growled.

"Well, no matter. If she is our Healer, the diamonds will kill her. Or they will turn her against the Goddess, to work for the

Droc'ri. For me. Don't worry. Bruce will take good care of her."

I stood stiffly, my jaw clamped. Was Sophia an untrained natural Healer like Ellara? Or was she more, as I suspected?

Garrick spun his glass of rose water, looking quite satisfied. "Now, do you have an antidote for the hex that these precious gemstones carry? We need to have something to offer the heads of state, after their countryfolk descend into their basest instincts and discard social mores." Garrick rubbed his hands together. "And murder each other."

"I'll work on finding one, Master. The Dark Lords' sorcery is indestructible. We may just have to *tell* the leaders we have a remedy."

"Ah! I like that plan even better!" He waved dismissively. "Get to work. We have a world to conquer." He stretched out his legs and leaned back.

"I'll make enough diamonds for all the important people, Master." But my mind was on how to free Sophia.

Garrick sipped his drink. "By the way, Rokan. I want you to go back to that band of untrained Healers in the Emerald Mountains. They have restored the Temple of the Crescent Moon as a place of the Goddess's power. I don't know what magic they have used, since they have not been initiated, but they are becoming a danger to us. We can't have them going around restoring the Goddess's sanctuaries. They are traveling deeper into the mountains, towards the remains of the Temple to the Six Winds. Find them and kill them before they do any more damage."

"Yes, Master." I bowed my head and withdrew.

I made a detour on my way back to my personal study. Deep beneath the rocky bluff that formed the back of the palace were the archives and a vast library. I had added to it over the years, and now it rivaled the Scholars' Guild collection. I kept the most priceless or damning documents here. I stood in the center of the room carved from sandstone and inhaled deeply. The smell of old manuscripts and the atmosphere of ancient knowledge had a calming effect upon me.

I went to the section where I had organized the ancient stories and myths of the Goddess and scanned the titles. I was looking for a particular tome that had referenced the legendary enchantresses. I searched, but the book was not where I had left it. Finally, I found it, tossed into the section where I kept the Droc'ri teachings. *Garrick! He has no respect! Was he researching the Bandrio'deirvi, too?*

I flipped through the book until I found a picture of a lovely woman. The caption read, Bandrio'deirvi, Leonini Enchantress. I turned the page and read: "*By embracing their shadow nature, the ancient Leonini became immune to the Dark Lords' magic. As a result, the Leonini bridge the worlds of the Goddess and the Dark Lords. They have created a magic far more effective than the Goddess's theurgy or the Dark Lords' sorcery.*"

I closed the manuscript slowly. I had never come across any proof that the Leonini actually existed. They were said to be the Goddess's children and to have seeded our planet, Gea, in the distant past.

I replaced the book in its proper location and slowly walked to my study. *Was Sophia really a Bandrio'deirvi? Were Margot and her friends? How does one become the master of them?*

I pushed Sophia from my mind and shifted to pondering what to do about Ellara. Without my Skeld I was at a distinct disadvantage, and the Alban shield drained my resources if I spent too much time using my Far Sight or engaging with her through Jack. I had noticed her polite resistance to Jack's attentiveness and her fierce protection of Thaddeus. Was she, like Margot, impervious to the web of discord Jack and I wove around her? She appeared to be making her own decisions, despite my best efforts. And Thaddeus was now uncontrollable — but not unpredictable.

My words cautioning Thaddeus that he would revert back to his original crippled state or worse if he let a Healer touch him had kept him under my thumb for years. When I told Thaddeus about how she had broken her vows to the Goddess, and killed a cleric, I thought I had effectively put him off of Ellara. I convinced Thaddeus that she had lost her powers as a result, and everyone she had healed or would heal would be cursed.

It would have been so much easier if she hadn't met the half-man captain. I had given him that name because he was only half a man when I met him. Everything from waist down did not function. He had smelled horrible. I wrinkled my nose at the memory. He still couldn't function as a man sexually. I had made sure of that. I smirked at the truth of the man who pursued Ellara. *That half-man could never be my rival! I know her. She still loves Sam. Ellara would never consider him for a pair'ti.*

The talent that made him a superb captain also made him a challenge. He was clever and willful. I had to kill anyone he cared for if they could not be turned against him, like Felicity. I had even returned him to a semi-crippled state. Yet, he still tried to circumvent me. It wasn't until I assassinated Matty's family, including his daughter, for whom Thaddeus had developed an affection, that I finally broke his spirit. When he was feeling particularly glum, I had taken him to a brothel in Zambril and proceeded to get him very drunk. In this weakened state, and with a little magic, I had persuaded him I could help him feel better. All he had to do was accept a small gift, a consolation for his loss. Finally, he halfway agreed. When he passed out from the powder the proprietress of the establishment had placed in his drink, I implanted the Kurat entity, which served to drain his will, make him feel unworthy and undeserving of love or of a mate. The invisible creature constantly reminded him how fragile his health was and how quickly he could return to his original, crippled, incontinent state if he disobeyed me, or sought love.

He was mine, now, even without the Kurat entity. I had never before considered him a threat. Who would want a crippled half-man? My control over him was rock solid.

Camila had served me well, but now Ellara had a confidence about her that I hadn't seen before. *It's that half-man. She's borrowing some of his essence.* I inhaled sharply. *She has merged with him!*

I groaned. I desperately needed to get to Alba and get control of the situation. I should have gone with Felicity. I could have used her magic to make a portal away and return to Tokurat before Garrick realized I was gone.

My Far Sight showed Felicity in the queen's quarters. As I watched, she turned away from inspecting the jars of lotion, brushes, and jewelry on the queen's dressing table and moved to caress one of Qadira's silk dressing gowns. A pair of Qadira's servants watched her suspiciously. The queen swept into the room. She took the letter Felicity handed to her and read it, then tossed it on a side table. It appeared that Qadira had asked Felicity to heal her, as she sat down, and Felicity moved behind her, placing her hands on her shoulders.

I smiled. Maybe the queen would trust the woman and use her to help take over Alba.

I searched for Ellara with my Far Sight and saw Ellara and Thaddeus returning to the bakery, looking quite pleased with themselves. *What had they done?*

Could I get Jack to provoke Thaddeus so that the captain would convince Ellara to leave with him? Once Thaddeus and Ellara left Alba, I could capture her wherever they landed. Watching them together made my blood boil.

I picked up a silver object from my desk and idly caressed it in my fingers. *I wonder how I can get her to welcome Jack into her heart? If Jack can get her to call the Goddess to heal him, I'll have her.* If I could travel to Alba, I would take care of Thaddeus once and for all, rather than relying upon Jack. Once again, I wished I had gone to Alba with Felicity.

THIRTY-SIX

ELLARA AND THE QUEEN

Araval

"What does the queen want?" I asked warily.

"She wants your support with Alba's problems."

Thaddeus muttered behind me, "Don't go. It's a trap."

I ignored him. I had just witnessed her force the king to sign a new edict. *What was she up to? Was she really trying to help the country?* "I will meet with the queen tomorrow. But it must be on neutral territory and no guards involved. And no attempt to capture me."

Jack beamed and rocked onto his toes. "I'll arrange it immediately." He headed up the street towards the castle.

"What do you think he and his master are up to now?"

"Don't go. The queen is not who she appears to be."

"Why do you say that?"

Thaddeus turned away and shook his head, muttering. "Already I have said too much."

I pulled him around to face me. "If I am to meet the queen, I need to know what to expect." I glared at him.

"Don't meet her. That's the best way to not be harmed."

"Thaddeus, you are really helpful at times, and I really appreciate that. Sometimes you withhold from me, hindering me. I need to explore every possible way to restore the heart of Alba. If meeting with the queen will be fruitful, I will do that. You are holding back secrets that could mean life or death for me."

"And me, if anyone finds out I revealed them." He refused to say more. We entered the bakery and he stretched out on the sleeping mat.

Determined to understand the queen, the next day I went outside to where Nana's friends gathered for their usual afternoon discussions. "Can you tell me about the queen?"

The nanas exchanged glances. Finally one volunteered, "She's a foreigner and doesn't understand our Alban ways."

"She's from the Desert Lands. Aren't women valued less than their male counterparts in that country? How did she end up becoming queen of Alba?" I asked.

One of the elders snorted. "The old king broke with tradition, embraced the Natuan religion, and married his heir to that woman."

It was obvious to me that the queen was a sore topic. "Why don't you like her?"

"The queens of Alba are like mothers to our country. They were typically Healers and chosen by the Gra'Bandia Council. They led the country with the wisdom and the backing of the Council. The country thrived for centuries."

"Then old King Theodopolis broke the tradition and now look what we have!" Another nana warmed to the topic. "Laws that break our country, foreign mercenaries who think they are the true rulers, a Droc'ri Grand Master who covets our country and wants to destroy the Goddess's last stronghold."

"She wants to meet with me. Do you think she will go against Lord Garth's master and bring balance back to our country?"

The nanas laughed. One of them placed a hand on mine. "Child, you really don't know anything about Qadira, do you? That woman's brother is the Grand Master of the Droc'ri. In Tokurian tradition, which is *very* patriarchal, he is her master. Always has been. She is supposed to kill King Leopold and give her brother the country."

"That's what she has done over the past fifty years. At first her father, the Suzerain of Tokur, started the practice to consolidate his control over neighboring countries. Her brother continued the practice of marrying her to the provincial leaders in all the countries on the mainland. She had to be married for a year and a day before she could inherit their lands and title. Very shortly after that, her husband would meet with a fatal accident or succumb to a fatal disease. She became known as the widow-maker. After a while, no one wanted to marry her."

"Until the sorcerer, Rokan, brokered a deal with the foolish old king."

"As the master of the woman, and since a Tokurian woman cannot own property or hold a title, her brother became lord and master over most of the world."

Someone else supplied, "Now her brother is Grand Master of the Droc'ri."

I perched on one of Nana's bread barrels. "What does she hope to gain from me?"

"Oh, probably to get you to assassinate our monarch. Then blame you for it. That's what she's done before."

"Except her magic doesn't work here. She'll want yours," another nana reminded the speaker.

"Magic? She has magic?"

"Child, that woman must be two hundred years old if she is a day! She has to leave every few months to go to Langon to rejuvenate. That's what the captain won't tell you."

My mind was a whirl. I thanked the nanas and returned to the kitchen, going about the mindless work of kneading dough and forming loaves. Thaddeus worked alongside me. Lines etched his face, but he made no comment.

With the loaves resting before baking, I asked Thaddeus if he wanted his healing session early. He nodded eagerly.

"I'd like to do something a little different. Are you willing to try an experiment?"

"Sure. Just don't hurt me." He winked at me.

I smiled at his trusting expression. "I promise I'll be gentle."

Typically, when I directed the Goddess's Radiance to a patient, I remained emotionally detached. I did not want to influence Her healing effects with my feelings, although I knew that the client could often feel my essential nature and state of mind. Now, Thaddeus sat in the wooden chair and I stood behind. I lay my hands on his shoulders. I started in the traditional way, opening to the Goddess and allowing Her energy to flow through me and into Thaddeus. Thaddeus's spirit joined with mine and the Goddess. He held back his emotions as well.

I moved to stand before him, straddling his legs. I pulled a small vial of rose oil from my pocket and lifted his hand, placing a drop in the center of his palm. I sat lightly on his lap, facing him, and placed his hand over my heart. I placed a drop of oil in my hand and placed it over his heart. I took deep breaths. I had never done this before and I really didn't know what to do next. I waited for the Goddess to guide me.

Thaddeus grinned. He slipped his hand under my blouse to come to rest between my breasts. I placed my hand over his. His spirit filled me. I followed his lead and unbuttoned his shirt partly so I could place my hand directly on his skin. He placed his hand over mine. I closed my eyes and watched with my second sight.

Around each of us was a sphere of energy. As we sat together, in the Goddess's embrace, our separate auras melded together, becoming one. The perimeter of our joined energy field became dense and contiguous.

"Summon the Goddess like you did when you restored me," I told him softly.

In a minute, the air around us vibrated. The border of our combined aura became a solid ring around us. I whispered the words that commanded the Goddess's protection. A network of fine lines wove between us. Thaddeus spoke the words and the boundary thickened. We said the words together and not only did the edge become impenetrable, but golden light flowed along some of the thin fibers that connected us at mind, heart, and soul.

When we finished, I smiled at him. "Did that hurt?"

He laughed. "No. Can we do it again? Was that the Ceangal Bandia?"

"No. Only a piece of the ritual."

The session with Thaddeus left me disoriented, and my sense of self shattered. I didn't know who I was. That had never happened when I merged energies with Sam. I retreated into the garden and sat on the ground, haphazardly picking weeds from the herb plots.

I sighed. I had done what I was willing to do to protect Thaddeus. Perhaps after I knew Thaddeus longer, I would complete the ritual. I hoped I now had the protective structure I needed to be able to channel the Goddess's Light, to purify the darkness invading our world.

Eventually, I returned to the kitchen to carry the freshly baked bread outside to Nana's customers. Thaddeus made new loaves and appeared completely unaffected by the Ceangal Bandia ritual.

I can hear your thoughts and sense you like never before, I heard in my mind.

So, we have a telepathic connection? I sent back.

That and more. I have your intuitive awareness and heightened senses. My body feels alive.

I suppose you heard my thoughts in the garden.

Of course. I like it! He added, *When you get yourself sorted out, you'll discover you have some of my talents, as well. It's a bargain like I've never experienced.*

After dinner, Thaddeus approached me and held my hands. "I know how you feel about me and you know my feelings for you. Will you accept me as your pair'ti?"

"I don't know, Thaddeus."

"But we have halfway committed to each other already."

"I did a partial Ceangal Bandia with you to protect you from the sorcerer who wants to kill you."

A shadow crossed his face.

"Thaddeus, only a few days ago, you believed I had cursed you and that you would revert to a crippled state if you associated with me, if I healed you, and especially if you succumbed to your feelings. Much of that darkness has been cleared from you, but more needs to be done. And I am not ready to replace Sam, yet."

"I can never replace Sam..." He rallied. "We make a good team. You need someone to support and protect you, especially now. I want to be that person. Admit it, you care for me."

My face burned. He was right. I did care about him. "We hardly know each other. The healing work makes me particularly receptive to you, and you to me. A relationship with me will not be what you have dreamed. We will push against each other, anger and worry each other. I had a lifetime to build trust with Sam and only a few days to do so with you. While I have not desired anyone but Sam, you have desired me for years. Only time will tell if the feelings between us endure."

"Will you at least consider becoming my pair'ti?"

I nodded. "I will consider it. However, we both have the same problem. You are not free to become my pair'ti, just like I am not free to become yours."

"What do you mean?" He looked worried.

"I cannot become your pair'ti because that sorcerer who is your master holds a piece of my soul. In so doing, he has bound me to him. I must find the piece of my soul that he holds and get it back before I can become your pair'ti." Through my connection to Thaddeus, his disappointment washed over me. "I care too much for you to ask you to bear this maledict. I will not have Rokan hunt you like he did Sam."

Thaddeus blanched. He pulled away from me as if I were a poisonous snake. "I'll never be rid of that ructabund! Even now, after you have chased his curse and evil creatures away, he comes between us!"

He rushed into the garden, leaned against the outer hearth-stones, and groaned. I understood the risk he had taken to rebel against the sorcerer's control, and his despair that it was all for naught. Rokan would punish him for his rebellion.

A short while later, I went into the garden. I found Thaddeus on the bench, head down and arms wrapped around his knees. Hopelessness radiated from him. I hesitated, then touched his shoulder. He didn't look up. "I don't know Rokan like you do. However, I have no intention of becoming his property, or allowing him to kill you as he did Sam. I don't want him coming between us. There must be a way to stop him and right the wrongs he has done."

Thaddeus didn't respond, but I sensed he listened. I sat down beside him and put an arm around him. "You are right. I have developed an affection for you. But to admit it, I feel like I am dishonoring my love for Sam. I love Sam with all my heart. It will take time for me to love you in the same way."

Thaddeus made a stifled sound, almost like a sob. He shifted and leaned against me.

I held him. "I thought about sending you away, but Rokan will probably try to kill you at sea."

He roused. "I don't want to leave you! I feel alive when we are together." He added wryly, "Especially when you are trying to get yourself killed. I know what you're thinking. Casting me out, even with a convincing display, will not fool Rokan. The display would have to be irrefutable. And that alternative leaves no room or hope for us to become pair'ti. Come with me. I have a cargo bound for Langon."

"I doubt that Rokan will be put off that easily. He will hunt us down. There has to be another way to get the sorcerer off our back." I caressed his cheek. "I want to live a meaningful life in a peaceful world." I had to admit, I enjoyed Thaddeus's company.

We sat together, each lost in thought. A growing dread crept into my belly. Jack's nasal tones interrupted us.

Nana came into the garden. "Jack says the queen will see you at Arty's Pub, near the castle. She is waiting for you now."

"Don't go," Thaddeus pleaded. "She will capture you."

"I'll be fine." But the knot in my stomach expanded.

We entered the kitchen, and Thaddeus warily watched Jack, or rather his master, who glared malevolently at the captain. Even the Goddess's protection still wouldn't stop Jack and his master from trying to kill Thaddeus. Sadly, I lacked a solution.

Jack bounced on his toes impatiently. "We must not keep the queen waiting."

I grabbed my cloak and tossed it around my shoulders. "I won't be long."

Jack gave Thaddeus a superior look and took my arm. I pulled away from his grasp. As we walked, I asked, "Tell me about the queen. How do you know her?"

"I know her from Tokurat. She is the Suzerain's sister. And very beautiful." He chattered on, but I wasn't interested in what he said.

"Why does she want to see me?" I pressed.

"To help the Alban cause." He rambled on about how the women at the pubs were being abused by the soldiers and it was getting harder to find a good woman now, since the best ones had escaped to Tokur.

I only half listened to him.

"Here we are." Jack guided me through a paint-peeled wooden door beneath a faded sign hanging by one chain. Inside, the small room was packed with men and women raising a drunken ruckus. The place smelled of ale, urine, and sweat. Jack ushered me through the crowd to a door concealed behind a soiled tapestry into a private cubicle that housed a table with a bench on either side. A woman leaned against the wall. The hood of her cloak concealed her features. A gloved hand twisted a goblet of cheap wine.

Jack bowed reverently to the woman. "Here she is, Your Majesty." He started to retreat.

"Stay, Jack." Her voice was low, and hinted at an unfamiliar dialect.

She indicated for me to sit. I noticed that she had Jack sit between me and the door, making it difficult to escape. I found myself sizing up the tiny room, its occupants, their strengths and weaknesses, and instinctively calculating escape routes. Is this what Thaddeus would do?

Yes. I am with you, I heard in my mind.

Thank you. I relaxed and faced the disguised woman. While I waited for the queen to speak, I continued to scan her with my Thaddeus-enhanced awareness.

"You are displaced from your home. So am I." She waited to see the effect of her words. "We are sisters of a sort." She pulled the hood back a few inches so that her face was partly illuminated by the flickering lamp.

"Why did you summon me?"

"As a sister in an unwelcome land, I wish to help you remain safe and alive. In exchange, I want your help with a matter I have not been able to accomplish."

"What matter is this?"

"You may have heard the rumors about me. My brother, the Suzerain of Tokur, has used me to steal countries through the agreements of marriage with my unfortunate spouses." Her fingers tightened around the stem of the goblet. "He has sent me to Alba, a land so foreign to my culture that I feel out of place. I am supposed to kill the king and hand over the country to my brother." She scowled every time she mentioned her brother. "Your sovereign is young and stupid, and deserves to die, but I don't want to kill this man." She sighed. "I am tired of this game my brother plays with my life. I just want to be left alone so I can live a normal life with someone I love." She lifted her gaze to mine and pleaded, "Will you help me be free of my brother and this cursed life?

Oh, she's good! I heard. *Don't let her fool you.*

"Why don't you kill the king, give your brother what he wants, and go live your life somewhere?"

She blinked at my words. "You would have your monarch killed?"

I shrugged. "You said it yourself. He is young, weak, and stupid. I'm sure one of the nobles would make a good ruler. Lord Garth maybe?"

Her eyes widened. Either she was a superb actress or the conversation wasn't quite what she expected. "Lord Garth answers to my brother. I hate the man!" she spat.

Actress, I decided. I smiled. "What, exactly, do you want from me?"

She leaned forward. "Kill King Leo!"

I took a deep breath. "You have more access to him than I do. And you have servants and assassins. Or Lord Garth could do it. Why me?"

"You went to see the king two days ago. Lord Garth said he was quite taken with you and asked for you several times after that. You can get close to him. Leo is unhealthy and weak. All it would take would be a pillow to smother him. Or you could use your dagger, some hemlock or spider venom." She watched me; her face unreadable. Her dark eyes glittered in the lamplight.

I pretended to contemplate her suggestion. "I would be charged with regicide and hanged or burned."

"I'll make sure you are pardoned, when I assume leadership of Alba."

"What if your coup for power fails and I am executed?" I shook my head. "I like living too much to risk my life in a desperate attempt for you to please your brother. I don't owe him anything. And I certainly don't want Alba to become another Tokur! I'm afraid I can't do what you ask."

"You just said he was a worthless king. And I'll protect you."

"Forgive me for being so blunt, but I don't have much faith in your protection. Our monarch is Alban and Goddess-born. There is hope for him. I will not kill him," I stated firmly.

She drew herself upright. "You dare to defy your Queen?"

"You are a foreigner in a strange land. You are isolated and alone in this quest. I will not help you." I stood. Jack remained seated, blocking my exit.

"I could have you arrested for attempted assassination."

"Yes, you could. And I could accuse you of plotting to murder King Leopold. That may be a common practice in your country, but it is not here." I placed my hands on the table and leaned towards her. "Whose word will the Peers accept? That of a non-native queen known to be the Widow-maker, or that of an Alban Advocate?"

"Ha! You're no Advocate, but a hunted Healer. I could turn you over to the clerics right now."

I straightened. "Yes, you could. And what would you gain? Have you ever thought about disregarding your brother's orders? What if you allowed yourself to accept that women have equal value to men and the right to live their own lives in freedom? The way I see it, Queen Qadira, you have an opportunity to break free from your shackles and follow your heart in a country that welcomes women. I ask you, will you help me to undo the laws that restrict womankind, that try to make Alba just like your homeland?" I stared at her, undaunted by her glare and the movement of her fingers as if drawing a magical spell. "Your magic doesn't work here, Qadira. Stop pretending to be the helpless victim in your brother's game. You have the opportunity of a lifetime at your fingertips. Claim your freedom. Align yourself with our king and help him cast out the usurpers. You will discover a different sort of meaning and a new magic in your life."

I turned to Jack. "Move." I commanded. When he didn't, I shoved him onto the floor and stepped over him. I muscled my way out of the establishment and into a circle of guards waiting in the street around the entry. A quick scan showed they were Lord Garth's men. Jack pinned my arms behind me.

"Take her!" Qadira said, moving before me and slapping my face. "You'll die for your insolence, woman."

I noticed movement behind the guards. Suddenly their legs collapsed and the soldiers tumbled over each other. I stomped on Jack's foot, leaned forward, letting his hold on my arms support me as I bent my knee and kicked upward into his groin. He squealed and released me. Invisible arms caught me, and together, Thaddeus and I raced down the street.

Several blocks away, Thaddeus whisked me into an alley, and he became visible. "I love having access to your abilities," he said.

"I see you are a quick study. What else can you do?"

"Only that. You showed me last night in the castle, remember." He sobered. "You sure have a way of rocking the boat. Qadira will want revenge."

I shrugged. "The words just came out."

Jack's following us. I heard in my mind. *We don't have much time.*

His master spies on us constantly.

I've been thinking about that. He held my face in his hands. *Do you trust me?*

I nodded. *It's hard not to, after working in the embrace of the Gra'yia like we have.*

He drew me into his arms. *I love you, Ellara. I always have. Whatever happens, will you remember that what I do is because I love you? You are more precious to me than my life.*

I had heard that phrase before, and Sam had died. Fear, like an iron fist, wrapped around my heart. *Thaddeus, what are you going to do? I don't want anything to happen to you.*

I was hoping you would say that. He pressed his lips tenderly against mine, like Sam did when he was leaving for one of his voyages. His spirit wrapped around me like a warm blanket.

Dread crept through my veins. The night suddenly became cold. I forgot about Jack following us, or my meeting with the queen. I knew Thaddeus was going away and I wrestled with this. *You're going after Rokan, aren't you?* I threw my arms around him. *He'll kill you.*

I want to get your soul piece back so we can have a life together. His fingers found the pendant with the spiral of gemstones he had given me a few days ago. He pulled it into the dim light. The stones winked. *Wear this always. It will protect you from any harm that might befall you, no matter its source, even if it is me. Let it be a reminder of my love for you.*

What are you trying to tell me? Determination radiated from him, as well as an equal part of apprehension. *What are you going to do?*

He cocked an ear. I detected the whisper of cloth and slow tread from a soft boot. *Jack is almost here. I need you to make yourself invisible and get about a block ahead of Jack. Then let him see you.* He stepped away. *Forgive me, Beloved.*

Thaddeus's words reminded me of Sam. I was reliving the events of Sheldon all over, only this time I thought I knew the outcome. Abandoning my reservations about Thaddeus, I circled his neck with my arms and stretched so I could kiss him. I let the love that had grown for him over the last few days wrap around him, whispering the words to command the Ceangal Bandia. Instantly, he merged with me and just as quickly drew away. *I will definitely be back for more of this!* Thaddeus slipped into the street and waited.

Following his instructions, I disguised myself and trotted towards the bakery. A block later, I let myself become visible and slowly walked the last distance. My mind was a jumble of conflicting thoughts, mostly dread of what was to come. A moment later, I heard running footsteps. I glanced back to see a man slam into Jack, knocking him off balance. Jack cursed at his attacker and lunged for him. The man sped towards me. It was Thaddeus. In a flash, he shoved me against the wall, knocking the wind from me.

I gasped, shocked. "Thaddeus, what are you doing?" I reached for our telepathic connection and met emptiness. Nor could I sense him.

In answer, he pressed his forearm into my throat, choking me. His face twisted in rage. "You'll pay for what you've done to me, Witch!"

THIRTY-SEVEN

ROKAN

Tokurat, The Desert Lands

Hurry up, Jack! Don't let him kill her. I pounded the desk with my clenched fist.

I would have done anything to be in Araval myself. I watched helplessly through Jack's eyes, trying to prod the rebellious Katz-paw to action. *Alba erodes my hold over Jack!*

Jack approached the violent scene slowly, still walking gingerly. *Don't be such a sissy. You have more important things to do than worry about your crotch!*

Ellara looked positively devastated and scared. She clawed at Thaddeus's arms and cried, "Thaddeus. What are you doing? Stop! You're hurting me." She shoved feebly against the strong man.

A wild-eyed Thaddeus raged at her. "I wanted to be free of that sorcerer and now, if I love you, I'll be bound to the very man I despise, and I'll be killed just like Sam was." His stranglehold tightened. Ellara gasped for air. "The Droc'ri was right! You are cursed. And you would trap me in your curse. You've been working for that devil man from the day we met! And I thought it was love! You've been using me just like your diabolical master! You're trying to bind me to him forever!"

"Thaddeus..." She wheezed, pushing against him, tears in her eyes. "This isn't you. That black creature must have control of you. Let me go."

He ranted, "Because of some trickery by you, I can't kill the monster that has ruined my life." He leaned closer. His tone was menacing. "You lied to me! You made me think I could love you, and you loved me. You're like all the other women in my life who have betrayed me. You've trapped me in your web of deceit, just like your evil master." He glowered at her. He wedged his body against hers and placed his long dagger under her chin. Ellara cried out as he drew blood. "I should kill you here and now! Kill you before another innocent fool falls into your trap."

Ellara stared at Thaddeus in shock. Her mouth fell open, speechless, and tears welled from her eyes. "It's not true. I have been honest with you. You know that. I couldn't hurt you," she croaked weakly.

Jack, stop him from killing her! But my ructabund agent refused to move. In fact, he seemed to be enjoying the spectacle, grinning and rocking onto his toes as he fingered his dagger. Frantically, I searched for what I could do to save the one who was my ticket to freedom. *She must not die!*

I grabbed my traveling talisman, but I'd never make it in time. I had to get Jack to intervene, but Jack disliked Ellara about as much as she abhorred him. *He's afraid of her. He's a disgrace to his assassin masters. Coward! This will be Jack's last mission.*

Ellara struggled with Thaddeus, trying to free herself from the suffocating hand at her throat. With a foot against the wall, she shoved against Thaddeus with enough force to dislodge his hold briefly. She twisted in his grip and whacked him over the ear. He yelped and renewed his efforts, anger distorting his features.

"Your sorcery won't work on me. You don't deserve to live for all the pain and suffering you've caused me." He pricked her neck with his blade. "I vowed I'd kill the next woman who betrayed me and broke my heart. You've done that, Witch!"

Why won't she defend herself? She could easily destroy Thaddeus with the power of the Goddess. I could capture her spirit, too, and she would be bound to me, finally.

Tears streamed down her cheeks and her lips moved, but I couldn't hear, through Jack, what she said. Whatever it was spurred Thaddeus to step back, holding her in place with a hand to her throat and his dagger poised to strike. "You don't deserve to live after what you've done to me," he snarled. Out of nowhere, a hand grabbed his raised arm and shook it. The dagger clattered to the cobblestones.

I released my pent breath. Who was that man who had become Ellara's savior?

Ellara slid down the wall to the ground, pulling her knees to her chest. She sat shaking and sobbing. The dagger with her blood lay at her feet. She held one hand to her neck, where blood seeped between her fingers.

Go to her, Jack, I ordered. Finally, the incompetent Katz-paw leaned over Ellara. But he didn't offer to help. Instead, he straightened and kicked her, and kicked again.

Jack stooped to pick up the blade, hefted it, testing its balance, then leaned over Ellara. "I may as well finish what Thaddeus started." She didn't even seem to notice him.

I shot to my feet, toppling my chair. Where was that stranger? The stranger, still wrestling with Thaddeus, had moved down the street. Thaddeus snarled, "Let me go. She must die."

Frantically I pawed through my talismans and clutched one, rummaged in a pocket for a strand of Ellara's hair, and incanted the words of power that would save her.

Ellara looked up as Jack thrust the dagger at her and rolled to the side, striking out with her feet at his knees. The blade dug harmlessly into the brick wall. She jumped to her feet, pivoted behind Jack, and kicked him forward into the wall. She snatched up the dagger and would have plunged it into his back, but she stopped, stared at it and Jack's crumpled body, then turned away, head hanging.

Thaddeus broke free from the stranger, turned back, and hurled at her, "I'll be back for you," then dashed into a side street.

The stranger approached Ellara and put a consolatory arm around her shoulder. He wore a dark brown tunic and leggings that magnified his athletic physique. The only object that interrupted his sleek lines was a dagger belted at his waist. Who was this man with long black hair flowing about his shoulders like a mane?

I settled back into my chair. My heart pounded from witnessing Ellara's attack. *If Jack weren't my only spy in Alba, I'd terminate him now.*

It surprised me that Thaddeus wanted to kill Ellara. For years, he had wanted love, a family, and to break free from his contract with me. Once again, Thaddeus's attempt to escape from me had failed. In fact, it had backfired so completely that he appeared to have broken at last.

I beamed, quite pleased with the turn of events. I never knew that holding a piece of Ellara's soul could work to my advantage, and in such an unexpected way. *Margot won't kill me because she doesn't want her mother to go to the Tiarna Drocha, nor will Ellara or Nana Magog for the same reasons.* I leaned back, steepled my fingers, and rested my chin on them. There was still a lot I didn't know about the relationship between Thaddeus and Ellara. *That idiot Jack is intimidated by her, and she is such a delicate-looking woman. It's unbecoming for a trained assassin.* Despite the instructions that I had given him to care for her in Alba, Jack thought she was too old and crotchety. He spied just enough to learn what I wanted to know, then made a beeline for the younger women at the Red Rose or other houses of pleasure.

I turned the sliver of clear quartz crystal over in my hand. I had used it to provoke Ellara to defend herself. It was only an inch long, just a few hairs thick, and shaped like a needle. The antiquities dealer had said it could pierce any aura with the intent of the sorcerer who could master the spirit of the tiny stone. It had taken a lot of study and years to tame and bend the crystal's powerful spirit to my will. I rarely used it, as every time I did, the crystal shrank in size. There were only a handful of uses left in the shard. The other limitation was that to work effectively, the user needed to have a personal item of the person they wanted to control. I had never used it before with Ellara. That she had been receptive to my command intrigued me. *What else could I make her do?*

Judging by her distraught appearance, Thaddeus had broken Ellara's heart. I had to make sure Thaddeus was really put off of Ellara. I caressed another talisman, this one a long, flat crystal wand. I leaned back and closed my eyes. I directed my attention to the *Lovely Lady.* Even though I couldn't see the activity on deck, through my magical spy portals I could hear conversations over much of the ship. I listened carefully to the voices.

"Let's go," Thaddeus growled.

"Cap'm, you look like you saw a ghost." Matty, the real captain of the vessel, exclaimed. "What about Ellara? Is she coming with us?"

"She's cursed and bound to that sorcerer who thinks he owns me and my ship!"

I do own you and your ship, Thaddeus. I always will. You will never escape me. I could punish you for trying to escape again. But this is better. Ellara has dealt you a crushing blow far more effectively than I could and destroyed your childish love for her.

Thaddeus angrily complained to Matty, "Now I find out I can't kill the sorcerer because he holds a piece of Ellara's soul. Nana Magog would kill me if I killed him. It would drag Ellara's soul into the Tiarna Drocha with that ructabund. And if she became my pair'ti, I'd become a target like her dead mate, Sam."

Thaddeus stomped into his cabin and I heard a slosh from his jug and thump on the table when he set it down. He muttered to himself, something about "gone forever," "can't love her," "she'll never love me." *Good. He's back under my control again. It's so satisfying to break his heart. Love makes a person weak and easily manipulated.*

THIRTY-EIGHT

ELLARA AT THE CASTLE

Araval

The stranger supported me back to the bakery. I hardly noticed him. My mind was fixated on Thaddeus's attack. I called to him in my mind, distress following my plea. I knew something was very wrong. That he would try to kill me still had my head spinning. I had trusted him.

The rage that had come over me when Jack attacked terrified me. It was similar to the wrath I had felt when the cleric, who turned out to be the sorcerer, had tried to steal Margot. My body shook uncontrollably. All I wanted was a safe place to curl up and hide.

Nana greeted us when we returned. She patted my arm. "I see you made it back safely. Come, Child. You could use a cup of tea." She shoved a steaming mug into my hands and guided me to a chair. She nodded to the stranger, who withdrew his support and departed. "Drink."

I perfunctorily sniffed the tea, then took a sip.

Nana stroked my back. "This will make you feel better. The Goddess is taking care of everything, Ellara. Let him go. He has given you what you need."

The tea did restore some of my sanity. I went into the garden, sat on the bench, and leaned against the warm bricks of the hearth. I looked into the star-studded night sky and thought of Sam. I imagined him as one of the bright stars that winked at me. I pulled my knees to my chest and wrapped my arms tightly around them. I couldn't feel Thaddeus. I reached with my Far Sight. He was almost to his ship. Energies swirled around him. I could not sense him. He had blocked me. A jubilant Jack followed the captain. Alone and abandoned, first by my beloved Sam, and now by Thaddeus, who I reluctantly had to admit had found a place in my heart, I sobbed into my knees. Eventually I stretched out on the bench, resting my body against the warm bricks, and escaped into sleep.

Songbirds announced the coming day. I awoke groggily, thinking last night had just been a bad dream. Someone had tucked a blanket around me. I smiled. That's something Thaddeus would do. I tossed the blanket aside and went inside, but there was no sign of the captain.

Already Nana was stoking the oven fire. She greeted me cheerily and pressed a mug of tea into my hands and a folded piece of paper. "This will help you see clearly." She pushed me in the direction of the garden. "Let the songbirds bring you the messages from the Goddess."

I returned to my favorite place against the warm bricks and leaned back, watching the inky sky fade gradually into the golden hues of dawn. Birds warbled and chirped, celebrating the new day. I sipped the tea. It contained a bitter herb I wasn't familiar with. But Nana was right. In a short time, the fog from my mind cleared.

I replayed the traumatic events of the previous night in my mind. I had refused the queen's request to kill the king. Lord Garth's guards had tried to capture me. Thaddeus had ingeniously rigged a line that rested upon the soldiers' boots and used the lamppost as a fulcrum to haul the men off balance. We had kissed and I knew he was going away. Then he attacked me and threatened to kill me. His dagger lay on the ground beneath the bench. I picked it up and inspected it. The tip had dried red-brown. I touched the scab on my neck where Thaddeus had drawn blood. I had been totally unprepared for his attack. He could have so easily killed me. But he didn't. Jack, on the other hand, had murder in his heart.

The note slipped to the ground. I picked it up and unfolded the small packet into a full sheet of paper. Precise letters flowed in straight lines across the page. I glanced at the signature and my heart ached.

Beloved, I hate myself for the pain and distress I caused you. I didn't want to hurt you. But I didn't know another way to prove to Rokan I was no longer a threat to him.

I couldn't warn you. The performance had to convince him. Rokan has to think I am still under his control. That is one of his weaknesses.

I have loved you since I first saw you some twenty-five years ago. During the last few days with you, feeling loved, accepted, and valued for who I am — not for what can be gotten from me — far exceeded my dreams. I will cherish the memory of our time together for the rest of my life.

I fear I have irreparably broken your trust and your heart. I don't deserve your love or to become your pair'ti. Please forgive me.

I love you with all my heart. I will protect you the best way I know how.

Thaddeus.

Tears spilled down my cheeks. My heart ached. Was he saying goodbye? I searched for Thaddeus with my Far Sight. His ship was somewhere at sea. He was slumped over a table covered with navigation charts, apparently in a drunken stupor. I still could not feel him. Bit by bit, I calmed my mind. All I knew for now was that Thaddeus had pitted himself against Rokan. The captain was keenly intelligent. I wished him luck and the Goddess's protection. Would I ever see him again?

I heard Jack's tenor voice greeting Nana. I tensed. *What's he doing out so early? It's barely daybreak. He's got a lot of nerve coming around after he tried to murder me last night!*

Jack's arrival started another train of thought. What was that force that urged me to assassinate him? It came from deep within me. I had never wanted to kill my daughter's thief. It had just happened. But what had driven me last night was malicious, evil. It left a bad taste in my mouth. That I could succumb so easily to vindictive destruction scared me. Luckily, I had come to my senses before I had done something I'd regret.

I went into the kitchen. "You look like you are ready to meet with the queen again."

"Huh?"

"Jack stopped by to say Queen Qadira will meet with you tonight at the same pub."

I sagged into a chair. Last night Thaddeus had had my back. Now I would have no one. "What's she want this time?"

"She wants to make a bargain with you, according to Jack."

I groaned. "Her bargains consist of murdering someone and capturing me."

"I think it might be a different bargain." The elder peered at me. "You have the young captain's powers now, just as he has yours. He's quite a resourceful man. Draw on his essence, his wit, and intelligence."

"Does it work when he is in a drunken stupor?"

Nana laughed. "Works even better."

"But I can't feel him."

"You don't need to feel him. You have formed a partial Ceangal Bandia. He is imprinted into your energy field, just as you are in his. You are inseparable now, and that is what makes both of you strong. Look inside yourself. You have access to not only your gifts, but his as well." Nana shoved loaves into the oven. She looked over her shoulder before she arranged them. "You have a new friend. He is across the street."

I cracked open the door and peeked out. A dark form moved in the shadows from the awning of a vendor's stall along the far side of the street. I walked towards the man. The closer I got, the more familiar he felt. "Boris?" I scanned him. "You're dressed differently from when you became a man at Cuilithe. What are you doing here?"

The man bowed his head, his thick black hair rippling with the movement. "Defending, you needed. I serve, willingly."

I hugged him. "I'm so happy to see you!" I ran my hand lightly across his shoulder and partway down his arm. His clothing had the smooth softness of hair. "Thank you for rescuing me last night."

He smiled and dipped his head again. I remembered from the Heartland that Boris, as a human, was a man of few words.

"Would you like something to eat? A place to rest? What can I get you?"

"I, fine." He planted his feet. "I, stay, watch."

Jack showed up shortly after I had started forming loaves, pleading to be healed. That he had the nerve to ask for healing after he had kicked and tried to kill me was beyond my comprehension. Without thinking, I snatched up Thaddeus's long knife. Uncensored words flew from my mouth. "I will not heal you, Jack. I will *never* be the mate of your master. Now get out, before I complete what I was ordered to do last night by your master!" *Why did I say that?* Thankfully Jack departed promptly. I retreated to the bench in the garden to calm myself and to ponder the significance of those words.

I spent part of the day studying Cleric Paul's translations. Thaddeus had read them and Nana said he had read Nana Magog's books as well. Thaddeus said he remembered everything he saw. We had argued about the necessity of performing the Ceangal Bandia when Nana said the ritual would make me be able to channel the Goddess more easily. He had flipped to the pages that talked about the benefits. What had taken me days, he had digested in an afternoon. It annoyed me that his mother had taught him the ancient Leonini language as well.

With thoughts of Thaddeus came a wave of sadness. I refused to wallow in my sorrow and searched for what I could do to distract myself. At least I didn't need to worry about Jack or his master constantly trying to eliminate the captain, and I could go about my plans unhindered by that burden. Still, I missed him.

I decided to experiment with invisibility. Why hadn't the soldiers noticed the rope wrapped around their feet? How had

Thaddeus placed it without their feeling it? When something was invisible, were the sensations such as weight or touch also concealed?

Nana didn't know the answer, so I made myself unseen and mingled with Nana's patrons. Sure enough, I could touch them, even gently push them a few inches to one side without their awareness. I spotted some of Lord Garth's soldiers coming down the street toward us. I waited until they were past us before I called, "Hey! Ructabunds! Gombeens!" None of them paid any attention to me. Daringly, I ran up to the last soldier and shoved him hard. He stumbled and bumped into the man in front. He spun around, but there was no one there. An argument ensued, and the man I had shoved defended himself by saying someone pushed him. The other man punched him and they moved on.

I retreated to Nana's and evaluated what I had learned. I observed I wasn't fatigued in the least. *"Thank you, Thaddeus,"* I sent to him.

I decided to go to the castle to see the king. I used my Far Sight to locate Jack sleeping under a tent at a campsite by the river. There was a woman with him. When she looked up, and in my direction, I recognized her. Felicity! What was she doing in Araval? And what was she doing with Jack? Why had he taken her to see the queen? Then it hit me. *Was Felicity going to assassinate the king?*

Troubled about the appearance of Felicity and satisfied that Jack wouldn't be following me, I headed towards the castle. I made myself invisible and followed a courier into the main entrance to the building. I suddenly realized that I could easily get lost. *Could I draw upon Thaddeus's memory of the fortress?*

I followed the messenger, hoping he would lead me to the king. Unfortunately, he went to Lord Garth's office. I couldn't resist easing into the expansive room that looked like a spartan military field office. Lord Garth, sitting at his desk, looked up sharply as the youth delivered a small package. The commander's eyes swept the room, passing over me. He hesitated and frowned, then continued his scan of the room. I held my breath, deciding it would be prudent to follow the runner out before I was discovered. Unfortunately, Lord Garth didn't open the package, but I did notice that the insignia on the messenger's uniform was that of one of the councilors.

I followed the young man to a common room adjacent to the kitchen. I retraced my steps and found my way back to the main passageway. Fatigue slowly settled over me. I knew I couldn't stay unseen much longer. Behind me was the Great Hall. It was empty. I remembered how we had gotten here from the king's private office and ran lightly down the hall. The imposing guard stood before the doors. I calmed myself and edged behind him, gently nudging him to take a step forward. I opened the giant door and slipped in. King Leo wasn't there, but a number of official documents lay on his desk. Quickly I scanned them, briefly wishing I had Thaddeus's ability to remember everything I saw.

One of the documents was for a new import tax on lamp oil from the Desert Lands. The money raised was to fund Lord Garth's military efforts and purchase "modern" weapons. It was signed and dated the night Thaddeus and I had been to see the king.

Another document, as yet unsigned, was a direct order to arrest all Healers and people practicing any form of herbal or bone-setting medicine. I grabbed the documents and stuffed them inside my shirt.

A page under a sheaf of papers caught my eye. I tugged the page from the stack. It looked like building plans. I heard voices outside the door. I scooped up the pile of unsigned documents and shoved them inside my shirt and ducked through the door into the king's bedroom. My invisibility faded. A quick scan revealed the monarch was not in residence here, either. Where was he?

The documents I had haphazardly placed in my shirt crinkled when I moved. I listened intently to the voices in the next room and risked using my Far Sight. Lord Garth was pawing through a stack of documents. With him were a couple of aids. "Where is it?" he growled. "I need to get him to sign those decrees today. What has that imbecile done with them? He's gotten more cantankerous since that wench came to visit him."

Instinct told me that he would search the king's bedroom next. I crept behind the magnificent tapestry map of Alba to the hidden door that Commander Fabian and I had used last time I was here. I stepped into pitch blackness, just as the men entered the room. I didn't move for fear of jostling something that would alert the hunters.

Finally, they left. I leaned against the wall and rested. Thaddeus may have given me his natural boldness, but I wasn't used to taking this sort of risk! I pulled the sheets out, smoothed them, and carefully folded them, replacing them once more inside my shirt. At least now they didn't rustle when I moved. I peeked into the room, crossed it, then cracked open the door to the private office. A short man sat in the king's chair.

I quickly closed the door and looked for something I could use as a torch to traverse the web of passages that eventually led to the outside. I heard heated voices in the other room.

"Get out of my chair, Garth," King Leopold demanded.

"What's wrong with you, Sire? You act like you have lost your mind. What have you done with the documents you need to sign?" Lord Garth's congenial tone took on an edge.

I smiled. The tincture I had given the commander to counteract the herbs used to drug the young man must be working.

"I'm tired of your telling me what to do, Garth. I'm king here and it's my job to decide what my country needs."

"Sire, I'm only here to serve. You are new to rulership, untrained, and undisciplined."

"My country is not a military campaign, Garth. Remember that. Now get out!"

"You've had a trying day, Sire. Here, let me help you to your bed to rest. We'll find those documents and you can sign them. They are for the good of your country."

"I'm tired of you, Garth. Now leave me alone. I have work to do."

The door opened, and two aides dragged the king into the room and settled him on his bed. One of Lord Garth's aides poured King Leo a cup of wine. From my vantage point, I watched him add a pinch of powder.

"Drink, Sire. It will make you feel better."

I made myself invisible and rammed the aide nearest to the cupbearer. He crashed into the man holding the cup, and the wine spilled on the king. Lord Garth cursed and cuffed both men.

"Now look what you've done, Garth. You've soiled my clothes. Get out!" King Leo's face was flushed.

"Worthless royalty," Lord Garth grumbled. "Get him to bed," he ordered his aides.

I retreated through the office, my concealment fading, and opened the main entrance doors. A King's Guard stood at attention. "Hurry! The king is in danger!" I tugged on his arm and ran back towards the door to the inner chamber. The Guard followed, calling for his comrades.

The guard burst in on Lord Garth and the enraged monarch, who twisted and kicked. But Lord Garth's orderlies were strong and determined.

The King's Guard poured into the room. I took the opportunity to escape the king's quarters after snatching a few more documents from the desk. Commander Fabian grabbed my collar as I slipped out. "What trouble have you caused?" he growled at me.

"Lord Garth's caused the trouble, sir. Come to the bakery when you are done here."

Safely back at the bakery, I spread the documents out on Nana's bed. Nana's retired Healer friends looked over my shoulder. Besides the warrant to arrest all Healers, and the new tax on lamp oil, there were a few more, smaller ordinances that didn't seem like much but had significant impact on small, women-run businesses.

"It seems that Lord Garth is trying to make his minions' activities legal," one of the nanas commented.

But what held our interest was an ordinance to fund some military activities in the country. Plans outlined barracks in each port town and major city. On the last page of the blueprints was an estimated survey of the timber in the Heartland and orders to harvest the trees to build the garrisons and sell the stumpage to pay for the labor and expenses of operating the fortresses.

The nanas stood transfixed. The Heartland was sacred. Never had a tree been cut down. Only the Gra'Bandia Council, in cooperation with the Heartland Caretakers, allowed a tree, once dead for at least ten years, to be salvaged. The wood was prized by metal smiths. Albans had become famous for their Heartland blades, fired from the magical wood. These highly coveted weapons were stronger than any other blade in the world. The metal never broke or lost its edge. The masters who forged these weapons were Mages, whose strength in elemental earth magic combined with the ancient wisdom of the tree to make these precious swords and daggers.

"This is sacrilege! This will destroy Alba."

"The Gra'Bandia Council must know."

I was skeptical of the Council, after my experience there. "I'll tell Nana Magog and she'll know what to do."

The tramp of soldiers' boots came to a halt before Nana Bean's shop. Quickly I folded up the pages and slipped them under the mattress. "How much should we tell the commander?" I addressed his pair'ti, Jillian.

"He is in charge of this country's well-being. He has guarded the way of the Goddess his whole life. He needs to know."

Nana opened the door. Instead of Commander Fabian, one of Lord Garth's lieutenants rested a foot on the stoop and straightened his gloves. A dozen soldiers accompanied him. His eyes swept the room. "Ah!" He stepped in, fake charm oozing from him. "You make my job so much easier. All of you nanas in one place."

The tall, fair-haired man dressed meticulously. He would have been handsome in his gold-accented red uniform, except for the lack of warmth in his large hazel eyes.

"What do you want, Morgan?" Commander Fabian's pair'ti asked.

"Why you, Nana. And the rest of you, to keep you company."

"What for?"

"I have a writ for your arrest." From his broad belt, he produced a small piece of paper folded neatly in half. A hand, gloved in unblemished deerskin, held it up for us to see. "And all the rest of you, especially the king's whore."

Nana Bean, almost as tall as the man, reached for the note. "I don't believe you, Morgan."

Morgan lifted his hand out of reach and motioned for his men to enter.

Without a second thought, I closed my eyes and imagined a protective barrier around the cottage, and silently spoke the words. The protective matrix of the Ceangal Bandia glowed in my inner sight.

Morgan turned to his men, who hadn't moved. "What's wrong with you lubb-oxes? Detain these old women." He leered at us. "It can't be that hard."

Jillian faced the officer. "Hand over the writ. If it is valid, we will go with you."

The man sneered at the woman. "I don't need a writ to arrest the lot of you!"

"Yes, you do." The nanas faced the man and stared intently at him. "Alba is a lawful land, and you and your commander have defiled our laws and our ways ever since you arrived here. Your dominion over us is coming to an end."

"Are those words of revolt, Nana?"

I recognized the tinny tone of Lord Garth. He entered the bakery from the direction of the garden. How had he gotten through my shield? Was he already inside and I hadn't noticed? I eased behind the other nanas, hoping to escape notice.

He scanned the occupants. "Where's that wench that the king favors?"

Does he know I'm a Healer? Goddess, protect me. Slowly I pushed through the women to stand before him. As indomitable as he presented himself, he was not much taller than me and was thinly built. Beady eyes studied me, probing beyond the surface. I averted my gaze and pulled in my aura as best I knew how, to make myself small. Out of the corner of my eye, I noticed Boris standing alertly, ready to defend me again. Black hair partly covered his face and, along with his clothing, which seemed to shift colors to match the background, he was hard to detect. *What could he do with all of these guards? He'd have to be a formidable warrior.* Unbidden came the memory of Boris, the horse, charging Lord Sengy's men in Sheldon, wreaking havoc amongst their ranks. And then the spectacular pinnacle of his prowess, when he had toppled Lord Sengy with a perfectly placed kick. I suppressed a smile as I imagined him charging through the ranks outside our door and lifting Lord Garth by his hair and shaking him like I had seen, when horses wanted to dislodge the dirt from dandelion roots. Except this man was bald.

A calloused hand grabbed my jaw and roughly lifted my head to face him. "You must be a witch. The king is possessed with you. Ever since you came to see him, he has not been himself." He plucked the white folded sheet of paper from Morgan. He held it up. "This writ ordering your arrest was signed into law this morning."

"What does the writ say?" one of the nanas asked.

"It orders the immediate arrest of all Healers and retired Healers and anyone practicing medicinal arts who is not sanctioned by the Natuan Ethnarch. It also prohibits women from owning and working a business or commercial endeavor in Alba."

The nanas exchanged looks. "I don't believe this new law is valid. Show me the document signed by the king."

Lord Garth puffed out his chest in a display of his superiority over the handful of elderly nanas. He released my chin. In that second of distraction, while he directed his intimidating air of authority towards the nana who had spoken, I snatched the note and darted behind the women. They closed ranks in front of me. I opened the piece of paper and held it up for all to see. Both sides were blank.

As one, the enraged nanas clamored and shouted at the two soldiers, shoving them out the door, and calling them names I had not heard before — names that made me blush. They stood on the stoop to the bakery and shouted insults at the soldiers. The nanas, joined by local citizens, redoubled their attack on the mercenaries and grabbed anything they could get their hands on, which for most were the cooling loaves of bread, to pummel Lord Garth's guards.

Commander Fabian pushed through the rebellious throng, coming face to face with Lord Garth, who thrust out his chest like a rooster trying to look important. "What is this about, Garth? Why are you harassing the citizens of Araval?" He scowled at the short man.

One of the nanas shoved the blank piece of parchment at the commander. "He came to arrest us with a blank piece of paper that he claimed was an order from the king."

The commander rounded on Lord Garth. "You go too far, Garth. I will not tolerate your behavior in my town, or in my country."

Lord Garth stepped back and taunted him. "What are you going to do, Fabian? You Albans are weak and don't know anything about fighting."

"The Zambril mercenary doesn't understand the Way of the Warrior," Commander Fabian replied calmly.

"Are you challenging me, Fabian?"

"I know you, Garth. You will cheat, steal, and bribe just to win. There is no honor in fighting you. You don't belong in Alba. Go back from whence you came."

"You'll never be rid of me, Fabian. This is *my* country, now. I will personally enjoy dismembering you limb from limb, after your precious city falls." He spun on his heel and marched off.

Commander Fabian's troop started to corral the soldiers, but the commander waved a hand. "Let them go."

The bakery became quite crowded with all the nanas, a few patrons, and the oversized commander. "Are any of you injured?"

His pair'ti responded. "We are unhurt physically, but that man is doing Alba a great disservice. His intentions become clearer every day. He means to destroy our way of life and our beloved island. We must stop him."

THIRTY-NINE

ROKAN AND GARRICK

Tokurat, The Desert Lands

On my scrying wall, I monitored Ellara and Thaddeus. Thaddeus reclined in his chair beside a table laden with sea charts, his head rested in an uncomfortable position over the back of the chair. A jug of rum lay on its side and rocked back and forth with the ship's movement. As he had done many times before, he had drunk himself into a stupor. Over and over, he muttered, "Kill Ellara. Must kill Ellara. She can go to the Mag Mell and join her dead pair'ti and never bother me again."

Was he serious? Were these the mutterings of a broken man? When I spied upon him later, Thaddeus had become violently ill, leaning over the side railing and retching. He looked ghastly. Matty carried him into his cabin and laid him on his bunk. The helmsman sat beside him, sponging his captain's forehead, and kept saying, "It's in the Goddess's hands, Cap'm. It will be alright." But Matty looked worried. If he was lucky, a very disillusioned Thaddeus would die from drink and a broken heart, and permanently be out of Ellara's life. When the half-man was with Ellara, he thought that he would be free. *He will never be free from my control. My magic is that strong. I control Ellara, too, even though she doesn't realize it. If she wants to get her soul facet back, she'll have to pledge herself to me!*

I sent Jack to charm Ellara. He arrived at the bakery the next morning, but Nana Bean said Ellara was still sleeping. When Jack returned later, petitioning her to heal his head where it had smashed into the wall, Ellara held Thaddeus's long blade in her hand. Her hand shook slightly. "Leave me alone. You *and* your master. I will *never* become your master's mate. I'd rather die first!" Through Jack, I saw tear tracks on her cheeks. I was sure Ellara was heartbroken, and vulnerable again. Was she sad because she really loved the captain? What's to love about that spineless drunkard? Or was she sad because she couldn't use him to go to the castle or to help her with the revolution her double was about to initiate. I was certain Ellara had healed him and most likely called upon the Goddess. She defended and protected him. Why? Was it just a Healer protecting her patient, or had she really fallen for him? Either way, Thaddeus was gone and she was ripe for the picking.

I studied the man who watched from the shadows across the street. His image kept shifting and I was forced to continually re-create the images on the wall. Who was the black-haired stranger who stood quietly watching the bakery and followed Ellara when she went out? He had the simple, unassuming look of an assassin. I needed to know more, but now that Thaddeus was gone and Jack didn't need to keep the two of them apart, he had resorted to spending more time with the ladies. It was a waste of precious time to watch through his eyes, and soon, I stopped bothering. *Ungrateful numbskull. He'll pay for his incompetence. At least he is still working on the other mission I gave him.*

I shifted the scene to Felicity. *Her resemblance to Ellara is remarkable!* She met with some of Jack's burly drinking buddies. They had sticks of explosives laid out on a table at a pub. She instructed the men to bind them into bundles with sailcloth. Then the rebels split into twos and each pair walked to key positions in the city, such as the water reservoir and the buttresses of the main bridge that connected the city with the rest of the country. They placed the destructive devices at the barracks of the King's Guard, the stables, and the treasury. Felicity made the devices invisible. Jack had told her that this would please me. I didn't want to see the town destroyed. But I rationalized that it could be rebuilt in a relatively short time.

I leaned back in my chair and clasped my hands behind my head, watching my agents lay the foundation for Araval's downfall. My mind wandered. Ellara had firmly rejected the queen's request to kill the king. That was exactly as I had anticipated. I had Ellara right where I wanted her. Now, I had to get Jack and Felicity to play the next act in the downfall of Alba. Rally the people into revolt. Lord Garth would help.

My keen senses caught the sound of soft slippers coming toward my study. I groaned. *What does he want this time?* Garrick was making a nuisance of himself. He entered my office and I put on a friendly smile.

"Have you found the youngsters in the Emerald Mountains, yet?"

I lowered my head. "No, Master. I was delayed due to some unforeseen events in Alba."

"Hm. Like what?"

"I'm training a new spy and Qadira wants to renege on your deal. She is thinking of switching sides and joining the Albans."

"That's what I heard as well." Garrick shook his head slowly in mock sadness. "She has served me so well for so many years. What would give her the idea to break her promise now? Does it have anything to do with a Healer who invited my sister to break her agreement to give me Alba? Qadira wants to keep the country for herself!"

I looked up sharply. *How does Garrick know about the private meeting last night? Who is his spy?* "I haven't heard that news, Master," I lied. "I know how important the conquest of Alba is to you, and I want to fulfill your desire as quickly as possible."

Garrick laughed. "You're not so well informed as you think. Never mind. I have my spies in Alba too. My sister has met with the Healer, who has proposed that Qadira break her agreement with me and seek freedom in Alba. Qadira is going to let the king live." He chuckled. "It appears this Healer has spirit and is very hard to catch. I want you to apprehend her and bring her to me."

I groaned inwardly. I knew what that meant. Maybe I didn't want to bring Ellara to Tokurat.

"Your Katz-paw in Alba is such a pansy. But he's doing his part in the downfall with your new Healer Katz-paw." Garrick's gaze strayed to the shifting scenes on my wall. "I see Alba's magic is weakening. You never could see so clearly before." He studied Felicity. "Is that the Healer who facilitates the toppling of the city?"

I nodded. "That is Felicity. Let me go and bring you the country."

"You'll be recognized, and the people of Alba will know the destruction of their way of life leads back to me. Then they will try to destroy me. No, let my unknown operatives in Alba do their job. It's better when people don't know who is causing the suffering. Then they fight with each other and I stand back and watch. Sort of like I do with you." He poked at me. "That was clever, using a Healer." One corner of his lips curled upward at a private thought. "My Droc'ri agents in Alba have everything under control. King Leopold will have a most memorable birthday this year." His fingers caressed the hilt of his dagger. "Then my agents will bring my sister to me. I'll take care of her." He grinned.

For a moment, I pitied Qadira for what her brother would do to her.

"You serve me best here, Rokan. I have a task for you that requires your immediate attention."

I bit my tongue and asked, "What do you need, Master?"

"You haven't gone to that band of untrained Healers yet. Why is that, Rokan? Are you afraid of them?" The wiry man watched me carefully. When I didn't answer, he continued. "I want you to take a band of Droc'ri and capture the young uninitiated in the Emerald Mountains before they can restore another of the Goddess's temples. Bring them to me. I want to taste their magic first before I kill them." Garrick smiled cruelly.

"Master, they will steal my magic and the magic of my Brothers."

"That's why I am sending you, Rokan. They know you and think they can control you. Unlike the others who failed to capture them, you can get close to them. Give their leader one of these." He lifted the lid to a small box revealing one of my disguised tainted diamonds. "I added something to make it especially destructive to them." Garrick smiled again. "I wish I could see what happens."

"You could come, Master."

"Oh, no. They're in a cold wilderness. I have too many duties to attend to here in Tokurat. There is so much to do in the dual role of Grand Master to the most powerful organization in the world and Suzerain to the Desert Lands and the countries north of us. Besides, you enjoy getting out for adventures."

I peered at Garrick. *What is he up to? He detests leaving his palace. Too many duties? His only duty appears to be telling me what he wants done.* "I don't need a band of Droc'ri to deliver this box. I can slip into their camp while they sleep and be away before they even notice. They don't keep watch."

"You'd better take them just in case you need help."

Garrick's afraid of them! I shrugged. "As you wish, Master. We'll leave at midnight."

FORTY

ELLARA AT THE BAKERY

Araval

Dinner time dispersed most of the gathered citizens. The nanas and Commander Fabian remained. Nana Bean stirred a big pot of stew and ladled some into bowls, which several women took outside to the King's Guard. I made a bowl of vegetables and took some bread for Boris. We sat side by side on the ground while he ate. He shared some of his bread with me. I sensed he was hungry and only took a few bites. He used the remaining bread to clean the plate. "Would you like more?"

He shook his head and climbed to his feet.

"Would you like to come in?"

Again, he shook his head.

454

I placed my hand on his shoulder. The way his hair fell over his shoulders and across his brow reminded me of Boris, the horse. He had faithfully protected me from harm then, too. "Thank you, Boris. I feel much safer with you around."

He smiled at me and dipped his head.

I spotted Jack and Felicity approaching the bakery. That she was companionable with Jack troubled me. *Is she working for Rokan, too? To what end?* I noticed the cuts on Jack's head had been tended. Did Felicity heal him? I didn't want them hearing what we discussed, so I waylaid them.

"What's going on in there?" Jack cocked an ear to listen.

"Nana is hosting a gathering of her friends. Something has come up that requires my attention. I can't go to meet Queen Qadira tonight. Can you postpone the meeting until tomorrow?" I glanced at Felicity, who watched me with a scowl.

Jack frowned. "She will be displeased. You do not want to anger her." He grabbed my arm. "She is your queen. You must obey her commands."

I twisted out of his grasp. "I will obey her commands, if they are reasonable, make sense, and don't involve killing someone. Besides, she will just try to capture me again. How can I obey a queen who is not honorable?" I nodded. "You can tell her that!" I moved towards the bakery. "Now, go. I have duties to attend to here."

Jack grabbed for me but found his arms trapped. He faced the stranger. "Who is this?" he demanded.

"Meet Boris. He is my new guardian. He still remembers how you tried to kill me last night. Boris doesn't say much but his prowess is unparalleled. Don't test him. You will come out the loser." I nodded to Boris, who released Jack slowly. "Now go, before I let Boris practice his art on you."

Jack was willing enough to leave, but not so Felicity. She stood toe to toe with me. Her anger washed over me. "Jack told me all about you. So, you're the one he loves!" she spat.

"Who?"

"I asked him to become my pair'ti, but he refused. It is you he wants." She lifted a hand and muttered a few words.

I steeled myself against her feeble magic, sensing to whom she referred.

"Felicity, I don't have a quarrel with you. I do not know you, nor do you have any reason to be jealous of me. Rokan can have you."

"How do you know him?"

"He is a sorcerer who hunts me. He has tainted the purity of your heart. Jealously is not becoming of a Healer."

She reached for my neck with both hands. Boris intervened. "Rokan is a powerful Mage. He is no sorcerer!" she snarled.

I shrugged. "He doesn't know how to love. He refused to mate with you because he doesn't want you to know he is a Droc'ri."

Her face flushed.

"Ask him, if you don't believe me. Have him show you his left inner forearm."

"You won't have him, Ellara. Nor will Thaddeus have you. I'll make sure of that!" She leaned closer. "I will destroy everything and everyone you love, Ellara."

"Rokan has already done that." I studied her. "Listen to yourself, Felicity. Are these the words of someone who has pledged herself to the Goddess?"

"I don't care about the Goddess. She is a false idol. I love Rokan. I serve him and him alone."

I was silent. Nana Magog's words passed through my mind. *"The Gra'Bandia Healers are not the honorable organization they once were."*

I shook my head sadly. "The dismantling of Alba is much worse than I thought, if Healers who have sworn to serve and defend the Goddess now obey the Droc'ri." I motioned to Boris. "Let her go." I turned my back on her.

"She's a witch," Jack told Felicity, as he dragged her away. His tiny smile suggested he was pleased that someone disliked me as much as he did.

Felicity was not intimidated and hurled back at me, "Camila will know what you have done, Ellara."

Jack glanced over his shoulder at the black-haired athletic man who stood beside me. When they were out of sight, I patted Boris on the back, and let my hand rest there. He shifted his weight into my hand, much like a dog when he wants you to scratch an itchy spot. As I had done with the horse, I rubbed along his shoulder blades and across the top of his shoulders. He sighed contentedly. That simple act helped to discharge the discordant energy left behind by Jack and Felicity. Across my inner sight flashed an image of the bridge crossing the Slant River and the waterworks that dammed the reservoir in a pile of rubble. *She's helping Jack destroy Alba!*

After I entered the cottage, I pulled Nana Bean aside. "Nana, how do I protect us from prying ears, without hiding the cottage in the process? I suspect Jack will be back to spy upon us."

Nana laughed. "It's simple. You know how to make the invisibility spell? It has four parts to it. The first phrase commands the cloaking. The last four words are the parts. Sound, sight, touch, and smell. All the magic is built upon a root command, such as hide, expand, contract, and reveal. Then you add whatever you are commanding, such as earth, fire, air, or water. Remember this and you can do any magic." She patted my arm. "The young captain has made you strong and resilient. He has been a blessing from the Goddess."

Quickly, I created the magic to hide our words, then returned to the conversation. The decrees were spread out on the bed. The commander, as the administrator of the laws of Alba, read the small print detailing the intent of the decree. He was frowning and shaking his head. "If these become law, it will destroy Alba."

"How do we stop it?"

Many voices chimed in. "Lift the curse on the king."

"Kill Lord Garth and his men."

"Refuse to follow the new orders."

"Reinstate the Gra'Bandia Council."

"Send the queen back to Tokur."

"Evict all the Natuan guards."

"Cede from the Ethnarchy."

One by one, the speakers stopped, and all eyes turned to me. "What do you say, Ellara? You are the only Healer among us who has the full backing of the Goddess."

I looked from one elder to the other. "You have much more experience at being a Healer than I do. I have no idea what I can do or what is possible." The vision of Alba's destruction distracted me. Tension wormed through my body as I digested Felicity's betrayal of the Goddess. How far had the integrity of the Gra'Bandia Healers degraded?

Someone snorted. "You've exposed Lord Garth for a fraud. You've refused Qadira's order to kill the king, you brought us information that we otherwise would not have known about until too late. And you are undermining the curse on the king as we speak. You underestimate yourself, Ellara."

"And in so doing, have thrown wood on the fire and put all of you in danger. I would not have more people die needlessly." I sighed. "The real culprit is unseen. It is the darkness that spreads across our land, a darkness that makes Albans give up the traditional way of the Goddess and become complacent. A darkness that makes them accepting of the wrongs that are thrust upon us. We have to find the source of that malicious shadow and destroy it. But I don't know where to look, or how to chase it from people's hearts when it has taken residence."

"It started in the mines," a nana volunteered.

"Alba's diamond mines. They became tainted about two years ago, when the young king married the Tokurian princess. I think that the sorcerer who comes now and then to Alba and arranged the agreement with the old king released a malevolent creature at the mines. Think about it. What better way to ruin our country than to destroy its primary resource?" Jillian said.

Murmurs of agreement went around the room. "Then wait for the taint to enter people's hearts, pass a bunch of decrees that remove our freedom, and give control to Lord Garth."

"We can't allow the Heartland to be harmed," someone said.

The herbalist said, "It's too late. The trees closest to the mines are losing their leaves and dying. We must stop this evil here and now."

"Can we go to the mines and undo the sorcerer's magic?" I asked.

"The Miners' Guild tried. Any who went died trying. Lord Garth is in charge of overseeing the mines."

I groaned. "How did he get so much authority?"

"He took it," Commander Fabian growled.

"If the curse was removed from the king, do you think he would stand up to Lord Garth and the council? Would he undo these new rules?"

Some heads nodded; others shook. "It will take the Goddess's blessing to remove the curse. You will be charged with witchcraft by the Natuan clerics and burned."

Cleric Paul's words came to mind. He had said that in ecclesiastical law, as well as with governments, the wording of a law was always subject to interpretation. Therefore, a person was not guilty unless it could be proven beyond doubt that a particular ordinance had been broken. And the only way that could happen was if the wording was very specific. "Commander Fabian, is there a law in the Alban registry that specifically forbids Healers from practicing their art? The law disbanding the Gra'Bandia Council wasn't specific."

The commander rubbed his chin. "Not that I recall. Nothing that specifically outlaws Healers to practice."

"So, it's an ecclesiastical matter? Is there a written document that formally acknowledges the Natuan faith as the national religion?"

The big man grinned. "You should have been an Advocate! But that doesn't mean Lord Garth and the perverted, pompously pious ass, Arkheim Aleas, will agree."

I lifted my head. "I believe it is worth the risk with the Natuan ecclesiastics. The Goddess will break the curse. We need our sovereign. He is a good man."

"King Leo's birthday is tomorrow night. Let's give him a present to remember!"

"There's only one problem. The public is not allowed. Only the courtiers and their wives," Jillian commented.

"Will there be entertainment?" I asked.

All eyes turned to me. "What do you have in mind? What can you do, besides have a spectacular performance of calling down the Goddess's wrath on Lord Garth?" Commander Fabian beamed at the prospect.

"Perhaps sing and dance for the king and his guests?" Dalela, proprietress of the Red Rose, proposed. "Ellara, if you can sing or dance, you can join us."

I rummaged in my haversack and produced a chanter, placed the reed into the wooden wind instrument, and blew a couple of notes.

Dalela smiled. "Come to the Red Rose tonight for a practice."

"I'll inform Lord Seth to invite a delegation from the Red Rose." The commander nodded. "King Leo will like this entertainment, and you will be able to get close to him." The commander rose to leave.

"Commander, what part do you think the queen is playing in this? I was supposed to meet secretly with her tonight to discuss a new proposal. Does Lord Garth answer to her? Would she stand against her brother?"

"Queen Qadira is a mystery. She's made several half-hearted attempts on King Leo's life. She hates it here, but she hates it even more back home. She despises Lord Garth, but she also commands him and his soldiers. I don't know what leverage she has on the man, or he over her." He shook his head.

"I think she is working with the sorcerer who arranged the marriage and the agreement with Tokur. I don't know what they are plotting, but I'd guess it's not going to be healthy for our country." I chewed my lip, hesitating. "I think they plan to destroy the city."

The man's eyes narrowed. "What makes you suspect this?"

"Watch Jack and the Healer who looks like me. He visits the queen and answers to a master in Tokurat. Jack is sometimes two people, and I know he is up to something, but I don't want to get close enough to find out. I think there is a mastermind pulling multiple threads of this plot to take down the Goddess and Alba." Very softly, I added, "Have a team inspect the reservoir and the main bridge abutments for explosives. Take a Healer. They may have been magically hidden."

The commander gave me a sharp look. He nodded curtly and exited the bakery. Outside, his deep rumble issued orders to his men. They hurried off.

FORTY-ONE

ROKAN AND GARRICK

Tokurat, The Desert Lands

I couldn't get the image of Ellara, devastated after Thaddeus's attempt to kill her, from my mind. The more I watched through Jack's eyes, whenever he decided to come around, the stronger the draw to her. She was vulnerable with a double broken heart, and ripe for me to swoop in and claim her. I fingered my traveling crystal. It would be so easy to travel to Alba, collect Ellara, and bring her someplace safe. The more I thought about it, the stronger the desire became. I calculated how long it would take. Could I hold the portal open long enough to walk to Araval and back before the crystal lost its integrity and it closed? I calculated it would be at least two hours and maybe longer if I had to hunt down Ellara, and the magic needed to keep the portal open for that long would destroy the crystal. I didn't want to risk ruining my only window into Alba.

I calmed my mind and focused upon Jack, urging him to bring Ellara to meet me at the portal in the forest, but he was well into his cups. I could not get him to budge from the ladies he had hired, funded by the money Qadira had given him. *He's useless to me!*

I searched for Felicity. She was with a group of men, placing explosives around the city. Through Jack, I had witnessed her accuse Ellara, and Ellara's response. She would not help me leave Alba.

I calculated again. How long would it take to get a ship off the island far enough to return to Tokurat? I scanned the Araval harbor with my Far Sight. A number of ships were docked, loading and unloading. If I could hire one of them... But the Alban captains could be very stubborn. Their ships were more valuable than gold and they pampered them like prized stallions. They departed when they were good and ready. That is what made Thaddeus so valuable. He was at my command.

I looked for the *Lovely Lady*. She was midway to Langon. I spotted one of Bruce the Terrible's pirate ships just off the mouth of the Slant River. Could I rendezvous with him to get me far enough offshore to transport myself and Ellara away? What if Garrick finds out? I'm supposed to meet with Garrick's men and attack Margot tonight. I don't have much time.

I drummed my fingers on the desk. I stood, carefully removed the papers and books I had been using, took a special cloth that neutralized any energetic signatures, and wiped the surfaces of the desk, chair, and books. I arranged my talismans so I could tell if they had been disturbed at a glance and re-shelved my books. I picked up my travel cloak and Garrick's box, reinforcing my protective spell before heading outside.

A figure blocked the corridor. "Rokan. Where are you going?"

I cursed silently, then dipped my head submissively. "Master. I'm going to find the untrained Healers."

Garrick moved closer to me. "But you said you weren't going to leave until midnight. Why now?"

"I need to locate them before I can take the Droc'ri to them. We don't want to wander around the wilderness all night looking for them."

"Very well. Your brothers will await you at midnight, here." He pointed to the floor. "Outside your study."

I hurried away. *Why was it so hard to focus? I used to juggle a dozen plots simultaneously without getting addled.* I arrived at my private abode away from the palace and sat on the bed, suddenly exhausted. It was hard to think. Automatically, I shrugged out of my tunic and put on the guise of the professor from Langon. Immediately, my mind cleared. I picked up the case Garrick had given me to deliver to Margot and a fog enshrouded my mind. I tossed the box from me. *What curse has Garrick placed on that stone? Is he trying to kill me? It wouldn't be the first time.*

I placed the packet far away from me and pondered my dilemma. It seemed to me that either the diamond was meant to muddle my mind so Garrick's men could finally kill me, or it would befuddle the minds of Margot and her friends so they could be captured and killed. Or maybe both. Neither option appealed to me.

I wove a protective spell around the box, then picked it up. A wave of dizziness passed over me. I tried a different formula, to no avail. Frustrated after the fifth attempt, I blasted it with black lightning. However, my lightning was gray. *What's wrong with my magic?* I raged. *I can't even destroy the confounded diamond!*

For the first time since I was a child, I acknowledged fear. Angrily I pushed my worries away. *I was the most powerful sorcerer in the world. I will be second to none!*

Irritably, I picked up the parcel and stowed it in my pocket. The effects of Garrick's magic were dulled, but it still scrambled my mind and distorted my judgment. I stepped out of my dwelling into the cooling night air. Outside the palace, a dozen Droc'ri waited. I opened a portal to a forest of stubby pine trees. Freezing temperature blasted us. "Let's get this over with," I growled to my Brothers. Just my luck that we traveled into a storm, I thought resentfully.

FORTY-TWO

ELLARA AND THE QUEEN

Araval

Practice for tomorrow night's performance went well. As I left the Red Rose, Jack accosted me. He reeked of wine. "Where have you been? I've been looking all over for you." He raced on, grabbing my arm. "What is so important that you make the queen wait? You will regret vexing her."

I jerked my arm out of his grasp. "Leave me alone, Jack." I started toward the bakery. Boris stood between Jack and me. I smelled fear. There was more at stake for him than he let on. What was he afraid of?

"Come on." He reached for me again.

I balked. "Is she planning on trying to capture me again?"

Jack shook his head vigorously. "No. Hurry up before she gets angry and leaves."

I allowed Jack to guide me to the same pub. I trusted Boris to defend me if needed.

Qadira sat in the same nondescript cubby-hole, wearing an old cloak that covered her fine silk tunic and wide leggings. Jack invited me to sit down, but he remained standing. The queen and I eyed each other. I was tired and not in the mood for games.

"Do not attempt to capture me again, Queen Qadira," I stated bluntly.

She laughed. "I had to test you, Ellara."

I watched her warily. "What are you testing me for?"

"To become my servant."

I stared at her in surprise.

She laughed. "Like I said before, I am a stranger in a strange land. I could use someone who commands some authority in this country. Unlike the puny Healer my brother sent, I need someone who is not afraid to stand by what she believes to be truth."

I puzzled over her words. *What is she up to now? What Healer did her brother send? Does she mean Felicity?* "And you want me to be your servant so I can do your dirty work, like killing the king?"

"Oh, much more. Garrick will never have this country. I want Alba for my own." She leaned closer. "I will destroy Alba before I let Garrick have it! Lord Garth takes orders from my brother, and I won't help him." Her lips twisted in distaste. "Garth is planning a military conquest, you know. Starting tomorrow, at the king's birthday. He covets this country as much as my brother." She made a sour face. "It appears my brother is tired of waiting, and is trying to force my hand." The corners of her lips curved up slightly.

"Lord Garth appears to be aligned with you and does your bidding."

"Yes, he does. That is because I am supposed to be assassinating the king so that he doesn't have to, but my brother has gotten impatient. The siren's call to become master of Gea has possessed him."

"Why do you need me?"

"Lord Garth suspects you are the Healer weakening the Droc'ri curse on the king. He is looking for you." Her voice softened. "I can tell him where you are, or I can keep quiet about you."

I laughed. "Lord Garth already knows where I am. He came to visit today. It was quite a spectacle."

"He just thinks you are the king's whore. He doesn't know you are a Healer. Imagine what he would do if he found out."

"I imagine he'd be delighted. I am not one of his favorite people."

470

She slammed her hand on the table. "You make light of this, Healer."

I leaned forward. "Then what are you trying to maneuver me into doing for you?"

We glared at each other.

"I want you to kill Lord Garth," she said very softly. "Tomorrow, when he tries to assassinate the king."

I shook my head. "There you go again, trying to get me to murder someone. Extermination is not my business. Get an assassin. That is what they are paid for. Besides, what makes you think I'll be in the castle for this assassination?"

She grabbed my hand. "You don't understand. Lord Garth is the link to my brother, who has orchestrated this conquest of Alba. My brother has spies here in Alba that secretly report to him everything that happens and everything I do. I do not know who to trust. I trust you more than anyone else on this forsaken island."

I raised an eyebrow. "So you want me to kill Lord Garth, then go assassinate your brother in Tokurat so that he won't execute you for failing in your quest?"

She smiled. "That will do for starters. And while you are at it, you can eliminate his Henchman, Rokan." She leaned towards me and lowered her voice. "I know you want to stop the systematic destruction of your country and your way of life."

I leaned back and extracted my hand from hers. "I'd love to kill Lord Garth and his master to stop what's happening. This is not the Desert Lands where problems are solved by just getting rid of someone. The problem facing Alba and the world will take more than assassinating two or three men. If you assume leadership of Alba, then what? How will you help our people rebuild and thrive? It's easy to say killing someone will solve the problem, but there are consequences to every action. Have you thought about that?"

Qadira drew back, pressing her lips together. "You would dare to reject my proposal, knowing full well I can have Lord Garth arrest you? You'd be tortured and burned for being a Healer."

"I neither accept nor reject your proposal. I say that before we act rashly, let's look at the alternatives and their consequences first."

"You Albans have no backbone!" She rose abruptly and pushed past Jack to exit the small space.

"Why do you annoy the queen?" Jack asked as he escorted me back to the bakery. "She could have you captured."

"Because she doesn't act like an Alban queen. She thinks everything is solved by assassinating someone."

"It's the only way to accomplish anything. Otherwise, it makes you appear weak."

"I didn't say Albans won't kill, but it has to be for the right reason. Qadira doesn't know her mind. The killings would be senseless."

"But you have a reason."

I was silent. Yes, I did have a reason. I would not break my Healer's oath to the Goddess just to satisfy the desire for vengeance. What would it take for my revenge to become aligned with the Goddess's wishes? Until then, I had to wait.

Back in the bakery, I lay on my sleeping mat and pondered the different pieces that all equaled a master conspiracy. *What have I gotten myself into? I have no idea how to break the king's curse! What did I just commit to? Even if I could undo the curse on the king, would he have the courage to oust those that wish to destroy our country, namely Lord Garth and his cohorts? The Natuan clerics need to go as well! What does Qadira hope to gain?*

Sleep eluded me and my mind drifted. I wished Sam were here to counsel me. I trusted his wisdom. I began to understand why he had said he was not up for this battle. I wasn't even sure that I was.

My thoughts turned to Thaddeus. I had been too busy during the day to give attention to a nagging feeling that he was in grave danger. With my Far Sight, I saw him lying on his bunk. Matty hovered over him like a concerned father. I let myself relax and sense him. Something blocked me, as if he had a shield around himself. It was not the darkness of the entity that the Goddess had banished. Had Thaddeus figured out how to make a shield to prevent Rokan from seeing him?

My intuition told me that Thaddeus was in trouble. I directed my senses to receive from Matty, and felt his plea for help.

I thought about sending my spirit, but Nana Magog had forbidden me from doing that, since the sorcerer could capture it. Besides, I wasn't certain that I could restore Thaddeus that way. I turned over all the new things I had learned. Matty's pleas became more insistent. More than anything, I wished I could be there. Nana Magog teleported herself to and from the Sacred Grove at Cuilithe. How did she do it?

I remembered a picture I had seen in one of Nana Magog's books of Goddess incantations. I got up, rummaged through my satchel, and pulled out the thin manual. I went to the hearth, tossed a piece of kindling on the coals, and blew until a small flame burst to life. In the dim light, I thumbed through the pages until I came to the drawing of a person in two places. My ability to read the ancient script was very limited, but I gleaned that this was a traveling spell. I whispered the words and the air shifted around me. I practiced saying the words several times until I was certain I had the sound sequences right.

I set the book on the table. I wanted to make sure I traveled to the right place. I needed something with Thaddeus's energetic signature imprinted on it. My protective talismans clinked. I touched the golden disc with the spiral of gemstones that Thaddeus had given me. It contained a strong impression of his essence and love.

I shivered. I never would have considered this action before, nor would I have known how to focus the Goddess's power. I had Thaddeus to thank for my enhanced abilities. What if... I pushed my fears away, surrendered to the Goddess, held the golden disk between my palms over my heart, and imagined myself beside Thaddeus on his ship. When the intention and location became one, I spoke the words that commanded the air. After a moment of disorientation, I became aware of cool air and movement under my feet. Wind whistled through rigging. I became aware of a big man supporting me where I stood beside Thaddeus's bunk.

"You came!" Matty would have said more, but I put my fingers to his lips.

A wave of nausea passed over me. My head cleared and I was able to stand on my own. I assessed the tormented man. His body burned. This was not a fever of the flesh, but one of his soul. His breathing was shallow and ragged, his pulses faint.

Immediately, I connected with the Goddess and let Her Radiance fill me. I brushed my hands over his body. Thaddeus squirmed and moaned. I placed my hand over his heart and sensed the nature of his malady.

I planted the kiss of the Goddess on the center of his chest, and let her Love flow through my hands to heal his broken heart. I received images that began with him as a young boy witnessing the rape of his mother and brutal death of his parents at the hands of Bruce the Terrible. And the capture of his friends for the slave trade, again by Bruce the Terrible.

Three years later, he was severely injured and left for dead in the sea when Bruce's pirates attacked the villager's knarr. He experienced a painful disillusionment about love from a young woman with a boy child. Cast out of the family with whom he recovered, the crippled youth had been forced to make his way alone in the world. His deformity had caused him to feel unworthy. Rokan cruelly crushed his dreams of loving and being loved. And now, the pain from the distress he had just caused me, and fear that I could never again love him.

Tears slid down my cheeks from the suffering that this man had endured and dropped on my hand over his heart. Thaddeus convulsed and choked, then started sobbing uncontrollably. I lifted him so that I could sit behind him and pillowed his head on my shoulder, like a mother soothing her injured child. I softly sang an unfamiliar song with words I had never heard spoken. I sang it over and over. In time the sobbing stopped and Thaddeus's breathing became normal and the fire in his body left. I still held him, even after the flush of the Goddess's essence faded. The rhythmic motion of the *Lovely Lady* lulled me, and I drifted to sleep.

Matty's return after taking navigational readings startled me awake. Matty nodded acknowledgment and went about his calculations. I slowly extracted myself and lay Thaddeus down. He slept peacefully. I followed Matty on deck.

After giving instructions to the helmsman, Matty led me to amidships. "The sorcerer spies upon us. When we transported your daughter several years ago, Margot said this was the safest place to talk."

That sounded like Margot. "I felt your call."

Matty pulled me into a bear hug. "I'm so pleased to see you! I was afraid he would die. The Cap'm just hasn't been himself."

"He will recover." I sniffed, my mouth watering at the aroma of food drifting from the galley below deck.

Matty grinned and left. In the predawn light, I took the opportunity to observe the crewmen, who scurried about the deck adjusting the sails for the new heading. They cast curious glances at me. The whole experience seemed surreal. Was I really on the *Lovely Lady*? Or was this all a very real dream?

Matty returned in a few minutes with a bowl of fish stew and rice. I moved aft to sit on a crate out of the wind. Matty sat beside me. He nodded to the crew. "Margot made quite an impression on the crew during that voyage."

I chuckled. "She has that effect." I knew she had traveled on other ships besides Sam's. She never mentioned the *Lovely Lady*. Belly filled and snuggled inside Matty's warm coat, I curled up on the crate and slept.

The sun was high when I awoke, refreshed. It had been a long time since I sailed with Sam. There was something purifying about sea air. I closed my eyes and listened to the creak of the vessel, the calls between the crew, the splash of water against the bow, and wind in the rigging. It reminded me of being with Sam. Tears filled my eyes. I had my own broken heart to heal.

Someone sat down beside me, put an arm around me, and kissed my forehead. For a moment, I thought it was Sam. I opened my eyes and brushed away the tears, to see Thaddeus. His smile warmed my heart. The tears returned, only these were tears of relief.

He brushed them away with a thumb and pulled me close to him. *I thought I was dreaming.* I heard in my mind. *I felt horrible for the despair I caused you. I was certain you could never love me after what I did. I'm sorry. Will you forgive me?*

I sighed. *I felt betrayed and abandoned until I read your letter. Still, your demonstration hurt. Don't ever do that again, at least not without warning me first.*

It had to be convincing. With your senses, for which I am grateful, I don't feel Rokan watching me as much now.

Did you have to almost die?

I didn't plan that. It was compelling, wasn't it? Thaddeus smiled wryly.

Don't do that again, either! We are Goddess bonded, at least partway. Together we are strong. If you die... I pressed my lips together. *You're lucky Matty called to me and I was able to come.*

I know. For that I am eternally grateful. He leaned against the bulkhead, pulling me close. *I've dreamed of this day for years. It fills my heart with joy to have you beside me sailing the seas.*

I exhaled slowly. *I wish I could stay. Are you aware of events in Araval?*

He shook his head, suddenly alert. *When I blocked you, I also could not sense you. What a lonely feeling after knowing your most intimate moods and thoughts.*

I sent him images of the last day's adventures. Thaddeus slipped off the crate and invited me to follow him into his cabin. He moved stiffly.

He wrapped his arms around me. *Stay with me. Let me take you away from all of that danger.*

I have to get back. I have a curse to break at the king's birthday party tonight.

He read my determination and groaned. *I'll have to save you from being burned at the stake by Arkheim Aleas.*

I hope not. According to Qadira, Lord Garth is supposed to assassinate the king at this party, too. I don't want that to happen. I want the king to rescind all the harmful laws.

Thaddeus looked dubious. *Well, that won't solve the world's problems, but it is a good start.*

I can't sit by idly and watch our country and the ways of the Goddess fall. I will do what I can. What about you? What are your plans?

We're destined for Langon. When I saw Sam that fateful night in Sheldon, he said that Kian was going to the Scholars' Guild to study and find a solution to the Droc'ri conquest. Since Kian has access to all of the ancient knowledge and the best minds in the world, I want him to research how to get your soul piece back.

Give him a hug from me.

He nodded. He cupped my face in his hands. *That you'd risk your life to come and heal me after I had wounded you... Now, more than ever, I want us to become Anam pair'ti. I will do what I must to make that possible.*

I stayed with Thaddeus a little longer, while his color and vitality returned.

Thaddeus, your attack on me was so unexpected that I was completely unprepared. I think that left me vulnerable to invasion by a dark force. I have cleansed and purified myself over and over to make sure I have no residue.

I never meant to actually kill you.

I know. However, Jack did.

I saw. Your rescuer was surprisingly strong and I couldn't get away from him to keep Jack away. I was relieved that you finally defended yourself.

It wasn't defense. It was a drive to execute him. I almost did. I'm terrified that force will overtake me again and make me do something I would never want to do. Like kill you. We need to complete the Ceangal Bandia.

Really? Are you sure?

Yes. I hesitated. For an instant Thaddeus's appearance shifted into Sam. I shook my head. *I can't. Not yet.*

At the look of relief on Thaddeus's face, I guessed that postponing the most intimate part of the Ceangal Bandia rite suited him as well.

Can we do like we did before? he sent.

I initiated the connection with the Goddess, uniting hearts and spirits. We held each other and let the touch of lips represent our physical connection. We spoke the words of the Ceangal Bandia to protect us and his ship, like I had done with Sam's. I imagined the protective shield for his ship included the light-bending properties that Boris had exhibited, so that when one looked directly at the *Lovely Lady*, it would be hard to see. Thaddeus was pleased. The more we surrendered our bodies and our individual essences, we became one energy, and the stronger the protective field around the ship and ourselves became. The shield reached its maximum density, and the presence of the Goddess within receded. We lingered in the satisfaction of our deepening connection. Reluctantly, we came back into our physical reality. Even more unwillingly, I withdrew from Thaddeus's reassuring embrace. It reminded me of how Sam used to hold me.

It was getting late. I turned my mind to how to return to Araval, without turning the *Lovely Lady* around and sailing back. I knew I could travel, because I had done so. But I had a strong emotional and Goddess-augmented connection with Thaddeus. How did Nana do it?

Let me help you. He sent me the image from another page in Nana's book. This drawing showed an opening in the air, like those the Healers at Cuilithe had used. I studied the words and said them softly. I repeated them until the air shimmered before us. I linked to the Goddess. I imagined myself in the garden behind the bakery. I honed in on a particular point in space. I spoke the words that commanded the air and the air shimmered, but no opening appeared. I glanced at Thaddeus. His energy joined with the Goddess and flowed through me. This time, when I said the words, a gap in the space before us opened to Nana's garden.

Before I could take a step, the hole in space snapped shut. What if I was only partly through when the portal closed? *I'm afraid to do this, Thaddeus. Teleportation is probably just as risky, but it worked to get me here. I must find a way to make it work to get back.*

Thaddeus didn't object.

Matty called to me and I had the talisman you gave me. Who can I use to attract me back to Araval?

Thaddeus shrugged. *Who do you feel closest to?*

Boris. The man who stopped you from killing me. He was, is, my horse. He's a Verndari shapeshifter. Now he has become my defender.

Thaddeus nodded. *Figures. How can I help?*

Do what you need to deceive Rokan, but don't block me again. To be of service to each other, we need to be able to sense the other.

You are not very good at deception. I may have to block you so that you remain upset.

I grimaced. I had to admit that Thaddeus was right. *I don't like deceit and misdirection. They are designed to manipulate people. I don't want any untruthfulness between us.* I traced a finger from his temple, along his jaw to chin. *I don't think I'll have any trouble pretending I'm sad.*

Thaddeus's expression sobered. *I will miss you.* He pulled me into his arms and softly kissed me. *I heard that Jack and a woman who is pretending to be you are stirring the people into a revolt. They have planted explosives to destroy the city if the queen doesn't kill the king tonight. Felicity will stab you in the back if she gets the opportunity.*

How do you know?

I have your Far Sight now. I heard rumors and I spotted Felicity with Jack before I left. He tightened his arms. *Araval is too perilous for you. Stay with me.*

It would be so easy to stay with him and see Kian. I wished I didn't have to leave. *I can't hide from this battle. I must return and fulfill my promise to Commander Fabian, and the nanas, for the benefit of Alba. Besides, Boris will protect me.*

I used my Far Sight to find Boris, who watched the bakery, even though I was not there. I couldn't just pop into view in the middle of the street. *Go to the garden, Boris.* I sent Boris the image of the garden behind the bakery, using the same communication method as when he was a horse.

Boris lifted his head, looked around, then calmly entered the bakery. When I next looked, he waited patiently in the garden. *Call for me,* I sent.

At the last minute, I sent to Thaddeus, *Let me know when you arrive in Langon. I will go to see Kian with you.*

Thaddeus caressed my cheek. *I look forward to it. Until me meet again.*

I waited until I had a strong sense of Boris, then opened to the Goddess and said the words that would carry me back to Araval. After a moment of disorientation, I became aware of the pungent scent of herbs. Boris caught me from falling. I leaned against him until the dizziness passed. I stepped back and thanked him.

He bowed his head. "Willingly, I serve you in whatever capacity you require."

I patted his arm and entered the bakery. I felt Thaddeus's spirit wrap around me. *Be careful tonight.*

"Thank you for your help." I paused. *I'm glad to sense you again. May the Goddess protect us.*

FORTY-THREE

ROKAN

The Emerald Mountains

I stepped through the portal and waited for my brother Droc'ri to emerge. Wind swirled heavy snow around us and whipped the trees. Widow-making dead limbs crashed down beside us. Most noticeable was the chill. I shivered. A quick glance at the other Droc'ri, who were not as warmly dressed as I, gave me a tiny measure of satisfaction. They grumbled. I shoved the tainted box into the pocket of the sorcerer closest to me and immediately, my mind cleared. I watched the man carefully to see if he showed signs of being affected like I had been.

"What are we waiting for?" Sid growled. "It's freezing out here."

I slowly pivoted, probing the night with my senses for Margot. "This way." I started in a southeasterly direction, picking my way through the trees. In a short time, we came upon an outcropping of rock in which there were a number of caves. There were no signs of horses or people.

"Where are they?" The others drew near Sid.

As if in answer, a brilliant light illuminated the sorcerers, including me. Warm, loving energy coursed through my body. I cried out, as did my fellow Droc'ri. One by one, they dropped to the ground, panting, then became quiet. I remained standing and stared at them in the unnatural light. I bent down to check if they were alive. As I watched, the bodies of my companions aged, then the wind blew the outer layers of their body into dust, and in a short time, the men were gone.

When I looked up, Margot and her friends stood before me. I met her stern gaze. "What manner of magic is this? You have killed my Brothers, yet I am still alive."

Margot shrugged. "The Goddess filled your Brothers with Her Loving Radiance. Like the others sent to capture us, they could not accept it. Why did you come carrying a poisoned diamond? To capture and kill us?"

It could have been Nana Magog speaking to me. Yet I detected nothing of the old Healer's essence about Margot.

"It was not my idea to capture or kill you. The tainted diamond also affected me." I scanned the energies of her friends. There was something different about them. They had become confident. I groaned inwardly. These young people were no longer children. Rebuilding the Temple of the Crescent Moon must have awakened and activated their innate abilities. Yet it appeared that all of their power was focused through Margot. *If Margot were out of the picture, could they still be so intimidating?*

Margot turned to one of the young women. "Excellent work, Bette. You can calm the weather, now."

Instantly, the blizzard and high winds ceased and the air in the forest warmed perceptibly. Margot beckoned. "Come, Rokan. We need to talk."

She turned her back and the group passed through an invisible barrier into one of the large caves. A cheerful fire blazed near the entrance. Deeper into the cave, the horses munched on grassy feed. *Where did they get that? There is no pasture for miles.*

Margot indicated that I sit. "Tell me why you are here."

"Garrick sent me to capture you."

She shook her head. "Why did *you* want to come?"

I started to say Garrick told me, but under the pressure of her intimidating gaze, I said, "I wanted to see how you were doing." I added, "I am impressed at how rapidly you rebuilt the Temple of the Crescent Moon. The Grand Master is worried that you will make the Goddess powerful again. Are you going to the Six Winds to rebuild *that* temple now?"

Margot didn't answer. Katarine offered me some water and a small plate of stew. "It's good to see you again, Rokan."

I took the proffered food and watched the group cautiously. I would not underestimate them again. "Am I your prisoner?"

Margot eyed me. "Do you want to be our prisoner?"

I shook my head.

The others settled down to sleep. Even Margot and Katarine lay down on a bed of moss. I was aware of their eyes on my back for a long time before they drifted off to sleep. Their nonchalance surprised me, especially since Margot had so decidedly expressed her dislike towards me during our previous encounter. Now, her energy was harnessed and focused like a sharp tool. I decided I'd stay with them for a while.

I surveyed the cave. A memory came into my mind of the caves in this area that were sanctuaries of the Goddess. This cave was the largest, with an array of geometric designs, lines and circles, and animals etched into the cavern walls, interspersed between brilliant blue, rose, green, and golden patches of rock. The cave had acted as a sort of relay point on a ley line, a Sprid'linya of the Goddess, that stretched from the Temple of the Crescent Moon to the Temple of the Six Winds. Of course, the Droc'ri had desecrated the shrine.

I surveyed the group, pondering whose life force I could feed upon. Towards morning, Katarine approached me, offering to share hers. She knelt before me and bowed her head. I touched her forehead and allowed her vitality to flow into me.

Suddenly, I was shoved roughly aside. Someone dragged me backwards. Margot stepped in front of me and declared, "How dare you feed on us and steal our life force!"

"It's alright, Margot," Katarine said. "I am willing."

Margot rounded on her friend. "What has he done to you, Kat, to make you think taking your essence is an acceptable practice? What else is he doing to you while he feeds? He does not need your life force, or any of ours. He has access to his own, just like we do. Just because he is lazy is not our concern. He can learn to connect to the Goddess for his vitality, like the rest of us."

Taken aback, I protested, "I need to harvest the vital force of another to live."

"No, you don't. Let go that facade you wear. You waste your vitality just to make yourself look young and handsome. Show your true self, Rokan." Her glare was unrelenting. Interestingly, it was not Margot trying to make me comply, which is what I would have done. Instead, it was a barrier that denied me access to her or the others.

"You need to go. Now." I didn't move. With a strength that surprised me, Margot lifted me to my feet and shoved me towards the perimeter of their camp. "If this is the respect with which you treat us, then you don't deserve our friendship." She propelled me forward. "Now go and be glad that the Goddess does not punish you."

I took a few steps, then faced Margot. Katarine tugged on her arm. "He needs our life force for his magic."

Margot opened her mouth for what I knew would be a scathing remark. Amazingly, she closed it, took a step back, and appraised me. I wished I could read her aura clearly so I could discern what was going through her mind. Finally, she said, "Do all the Droc'ri have to feed on innocents to maintain their magic?"

"It is a common practice," I replied. "It keeps us healthy and virile. It is the Droc'ri way to demonstrate our prowess through physique. A young, strong body means powerful magic."

Margot snorted. "Why don't you get your vital energy from the Goddess?"

I smiled at her, although I knew my charm had no effect on her. "Healers do it, too."

She made a face, then nodded slowly. "You and Nana Magog must be about the same age. She does not go about feeding on willing or unwilling subjects, yet she retains a strength and vitality that matches your own. It's obvious that you and your Brother sorcerers have this practice to satisfy your egos." She leaned forward. "Let go of this illusion of youthful vitality and show me your real appearance."

490

I cringed. I had never revealed my two-hundred-year-old form to anyone, not even to myself!

She eyed me. "You can let it go voluntarily, or the Goddess will strip you of your glamour. Which do you choose?" When I hesitated, she stretched out her hand and pointed her index finger at me. She read my reluctance. I had no doubt she would follow through with her demand if I withheld.

"You ask me to break my Droc'ri vows," I growled at her.

She was not intimidated. "You hide from yourself, Rokan. Your life has been a practice of deceit and illusion. If you want the right to call us friend, you must not pretend to be someone you are not."

"You will shun me."

Margot shrugged. "Try us."

I didn't want to drop the illusion I had maintained for at least one hundred fifty years. But she had more patience than I would have given her credit for, and eventually, I let my youthful physique slip. I was keenly aware of all eyes upon me. I thought revealing my aura was vulnerable. Unmasking my true, elderly form was akin to a death sentence. *How could this wisp of a girl compel me to do something I had never before done?* Angrily I lashed out at Margot, smiting her with an invisible hand. But my power dissipated around her, captured by that strange magic that Margot and her friends conjured.

"He's not so bad," I heard someone mutter. "Now we can see the real Rokan and not some fiction he uses to confuse others."

Someone else agreed. "Now his energy matches his physical appearance."

"He doesn't look like a Droc'ri sorcerer." Katarine laughed. "No one would ever know or recognize him."

At first, I was angered by their comments, but the non-threatening atmosphere surrounding me was calming. I looked down at my body. My tunic hung loosely on a bony frame, held erect through sheer will. Wrinkles laced the skin over the raised tendons and gnarled joints of my hands. Silvery strands floated around my face. I had prided myself on my hair. I started to mutter the words that would restore me, but Margot stopped me with a hand to my chest. I inhaled sharply, wary of what she would do to me in my powerless state.

She smiled, as did all of her companions. "At last, we see you without one of your many disguises, Rokan. It took a lot of trust and courage for you to reveal yourself. I respect you for that."

Her words took me aback.

The rest of the group swarmed around me, patting me. Their demeanors had shifted from wary acceptance to genuine respect and ease. Slowly, I found myself relaxing.

"I think we should call him Nan Rokan," someone said.

Murmurs of assent followed his words. I stared at the untrained Healers, one at a time. They regarded me with a reverence that I had never experienced before. It both pleased and unsettled me.

Margot inspected me. "The Droc'ri live in deceit and dishonesty. It takes all of your energy to pretend you are bigger, better, younger, wealthier, and crueler than anyone else. You waste your vitality and that of those you feed upon to keep an unnecessary glamour just to make you think you are strong and invincible. Just be who you are and you will have more energy to use when it is needed."

I straightened.

Margot leaned closer. Her tone turned serious. "If you want to remain with us, you will wear your true form, and you will show your aura. We will not provide you sustenance to maintain the false you. You may not feed upon any of us. Is that clear?"

I nodded slowly, meeting the intensity of her gaze. I grinned inwardly. She made me feel alive, even if I lived in a two-hundred-year-old body.

With a word, I adjusted the sizing of my clothes to match my body. However, my legs tired. A couple of women escorted me to a log, where they helped me ease onto the hard surface. "Don't worry. You'll get used to your new body," one of them encouraged. "You still have your magic."

I did. Testing my connection to the elements, I aimed a finger at the fire, and it exploded into flames that reached high into the sky. I grew a bed of moss on the log to cushion where I sat. I felt elated. My magic flowed effortlessly. Maybe these untrained initiates were wiser than they knew.

I stayed with Margot and her friends, first at the cave, while they rebuilt the sanctuary, then at another shrine a day's ride south. She had a map of the mountains. Small X's noted the four locations they had restored from Langon southwards.

That evening, I commented, "The Grand Master sent me to stop you from restoring these temples. Do you know the significance of what you are doing?"

Margot shrugged and glanced at the others. "We are rebuilding what you destroyed."

"Do you know why they were destroyed?"

She lowered her eyebrows. "Probably in an attempt to weaken the Goddess and Her Healers so the Droc'ri could become more powerful." She pointed at me. "You can atone for some of your evil deeds by helping us restore the Temple of the Six Winds." She poked her finger at a point on the map. "That is, if you have the courage to face the Goddess and plead for Her mercy."

"The Temple of the Six Winds is in the Desert Lands, in the country of Nesbit. How are you going to get there? It's through hundreds of miles of inhospitable terrain."

"Same way we got here." Margot refused to say more.

I entertained the young Healers with stories about my travels, about the life of a Droc'ri and legends about the Goddess. During the day, I guided each person in the use of their talents and warned of the consequences of misuse of that power. I moved stone and cemented it together with elemental magic, and showed the youths how to do that. What had taken them three days at other sites, they achieved in one, because of my assistance and tutoring. It pleased me how easy and accessible my magic became.

For their part, the young women and men treated me with a respect I had never known, bringing me food, making sure I was warm and comfortable. Even stranger, the persona of the all-powerful Droc'ri sorcerer eroded so that I saw myself through their eyes as an elderly, wise scholar. They sought information about the history of the temples, the lands through which we traveled, and the significance of each temple they had restored. I delighted in sharing my vast knowledge. Previously, as a Droc'ri, I had commanded respect through fear. Now these uninitiated gave freely to me, not because I required them to do so, but because it came naturally.

Even though my voice was soft and thready, it appeared to motivate my companions more effectively than the deep resonance I had projected in my disguise. My time with the Healers caused me to question everything I had learned and practiced as a Droc'ri. With a shift in my perspective, what I had believed was weak was actually a strength.

The world Margot and her friends had created seemed surreal, as if I had stepped into a fantasy land that had lain hidden and dormant within my innermost being. I didn't want to leave it and return to the cut-throat world of vipers in the reeds, domination, and manipulation, which was the norm for a Droc'ri. In that existence, I could never relax. I always had to watch my back. I could not trust anyone, much less rely upon anyone's help. It was a dog-eat-dog world where survival meant being the most powerful, resourceful, ambitious, and ruthless.

When it came time for me to return to Tokurat and report to Garrick about their magic, each person came up to me, thanked me for joining in their journey, hugged me, and kissed me on the cheek. Even Margot, who still kept a watchful eye on me, approached. She didn't hug or kiss me.

"Will you help us restore the Temple of the Six Winds?"

I regarded her, longing to remain with her and her friends. We had worked together for two days, rebuilding as many temples. I found myself saying, "You have three more temples on this ley line — this Sprid'linya of the Goddess — before you reach the Desert Lands. When you reach your destination, I will come and help you." *What would I tell Garrick?*

"Rokan, you are a man between worlds, bridging the worlds of the Goddess and the Dark Lords. It is a dangerous path you walk, filled with difficult choices that pit your beliefs against your desires, and it threatens to rip you apart. It takes courage, determination, and resilience. You are blessed by the Goddess to bring balance to the realms." She thought for a minute. "Come to us when you need a reminder of what can be."

Her words touched a chord and pleased me. She publicly recognized and acknowledged my efforts and abilities, something neither Garrick nor any of the Droc'ri had ever done. After all, doing so would be admitting frailty, and the Droc'ri *never* acknowledged weakness. I dipped my head to her, stepped a few paces away, and created a portal. I assumed the illusion of my imposing prowess, but before I stepped through the portal, I let it slide away. I smiled to my audience, then passed through the opening into the hot, dusty streets of Toku-rat, resolving to help Margot and her friends bring a harmony between our respective approaches to living. Vibrant life flowed in my veins, even if my elderly body didn't show it.

Before the portal closed, I heard Margot say, "Let's go. If we are lucky, we will reach the Temple of the Six Winds in three days."

FORTY-FOUR

ELLARA AT THE CASTLE

Araval

F inally, the evening for the king's party arrived. Nana gave me a blessing of protection from the Goddess. Under the cover of darkness, I climbed over the garden wall and trotted to the back entrance of the Red Rose. Boris followed.

I knocked lightly, and immediately, the door opened. One of the women guided me to the dressing room, where I was given an elegant, embroidered blue and gold gown that clung to my curves. Pale blue silk veils, flecked with gold, fastened at my shoulders, and floated as I moved. Another lady plaited my hair into layers atop my head and held everything in place with long jeweled pins. Yet another painted my face with blush powder, reddened my lips, outlined my eyes, and defined my eyebrows with a charcoal pencil.

I stared at the woman I had become in the mirror and hardly recognized her. Dalela draped a blue velvet cloak over my shoulders and gently lifted the hood over my head. We exited the building and climbed into the waiting carriage. Squeezed together, warriors of beauty and elegance, we boldly headed into enemy territory.

Even though everyone appeared calm and confident, I sensed apprehension from the ladies. Dalela placed her hand on mine. "All will be well. You don't look like a Healer. We'll watch out for you."

I swallowed and tried to relax. I had made Dalela's acquaintance only a few days ago. Almost immediately, a kindred connection developed between us. She recognized me as a Healer from the beginning. In exchange for tending her ladies' wounds, inflicted by Lord Garth's brutish soldiers, she offered me private baths, delicious meals, wise counsel, and friendship.

When we arrived at the castle, the sounds of revelry suggested the festivities were well underway. Servants escorted us to a room adjacent to the great hall. Several minstrels tuned their lap harps and the acrobats stretched. All eyes turned and watched the twelve enchantresses enter the room. I felt self-conscious and certain I'd be discovered.

We moved to one corner of the room, removed our cloaks, and touched up our hair and face paint. We waited, listening to the cat-calls, whistles, pounding, and claps from the hall. We were to be the last of the entertainers. As time dragged by, fear reared its paralyzing head and ate away at my resolve.

Finally, the troubadours went into the hall, and we were alone in the room. Dalela whispered to me, "Can you give us the blessing of the Goddess?" She glanced at the others who sat stiffly, picking at invisible lint on their gowns, spinning rings on their fingers, or tapping their toes. "I think we could all use Her Gra'yia."

I peered around the room, then closed my eyes and invited the Goddess to guide and protect us. Immediately, She chased away my anxiety and filled me with confidence. I asked Her to provide me the opportunity to dissolve the curse on King Leopold tonight and to protect him from assassination.

We stood and flexed our bodies. I checked the double reed for my Alban-carved, wooden chanter for cracks, which would make it squeal. I flexed my fingers above the small holes spaced in the hollow wood cylinder, then played silent scales to limber up. I slid a soft cloth along the length of the instrument, buffing the reddish wood to a luster, then shined the brass flare at the bottom. Finally, I tested the straps on the brass finger cymbals for snugness and fastened them to my thumb and middle finger like giant rings. When I needed them, I could simply rotate them into position.

The minstrels returned from their performance, chatting animatedly. They had been invited to the feast and hastened to set their instruments down and reenter the great hall.

A servant beckoned us to follow him around to the main entrance of the festive chamber. I held back and walked with a green-gowned lady who carried a circular hand drum.

A cacophony of sound greeted us at the doors. The expansive room was filled with people sitting or reclining at long tables placed near the walls and laden with trays of meat, decanters of wine, bowls of soup, dishes of colorful fruits and vegetables, and platters of pastries, cakes, and bread. It smelled heavenly.

Bright banners along the walls filled the spaces between tapestries that hung from ceiling to floor depicting detailed hunting scenes. The tables formed three sides of a rectangle with a broad space in the middle, which was used by the servants and performers. Facing the main entrance was a raised dais upon which the king's table rested. It was not so heavily laden with food. Instead, the nobles seated there were served from a sideboard behind.

I recognized King Leopold, taller than the guests to either side of him. Pale hair softly curled around his neck, highlighting his ruddy, clean-shaven face. The Natuan gold band on his head kept his hair in place and indicated his status. His jacket matched the red and gold of the fighting winged-lion family crest on a banner behind his high-backed gilded chair. He held a golden goblet. He looked splendid.

Beside him sat a glamorous woman with strawberry blonde hair arranged high on her head. A thin circlet of rank graced her head, and her many jewels sparkled in the lamplight. For all of her beauty, Qadira's polite smile didn't reach her eyes.

She seemed to be watching someone in the crowd. I couldn't see the object of her interest among the guests. She presented herself differently than the queen I had met at the pub.

An elderly gentleman sat to the king's right. "That's Lord Seth," Dalela whispered. "He's the king's advisor. He served the old king, too, and I believe he is still loyal to the Gra'bandia Council."

I glanced at the slender bald man, with a stern expression and a scar stretching from temple to chin, sitting next to the queen. I noticed that Lord Garth didn't sit on the king's side of the table. I hoped he wouldn't recognize me.

Behind and to one side of the king stood Commander Fabian, resplendent in his military finery, making Captain Morgan, who stood behind Lord Garth, look slovenly by comparison. Commander Fabian dipped his head imperceptibly in acknowledgment.

It was late, and the guests had consumed many cups of wine and ale. Loud voices assailed our ears. A servant struck a gong, and a booming voice announced us. Before we entered, Dalela started singing. After the first verse, we picked up the chorus and entered the room, still singing and moving regally in time with the melody.

Silence descended over the room. The servants paused in their tasks, and guests stopped chewing or drinking. The king's attention riveted on us. We repeated the song several times, turning it into a round and harmonizing, as we paraded before the audience. We stopped before the royal table, where

Dalela bowed and said, "Greetings, good King Leopold. We wish you a blessed birthday."

The young king closed his mouth hurriedly and nodded curtly.

Courtiers stared at us, some with kindly expressions, some lustfully. Lord Garth, though, frowned. He leaned to his neighbor. "Who invited them?" he growled.

It dawned on me that all the other entertainers had been men. I took a deep breath. *I have a duty to perform, and I will not let anyone distract me from it!*

King Leopold flicked his fingers. "Go on with the entertainment."

Dalela bowed again. The drummer and I stepped to one side, and we played several folk-dance melodies. Dalela's songbird notes stirred the listeners, and soon the courtiers sang softly or clapped their hands in time with the music. The rest of our troupe danced.

Then the women split into pairs or fours and incorporated some of the ancient ritual dances into their routines. I played the chanter or finger cymbals and observed the crowd. King Leo drank in the seductive movements, as did many of the other men. The ladies of the court and Qadira wore reserved expressions. Lord Seth, who sat next to the king, beamed with childlike delight, especially at the latter dances.

Then our time was up. The audience applauded, hooted, and pounded the tables with their goblets for more. Dalela had anticipated this and hummed the first few bars of an old ballad from the days when Alba thrived. I accompanied her with the baleful tones of the chanter, and the rest of our group formed a wide half-circle behind us and sang the chorus or hummed softly in the background.

Dalela and I were about the same age. A certain grace and wisdom come from enduring life's experiences, which a younger woman can't equal. It was with this inner self-possession that Dalela and I orbited each other like the sun and the moon in simple, flowing circles as she sang and I played. The Goddess filled me. My aura merged with Dalela's and expanded to encompass the room. Time stood still.

> *Sun caresses the land*
> *With a gentle hand.*
> *River, mountain, and tree*
> *So that human in sacred union, we can be*
> *United woman and man*
> *Free and without ban*
> *To thrive for the benefit of all*
> *Alba, Goddess home, call.*

The others joined in for the chorus.

> *Cro'i an Bandia. Cro'i an Bandia.*

When we finished, the haunting melody lingered in the air. Then stillness so profound that one could hear a pin drop descended over the feast-goers. Dewy-eyed women and men stared at us. Lord Garth, who had half risen from his chair, slowly settled back onto the seat. *If he knew the significance of that song, he would not be so complacent.*

The king clapped loudly. The rest of the room followed suit enthusiastically, pounding the tables and whistling.

"That was delightful," he pronounced. "Come, sit with me for a while." He patted the table next to him.

Dalela and I exchanged looks and we glided around the table, keeping as much distance from the scowling Lord Garth as possible. She squeezed my hand encouragingly and nudged me to sit next to the monarch, in the seats that Lord Seth and his neighbor had vacated.

I smiled sheepishly at King Leo and busied myself with arranging my dress. I was aware of all the eyes on us and read hope in the faces of the women who had helped me gain this opportunity. I knew I had to get my hands on the king's crown, but I had not a clue as to how to perform that feat discreetly. I also didn't know just what the Goddess was going to do. I hoped it would be quick, like when she had dissolved the entity that had fed on Thaddeus.

"I haven't heard 'Heart of the Goddess' since I was a child. My mother used to sing it to me."

Dalela responded. "I'm glad it pleased you, Sire. That was our one desire."

He drank from his cup and sighed. "Those were such joyful times."

"Things have changed dramatically," I volunteered. "Do you wish we could live in those joyful times again?"

He turned to look at me and slowly nodded. "I dream about it all the time, but alas, I cannot bring back the past."

I stared at the food before me, at a loss for what to say or do next.

"How rude of me. I haven't offered you refreshment after your captivating performance." The king waved towards the dishes before him. "Help yourself."

He swirled the liquid in his cup slowly. I reached for a biscuit. "Alba has been such a wonderful country to call home," I said. "Especially as a woman who has the freedom to creatively express her best talents, alone or together with her pair'ti. Wouldn't you say that system has worked well for years, Sire?"

He shot me a glance, then took a long draught from his goblet.

"During the last few months, Alba has lost its sparkle. Have you ever thought of a happier future, based upon past times when Alba thrived?" I asked softly.

He choked, then coughed profusely. Suddenly the room became silent. I made myself chew, pretending that I was only making idle chat and not uttering potentially treasonous words. Lord Garth's chair scraped on the marble floor and his uneven footsteps drew near.

Lord Seth intercepted him. "Garth, have you had any of the crème custard yet?" He nudged the old soldier with his elbow.

"It caresses your palate like your lover..." he trailed off at Lord Garth's growl.

Dalela grabbed my hand. We rose and bowed. "It has been a pleasure to enjoy your generous hospitality, Your Majesty. I am afraid we bore you with topics not fit for your birthday." She tugged on my hand. As I eased away from the dais, a breeze from a passing servant lifted the veil that covered my gown. It snagged on the raised Natuan symbol cast into the golden band that encircled the king's head. I had almost tugged the symbol of office from him before I realized the fragile fabric was caught. The crowd gasped.

Apologizing profusely, while trying to maintain some dignity, I worked to disentangle the sheer cloth that had gotten caught in a fold of the metal. Guards grabbed me, which resulted in the crown coming completely off King Leo's head. A roar filled the room. The king's chair screeched on the marble floor as he stood abruptly and snatched for the golden symbol of his authority as it clattered to the floor.

I bent to retrieve it at the same time as he did and our heads clunked together. Automatically, I reached for his arm to keep from falling over and felt the Goddess's power sweep through him and the crown we both held, much like what had happened when the Goddess destroyed the entity attached to Thaddeus. Still clutching his sleeve, we rose together, staring at each other in shock. Angry murmurs ran throughout the guests. I carefully disentangled the fine silk from the metal and slowly handed the king his crown. I bowed my head. "Please forgive me, Sire." I glanced around at hostile faces.

"We wanted to make your birthday memorable, but not exactly like this." I smiled shyly at him.

He continued to stare at me, recognition dawning in his eyes. He burst into laughter. He pointed at my hair, which had slid from its lofty heights. He sat back down into his royal chair and handed me the crown. "You may as well restore what you destroyed a moment ago." He nodded to the crown. "Put it back on."

I lifted the golden band with the Natuan symbols. The taint that I had noticed the first time I saw the king was gone. I smiled at him, and silently incanted the blessing that would give him the courage and strength to rule our country in the way of the Goddess. I placed it gently on his head. I leaned close to him. "You really need a new crown. This one doesn't do you justice!"

In a flash, he caught my hand, gazing into my eyes, as he lifted my hand to brush my fingers with his lips. "Thank you," he said softly. "Come to me tomorrow."

Surprised murmurs traveled through the gathered courtiers. Lord Garth tried to move past Commander Fabian, who had placed his massive body between the old soldier and the king.

King's Guards crowded in the narrow walkway between the king's table and sideboard blocking our retreat. Dalela nudged me forward. We slipped behind King Leo's chair and by Commander Fabian, intent upon making a hasty exit. I held the locks of my hair so that my face was partly concealed from Qadira and the mercenary.

Lord Garth pushed past Commander Fabian and wrapped strong fingers around my arm. I couldn't tug free without exposing my features.

Just then a massive gray tabby cat rubbed against Garth's legs, purring loudly. Garth stepped back in horror, his eyes fixed on the cat, yet not surrendering his hold on me.

Boris? The cat turned his steady gaze on me. Blinking once, he wove between Lord Garth's legs, purring even more loudly, and arching his back to rub against the old soldier's knee. The cat leisurely stretched so that each paw rested gently on the man's thighs near his groin and stared into the man's face with unblinking golden eyes. The old soldier tried to back away, scowling. He reached for his dagger.

While Lord Garth was distracted, Dalela tugged my arm and we edged forward. Noticing our movement, he opened his mouth to speak and tightened his grip. The cat sank claws deep into his legs. Lord Garth roared, and thrust his dagger at the creature, who darted out of the way. I pulled free and we scurried out of the great hall, the cat trotting behind.

"Seize them!" Lord Garth shouted to his soldiers. "Don't let them leave the castle."

Commander Fabian's deep voice commanded, "You have no right to interfere with the citizens of my town, Garth. Call back your men, or my guards will detain them."

Judging by the shouts, crash of tables and platters, and then ring of clashing steel, it sounded like the birthday celebration had turned into a contest of power between the rival commanders.

Leaving the castle by the same unmanned portal that Thaddeus and I had used, we raced along the backstreets to the Red Rose. In the safety of the dressing room, I heaved a sigh of relief and hugged Dalela. "Thank you, Dalela."

"You certainly made an impact! You were marvelous!" She kissed my cheek.

"The king recognizes that the darkness that inhibited him is removed. This new freedom puts him in more danger, now," I commented. "Rumor has it an attempt will be made on his life tonight."

Dalela nodded. "We heard that, too. He has an assassin who protects him. Let's hope Somchi lives up to his reputation."

I hugged the other women. "Thank you for your help. It's not over. I hope you don't pay the price for my actions tonight."

My companions removed their cloaks, touched up their face paint, combed their locks and returned to the main rooms of the Dalela's establishment. I removed the hair piece, then shrugged out of my lavish garments and dressed in plain tunic and trousers. As I scrubbed away all vestiges of the face paint, I commented, "The king wants to meet with me tomorrow. What do you think he wants?"

Dalela shrugged. "Maybe he wants your help in taking back his kingdom from Lord Garth and his master." She shook her head. "Lord Garth will not be happy about the events of

tonight. He recognized us and knows where we come from."
She leaned closer to me. "He has a favorite here."

I paused in belting my dagger and small medicine kit. "He
does? I wonder what kind of lover he is?" I had never considered the man may have a softer side. "Maybe he will not
pursue discipline for our adventure tonight."

The door opened and one of Dalela's ladies looked in. "Ah,
good. You're still here."

"What's wrong, Elsie?" Dalela asked.

"Two of Garth's soldiers beat Maia. Can you tend to her,
Ellara?"

I nodded and she supported the woman into the room. The
injured woman sat gingerly into a chair.

After assessing her condition, I asked my spirit healing team to
rebalance her aura from the trauma she had endured. While I
rubbed salve on the bruises, cleaned the cuts and applied
healing ointment, Dalela continued, "Rest assured, Ellara.
Lord Garth will seek retribution for the removal of the curse
from the king. He will turn the city inside out looking for you.
His master will be very angry. Garth will try to kill the king
just to curry favor with the foreigner."

Dalela left the room while I finished tending to the injured
woman. She returned in a few minutes carrying a sack filled
with food, a small cookpot, and a couple utensils. "You are not
safe here. Leave for a couple of days until things quiet down
in Araval. I'll tell the king you will meet with him when it is

safe. Boris is waiting for you outside and will take you to safety."

She tossed a travel cloak over my shoulders and pulled the hood over my head. She cracked open the back door. In the distance, we heard the tramp of soldiers' footsteps. Screams and shouting came from the parlor and dining hall in the Red Rose. Dalela shoved the sack into my hand. "Go, while you can. You must not get caught. We need you to break the curse on our country."

Keep reading for the first chapter in the next spellbinding installment of The Chronicles of a Fractured Soul...

A SNEAK PEEK!
CHAPTER 1 - ELLARA

Araval, Alba

The screams and surly voices coming from the salas of Dalela's establishment drew nearer. The door burst open and red uniformed guards poured into the dressing room, capturing the ladies who lingered after our performance at the king's birthday celebration. Dalela, proprietress of the Red Rose, shoved me out the back door onto the street. I grabbed her hand, dragging her after me.

"Don't let them escape. After them," a guard roared from inside.

A discordant tramp of soldiers' boots came from up the alley. They were Lord Garth's men, undoubtedly following their commander's orders to capture the enchantresses from the celebration and especially the one who shattered the Droc'ri curse on the king. They searched for me.

Soldiers posted in the wide alley behind the Red Rose swarmed towards us. I pulled on Dalela's hand. "Come on. We must not be captured."

A sleek, long-legged hound detached from the shadows and intercepted the guards who pursued us. Men tumbled over each other, cursing as they tried to pursue us and deal with the elusive canine that nipped at their hamstrings and wove between their legs so that they slashed at their companions.

We ran towards the river and away from the melee. Soldiers pounded towards us from a cross street. Others poured up from the port. "There's a narrow path between those two brick buildings." Dalela pointed about half a block down the street. "We won't make it."

I pulled her into the deep shadows next to the wall and calmed myself enough to speak the words to make us invisible. Sticking to the shadows, we inched our way toward escape.

The three groups of soldiers swarmed together, milling about like a flock of chickens. Guards brushed against us. I held Dalela's hand firmly, and we froze, barely breathing.

"They are trapped. They're here somewhere," one man said. "Where's the lantern. Inspect every nook and cranny. They won't get away."

The soldiers drew their swords and systematically started probing along the walls. I closed my eyes and prayed that my invisibility shield would be impermeable. Movement caught my attention. A cat trotted along the far side of the street, tail high in the air, as if it didn't have a care in the world. It was the same gray cat who had distracted Lord Garth at the king's celebration, allowing us to escape the castle. Surprisingly, the soldiers didn't notice the small animal.

The men drew closer. My mind raced. I had no idea what would happen if a soldier shoved his sword at the invisibility shield. Would it bounce back or would it penetrate and kill us? We held our breath. The tip dug into the brick beside me. Then the man stood before us. As he thrusted, the cat yowled as if its toes had been stepped on. The man lurched back in surprise and the feline scampered off. "Stupid cat," he growled.

His comrades jibed, "Scared of a kitty?"

"Thank you, Boris," I sent to him. While they were distracted, we scooted along the wall, and in minutes we had crossed the street and slipped into the narrow gap barely wide enough to squeeze through. We felt our way along the walls of two-story buildings and finally came to where it intersected another alley. Boris, in his human form, waited for us there.

"Go on. I can manage from here," Dalela said. She squeezed my hand. "Goddess protect you." She darted into the alley and headed towards the river.

Boris nudged me forward. We threaded our way between the buildings for another couple of blocks to a main street that connected the wharf with shops and merchants' warehouses.

As we crossed the street, we spotted a group of men. In the dim light, I could not tell whether they were Lord Garth's soldiers or ordinary citizens. But I recognized Jack's tenor voice.

The men appeared to be quite pleased with themselves. "It will be spectacular," Jack was saying.

"At dawn, the town will go boom!" a deeper voice exclaimed.

I tugged Boris's arm. I silently spoke the words that would make us invisible and crept closer. A cloaked woman glanced directly at us. I froze. Felicity! Was she helping Jack?

Felicity had falsely accused me of working for the Droc'ri sorcerers at the Gra'Bandia Council meeting at Cuilithe, and I suspected she had contributed to the Doyen's declaration that I was cursed. The Doyen had forbidden me from ever using my healing talent again and had even tried to strip my gift from me.

I didn't know if, as a newly blessed Healer, Felicity could see through my spell. I eased behind the muscular form of Boris, hoping that the light-bending properties of his clothing would confuse her senses.

I had observed that passersby didn't appear to notice Boris where he stood across the street, motionlessly watching the bakery where I helped Nana Bean make bread, discreetly tended to wounded citizens, and slept. Even when he walked down the street with me, people's gazes slid past him to me. It was part of his magic as a Verndari shape-shifter.

"Come on," one of the men said. "We have three more to place. Let's get this done while everyone is hungover from the feast."

We watched the group split up. Two men and Jack headed uptown towards the castle, and the other two and Felicity returned to the docks. I indicated to Boris to follow the group heading up the street. He shook his head. I sent him the image of following them and then returning to me. "I'll be safe," I whispered. "I want to see where they go. We cannot let them destroy our city."

He reluctantly followed, keeping a safe distance. I stole behind the group heading towards the river, maintaining my invisibility shield and sticking to the darkest shadows.

At this time of night, few people were about. The wharf was empty except for a stray sailor returning to his bunk aboard his ship. Downstream were the calls of dockworkers loading the last cargo and fastening it down in preparation for departure on the next tide.

Felicity and her two companions stole across the open space towards the massive stone bridge that arched across the Slant River and connected Araval to the farmland south of the capital. They climbed down the bank to water's edge. After a time, they returned, brushing off their hands, and one of the men said, "One more to go. Where do you think?"

Felicity was silent. "What would hurt the most?"

"Destroying this bridge will stop all commerce. Jack is destroying the waterworks. That should cripple the city, I'd say," one of the men volunteered.

"It has to be somewhere the king's commander wouldn't expect."

"The castle?" Both men chuckled, one raising and spreading wide his arms dramatically.

"No. What do these people treasure?"

The men shook their heads. "The Goddess? The Heartland? Their freedom?"

"Come."

After letting them get a good head start along the open stretch of waterfront, I followed to a grove of ancient trees near the castle in the heart of Araval. Felicity surveyed the trunks supported by tall, above-ground roots, then selected one in the center of the grove and indicated to dig under a massive support. Soon the men were finished, and after wiping their hands on their pants, one said, "Let's go to Arty's Pub and see how Jack did."

Fatigue weighed on me. It had been a long day, starting with teleporting myself to the *Lovely Lady* in the wee hours of this morning to save Thaddeus's life, then returning to Araval to break the Droc'ri curse restricting King Leopold's ability to rule Alba, and now this. But I was not about to allow Jack and Felicity to destroy our city or our country.

I went to the tree where they had concealed the sack. The ground looked undisturbed. If I had not seen them place it, no one would have known anything was there. I passed my hand around the base of the tree, but could not sense anything. How had she hidden it? This was not the usual Goddess magic.

I leaned against the tree and sighed. Urged toward a raised root partway around the trunk, I felt in the earth. Digging quickly in the loose soil, my fingers brushed across rough burlap. I tugged, but it was wedged under a root. I scooped away more dirt and was finally able to pull the sack free. Carefully, I opened the heavy bag and felt along tubes about a foot long formed from sailcloth and connected to a cord. I removed the fuse from each cylinder and slung the sack over my shoulder. I stood, wondering what to do with the explosives.

I walked several blocks until I came to a blue house that stood alone among a row of two-story buildings. A sliver of light escaped from the shuttered windows. I tapped lightly on the door, which swung open immediately.

Commander Fabian's pair'ti stared at me, frowning. "Where's Jules?"

I shook my head. "Last I heard, he and Lord Garth were crossing swords in the great hall."

"Jules detests that man!"

"Jillian, we have a bigger problem." I lifted the bag of explosives.

She drew me into her cottage. In the lamp light, we peered into the sack and pulled out a dozen tightly wrapped tubes containing black powder. While we inspected them, I told her where I had found these and that there were more around the city, set to detonate at dawn. She gave me a stern look, then grabbed her shawl. "Let's go."

We walked up the street another block and she knocked on a door. Almost immediately it opened and we were ushered in, as if the woman had been expecting us. Jillian explained the situation, and the elderly nana followed us out the door. We split up. The nana turned toward the castle, and went off, and Jillian and I returned to the river to locate the device under the bridge.

Before we had finished, Boris showed up carrying three gunny sacks. He helped us remove the one shoved under the bridge buttress and we retreated to Jillian's house. "As commander of the King's Guard, Jules needs to know about this," she commented. She turned to me. "Garth's men are looking for the woman who broke the curse on the king. Go back to Nana Bean's bakery."

"Garth knows I am staying there."

"You don't look anything like the woman who broke the curse. He thinks she is one of Dalela's women." She patted my arm. "You'll be safe there, at least for tonight." She cocked an ear. "Garth's men have captured eleven of the women who went to the castle. They scour the town for the twelfth."

"But..."

"I know the arrogant man, all too well." She peered at me. "Child, you need to remain free."

I surveyed the room. Jillian's house was designed much like Nana Bean's bakery, with an open space, a sleeping area, a storeroom, and a big hearth. Instead of a large table like the one that Nana Bean used for making bread, there were a pair of large, comfortably padded chairs sitting before the fire. "How about I stay here?"

Jillian shrugged. "Suit yourself. Garth might come here looking for Jules, though. Get some rest. I'll see to the rest of the explosive weapons."

After the nana departed, I nestled into one of the chairs, and almost immediately drifted off. I started awake when the door burst open, and groggily squinted at the figures partly illuminated by the dim glow coming from the hearth. The smell of ale and garlic wafted over me.

Felicity, Jack, and a half-dozen of their co-conspirators packed into the room. Jack spotted the sacks Boris and I had collected, motioned to his companions and they swarmed to collect them.

I shot to my feet as Felicity lunged at me. She shoved me back into the chair, hands reaching for my throat. "You cannot save your pitiful city, Ellara. For every one of the explosives you find, we will just find another place to put them. Your city will fall," she spat. "And so will your king and your heretical Goddess tradition."

A commotion at the back of the crowd broke her concentration long enough for me to shove her off. Men jerked backwards and fell onto the street until Boris stood behind Felicity and Jack. With a swift movement, he captured their arms and pulled them behind their backs. He looked to me for instructions.

I climbed to my feet and brushed myself off. "Felicity and Jack. I will not allow you to destroy our homeland." I walked slowly towards them, raised palm facing outward. "Your actions cannot go unpunished."

Jack tried to back away, but Boris restrained him. Felicity's face reddened. "I will destroy everything you love, Witch. Then I will destroy you."

I nodded to Boris. While he dragged them out of the cottage, I collected the gunny sacks the men had grabbed. Jack's cohorts clambered to their feet, and eyed Boris, who had placed himself between me and the men. He easily contained Jack and Felicity, who struggled against his grip.

I moved to stand before each man and studied them. "What has happened to your hearts to make you betray your country? What has happened to your respect for all life that you would attempt to destroy our city, our country, our way of life?" I looked into each man's face, seeing into their souls with the gaze of the Goddess. They squirmed, lowered their heads and shuffled their feet. "You have been raised in the Goddess tradition. You have benefitted from the equality between man and woman. What worm has crawled into your heart to cause you to act against your innermost principles?"

As I spoke, I passed my hand over each man's chest, feeling the tingle of the Goddess's Loving Radiance pass through my hands and into the men. They stopped shuffling their feet and lifted their heads, meeting my gaze. "Go home to your pair'tis. Remember the harmony we have lived in for centuries. Remember how the Goddess has supported us so that we have thrived. Do not listen to the corruptive words of the foreigners who would strip away our freedom to satisfy their own greed. You know the way of the Goddess. Listen to Her with your hearts."

I finished the clearing and restoration on the half dozen men, stepped back, and watched. One by one, they nodded acknowledgement and turned toward their homes, moving quietly away.

I turned my attention to Jack and Felicity, weighing the odds of getting them into the custody of Commander Fabian and the King's Guard.

Boris lifted his head, looking uptown. Then I heard the discordant tromp of boots. Garth's men. Unlike Commander Fabian's guards, who marched in cadence to the sound of one step, Garth's mercenaries, like everything else they did to gratify their desires, marched to their own rhythm.

Jack and Felicity must have heard, too. They shoved and struggled against Boris's iron grip. In a swift motion, Boris snapped his hands against the sides of their necks and they tumbled to the cobblestones. We scooped up the sacks and hastened away.

As we ducked from one pocket of shadow to another, I slowed. Finally, I had to stop and rest. Boris urged me onward, adding my two sacks to those he carried. That helped, but I could barely make my legs move by the time we reached a thicket on the outskirts of Araval.

"Droc'ri magic," Boris supplied. "Poison magic." He pointed to a moss-covered patch of ground, backed by the massive trunk of a tree. "Sleep. I watch."

As I settled onto the earth and pulled my cloak around me, I wondered aloud, "Is Felicity using the Dark Lords' magic? How could she ever have been blessed by the Gra'Bandia Council as a Healer, as one who works solely with the Goddess's theurgy?"

"Nana Magog correct. Council corrupt."

Book Two in the Chronicles of a Fractured Soul is coming soon from Empower Press! Sign up for Lany's newsletter to be the first to hear release news.

GLOSSARY

Mythical enchantress immune to the Dark

Merging of body, heart, and spirit nd the Goddess to establish a protective y connect the couple

rt of the Goddess

the Heartland

D al beings from another dimension

Dr ers, agents of the Dark Lords

Far' nt, usually the Healer's pair'ti, who s ody the Goddess's energies

Gra'B ua Healers and Mages: Representatives of the Loving Goddess

Gra'yia: Healing energy composed of Divine Love

Lig'yia: Purifying energy composed of Divine Light

Pair'ti: Mates, spouses

Pell: Ball

Rith Bac'croi: Heart-binding ritual that an initiate goes through to become a Droc'ri

Shaedid: Weasel, insult

Sprid'linya of the Goddess: Spirit lines, grid of ley lines on the planet

Tiarna Drocha: Realm of the Dark Lords

Verndari: Alien race of guardians for the Goddess. One branch is the shape-shifters.

GLOSSARY

Bandrio'deirvi: Mythical enchantress immune to the Dark Lords' magic

Ceangal Bandia: Merging of body, heart, and spirit between two people and the Goddess to establish a protective barrier and to powerfully connect the couple

Cro'i an Bandia: Heart of the Goddess

Cuilithe: Sacred Grove in the Heartland

Dark Lords: Non-corporeal beings from another dimension

Droc'ri: Dark Kings. Sorcerers, agents of the Dark Lords

Far'degan: Masculine element, usually the Healer's pair'ti, who supports the Healer to embody the Goddess's energies

Gra'Bandia Healers and Mages: Representatives of the Loving Goddess

Gra'yia: Healing energy composed of Divine Love

Lig'yia: Purifying energy composed of Divine Light

Pair'ti: Mates, spouses

Pell: Ball

Rith Bac'croi: Heart-binding ritual that an initiate goes through to become a Droc'ri

Shaedid: Weasel, insult

Sprid'linya of the Goddess: Spirit lines, grid of ley lines on the planet

Tiarna Drocha: Realm of the Dark Lords

Verndari: Alien race of guardians for the Goddess. One branch is the shape-shifters.

AFTERWORD

REFLECTIONS

When a book captures my heart, I want to keep the story alive a while longer. Often, I let my imagination explore the private lives of the characters that inspired me and recreate the narrative with me in it. I explore how I would have responded to the situations described in the book. This allows me to extract more meaning from the story, take the resonant bits and pieces, and adapt them in my daily life.

You're invited to explore your experience with the story.

What themes in the narrative resonated with you?

What characters could you relate to and why?

What was your main take-away from the story?

What areas of your life do you wish you could heal?

If you had free access to your talents and the courage to live them, what areas of your life would you change?

I'd love to hear your perspectives. You can contact me at www.lanymarie.com.

You're invited to sign up to receive periodic insights into Ellara's private life that are not in the book, the personal challenges she had to overcome, and some of her daily practices to become the Healer that she is. Go to www.lanymarie.com to learn more.

ACKNOWLEDGMENTS

Writing is a way of expressing what is not normally seen or recognized within one's self. If you want to get to know yourself, write a fictional story with a surrogate character to represent yourself. You will discover that all of the characters have bits and pieces of you and exhibit aspects of your beliefs and life experiences in their personalities and behaviors. I would not have discovered this without the help of a team of mentors and editors.

It is with heartfelt gratitude and appreciation that I acknowledge my mentors who have guided me and my characters into more than I thought we could become, and who helped bring this story together.

Doc Kelley, who told me I needed to turn my story into three books and explain what I meant with certain terms and behaviors of my characters in my original draft.

Jackie Wolfe, who brainstormed with me to create the world of Gea, the magic of the Healers, and the Droc'ri's beliefs and traditions.

Teresa Funke, who patiently pointed out the inconsistent behaviors between my characters and what they should know and do. In other words, they needed to grow up. She helped me go from relating to the world through my head to experiencing the world through being in it and observing actions and feelings.

Mia Manns, who gently supported me to complete the book, not only pointing out what needed more explanation and what could be left out but acknowledging the parts that worked.

My sweetheart, Tom, who listened to all my ideas and plot problems, generously allowed me the uninterrupted time to work on my story and shared his wisdom from over fifty years of working on the Willamette River about shipping, boats, and transporting products on the water.

My daughter, Heather, who prodded me to make the story more compelling.

My son, Kelly, whose presence inspired me.

My sister, Barbara, who urged me to make the horse magical, and to have other animals with special powers.

Larry Martin, who poked, prodded, and supported me with energy work to evolve my consciousness. Only then could my characters evolve.

Scooter, my Italian Greyhound, whose daily duty became to make sure I took him for a walk and didn't forget to eat. It was during these walks that I often was able to resolve a problem or receive an inspiration.

My friends whom I bounced ideas off of and who inspired me.

The publishing team at GracePoint Publishing.

And to all the people and public figures after which I modeled my characters' traits and behaviors.

A special thanks to my non-physical team of guides, teachers, angels, and masters, and Alena-Sophia, the spirit of the story.

From my heart to yours, thank you.

AUTHOR'S NOTE

Life is a gift. It invites one into a perpetual quest for the answer to "who am I *becoming?*" followed by, "how do I share who I have become?" Through the power of words that form a narrative, a reader gains a window into the essential nature, and the life experiences, of the author.

Born and raised in Oregon, I spent my life exploring the magic and mysteries of life, not only my own, but those of other people, cultures, and places. As a child and an avid reader of sci-fi and fantasy and a dyed-in-the-wool Trekkie, I love stories where the hero or heroine discovers their hidden powers.

When I was young, I dreamed of healing people with a thought. Believing in such gifts never went away. When I was about nine, I was blessed with psoriasis. Of course, at the time, it didn't seem a blessing at all, and my family and I tried everything to get rid of it. The research and education led me outside of conventional medicine and into Eastern and Western healing arts and traditional ways. Following and studying more deeply, I discovered indigenous energy and spiritual traditions, thereby revealing my own innate talents of a highly empathic and psychic nature. Perhaps I *could* heal myself; at the very least, I gained a useful tool to understand myself, others, and the natural world around me.

Believing there was more to this life than physical existence, I delved into divination arts, discovering and uncovering the Celtic wisdom of my ancestors, Astrology, shamanism, Human Design, Numerology, Akashic Records, and mediumship, interweaving and connecting me back to this innate truth: we are all healers. It has been my interests, beliefs, trainings, and connections with others that provided me the wisdom and insight to share with clients and readers directly.

Living in a place that nurtures my soul, flanked by my sweetheart and our Italian Greyhound, and coupled with profound conversations enjoyed amongst our adult children, I thrive.

You can contact me at www.lanymarie.com.

ABOUT THE AUTHOR

Lany lives on the Oregon coast with her sweetheart and Italian Greyhound. After years of exploring the healing arts, she decided to surrender her professional life in business and pursue her life-long dream of writing a fantasy novel. When she is not editing and re-writing, she loves to walk through magical woods and eat cream puffs.

Find her at www.lanymarie.com.

WANT TO KEEP READING?

For more breathtaking fiction, visit Empower Press at www. gracepointpublishing.com.

EMPOWER
P R E S S

Made in the USA
Monee, IL
17 July 2021